THE MOAI ISLAND PUZZLE

KOTŌ PAZURU

Paul Halter books from Locked Room International:
The Lord of Misrule (2010)
The Fourth Door (2011)
The Seven Wonders of Crime (2011)
The Demon of Dartmoor (2012)
The Seventh Hypothesis (2012)
The Tiger's Head (2013)
The Crimson Fog (2013)
(Publisher's Weekly Top Mystery 2013 List)
The Night of the Wolf (2013)*
The Invisible Circle (2014)
The Picture from the Past (2014)
The Phantom Passage (2015)
Death Invites You (2016)

Original short story collection published by Wildside Press (2006)

Other impossible crime novels from Locked Room International:
The Riddle of Monte Verita (Jean-Paul Torok) 2012
The Killing Needle (Henry Cauvin) 2014
The Derek Smith Omnibus (Derek Smith) 2014
(Washington Post Top Fiction Books 2014)
The House That Kills (Noel Vindry) 2015
The Decagon House Murders (Yukito Ayatsuji) 2015
(Publisher's Weekly Top Mystery 2015 List)
Hard Cheese (Ulf Durling) 2015

Visit our website at www.mylri.com or
www.lockedroominternational.com

THE MOAI ISLAND PUZZLE

Alice Arisugawa

Translated by Ho-Ling Wong

The Moai Island Puzzle

This book is a work of fiction. The characters, incidents, and dialogue are drawn from the author's imagination and are not to be construed as real. Any resemblance to actual events or persons, living or dead, is entirely coincidental.

First published in Japanese in 1989 by
Tōkyō Sogensha Co., Ltd. as Koto Pazuru
KOTO PUZZLE
Copyright © 1989 by Alice Arisugawa
English translation rights arranged with Tōkyō Sogensha Co., Ltd.
English translation copyright © by John Pugmire 2016.

All rights reserved. No part of this book may be used or reproduced in any manner whatsoever without written permission except in the case of brief quotations embodied in critical articles and reviews.

For information, contact: pugmire1@yahoo.com

FIRST AMERICAN EDITION
Library of Congress Cataloging-in-Publication Data
Arisugawa, Alice
[*The Moai Island Puzzle* English]
Koto Pazuru/ Alice Arisugawa
Translated from the Japanese by Ho-Ling Wong

Dedicated to Yoshitaka Miwa

Contents

Introduction
Dramatis Personae
Prologue: Puzzler
Chapter One: Jigsaw Pieces
Chapter Two: Locked Room Puzzle
Chapter Three: Bicycle Puzzle
Chapter Four: Moai Puzzle
Chapter Five: Suicide Puzzle
Challenge to the Reader
Chapter Six: Jigsaw Puzzle
Epilogue
Translator's Notes

Introduction:
Behind *The Moai Island Puzzle*
Sōji Shimada

Alice Arisugawa's *The Moai Island Puzzle* is a mystery masterpiece which was first published shortly after Yukito Ayatsuji's *The Decagon House Murders*, for which I also wrote an introduction, explaining the origins and significance of *honkaku* ("orthodox"), the Japanese form of the Golden Age puzzle-plot.

In my introduction to *Decagon* I explained that *honkaku* refers to a form of the detective story that is not only literature but also, to a greater or lesser extent, a game. It follows the concept of "a high degree of logical reasoning," the key prerequisite for the most exciting form of detective fiction as proposed by S.S. Van Dine, a prominent figure of the English-language Golden Age of detective fiction during the 1920s. I explained how, after World War II, novelists like Akimitsu Takagi and Seishi Yokomizo wrote several excellent *honkaku* detective novels, but that the arrival in the 1950s of "the social school" of Japanese mystery fiction dried up interest in *honkaku* mysteries almost overnight. This school, led by Seichō Matsumoto, emphasised "natural realism" in which the motive that led to the crime and the depiction of the psychology of the criminal were the most important elements.

The "winter of the age of *honkaku*" lasted until the early 1980s and ended with the publication of my own humble work *The Tokyo Zodiac Murders* (1981), followed by Ayatsuji's *The Decagon House Murders* (1987). Because of the thirty-year hiatus, this new Japanese mystery scene was dubbed the age of *shin honkaku*, or "new orthodox." One of the most important works that made the inauguration of this new age inevitable was Arisugawa's *The Moai Island Puzzle*, first published in 1989.

The term *honkaku* was actually coined in the mid-1920's by Saburō Kōga, but it was Edogawa Rampo, in his essay collection *Gen'eijō* (The Phantom Castle), who first applied the term *shin honkaku* to the style of British post-Golden Age writers of the 1940s, such as Michael Innes, Margery Allingham and Nicholas Blake.

Starting in the 1960s, Yomiuri Shimbunsha started publishing a series of mystery novels dubbed *Shin honkaku suiri shōsetsu zenshū* (A Complete Collection of Shin Honkaku Mystery Novels). Ironically, it was Seichō Matsumoto himself who was responsible for the supervision and commentary of the series. He used the term *neo honkaku* in a retrospective on the emasculation of the Japanese mystery novels after the age of the social school. But the term did not catch on, probably because the Shimbunsha collection in its ensemble was not impressive enough to spark a revival of *honkaku/ shin honkaku*. In fact, the term *shin honkaku* did not finally take hold until the 1990s.

The age of *shin honkaku* is one of development of unexplored territories and, looking back now, we can identify two distinct routes from which writers could make their way to these exciting frontiers. One was to make a debut via the Kodansha Novels line of publisher Kodansha, headed by the famous editor Hideomi Uyama. I, too, was involved with this route in a consulting capacity. Mr. Uyama and I would have discussions about the quality of the works and how they were shaping up, and once publication had been decided, I would write the introductions and the marketing slogans for each of the works.

The other route was through publisher Tokyo Sogensha. Former Sogensha company director Mr. Yasunobu Togawa, who was an editor at the time, was the focal point of this project, with *honkaku* mystery writer Tetsuya Ayukawa acting as consultant. This would evolve into the Tetsuya Ayukawa Award for newcomers. Every year, a talented writer is able to make his first step on the route to success thanks to this award, and Alice Arisugawa was one of those to make his debut on the *honkaku* mystery scene through this route.

Yukito Ayatsuji began his writing career with *The Decagon House Murders* in 1987, while Alice Arisugawa began in 1988 with *Gekkō*

Gēmu (Moonlight Game). The latter had been submitted for Kodansha's Edogawa Rampo Award, but because it failed to pass the first round, it was published through Tokyo Sogensha.

The Tetsuya Ayukawa Award started in 1990 and it was in the ceremony hall that Kaoru Kitamura, Taku Ashibe, Yukito Ayatsuji and Alice Arisugawa all met. Their social calls continue to this day, and Ayatsuji and Arisugawa have become close friends after working on the original scenarios for *Anraku Isu Tantei* (The Armchair Detective), a whodunit TV drama.

Other well-known novelists who started with Tokyo Sogensha are Kaoru Kitamura, Taku Ashibe and Reito Nikaidō. Nikaidō, however, did the exact opposite of Arisugawa: before making his debut with Tokyo Sogensha, he moved to Kodansha.

Among those who took the Kodansha route are Rintarō Norizuki, Shōgo Utano, Yutaka Maya, Yasuhiko Nishizawa, Natsuhiko Kyōgoku and Hiroshi Mori. In the early days, the term *shin honkaku* as coined by Rampo was applied exclusively to Kodansha newcomers, but eventually it was also used for writers from Tokyo Sogensha, and had become a genre-defining term by the 1990s.

Like just about every *shin honkaku* writer, Alice Arisugawa was originally a member of a university mystery club, but not the Kyoto University Mystery Club made famous by *The Decagon House Murders*. Arisugawa, on the other hand, came from the Mystery Club of Dōshisha University, also located in Kyōto. As to why only amateurs debuting from university mystery clubs became the founders of the extraordinary phenomenon known as the *shin honkaku* movement, that is an important question which holds lessons for the future. The answer might be found in the Aesopian tale I recount below.

In the 1920s, when Edogawa Rampo imported the Edgar Allan Poe-Arthur Conan Doyle style of mystery novel which started in the West, and new Japanese writers gathered to solidify the form of this new genre, the scientific revolution which had given birth to the detective novel had not yet arrived in Japan. In the absence of scientific inspiration, Rampo turned to the grotesque haunted house attractions of the Edo period (1603-1868). To compare it to a British example: he employed a style reminiscent of the terror people experienced for the Elephant Man. Such grotesque horror does appear to some extent in Poe's and Doyle's works, but to nowhere near the extent of the Japanese mystery novels. Eventually, Rampo's followers started going too far, even introducing the pornographic tendencies of Edo period entertainment fiction into their novels.

Whereas Poe and Doyle used the shocking elements from pre-modern times as a jumping board to proclaim the intellectual victory of the scientific revolution over pre-modern times in their tales, Rampo used the pre-modern Edo period as an inspiration stressing the vulgarity of the "Edo mass culture," which was devoid of scientific deduction. As a consequence, Japanese mystery authors were looked at with contempt by authors of pure literature at the time, purely because of the vulgarity which offended their morals. Hence the belief that mystery fiction was just lowbrow entertainment found its way into Japan's literary world, as well as with the readers.

It was the post-war emergence of the social school of mystery fiction pioneered by Seichō Matsumoto which saved the genre. Focusing on the motive behind the crime and the psychology of the criminal, this new school managed to improve critical reception of mystery fiction and give pride back to genre writers, while maintaining the sales numbers of the Rampo era. The superiority of the Seichō style was accepted by the literary world, changing the literary scene virtually overnight. Professional writers hastened to get on board with this new trend, and what was then being called *honkaku* mystery was thrust together with the Rampo style and shunned. *Honkaku* and the Rampo style are not the same, but at the time nobody was interested in clarifying the matter. In the period before World War II, unsuccessful *honkaku* writers had been in contact with Rampo, who was seen as a pioneer and a leader in the genre, and Rampo himself had written *honkaku* short story masterpieces in his early years, which he himself and the readers loved. So the confusion of *honkaku* with the Rampo style seemed natural enough, but none of this mattered because the topic had become taboo.

These complex circumstances affected the Japanese literary world profoundly, leaving deep scars and purging *honkaku* writers; any professional writer associated with *honkaku* was quickly ostracised. So it was that in the 1990s, after the tide started to turn and the popularity of the "social school" started to fade following the publication of my own *The Tokyo Zodiac Murders* and *Naname Yashiki no Hanzai* (*The Crime in the Leaning Mansion*), professional writers capable of taking up the challenge of writing their own *honkaku* mystery stories were nowhere to be found. Thus it fell to the amateur writers from the university mystery clubs, untainted by the past, to pick up the gauntlet.

Before describing the evolution of this movement in Japan, however, it is important to know what happened in the West to the movement known as Golden Age Detection. This genre of mystery fiction, which builds on logical reasoning, had come to a surprising end, ironically because of S.S. Van Dine's rare talents. Declaring that the detective novel was the only form of literature that put the reader to work, he had argued that "a deduction game emphasising fair play within a limited setting" would be the story structure with the best potential to result in masterpiece mystery stories. He focused his own writing on this form, and the success of the Golden Age of Detective Fiction proved him right. But when the elements of the game are too severely limited and the building materials are all the same, only the first few builders will get all the glory and there will be an over-abundance of similar novels, which is what happened. Further contributing to the decline of the puzzle plot novel was the emergence of Hollywood and visual entertainment—itself the result of scientific development—which allowed people to enjoy mystery fiction in a more passive manner, without putting the viewer to work.

The Japanese university students who started writing mystery fiction were aware of what had happened in the past on the other side of the ocean. Making sure they didn't limit themselves too much, they bravely pushed the frontiers of the format, carefully picking the most flavourful elements for their own dishes. This is the best way to explain the essence of 1990s *shin honkaku* writing, of which *The Moai Island Puzzle* is a prime example. The simple, attractive, setting is a limited stage: a lonely island where nobody from outside, not even the police, can interfere. Potential suspects are introduced one after another in a fair way, with a narration free of any falsehoods, to the young members of the Mystery Club who arrive on the scene by boat. The amateur detective is given the important duty of looking for hidden treasure, investigating several murders—including an impossible one—and finally identifying the murderer, using clues that are also available to the readers. This setting is an alluring one that should attract anyone with a love for mystery fiction. *The Moai Island Puzzle* is a soup made from Van Dine's country house mystery, with a dash of pirate treasure hunt thrown in.

Now let us turn to the author of this work himself: Alice Arisugawa. He was one of the amateur writers who made his debut as described above. He had one clearly-defined ambition when he started his writing career: he was determined to be the successor to Ellery Queen. He made that clear to everyone around him when he first started, and it is still his goal today. Yukito Ayatsuji, a member of the Ellery Queen Fan Club, got wind of Arisugawa's declaration and read his debut novel, *Gekkō Gēmu* (*Moonlight Game*). At that time, Ayatsuji was not convinced, but after reading Arisugawa's second work, *The Moai Island Puzzle*, he was won over. Thus, in order to discuss Arisugawa's style, it is also necessary to analyse the writing style of the American giant.

As so many scholars in both the United States and Japan have pointed out, the charm of Ellery Queen's detective stories lies in the spirit of fair play, the beauty of the surprising, but clever clues and the intellectual and cool logical reasoning culminating in the Challenge to the Reader. The Queen cousins had no particular interest in shocking conclusions or witty writing. What they loved was intellectual excitement, such as when something seemingly innocent eventually evolves into an essential clue. Arisugawa has embraced the Queen tradition and worked on perfecting this element, which he considers the most alluring point of detective novels.

In *The Moai Island Puzzle,* he has no interest in dumbfounding the reader with something shocking at the end of his meticulously constructed tale of mystery solving. A murder without any showy elements happens and, by introducing expertly placed clues, he coolly constructs a chain of logical reasoning with mathematical precision. The reader will be touched by the calm way in which the detective, Jirō Egami, using a normal, everyday style of speech, exposes the murderer. The explanation is done without any eccentric behaviour but readers will experience a serene intellectual astonishment and a silent respect for the mind of the author who was able to come up with the logic leading to the identification of the murderer. Arisugawa considers this mathematical, proper process of logical reasoning more important than a showy performance.

This leads us to another aspect of an Arisugawa novel: the type of detective. Roughly speaking, there are two types of great detective in mystery novels. On the one hand there is the dramatic hero detective, and on the other there is one of the characters who just happens to be given the task of explaining the truth to the readers.

The archetype of the hero detective is, of course, Sherlock Holmes. To my mind, almost any detective character will automatically turn into a Holmes-like hero type whenever they appear in films or TV dramas. This is because the visual medium simply doesn't allow for a protagonist who is as expressionless as a machine, silent, lacking in vigorous action, and forever lost in thought. Detectives in TV dramas are almost all active, cracking witty jokes, talkative during investigations, and at times even acting peculiarly to attract the attention of those around them. And in the visual medium, the ability offered by the printed form to flip back several pages to check up on a piece of evidence, is severely limited. As a consequence, there is a limit to how elaborate the logical reasoning can be.

The mystery-solver detective, who silently bears the task of solving the mystery without being extrovert and talkative, is a type whose existence is thus only possible within a bundle of printed pages. It is there where he can make best use of his typical, attractive intelligence to do cool-headedly whatever is needed to solve the mystery. The question of why is an interesting one, but for some reason you find this type of detective often in Japanese mystery novels. You will come across this type in Western mystery fiction also, for example Jacques Futrelle's famous The Thinking Machine. However, even these reserved types turn into hero types whenever they are adapted for the screen.

There is another reason for Arisugawa's use of this latter type of detective. The Ellery we follow in Ellery Queen's novels isn't an eccentric character either. But what is extremely important is that Ellery has no need for a Watson. The reason why so many detectives need a Watson is because they need to be heroes. The Watson character emphasizes his own normality, while expressing surprise at Holmes' genius. Each time Watson is astonished and praises Holmes, he makes Holmes more and more of a hero.

As for the path Alice Arisugawa chose as a follower of Ellery Queen, it appears to me he has gone for similar methods to those of his mentor. One should consider his detective, Jirō Egami, a character who is simply tasked with laying out an impressive chain of logical reasoning. But Egami has one big, but clearly defined difference with Ellery. That is the existence of Alice, the narrator of the story and Egami's Watson. Like his mentor Ellery, Alice Arisugawa has a character sharing his own pen name appear in the story, but unlike the mentor, who gave his name to the detective, the student-writer Arisugawa decided to give his name to the Watson character. One can sense Arisugawa's reserved personality here. Even though Arisugawa uses the same methods as Ellery Queen, one could even make the guess that somewhere, he also secretly wishes his detective could act more like a hero. If my reading is correct, Egami might become more like a hero-detective in the stories that follow *The Moai Island Puzzle*. Or perhaps, this was a way for Arisugawa to graduate from his mentor's methods.

Dedicated to my New York friend John Pugmire.

Sōji Shimada

Tokyo, 2016

Dramatis Personae

Maria Arima – Second year student of Eito University.
Tetsunosuke Arima – Maria's grandfather.
Ryūichi Arima – Maria's uncle.
Hideto Arima – Ryūichi's eldest son.
Reiko Arima – Ryūichi's adopted daughter.
Kazuto Arima – Ryūichi second son.
Kango Makihara – Ryūichi's brother-in-law.
Sumako Makihara – Kango's daughter.
Junji Makihara – Sumako's husband.
Toshiyuki Inukai – Ryūichi's half-brother (same father).
Satomi Inukai – Toshiyuki's wife.
Yūsaku Sonobe – Doctor.
Itaru Hirakawa – Painter.
Jirō Egami – Fourth year student of Eito University.
Alice Arisugawa – Second year student of Eito University

Names follow western convention: given name followed by family name. N.B. Alice here is a male

Kashikijima

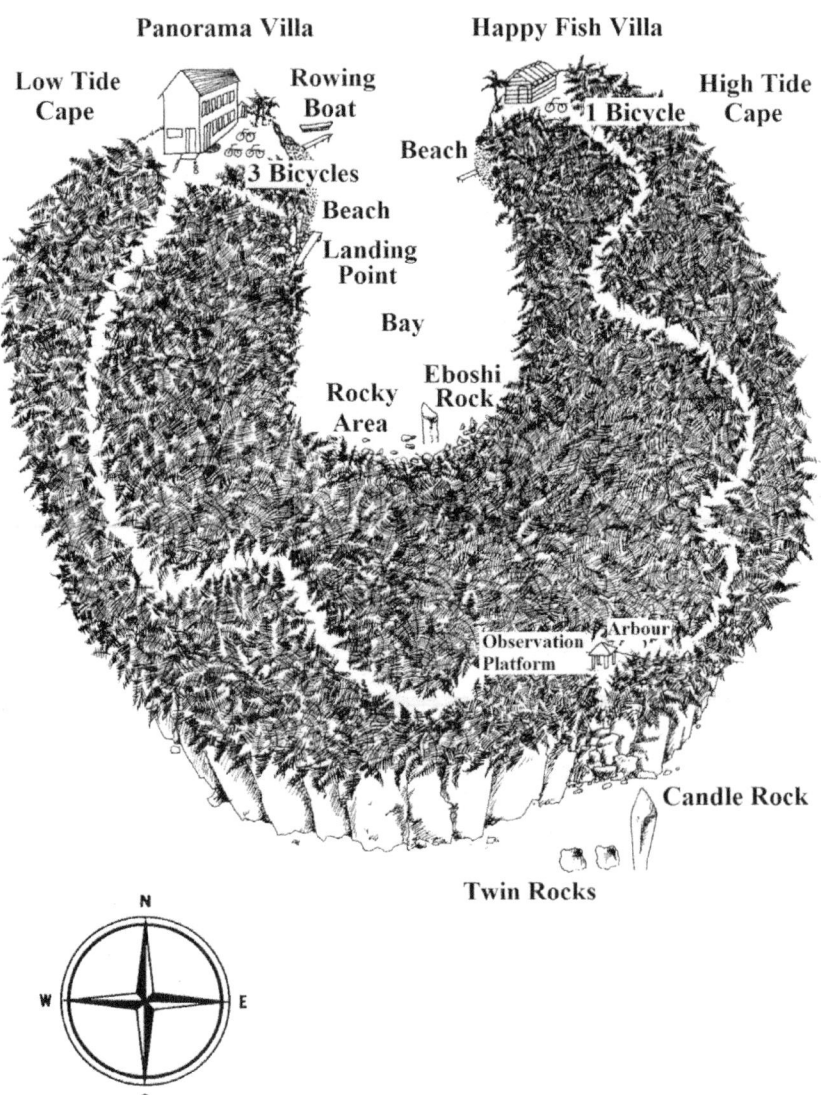

PROLOGUE: PUZZLER

Obligation Law, my second period class, had ended. Hungry students quickly crowded in front of the exit in an effort to make their way to the cafeteria, making it impossible for anyone to leave. Patient as I am, I decided to sit down on a seat near the exit and wait until the congestion was over.

'You always do everything at your own pace, don't you, Alice?' said a voice that came from above my head. I turned—my head still resting on the table—to see a pair of cute, round knees peeking out from a dark check-patterned mini-skirt. I raised my head to look at a familiar face.

'Maria? Perfect timing.'

It's only the start of the story, but already two curious names have popped up, but please read on. Don't get exasperated.

My name is Alice Arisugawa. I'm a second year law student at Eito University. I'm Japanese and I'm male. The girl with semi-long russet hair looking down at me is Maria Arima. She's also a second year law student at the same university. Maria is also Japanese, but, unlike me, she's female.

Eito University, where this conversation was taking place, is, as you would expect, located in Japan. In Kyōto to be exact, the ancient capital boasting a 1,200 year history. The campus is located across from the Imperial Palace. So how did two people bearing such exotic names come to meet in this age-old city? It must have been a prank of the gods.

'Remember Mr. Egami and the others said they had no classes in the morning today? They're probably already waiting for us. We should go.'

Egged on by Maria, I got up from my seat. She always claimed her speciality was making her way quickly through crowds, and she did indeed wriggle skilfully through the waves of people. I yelled for her to wait for me, as I tried to follow her by elbowing my way through.

Café Lilac was located slightly north of the intersection of Imadegawa-dōri and Shinmachi-dōri. For a café in this student town, Lilac was certainly nothing outstanding, except for their delicious *tarako* spaghetti. That, and the fact that we could hang around there for hours, was what gave the place its charm and why it had become our usual hang-out place. It was our very own Villa Lilac[i].

'See, they're already eating.'

As soon as she'd entered, Maria had spotted our friends and walked straight over to the table next to them.

Our three seniors were already wolfing down their *tarako* spaghetti, a dish which never seemed to bore them.

'They're here, they're here,' said Oda, with his mouth full. 'We've been waiting.'

'Sorry we're late,' said Maria, pulling a chair from an adjacent table and sitting down. I grabbed the empty seat next to Egami.

'Have something to eat first.' Mochizuki, who was sitting opposite me, raised his hand and hailed the waiter.

The five people gathered there all read mystery fiction as a hobby, and love the genre more than anything in the world. The same five people also make up the complete member list of the Eito University Mystery Club. The "elderly" man sitting next to me was club president Jirō Egami, a fourth year philosophy student. Because he was our senior, Maria and I addressed him as "Mr." He'd been enrolled at Eito University for seven years already. His long, wavy hair touched his shoulders as he silently but expertly moved his fork. Across from him sat Kōjirō Oda. He was a third year economics student and always had his motorcycle and hard-boiled crime fiction on his mind. He had a refreshingly short haircut. The person with the silver-rimmed pair of glasses next to Oda was Shūhei Mochizuki. He too was a third year student of economics, forming a dynamic duo there with Oda. Mochizuki, however, was an Ellery Queen freak, only interested in classic detective fiction.

Until last spring, the club had consisted of just four men—those three seniors plus yours truly, Alice Arisugawa—but then Maria had joined. Our family names are Arima and Arisugawa, so we have consecutive student ID numbers. We were also in the same language classes and she was actually the first girl to talk to me here at the university. But I hadn't realised she was such a passionate mystery fiction fan until we'd known each other for more than a year.

I'd been chatting with the seniors in the student hall lounge one day, when Maria had come by to borrow my notebook. We were just in the middle of a conversation about Dorothy L. Sayers, and Mochizuki had been wailing that he badly wanted to read Sayers' out-of-print masterpiece *The Nine Tailors*, when Maria asked him simply: 'Would you like to borrow my copy?'

He'd reached out with his right hand, crying 'Please!' and fallen off his chair.

So that's how the Mystery Club gained its first female member. Maria hadn't known I was a member—in fact, she hadn't even known of its existence. Naturally, we men all welcomed her wholeheartedly. Spring had finally arrived at the Mystery Club.

'Anyway, Mr. Egami and Alice sure are lucky guys...,' said Oda, as he wiped his mouth with a paper napkin. 'A week-long holiday on an island in the south. Wish I could've gone instead of staying here.'

'Me too,' added Mochizuki. 'Maria, why didn't you tell us a bit earlier? If you'd been planning to ask us anyway....'

The "plan" was an invitation to a villa owned by Maria's uncle Ryūichi Arima, located on an island fifty kilometres to the south of Amami Ōshima. As if a summer holiday on an island wasn't perfect enough, there was also to be a fantastic event.

'Too bad for you both,' I said with sympathy. 'But, Nobunaga, you can't possibly skip out on your sister's wedding. And Mochi, you already paid 200,000 yen for your driving school.'

Nobunaga was Oda's nickname, after the famous warlord Nobunaga Oda.

'Can you believe my sister? Holding a wedding in the middle of summer, just because she's having a baby....'

Mochizuki complained as well:

'What about me? I've been planning to go home and get my driver's licence for over a year now, so I can't make the trip. Talk about bad timing!'

He slammed the table, and the waiter bringing Maria's and my *tarako* spaghettis raised his eyebrows.

'I don't even care that much for an island holiday. Save some dough and you can go anytime,' said Oda as he leant over the table. 'But a treasure hunt is something else.'

Precisely. The treasure hunt was the fantastic event included in the trip.

'You two said you'd at least like to take a look at the map, so I brought it with me. But I don't think you can deduce anything with only the ma—'

'You never know. Show us, show us,' pleaded Mochizuki.

Even though our spaghettis had finally arrived, Mochizuki didn't even give Maria time to pick up her fork. I was tempted to remark how different his behaviour was from just moments before, when he'd kindly called the waiter over for us, but I guess it can't be helped.

Holding a treasure map in front of a mystery fan is like holding out a red rag to a bull.

Maria, too, gave up on any attempts at resistance, undid the fastener of her shoulder bag and pulled out a map neatly folded in four.

Not only Mochizuki and Oda, but even Egami leant forward over the table. This was also the first time I'd had a chance to see the map myself. Our four heads were all clustered at the centre of the table.

'But that's...,' I muttered in surprise.

Kashikijima Island looked like a horseshoe, or perhaps the horns of a bull, almost enclosing a small bay. There were capes on the left and right sides of the bay, and on each of them a picture of a house had been drawn. The two houses were connected by a single road which followed the shape of the island. Judging by the map, I imagined that travelling between them had to be extremely inconvenient. There was no other obvious residence on the island, but there were several strange marks scattered here and there on the map.

'The house on the left—or to the west,' said Maria, 'is where we'll be staying: Panorama Villa. Across the bay, on the eastern side of the island, is Itaru Hirakawa's Happy Fish Villa. There are no other houses on the island.'

She began to explain what else was on the island, but Mochizuki cut in.

'Wait a sec! I'm more interested in these marks here. I assume they represent the famous *moai* statues?'

The look of resignation on Maria's face meant she knew she wouldn't be able to start her long-awaited lunch for the time being. She put her hands on her knees and cleared her throat.

'Yes. But even though we call them *moai* statues, they're actually quite different from the stone ones on Easter Island. These are made of wood.'

'Are they big?' I asked.

'Not really. About as wide as a telegraph pole, and measured from the ground up, they're about one metre high. Faces resembling those of the Easter Island *moai* statues have been carved in the wood, but not very accurately. They look more like one of those Enkū statues[ii].'

'Enkū's *moai*?' Egami laughed as he lit his Cabin cigarette. 'How many of them are there?'

'Twenty-five in total. I heard that most of the statues on Easter Island are facing away from the ocean, but these wooden *moais* are all looking in different directions. I suspect it has something do with the mystery. They might be the key to unlocking the secret.'

Four pairs of male eyes were fixed on the map on the table. While we were all lost in thought, Maria quickly started wolfing down her *tarako* spaghetti as if she was slurping *soba* noodles at a street stand, and I quickly followed suit.

'There's not much we can say with nothing but this map here, but it certainly looks like an interesting puzzle.' Club president Egami's interest was also aroused, it appeared. 'I guess your grandfather was quite a character, Maria.'

Maria nodded rapidly, a long strand of spaghetti dangling from the corner of her mouth.

'Yes, he was a bit strange. He was quite a puzzle fanatic. He was especially fond of the ones by Sam Loyd and Lewis Carroll, and was an avid collector of the originals. He had a busy life as a businessman and puzzles were how he relaxed.'

Maria's grandfather, Tetsunosuke Arima, was the founder of ARIMA, a medium-sized stationery manufacturer. The company had started out in Ōsaka, but had moved to Tōkyō in the 1950s. They'd begun with paper materials, but nowadays the company had grown so large they handled all kinds of office automation machinery. Tetsunosuke had retired from his position as president when he'd turned seventy, leaving the management of the company to his three sons. He'd passed away five years ago and ARIMA's current president was now his eldest son, Ryūichi. His second son, Ryūji, was vice-president and the third son (Maria's father) Ryūzō was senior managing director. In other words, the stereotypical family firm.

Maria had been born and raised in Tōkyō, but she'd failed all of her entrance exams for universities in the Tōkyō Metropolitan Area. Eito University was the only place to have sent her an acceptance letter, even though she'd only taken the exam by chance, combining the exam with a short holiday in Kyōto. She'd somehow managed to persuade her anxious parents to send her to study in the ancient capital.

'Did your grandfather also make his own puzzles?' I asked.

'No, he was simply a fan of solving them. Crossword puzzles, mathematical puzzles, mazes, you name it. Oh, and jigsaw puzzles, too. My late grandmother used to say that he'd often stay up all night struggling with a puzzle. This *moai* puzzle is the only one he ever devised himself. But we only found out about the map after he'd passed away; it was enclosed with his last will.'

So it was a parting puzzle entrusted to his lawyer. Tetsunosuke Arima had certainly been fond of jokes. Not surprisingly, he was also the one who gave his granddaughter her name. Officially, Maria is named after Saint Mary, because they share the same birth date, September 8th. But the real reason for the choice of name is that Maria Arima is a palindrome in the Japanese syllable alphabet: *ma-ri-a a-ri-ma*. Her jokester of a grandfather had certainly made life hard for her.

Mochizuki stared at the map with his arms crossed, wearing a puzzled expression. Then a thought appeared to occur to him and he asked Maria: 'By the way, what kind of treasure is it? Jewels or suchlike buried somewhere?'

'Jewels,' replied Maria. 'Grandfather loved his birthstone, diamonds. Grandmother was born in April, so my grandfather gave her diamond jewellery for wedding anniversaries, birthdays, anything. When she passed away he took most of the collection and hid it somewhere. He told the family he'd tell us where he'd hidden it before he passed away, but he died suddenly of a stroke five years ago without having told anyone about the hiding place. Even at a low estimate, the diamonds he hid are worth five hundred million yen, so that had us very worried for a while, but then this treasure map appeared. He'd entrusted it, together with his last will, to the family lawyer.'

'All of you were probably surprised, eh?' said Oda.

'You bet! Grandfather had said he'd hidden the diamonds, but we thought he'd placed them in a safe-deposit box at some bank or other. Imagine our surprise when we found out he'd childishly buried them somewhere on the same island as our holiday villa! Building a villa on a deserted island is already a bit odd to begin with, but I guess it was done out of admiration for *Treasure Island*, which had been such an influence on his life. There are coconut and fan palms planted around the other family mansion in Seijō back in Tōkyō as well, giving it a tropical island feel.'

'So you've already hunted high and low and couldn't find it,' said Mochizuki, 'and now it's up to the great minds of us Mystery Club members to take up the challenge and solve the mystery.'

'Well, the minds of the *best* members of the Eito University Mystery Club, anyway,' I added, to which Mochizuki responded with a growl:

'What are you saying? You just have more free time than me and Nobunaga. Damn, the likes of Alice chosen over me. Hah, I don't even need to set foot on the island. I'll figure out the location of the treasure with just this map here.'

No, no, Maria gestured as she shook her head lightly. 'I think that'd be impossible, Mochi. The locations of the *moais* are marked with an X on the map, but the directions the statues are facing are all slightly different. And that seems to be significant. I suspect you'd need to know which way they're facing in order to solve the mystery. Actually, he said precisely that….'

She suddenly closed her mouth. Since that seemed rather unnatural, Egami asked her what was wrong.

'Actually…my cousin Hideto did his best to find the treasure, in the summer three years ago. I was also staying on the island at the time. He was very close to solving the mystery. I still remember he came to me very excited, five days after he'd begun his search. "I went around to check which way the *moais* were facing. Maria, I think I'm onto something," he told me. My cousin didn't mention anything more than that, but when he told me this, I remembered my grandfather had brought a surveying engineer with him when he'd had the statues installed.'

'I see,' said Mochizuki, 'but your cousin didn't find it either, right? So he was on the wrong trail, too.'

Maria lowered her voice.

'Actually, he died. The day after he talked to me with such confidence….'

'He died? That's awful. But how?'

'He drowned at sea. He was a very good swimmer, so I couldn't believe it. It was a real shock.'

Maria looked mournful. For a moment, a shadow darkened our happy talk, but she quickly looked up again and smiled.

'Sorry, it all just came back to me again. He was seven years older than I and always very nice to me. We always spent a week together in the summer, so his death really hit me.

'But let's change the subject. I hope you, Mr. Egami and Alice, will do your best to find the treasure, so the spirit of my cousin won't have any lingering regrets about it any more. I want to be able to tell him we finally found it.'

I wasn't sure how much Maria was expecting from our brainpower. I'd been mumbling about wanting to go somewhere far away for the summer, when she invited me to her uncle's villa, and said we could go on a treasure hunt. But perhaps she was really hoping we—or more precisely, Egami—would turn out to be the ace up her sleeve, who would solve the mystery that had baffled so many before us. Talking about helping her cousin's spirit might have sounded exaggerated, but it might be how she really felt about the whole business. If so, I'd need to give it my best shot.

'A great responsibility for you, Mr. Egami.' Perhaps Oda was thinking the same way I was as he said those words and tried to read Egami's reaction. Mochizuki was still staring at the map, even though Maria had said it was impossible to solve it just with that. I was sure he was going to ask her if he could make a copy of it.

'Mochi, although I still believe you have to be on the island yourself in order to solve the puzzle, instead of here on the mainland, I'll give you a hint. It might be the key to solving the whole thing.'

'A hint? Why didn't you say so earlier?'

'It was written in the last will which came with the map. "The person who solves the evolving puzzle, will inherit the diamonds." It specifically said "evolving puzzle."'

'An evolving puzzle? What does that mean?'

'It's the key to the puzzle precisely because it's not that simple. I have no idea what it means either, and everyone else also racked their brains about it.'

'Ah, I see. Okay,' mumbled Mochizuki, a satisfied expression on his face. 'I might need to wait for your report on the investigation on the island before I can solve it all, but I'll try to get as close as possible just by using this map and your hint. I'm not expecting much from Alice and Mr. Egami, so I'll be waiting for your report.'

'Every morning, while it's still cool outside, you'll need to remind yourself that the map's your summer companion,' joked Egami.

After we left Café Lilac, Mochizuki went into a bookshop on the corner, where he made a copy of the map and bought Darwin's *The Origin of Species*.

CHAPTER ONE: JIGSAW PIECES

1

August 2nd, departure from Ōsaka.

Flight JAS 933 arrived at Amami Ōshima Airport at ten minutes to ten. Our trip through the sky had been a short one—just under two hours—but the real ordeal was yet to come. I got a bad feeling about it when we boarded the chartered motor yacht at Naze Port and, as I had feared, the boat rocked. There was a long—very long—three-hour voyage ahead.

'Uugh, I'm feeling sick.'

Above me, I could hear the captain whistling a merry tune as I lay slumped on the bench seat of the main cabin. I'd taken some motion sickness pills beforehand, but I still didn't feel well.

'Alice, are you all right?' asked Maria, who was seated in a lounge chair on the other side of the table. It could have been her constitution, or her familiarity with the voyage, but she was completely unaffected. Egami was absolutely fine as well, and was up on deck staring at the sea. I was the only one in such a pathetic state.

'How can you be seasick on such a fine day? There's not a single wave out there. Kids these days. No perseverance.'

Those frustrating words were uttered by Yūsaku Sonobe, a balding doctor in his fifties who, like us, was a guest at Kashikijima's Panorama Villa. We had met him at Naze Port.

'Dr. Sonobe, please don't give me a lecture on perseverance. This is just the way my constitution works. Don't they say Admiral Nelson also suffered from seasickness his entire life? I—I'd be happy if you'd dispense with such unscientific talk.'

I said this as I desperately tried to suppress the nauseating feeling in my chest. The good doctor snorted in amusement.

'I see you're a smooth talker. But you're absolutely right, there are people who just can't get used to motion sickness because of their constitution.'

'I—I'm only bad with boats.'

'Okay, we know, so let's drop this now,' said Maria, going up the narrow staircase to the deck, leaving the doctor and me alone together.

'Mind if I smoke?' he asked as he took out a pipe. I was surprised he was polite enough to ask a youngster like myself, so my reply was a bit late. My first impression of him was that of an old geezer with a sharp tongue, but he turned out to be quite the gentleman, not a difficult eccentric at all.

'Then I don't mind if I do. Physician, heal thyself, they say, but I just can't give up the habit.'

With a practiced hand he stuffed the tobacco into his briar pipe, lit it, inhaled deeply once and, with a contented expression, blew smoke towards the ceiling. I felt a sense of admiration for the self-confidence and dignity of this middle-aged man who had found success in life.

'Doctor, do you come to the island every year?'

'No, I'm invited once every three years. Unlike you, I live in Yokohama, so it's too far to come every year. Anyway, skipping two years between visits is just about right, for by the springtime I've already become excited. I don't swim, I don't fish, I just spend six days doing nothing at all, but it's the perfect rest for body and soul. You might not guess it from my appearance, but I'm actually the director of a private hospital. Usually, I'm completely worn out, overwhelmed by work, other miscellaneous affairs and I don't know what. If I don't get new life blown into this body once every three years, it's my heart that'll stop working before those of my patients.'

He started to become more talkative, possibly because we were coming closer to the island. A six-day holiday from all the busy work. And when it's over and he returns to Yokohama, he'll probably find six days of work piled up waiting for him. That wasn't the case with me. I felt a little bad because of this luxury of mine, as if I was some sort of nobleman.

'Are you the Arima family physician?'

'Not precisely. My father was good friends with the former head of the family, Tetsunosuke Arima. They came from the same town. They were also team-mates in the Keiō University boat club. And my father happened to be a doctor as well. The current head of the Arimas, Ryūichi, and I are the same age, and I used to come to the island all the time with the whole family. So, well, I guess you could call me a childhood friend who also happens to be a doctor,' added Sonobe, as he waved his prized briar pipe in front of him. The smoke that came drifting from his pipe had a sweet and enticing scent to it, and even though I didn't smoke myself, I didn't find it unpleasant at all.

'To tell you the truth,' he began again, and his face lit up, 'there's another thing I always look forward to. Young people like yourself also stay here and I find it very stimulating to exchange ideas with them. Their stories are sometimes naive, but occasionally it is I who learns something. Speaking of which, it'd be a pleasure if you and that long-haired senior of yours would have a drink with me.'

'I'm sure we'd love to.'

Perhaps it was the chat that had helped, or maybe because my stomach was completely empty now, but I felt a lot better. I remembered Maria saying the wind felt nice, so I thought about joining her on deck too. I said so to Sonobe, who showed his yellow teeth as he laughed.

'That's good to hear. Take a look outside.'

I climbed up to the teak-tiled deck, where I had to close my eyes because of the surprisingly strong wind. Egami and Maria were standing side by side, and his long hair and her russet hair were dancing around like flames.

'Hey, Alice, feeling better?'

'How long before we reach Kashikijima?'

'Two and a half hours ago, I told you it'd take three hours, so even you should be able to work out it's another thirty minutes. But look, Alice, you can already see it over there.'

Maria pointed directly ahead, her eyes squinting as she looked into the distance. The azure sea and the sky, which resembled a rainbow of varying shades of blue, filled my view completely. I could just make out some black spots floating on the horizon. 'So that's it,' I muttered.

'I'm getting so excited,' said Maria. 'I haven't been here for three years. And this time, I've got you and Mr. Egami, two splendid men, with me.'

She pushed away the dishevelled hair that had covered her face and looked straight up at the sky. There was not a single cloud up there.

2

Kashikijima was a fairly flat island, with tropical plants growing all over it. The boat went halfway around the island. As we looked starboard towards the place we'd be staying—Panorama Villa on the western cape—the yacht slid into the bay. We were told the only place boats could land, even within the bay, was near the tip of the western cape, which was called Low Tide Cape. The boat slowly made its way towards the landing place and finally reached the shore.

After dropping us off, it turned around immediately to return to Amami. It left quickly and wouldn't be back until the day we were scheduled to return to the mainland, five days hence. As I watched the boat disappear into the shadow of the cape, I felt a slight unease.

'If you get homesick now, there's no way back, you know.'

It was Maria. I replied: 'Don't think I'll get homesick, but what if somebody suddenly turns ill? And I guess sometimes people get hurt, too, don't they?'

'Alice, I'm not sure whether you're just worrying too much or have too much common sense, asking these silly questions just at the very moment we're landing. Dr. Sonobe is with us too, so don't worry.'

'I know he's here while we are, but what happens after he's gone? Anyway, he's here on holiday. It's not as if he's the family doctor.'

Maria sighed. 'Then let me put your mind at rest. There's a wireless transceiver here. My uncle and cousin are both licensed amateur radio operators, so they can call for help in case of an emergency. Happy?'

'I guess so.'

Egami and Dr. Sonobe were walking a bit in front of us. Sonobe was looking up at the taller club president as he was talking.

'So I heard you're in some detective fiction club, eh? I'm not really interested myself, but it's certainly exotic. The act of reading books is itself an utterly unproductive one, of course. Particularly if you're only reading mystery novels, well, that's just plain debauchery and dissipation. When I was young, I dabbled a bit with German literature, but detective fiction, that's something exotic. Anything goes there.'

I wondered whether the chatty doctor wasn't in some kind of manic state. My taciturn senior merely mumbled responses under his breath. At the rate the doctor was going, he would probably invite us to have drinks with him that very night.

We plodded our way up the narrow path leading from the landing place up to Panorama Villa. The sun was still shining fiercely and I felt perspiration dripping down my back. After a hundred metres we reached the top of the hill, where the path widened. An early American style two-storey building stood there, its weatherboards painted white—Panorama Villa. It was long and narrow, with a terrace and large French windows overlooking the bay.

'Yay, we're finally here, everybody.'

Maria was the first to run to the door. She had just grabbed the knob when the door opened from the inside.

'Oh, Reiko, hello!'

'Welcome, Maria, it's been a while. The long trip must've been tiring.'

A woman with a neat short haircut stepped outside. She wore a sleeveless one-piece dress with an ethnic pattern, an ethnic-inspired necklace and thick, wooden bracelets around her wrists. They made her slender white arms look even more fragile.

'I'm here again, Reiko. Good to see you looking so happy.'

A smile appeared on Sonobe's face as he greeted her. The woman they called Reiko bowed her head slightly and thanked them simply.

'Reiko, these two are friends from my university club. My senior, Mr. Egami, and Alice Arisugawa, the same year as me. We're in a detective fiction club.'

'Nice to meet you. I'm Maria's cousin, Reiko Arima. Thank you for always taking such good care of her.'

'No, she's the one who takes care of us. Nice to meet you, too.'

Following Egami, I greeted Reiko in turn.

'Oh, sorry for keeping you here at the door. Please step inside. You can put these slippers on.'

We stepped into a large hall. To our right, next to French windows overlooking a terrace, stood a rattan table and chairs. The windows were open, white lace curtains swirled in the wind and we had a partial view of blue sky and sea. Immediately to our left, in the far corner, was a television set with chairs facing it. To the back of the hall to the left, next to open doors leading to the dining room, was a spacious staircase which led to the floor above and, next to that, a table with a glass top. To the right of the dining room was a long corridor leading to the rear of the house with windows in the right hand wall overlooking the sea.

'Please have a seat over there by the windows. Let's have something refreshing before I show you your rooms. You can put your luggage here against the wall. Ah, Maria, it's okay, you sit down too. I'll be right back.'

After Reiko had offered us some very nice seats and stopped Maria from getting up again, she went into the dining room. I found myself inadvertently staring at her retreating figure walking elegantly away with her back stretched and her shoulders gently rocking.

'Reiko is really a wonderful person, don't you think?' Maria said, as she looked at both me and Egami. My senior only answered with a smile, but I nodded vigorously.

'You could be forgiven for saying: "That's my cousin. Beauty runs in the family,"' I said, but Maria shook her head.

Interior of the Panorama Villa

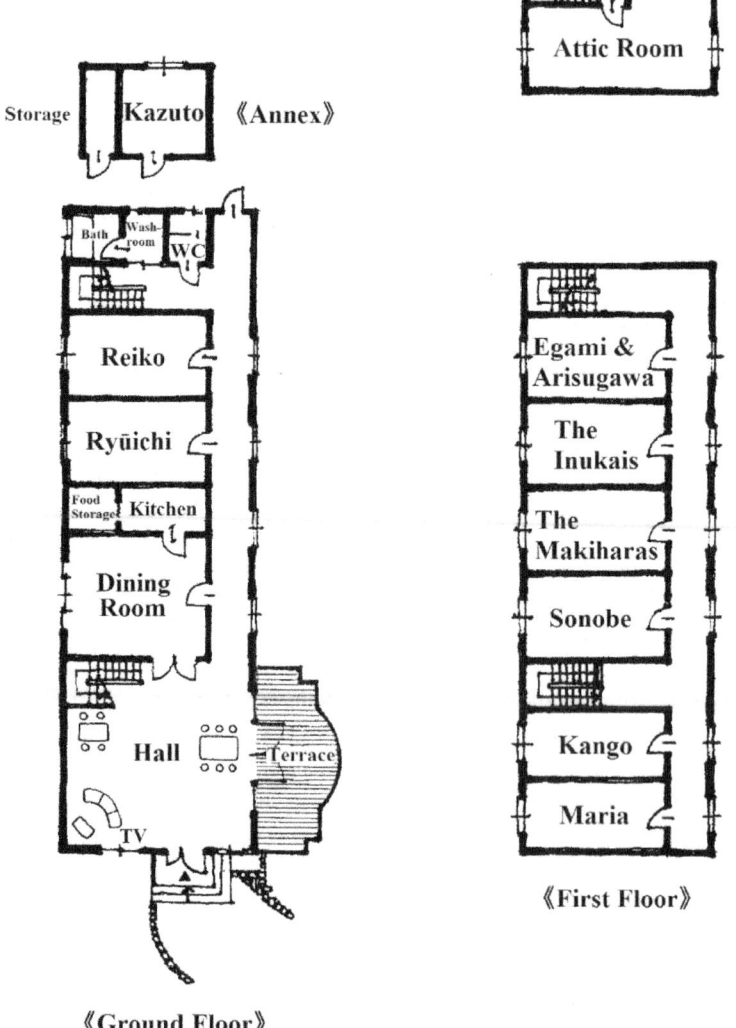

She looked rather sad as she replied: 'To be honest, Reiko and I don't share any blood at all. I told you about my cousin who died in an accident here on the island three years ago. Well, his name was Hideto, and Reiko was his fiancée. Hideto's death was so sudden that Reiko was stunned by it. She became neurotic and had to be admitted into an institution for a while. She couldn't even talk any more and there was a period when I couldn't bear seeing her like that. After a year she finally recovered and that's when my uncle adopted her as his own daughter. Hideto was of course in love with Reiko, but my uncle was also quite fond of her. They had shared their pain over the loss of Hideto and overcome that together, so my uncle had grown very attached to her and considered her part of the family. It might be strange to say this, but it was also lucky in a way that Reiko was all alone in the world, both her parents having already passed away.'

Sonobe had been nodding as he listened to Maria, and when she paused, he added: 'I'm happy it turned out as it did.'

'I'm very fond of her, too.' Maria added and, just at that moment, Reiko appeared in the hall again, bearing a tray with four cups. As she served us, the ice cubes in the cups made a refreshing clinking sound.

As I stared out of the French windows at the wide sea which stretched as far as the horizon, I couldn't believe that only yesterday, I'd still been in Ōsaka, the city of clamour. This extreme change in environment almost had me disoriented. For a while, everyone remained silent, and only the rhythmic sound of the waves reached our ears.

'Where's Arima? And the others?' Sonobe asked.

'My father is having his afternoon nap at the moment. Mr. Makihara and the Inukais are visiting Mr. Hirakawa at his villa. Kazuto, Sumako and her husband are down at the beach, I think.'

'Oh, so Mr. Inukai and his wife are here this year, too? That should be fun.'

The doctor took out his briar pipe in leisurely fashion.

'This will be the first time I'll have met Sumako's husband. Apart from him and Mr. Egami and Alice here, all the faces are the same as three years ago.'

Sonobe hadn't noticed that Reiko had cast her eyes down. Maria, too, felt uneasy and had turned her eyes towards the view beyond the windows. Mr. Egami had noticed their reactions as well, but Sonobe remained oblivious and calmly lit his pipe. It had slipped the doctor's mind that one person who had been here three years ago actually wasn't there. It was probably better to avoid the topic of "three years ago" in front of Reiko. I even started to feel bad for having been so inconsiderate as to get all excited about a treasure hunt.

3

There was a knock on our door.
'It's Maria. May I come in?'
Egami replied in the affirmative.
The door opened and Maria entered, wearing a tank-top that showed off her shoulders and her chest.
'I see the two of you have already changed into something more comfortable. This room is comfortable too, don't you think?'
'Yes, nothing to complain about.'
Egami remained seated on his bed as he stretched his arm out to open the half-open bedside window completely.
'You can even see the sea from here.'
'You can see the sea from all the windows here in Panorama Villa. The sea is all you can see, in fact. But what I love best here are the nights. It's as if this small island turns into its own separate world, drifting away in the universe. It's lonely and frightening, but after a while, all kinds of thoughts well up from inside you and, at that point, it feels as if your body fades away as well. It's really a mysterious feeling. You become smaller than a speck of dust, but despite that, you can still feel your body as you're being lured by the sound of the waves and slowly wash away. I feel this sensation every night.'
Maria's eyes were shining as she looked far away beyond the window. It was rare for her to talk like that without any signs of embarrassment. Okay, I planned to enjoy the same experience that very night.
'We can go swimming tomorrow. And look for the treasure as well.'
She'd suddenly turned back from a dreaming maiden to her usual brisk self. 'I'll show you the house first and then we'll take a quick look around the island. Oh, but all of our bicycles are gone now.'
'You have bicycles here?' I asked.
'Yes,' replied Maria. 'It's a small island, but it's shaped like a C, so it takes ages to walk to the cape on the other side of the bay. If you wanted to walk between the two capes, it'd take about an hour and a half. So, by way of public transport, we have three bicycles here at Panorama Villa. We're on Low Tide Cape. The cape on the other side

of the bay is called High Tide Cape, and Happy Fish Villa, the holiday home of Mr. Hirakawa, the painter, is built at the top of it. Mr. Hirakawa has his own bicycle, too.

'Cycling around the island is fun. I'd been thinking of taking a tour now in preparation for the treasure hunt tomorrow, but all of our three bicycles are gone for now.'

'Ah, Reiko mentioned that, didn't she?' Mr. Egami recalled. 'They're being used by Mr. Makihara and the Inukais at the moment, as they're visiting Mr. Hirakawa.'

'Haha, you're good at remembering names. "Mr. Makihara and the Inukais." As if you've met them before. Yes, you're right. They've taken all three bicycles now.'

'Ah well,' I said, 'cycling around the island is something we'll have to look forward to tomorrow. Let's explore on foot today.'

'Okay, then let's go.'

Our room was at the end of the hallway on the first floor, and if you turned left coming out, you would find the back staircase which led downstairs, as well as up to the attic room. Turning right, you would see three doors between you and the main staircase leading down to the entrance hall. On the other side of that staircase were two more rooms. On the wall side of the hallway were as many windows as there were doors opposite, looking out over the sea, just as on the floor below.

'Look, that's High Tide Cape over there,' Maria pointed out

On the eastern cape on the other side of the bay stood another villa, as if the two cliffs were twins. The distance as the crow flies would be about three hundred metres, at a guess. If the sea hadn't been there, you could have walked the distance easily in a few minutes, but if you took the road that followed the C-shape of the island, it would take you an hour and a half. Even the closest and only neighbour lived quite a distance away on foot.

'You see there's a building on the very tip of the cape, just as we are here? That's Mr. Hirakawa's Happy Fish Villa. It's a lodge-style construction, quite small but fancy.'

'Where does Mr. Hirakawa usually live?'

'He's from Tōkyō. He always stays here from the end of July until mid-August, timing his stay every year to coincide with the period when we and our visitors are here. Because it would be rather expensive to have food shipped in for just one person.'

'Does he paint landscapes? Or is he like a Japanese Gauguin? There don't seem to be any native women here on the island.'

'Landscapes are his *forte*, but that's not all he does. I have another cousin, Sumako Makihara, and three years ago he painted a portrait of her.'

'Oh.'

There it was again: *three years ago*. The last time Maria visited the island was three years ago, so I guess it's only natural, but still... those words nagged at me somehow. It was as if there was a first chapter to this whole story, a chapter only Egami and I hadn't read.

'Are all the rooms on this floor occupied by guests?' asked Egami, as he looked at the row of six doors and the small staircase in the back. 'And isn't there an attic room as well?'

'The attic room's not a bedroom. It's filled with the shells my grandfather occasionally collected, and some of his books on puzzles which we never got rid of. It's basically a storage room. But that's something for later, let's go downstairs.'

We followed her down. She explained that the room next to ours was occupied by the Inukai couple, Toshiyuki and Satomi, and next to them were Sumako Makihara and her husband Junji. Yūsaku Sonobe's room was just before the main staircase, on the other side of which were Kango Makihara's room and finally Maria's. So hers was the farthest from ours.

'How do you know?' I asked. 'Had you already heard how the rooms were assigned before we came here? You've had no time to ask anybody since we arrived.'

'Oh no, it's not as if I heard about the room arrangements beforehand. But the people here this year are almost the same as three years ago, so I just assumed the room assignments would be the same. The only differences between now and then are that Reiko occupied the room Mr. Egami and you are in now, and that Sumako used a twin room all by herself.'

'So Reiko is staying downstairs this year?'

'Yes. Three years ago she stayed in a guest room because she was Hideto's fiancée. She's probably staying in the room in the rear of the downstairs corridor this year. It's the room Hideto used three years ago. So Reiko and my uncle are downstairs. Kazuto has a room in the annex.'

How would Reiko feel in the room of her deceased fiancé? Wouldn't the pain she'd almost forgotten well up again from within the depths of her soul? Or would she find comfort, immersing herself in sad feelings of nostalgia? Either way, it was definitely no business of mine.

At first I'd assumed that the famous paintings hanging in splendid frames on the wall of the main staircase were replicas, but on my way down I realised I was wrong. Rembrandt's *Night Watch*, Monet's *Water Lilies*, van Gogh's *Cypress*, Renoir's *Young Girl Bathing*, Seurat's *A Sunday on La Grande Jatte – 1884*: they weren't replicas but completed jigsaw puzzles of 2,000 pieces or more. I guess they were high-grade puzzles, because they were very well made.

'Alice, did you think those paintings were were real? There isn't a single painting in this whole house. Everything hanging here is a completed jigsaw puzzle. I told you my grandfather was crazy about them. Do you want to try one out?'

'I'll pass. I'm shuddering at the mere thought of coming all the way here to a sunny island, only to struggle with a pesky puzzle. Ah, sorry, I shouldn't have said that.'

Maria didn't seem to mind. 'You're right. But a jigsaw puzzle isn't really that boring. An unfinished jigsaw puzzle has been laid out on the big table next to the staircase downstairs. You know, just as they have as a form of recreation on luxury cruise ships.'

'Sadly enough, I've never been on any.'

'Neither have I. But it's a way of getting the guests to play together. I took a peek just now, and this time we're building Rousseau's *The Snake Charmer*,' Maria explained, as we descended the staircase.

On the pipe-legged table with the glass top, you could already see parts of some flourishing tropical plants and the full moon.

'Is your poor head starting to hurt, Alice?'

'No, looks fun, actually.'

I'd changed my mind. My first impression when I saw the completed puzzles in the frames was that it looked like it'd take too much effort, but seeing the pieces of this incomplete puzzle seemed to lure me. The view of thousands of pieces in a disorderly state was something to behold.

Reiko appeared from the dining room with a glass of orange juice on a tray.

'Oh, are you going out for a walk?'

'Yes,' replied Maria. 'The bicycles aren't back yet, I assume?'

'No. Mr. Inukai and the others will stay at Mr. Hirakawa's until the evening. Sumako said she'd be back to prepare for dinner, but she's not here yet.'

Maria offered to help but Reiko declined: 'That's okay, Maria. You've just arrived, so today you just act like a perfect guest. I'll have you working on lunch and dinner from tomorrow on.'

'Okay,' said Maria simply. Then Reiko noticed that her eyes were fixed on the orange juice.

'This? Father's awake now, so I'm taking this to him. It's his daily routine to sleep for two hours after lunch and then have a cold glass of orange juice.'

'I'll say hello to uncle later then. Reiko, you'd better go now, the ice cubes are starting to melt.'

'Okay. Have a nice walk.'

Reiko gave Egami and me a warm smile and saw us off.

'Reiko's so bright again,' Maria said to herself as we exited the villa. 'She was still so depressed even after she'd recovered from her neurosis. Even when she smiled, it was always a weak smile, and it almost hurt looking at her.'

'You're quite concerned for her,' said Egami as he shot a glance behind him. 'Is she the sister you've always wanted? I do agree she has something feminine which you lack.'

'Am I so un-girl-like? I'm sort of surprised. Nobody has ever said I was boyish, not even when I was a kid.'

'I never said you were boyish. I'd say you were a shy, girlish boyish girl.'

'Mr. Egami, what does that even mean? That makes no sense at all.'

'I think it was quite a striking expression.'

My unwanted opinion was answered by a glare from Maria.

As well as the small path leading down to the landing point, there was another one to the rear of the villa that led down towards the open sea. I couldn't see where it went because the lady palms growing on this side of the path blocked the view.

'Oh, that path leads down to the beach.' Maria had quickly caught my expression and explained immediately. 'The island only has a couple of beaches where you can swim. The beach down here, and another one directly beneath Mr. Hirakawa's Happy Fish Villa. If we went down there now, we'd see Sumako and the others, but let's save the greetings for later. I'll show you the *moai* statues first, as a preliminary inspection for tomorrow. Behold their dauntless countenances and set your fighting spirit ablaze!'

'Dauntless, countenance, blazing fighting spirit....'

'So?'

'Not very appropriate words for a girl.'

'You're close to getting kicked, Alice.'

4

The path curved gently to the right, with trees blocking our view of the bay to our left. After a while, the sea appeared on our right. It was probably just an illusion, but the faraway horizon appeared to be curved and I stopped in my tracks in awe of the magnificent view.

'Keep moving, Alice. There's a spot with a nice view up ahead.'

There she was, interrupting a person who was busy being deeply moved by the island on his first visit. Oh well. I guess Maria was just innocently trying to appeal to me by telling me she knew a place with an even better view. No way I'd ever think of her as not cute.

We continued down the gentle slope.

'Let's see, there should be one over there…. Oh, look, there it is.'

Maria stopped, and pointed towards a row of thinly-scattered black pine trees. The sun reflecting from the sea allowed me to see only a dark silhouette, like a needle sticking out from the edge of the cliff.

Maria went into the grass, carefully minding where she put her feet. I nonchalantly tried to follow her into the grass, but she stopped me.

'It seems to be okay here, but I'm being very careful. Watch where you place your feet. There are yellow-spotted pit vipers on the island.'

I pulled my foot back hastily. It's nothing to brag about, but I hate snakes. I even jump when the random page of an encyclopaedia I open turns out to be the one on snakes. And did she say yellow-spotted pit vipers? Wouldn't they, like, represent Japan in any international venomous snake competition? Dark clouds quickly gathered above my previous image of this paradise-like island.

'Oh, you don't need to be so afraid. It's not as if they're slithering around everywhere. To be honest, I've only seen them twice. And only far away in the bushes, crawling away quickly. Walking out at night is scary, but during the day you don't need to be afraid of stepping on them by accident. But being careful never hurts.'

'Just to be clear, I've no intention of losing my life looking for hidden treasure.'

I followed Maria and Egami. About ten metres from the path, the cliff offered a sheer drop into the sea. There were no railings, of course, so I moved to the edge timidly and peeked down below. Fifteen, sixteen metres below, waves came surging in from afar, broke on the shore and turned into white foam.

'Alice, that's dangerous,' said Maria from behind me. 'Anyway, look at this *moai* here, standing in silence, guarding the secret to the location of the treasure.'

I turned round, and saw Maria pointing eagerly. Egami put his hand on his hip and looked amused at this so-called *moai* statue.

'It's pretty well made, actually.'

Just as she'd told us, the statue was about as wide as a utility pole and about one metre high. It was probably made from pine wood. A chisel had been used on the midsection, and, while the face had been cut out rather roughly, it had indeed more or less the same face as those famous stone statues on Easter Island. Dauntless countenances, Maria had said, but considering their drooping eyes, long, thin noses and lips sticking out, cute might have been the better word. A *jizō*[iii] statue of the southern islands.

'Even if it doesn't turn out to be the key to the puzzle, don't you think it's a good mascot for the island? Statues exactly like this one are spread all around the island, but even though they know where the treasure is, they won't tell anyone. Stupid dwarfs.'

Egami touched the statue's face and back lightly. That was his habit. Once, when we visited an old temple in Kyōto, he also lovingly touched the black pillars and gates that had stood there for hundreds of years.

After he stopped stroking the statue, Egami crouched down and looked it in the eye. He was probably trying to find out what was reflected there. Maria and I stood behind him and peered in front of us, over his head.

'But there's nothing reflected there but the bushes on the other side of the road.'

'Of course,' replied Egami, still looking at the statue. 'Maria, is there anything interesting over there, on the other side of those trees?'

'Just the sea.'

Egami let out a low 'I see.' He got up slowly and brushed the dust from his knee. 'And you said the *moai* on the island all look in different directions?'

'Yes. At least, it's not as if I've checked every one of them, but I think Hideto did.'

'Just before he died?'

'Yes. He spent his last three days going around checking all the *moais*. He'd invited Reiko to the island, so he might have wanted to impress her. He was someone who would get totally focused on one thing. And of course, since it was a question of diamonds buried somewhere, I imagine he wanted to find the treasure and give it to his fiancée.'

'I can understand that,' I said.

'Grandfather was a very impressive person, so I think Hideto also wanted to take up the challenge and beat him at his own intellectual game. How's that for the psychology of a man in his twenties?'

'I can understand that,' I said again. I was precisely twenty.

'How old was Hideto when he died?' asked Egami. Maria opened her eyes wide as she looked up to the sky and thought.

'Twenty-four. Reiko is twenty-six this year, so she was twenty-three at the time. They were really the perfect couple.'

'And Hideto was just one step away from the answer, you said. Had he in fact already solved the puzzle?'

Maria tilted her head slightly as she fell into deep thought again. For my part, I was happy to appreciate her rich repertoire of gestures and expressions.

'I don't think he'd solved it. I don't remember what he said exactly, but it was something like "The key lies in the direction the *moais* are facing," and "I think I'm onto something." He came to me one night after dinner, while I was washing the dishes, and whispered that to me contentedly. He drowned shortly afterwards. "When I've found the treasure I'll give you a pair of earrings as a present." Those were the last words Hideto spoke to me. I made fun of him. "You sound confident. Tell me that when you've found the treasure and brought it back with you."'

'Don't get all teared up, Girl Detective.' Egami pointed his finger at Maria. 'Don't get all emotional. You're doing this for your cousin, remember?'

'Yes. This girl detective will do her best.'

Maria looked up and smiled. She loved being called a girl detective by Egami and had always been disappointed that girls couldn't get into the Boy Detective Club[iv].

'Did Hideto perhaps hint at something? Like what direction, or what kind of place, or how the treasure was hidden?'

'Nothing like that. But let's stop guessing and accept the challenge of the puzzle head on. It's a puzzle made by a human, so it must be possible to solve it. Mr. Egami, please use your brains to help us. You too, Alice.'

'If it's for you….'

I wanted to be of help, but to be honest, I had no confidence I could. I was good at crossword puzzles, but I had no idea where to even begin with this puzzle and if I'd come across it in a book, I'd have gone straight to the page with the solution. I hoped she wasn't expecting too much of me.

'Okay, here's the plan.' Egami turned round and faced the sea. 'Let's put our faith in Hideto and go around investigating the directions the statues are facing. Starting tomorrow we'll check out every *moai* on the map, one by one.'

'Roger,' said Maria and I in unison.

Egami's eyes were fixed on the sea, which shone brightly with diffused reflections. Maria and I faced into a sea breeze. The three of us stood there for a while, without a word being spoken.

5

We returned to Panorama Villa as the sun started to set. It was past six, which was still before the summer sun would disappear completely in the south.

A man and a woman, both under thirty, were seated in the rattan chairs near the window, while Dr. Sonobe was sitting in front of the glass-top table, crouching over the jigsaw puzzle.

'Maria, welcome back.'

The woman by the window greeted us when she saw us. The man sitting across from her turned to look at us as well.

'It's been such a long time, Sumako. Hello, Junji.'

'Glad you could make it.'

Maria introduced us to her cousin and her husband. Sumako Makihara was eight years older than Maria. Her wavy hair was still wet, as if to prove she'd been swimming until a few moments ago. Her face had well-defined features and the eyeliner and red rouge she had just applied were vivid.

The gaudy, flower-patterned one-piece she was wearing and the cork necklace she had around her neck looked fancy. Her crossed legs were also nice to look at.

Junji Makihara didn't make as smart an impression as his wife Sumako. Beneath his short, stubby hair was a swarthy face which didn't look clean because his moustache hadn't yet grown out fully. Unshaven spots all over his chin also stood out. But I wouldn't describe his face as primal. He wore a garish yellow Aloha shirt, and a necklace with a coin formed in the shape of a wave was hanging from his thin neck. The legs that stuck out of his white Bermuda shorts looked weak. Hold it. Writing my impressions down like this makes it seem as though I became very biased against him in mere seconds. Even taking into account that people aren't always dandy-looking when they're relaxing, there was nevertheless a difference in class compared to his beloved wife.

'So these are your male friends? One on each side.'

'They're my friends-slash-detectives.'

Maria introduced Egami and me to the couple. Sumako laughed heartily when she heard we were detective fiction fans who had come to the island to solve the *moai* puzzle.

'Maria, are you still into detective stories? You've been reading them since you were a kid. I remember your parents often complained about it. "It's good she's reading books now, but I'm not sure about the shelves being filled with bloodthirsty titles with the murder of this or the tragedy of that."'

'Oh, sorry. I forgot your friends also read them.'

Sumako shrugged unassumingly, put a menthol cigarette in her mouth and lit it.

'But I'm looking forward to seeing how you'll manage. If you three put your heads together, you might really solve the mystery. Don't you agree?'

For some reason, the "you" was referring to me. I decided I'd keep silent if she ever called me "little Alice," but answered with just a simple 'Yes.'

'You can count on us.' Maria clasped her hands together behind her back and straightened herself. 'You're just saying sweet words now, but that's because you don't know how sharp our Detective Egami really is. Just a while ago, when I was coughing because of a summer cold, I added one or two coughs at the end on purpose, but he saw through me. "Two of them were fake," he pointed out. I was so surprised.'

What does that have to do with looking for a treasure? the expression on Sumako's face said.

'I'm looking forward to your exploits,' joined in Junji. 'I'd do anything to get my hands on the treasure, but I'm really bad at puzzles and difficult things like that, so I've given up. If you do find the diamonds, I'll be content simply to look at them.'

'We'll definitely find them. Right, Mr. Egami?'

'I wouldn't say definitely.'

Maria looked slightly disappointed by his common sense reply.

'Oh, today's going fine!'

A voice yelled out from the other side of the hall. The doctor smiled happily as he entertained himself with the puzzle.

'Err, this one maybe? Hm? If it's not this one, then I've another one here. A piece with the reflection of the moon in the river.'

Perhaps he was speaking out loud on purpose so we could hear him. As he was digging through the pile of uncompleted puzzle pieces, he mumbled something.

'Hmm, that doctor sure is having fun,' said Junji, with a bored expression. 'I just don't understand what's going on in people's minds when they're playing with jigsaw puzzles. You have a perfectly fine picture which you cut up in pieces and then you have to work to put it together again. Only someone with too much time on his hands could've come up with that. The completed puzzles are hanging in the staircase, but instead of pictures filled with cuts, normal replicas or posters would've looked much better.'

His way of speaking was certainly crude. Even so, he'd lowered his voice so the doctor wouldn't hear him.

To me, it sounded as if Junji had also been criticising detective fiction. Mystery writers rack their brains to come up with some never-before-seen trick or strange case, and then they break it up in pieces and then pretentiously build it up again step by step. And readers enjoy witnessing this meaningless process. Junji would have wondered what kind of person had come up with that, too.

'You're having a fine streak, doctor.' Maria ignored Junji and called out cheerfully to Sonobe.

'Yes, I'm on a roll. Arima's reading a book in his room. Have you greeted him already?'

'I'll go and see him now. I'll be right back.'

Maria left us and went into the hallway. She herself was probably under the impression she was walking normally, but she never walked in a straight line. I stared at her receding figure as she waggled her hips.

'Have a seat over here. You two fellows shouldn't keep standing up all the time.'

Following Sonobe's offer, we sat down on the seats opposite him. He was apparently on a good streak. I picked up a piece that looked like part of the night sky, but I couldn't find where it fit.

'I think this is the head of the snake.' Egami moved one piece in front of him. 'Doctor, I'll leave that spot with the water to you. I'll do the snake.' The doctor nodded in silence.

Egami dexterously gathered a number of pieces in front of him which looked like parts of the dark figure of a snake. He didn't try to put them together, but only kept on gathering similar pieces.

'Hmm, I see you know the basics of puzzle solving,' said the doctor after he'd taken a peak at Egami's work.

I shot a glance at the Makiharas. The husband had a wry grin on his face; the wife was blowing peppermint-flavoured smoke towards the open window.

6

Sonobe, Egami and I stayed in the hall, busy with the jigsaw puzzle, until the seven o'clock dinner. After greeting her uncle, Maria had returned and gone to the kitchen to help Reiko, after which a tired-looking Sumako also stood up and followed Maria. Junji sat near the window for a while, but then, obviously bored, he stepped outside.

Just before seven, I heard the sound of bicycles stopping in front of the house. It was probably the three who'd returned from their visit to the artist Hirakawa's Happy Fish Villa.

The door opened to the accompaniment of a man's voice.

'Maria was supposed to bring two of her friends, I believe? And Doctor Sonobe should be here too. It's been a while since I last saw him. Ah, here they are. Welcome, Doctor.'

The man who came in greeted the doctor in a hoarse voice. He looked over sixty and, unusually for that age, was nearly six feet tall. His hair had turned almost completely grey and many wrinkles were chiselled into his face, but he had a healthy complexion. As he walked slowly towards us, I noticed his long and dignified stride.

'You look good, Kango. You always stay so young, while I am only turning older and older.'

'Nonsense. I've heard all the stories about the energetic doctor who's still busy swimming in the sea of neon lights in Yokohama's Isezakichō district.'

'Ha, that's a good one. I stopped doing that a long time ago. I'm just an old geezer who doesn't even know what he's living for.'

Having said that, Sonobe introduced Egami and me to the man.

'Pleased to meet you. My name is Kango Makihara. I'm Ryūichi Arima's brother-in-law, and also Maria's uncle. I hope you enjoy your stay here.'

He held out a large-boned hand which both Egami and I shook as we greeted him in return.

The other two were a couple. They were in their mid-thirties and both small in stature. They introduced themselves politely. Toshiyuki Inukai had a childish face, save for his thick black eyebrows and was wearing a plain white T-shirt. He was only thirty-six, yet was apparently already a restaurant owner with nine chain outlets in the Fukuoka and Saga prefectures. I was surprised to learn he was the younger brother of the sixty-two year old Ryūichi Arima.

'Naturally, we don't share both parents. I'm his half-brother.' He started to answer the question that had popped into our minds. 'We have different mothers. I'm the son of my father's mistress when he was already in his fifties. But my father and the Arima family have always treated us well. After my mother's death, I got a great deal of financial support from the Arimas too and opened a restaurant in her home town. This is our second visit here on the island and it's really a fantastic place to be.'

His wife's name was Satomi. She was wearing a sleeveless, whitish summer sweater and a knit skirt. She had a very Japanese face, long with round cheeks. Her hair had a hint of chestnut brown, but unlike Maria, she probably dyed hers. Still standing, Toshiyuki told the story of how they met, while Satomi listened as she unconsciously played with the ring which fit loosely around her ring finger.

So, how many people had we been introduced to at this stage? Reiko Arima, Junji Makihara, Sumako Makihara, Kango Makihara, Toshiyuki Inukai and Satomi Inukai. Six, not counting the two we had yet to meet in this house: the owner, Ryūichi Arima and his son, Kazuto. We would probably meet them at dinner.

Reiko appeared out of the kitchen, wearing an apron.

'Welcome back. Dinner's almost ready, so please wait just a little longer. Meanwhile, I'll bring you some iced tea.'

'I'll pour,' said Satomi, shaking her wet hair. 'I'm sorry, Reiko, for staying away all the time. I'll wash up today.'

'No, you just behave like a real guest. But I really appreciate your thoughtfulness.'

The two women kept thanking each other as they disappeared into the kitchen.

'I feel bad for the women, but we useless men will just have to sit here and wait,' said Kango as he went over to the window and let his large body slide into a rattan chair. Toshiyuki Inukai sat down opposite him. Satomi brought out some tea for all of us.

'Now might be the time we rely on the ladies, but it might become the time for the men to work soon,' said Sonobe as he started on the puzzle again. 'Maybe we should have these two young men help as well.'

'With what?'

'A typhoon. The news this morning said that Typhoon No. 12 was to the south of Ishigaki Island. It was moving at high speed towards the north-east, so it might arrive here sometime tomorrow night.'

Now that he mentioned it, I'd heard the typhoon alert as well. But it wasn't as if we were staying in tents, so I thought it'd be kind of fun to experience a real-life typhoon on a remote island in the south sea.

But now, slightly worried, I asked the doctor: 'Have you ever experienced a typhoon here on the island?'

'We were hit really hard by one over ten years ago, but that's all.'

'What happened?'

'Well, there was a lot of rain of course, but it was especially the wind that was incredibly violent. We lost almost all the phoenix palms planted in the back of the house. The antenna of the wireless transceiver was also hit and, even after the typhoon had left, the sea remained so rough with high waves that the rescue boat was delayed for two days before it managed to reach us.'

'That was a really heavy one.' Kango's hoarse voice came from across the hall. 'And it came in the middle of the night as well. We have a generator here, so we had no fear of a power failure, but the whole house creaked and we were quite anxious.'

'The house is in an exposed position on the edge of the island and on a hill as well, so it's a sitting duck for the wind. I was already busy working out in my head what to grab hold of if the house started falling apart.'

'It was then that my father-in-law….'

Sonobe and Kango were holding an excited conversation across the hall about the event ten years earlier. I added the occasional 'Wow' and 'Oh,' while Egami concentrated on sorting out the jigsaw puzzle pieces he needed. He wasn't particularly interested in jigsaw puzzles, but once he started something, he couldn't help but do his best, which was one of the reasons I respected him so much.

'Sorry to have kept you waiting, everyone. Dinner's now ready. Come into the dining room,' said Reiko as she appeared in the hall. Maria came out as well, also wearing an apron, saying 'I'm going to call uncle.' She waved to us and walked quickly away.

'I went all the way to High Tide Cape by bicycle today with the Inukais, so I'm starving.' So saying, Kango led the men into the dining room.

7

Twelve faces gathered around the large dining table which appeared to have been made from oak. It was our first time here and we'd only just arrived, so we were led to the seats for the guests of honour. I was the youngest of all those present and also of a lower standing, so it made me uncomfortable. But the menu was a delight.

'Today we have no less than four guests from afar. I'm happy you came all the way to our little island. I hope you'll have a relaxing time,' said Ryūichi Arima in a welcoming manner. The elderly gentleman, with his grey hair combed back, had friendly eyes and a surprising air of modesty.

'Thank you for always taking care of my niece, and please enjoy your time here.'

As Ryūichi said that, he bowed his head slightly in the direction of Egami and myself. As we would be his dining guests for a week and had no recollection of taking good care of Maria, we returned the gesture with some embarrassment.

'I was surprised that Maria's friends turned out to be two men. I'd heard she would be bringing two private detectives to look for the treasure, and seeing how bright these two look, I somehow feel assured.'

It was Kazuto Arima who had grinningly spoken those words, sitting opposite me. He had narrow shoulders and bangs of hair reaching his eyebrows. He was Maria's cousin, five years her elder, and the younger brother of the deceased Hideto. He spoke in a tenor voice, the tips of his fingers pinched around a cigarette.

'I'm afraid I let my imagination run riot, and was all excited from this morning on, expecting two spirited female college students to turn up. Nobody had told me Maria's friends were men, so imagine my surprise when I came down here to the dining room. I actually saw the three of you come back from your walk from a window on the floor above. Just a glimpse of you coming inside. The only thing I saw then was your head, Mr. Egami. I never doubted you were a woman. Just thought that you were a rather tall one. Long hair suits you, but don't you want to cut it short at least in the summer? The heat would make me go crazy.'

He was a talkative man. I was not very appreciative of people who made comments about other people's hair. He wasn't talking about me, but I almost wanted to tell him to lay off with the Mohican cuts and pigtails.

'I don't cut my hair at any time of the year. There's spiritual power residing within each strand of hair, you know,' replied Egami with a solemn expression.

Kazuto was taken aback for a second by this unexpected answer, and I had to suppress my laughter as the corners of my mouth were twitching. I shot a glance at Maria, whose shoulders were shaking.

'They often say something like that in the West,' Sonobe said, with a straight face. 'The source of one's power lies in one's hair. Do you know the story of Samson and Delilah? I wonder if it's exclusively a Western tradition?'

With the discussion starting on a topic he didn't even begin to comprehend, Kazuto kept his mouth shut. He was twenty-four, but still a student. He had failed his entrance examinations twice, had gone abroad for a year on an exchange program, and was now in his third year. But I had no comment about that. Egami, our club president, was twenty-seven and in his fourth year, and I didn't want to comment about that, either.

'By the way, Mr. Inukai, I heard you were going to open a restaurant in Kokura this autumn?' said Sumako. Toshiyuki Inukai stopped the fork he was moving to his mouth in mid-air.

'Yes. Someone introduced me to a great property and, while it wasn't easy to acquire, I simply couldn't let it go. I keep pushing myself on, I suppose it's just who I am.'

'But you know what's exciting?' Satomi picked up after her husband. 'When we were visiting Mr. Hirakawa this afternoon and told him about it, he said he would make a painting for us to put up in the new restaurant. "What about a large painting of the *shiranui*[v] lights of the Ariake Sea?" he asked.'

The couple looked at each other and smiled. Toshiyuki continued his tale, his fork still poised in mid-air.

'The restaurant is scheduled to open in November, so he couldn't finish it by then, but I'd never dared to dream he'd offer us a painting.' Toshiyuki eagerly continued talking about his restaurant, but Sumako had lost interest halfway through and paid no attention to him anymore.

When Junji Makihara wasn't silently moving the food into his mouth, he was swigging beer like water. His swarthy face had turned red. Kazuto had decided we weren't much fun to talk to, and had turned away to start a one-sided conversation with Reiko about the films of the summer. Ryūichi initially talked to Maria and us about the life of university students nowadays, but after he'd poured a glass of beer for his old friend Sonobe, the two of them started to have a lively discussion about all that had happened in their lives of late.

It was a peaceful dinner. We had ice cream and coffee afterwards.

After that, Kango and Junji moved to the seats in the corner of the hall in front of the television, which only showed NHK[vi]. They watched a foreign travel programme with their arms crossed and without exchanging a single word. Sumako said she was tired from swimming and had gone upstairs, as had Toshiyuki Inukai, while Kazuto sat in one of the rattan chairs near the windows, reading. Sonobe, who'd invited us for a drink and a talk earlier, had become engrossed in conversation with Ryūichi and the two of them had retired to Ryūichi's room. Reiko and Satomi were doing the dishes, and Reiko had stopped Maria from helping them.

'You really don't have to help today. Go and talk to Mr. Egami and Alice about how you're going to spend your time tomorrow.'

Maria finally gave in. With a 'Let's go,' she invited us upstairs. She said she'd show us the attic room, which would be interesting because of all the junk there. We went up the stairs in single file.

'Welcome to Panorama Villa's toy box,' said Maria as she opened the door. The boarded room contained only bookcases with doors and, on two of the walls, display cases for shells. It was a bleak space without a single chair. I'd expected a dirty, stuffy room, but it had been cleaned up nicely, with not a speck of dust in sight.

I peeked inside the glass display cases and saw over a hundred shells lined up on cotton wool. The ratio between spiral shells and clams was about three to one and they were meticulously assorted by family, such as ear shells, moon shells and ark shells. Each of them was accompanied by a card that noted the name and the day and place it had been found, but they had all turned yellow. It was sad to see such a collection after it had lost its master.

Curious as to what kind of books were in the bookcases, I walked over to one, but I stopped when I noticed a rifle leaning against the wall by the door.

'Is that for decoration? Or is it a real functioning rifle?'

'It's real enough,' said Maria, as if that was perfectly normal. 'Why don't you try sniffing the barrel? I bet Kazuto has been blasting away all summer, so it should smell of gunpowder.'

Having never touched a firearm before, I gingerly pointed the barrel towards my face and brought it close to my nose.

'You sure have guts, Alice. That's dangerous: it might be loaded.'

As soon as Maria spoke, I hurriedly turned my face away. That apparently looked so funny, even Egami started to laugh.

'You look so cute,' Maria said cheekily. 'But you really should be more careful. Still, it's really unique to see someone so afraid of rifles putting one right up to his face.'

'Shuddup.'

I changed my grip on the rifle and pointed it at Maria's chest. Her expression changed. 'Stop it,' she said, hiding behind Egami and repeating her plea. I guessed that confirmed the rifle was the real deal. As this was starting to become a very unfunny joke, I pointed the rifle up at the ceiling. With that one movement, I felt like a soldier for a moment and I experienced a kind of fear of the power involved.

'Using our club president as a shield. You're quite the one.'

'You can't talk. It's crazy to point a rifle at someone.'

Maria remained behind Egami as she spoke. It's safe to come out, I thought, but she might still be on her guard because I was still holding the rifle. I hadn't held it long enough to get the feel of it, but I put it back against the wall anyway, with some reluctance.

'I'm sorry.'

Maria appeared from behind Egami and let out a big sigh.

'Even Kazuto has more common sense than you.' She was still mad. 'And he's frightening enough.'

'So this is his rifle?' asked Egami and Maria nodded.

'Yes. He got it from one of his friends. But he has no licence or anything. So he's in violation of the Swords and Firearms Control Law. But he doesn't take it off the island, just shoots at practice targets as a form of stress relief, so everyone on the island keeps it a secret. Heck, he lets anyone else take pot shots as well.'

'Have you used it yourself?' asked Egami.

'Two or three times. I'm also guilty, I guess. We're all accomplices…oh, except for Mr. Inukai. He used to be into clay target shooting when he was still at university, and, while he doesn't own a rifle, he still has a licence.'

'Mr. Inukai? The restaurant owner? That doesn't fit his image at all'.

'He's not tall, but he's quite the sportsman, actually. He's also the best swimmer. Very different from someone else I could name.'

'Are you talking about me? I'm quite good at swimming, I'll have you know. Only I'm not very fast. Must be my personality.'

'Not you, Alice. I was talking about Kazuto. He just sinks.'

To me it seemed as if Maria had little affection for her cousin. It was the opposite of how sad she always looked when she spoke of the deceased Hideto. I didn't like Kazuto's rude way of talking either, but I also had the impression he was not that bad a person.

'Aha, all books on puzzles.'

I turned round to see Egami in front of one of the bookcases, reading the titles on the spines one by one.

'There are a lot of interesting books there. You can take one with you to bed and spend the night puzzling,' suggested Maria, but Egami shook his head and closed the book he was holding.

'I'll pass. I need to rest and be sharp for tomorrow. Why should I spend time on one single puzzle, when this whole island is one?'

'If that's your argument, why spend time racking our brains over puzzles when life itself is one?'

No. That wasn't it.

There's no need to build a labyrinth when the entire universe is one.

Thus wrote Borges.

8

Maria's description "Panorama Villa's toy box," had been exaggerated. There was nothing much of interest there, so we decided to go to Maria's room to decide on our plans for the following day. As expected, her room was the same as ours, except that it only had one bed, but it had the same wallpaper and curtains.

'Breakfast is served between seven-thirty and eight, so keep that in mind,' she began energetically. 'But what will we do after that? We could swim for a while after breakfast. Or we could go around the island by bike?'

'Personally, I'd prefer to take a look around the island first,' I replied. 'And not just going around at random, but checking the direction each *moai* is facing.'

'That'll be difficult, you know. Not all of the statues are standing near the road. Oh well, let's go cycling tomorrow then. We can check the statues we can reach without trouble and also visit the island's best spots. There's a hill where you can overlook the whole island and there are also some strangely shaped rock formations. We could also visit Mr. Hirakawa on the way. We'll go swimming in the afternoon.'

And with that, the meeting was over. She'd decided the next day's schedule all by herself. Neither Egami nor I were shrinking violets, like those people who go to a restaurant and order the same as everyone else, but discussions tended to end quickly and smoothly with Maria around. Like now.

'I think I'll go to bed early tonight. I did bring Ruth Rendell's latest with me, though.'

'Rendell? She's good, but I don't get as intrigued any more as when I first read her books.'

'Alice, don't be so demanding. There's nobody else who can write like her. I'm going to do an essay on her for the club magazine's autumn issue. Rendell is a master of the art. Don't you agree, Mr. Egami?'

A lively discussion on contemporary British mystery fiction started. In the end it all came down to the personal preference, so I'll omit the details here. The topic changed several times. And while we were considering Colin Dexter's capabilities as a writer of puzzle plot mysteries, it happened.

'You can't.'

We all heard the voice saying those words and we all went quiet at the same time.

'You can't. Dad's finally having a good time with this holiday, so I don't want you to make him angry again. What are you thinking, bringing up money now? Your timing couldn't be worse.'

'But I want to talk about it now because he's in such a good mood and won't be so difficult about it. It seems your dad hates me quite a bit, but if his cute daughter asks him, he'll open his wallet, even as he complains in that sweet voice of his.'

'I don't want to ask him. How about asking him yourself?'

'You can't say no, just because you don't feel like it. You're saying I should ask him myself? That's a good one. The moment he realises what I'm there for, he'll come at me with a barrage of lectures. In that sweet voice of his, of course. Asking him myself is the worst possible way to do it.'

'You're always like that. You and dad always get along so badly.'

The voices were coming from right below the window. It was the couple Junji and Sumako Makihara. They were trying to hold a conversation quietly and in secret, but the topic soon had them subconsciously talking louder. They hadn't realised there was anyone in the room right above them.

'Yes, I really can't stand him. All through the year he's looking around for someone he can lecture. And loudly, too. He's the type you absolutely don't want as a father-in-law, and that's a fact.'

'Please, stop it. He's my dad. I can't take it. You and he are my only family left in the world, but seeing you two hating each other.... It really hurts.'

'Is it that difficult for him to lend his daughter and her husband five million yen? He's got piles of the stuff. My business might be peanuts compared to the Inukai restaurant chain, but it's my own, which I finally managed to set up with the money I saved from driving a truck around for five years.'

'Yes, I know, that's why—.'

'I won't have my place taken from me just because of a mere five million yen debt, damn it!'

'Let's leave this for now, Junji. You're getting all worked up.... I understand, and I will talk to dad. Sometime while we're on the island.'

There was a brief pause in the discussion.

'As soon as possible.'

'Yes. I'll try tomorrow... Don't forget that in this world, the one I care most for is you.'

'I care for you too...'

The sound of clothes rustling. Signs of hugging. The noise of footsteps receding.

We were left behind in our silence.

I coughed. 'We were eavesdropping. That's bad.'

'Since their talk reached us upstairs, there was not much dropping. And eavesdropping sounds so disreputable.' Maria brushed my concerns away. 'But that was funny. All three of us shutting our mouths the moment we heard them talking in secret. I wonder whether that's normal human behaviour.'

If the two of them had realised there were people in the room above during their secret talk, it would've been embarrassing for them. We were just being polite.

'Mr. Makihara was crying about his business, but I didn't even know he had one. Is it a restaurant like Mr. Inukai's?' asked Egami as he looked at the star-filled sky outside the window. The velvet night sky was crossed by the Milky Way.

'Junji owns a small bar. As he said himself, it's quite different from Mr. Inukai's restaurant chain. But it appears as though business isn't going well. He might not be able to repay his debts.'

'But I do feel bad for Sumako. Having your husband and father with so much bad blood between them is enough to make you sick. Maria, when you choose your husband, you'd better have a fortune-teller tell you the compatibility between your future husband and your father.'

'Sumako's situation is extreme. Just listening to it makes me tired. She always lived her life freely before, but I guess now she's stuck in a dead end.'

Maria explained that, after a free-wheeling adolescence, Sumako had taken up the same occupation as Florence Nightingale, whom she admired greatly, but had given up after a year and entered university at the age of twenty-three to study law. She'd become interested in art and had posed for Hirakawa on this very island. For a time, she'd been attracted to the middle-aged painter. Then, after she'd moved on again, she'd met Junji, the brother of one of her friends.

'They fell in love immediately. Junji asked her to marry him after three months of dating. Unfortunately, Uncle Kango didn't like him at all. He'd been casting nets around for a suitable husband for his daughter, but the men he had in mind were all elite employees of commercial banks or general trading companies, or in line to become the second generation presidents of a company.'

'What kind of business is your uncle in?' I asked.

'He opened an accounting firm with a friend when he was in university. It's not a big business, but he's fairly wealthy and owns quite a lot of land in the metropolitan area. Anyway, my uncle has been looking down on Junji since they first met, and has no qualms about saying hurtful things to him.'

No wonder Junji was so bitter.

'But Junji puts up with that for a reason. Uncle Kango didn't object when Junji married into the Makihara family, probably because he wished his dear daughter to be happy. He's saved Junji's bar before and I even heard he'd bailed Junji out after he'd lost a fortune playing *mah-jong*. So Junji shouldn't act like such a bigshot either.

'It must be really tough for Sumako. I guess she persuaded the two of them to come to the island to patch things up, but as things have turned out, she needn't have bothered.'

Maria let out a big yawn. She wasn't making fun of Sumako's troubles, but was simply exhausted.

Night descended on the island. It came twice. The first time was when the sun set. The second time was when the lights disappeared from the bedrooms.

Claiming a lack of sleep, Egami said he'd go to bed early as well, so at eleven he switched off the light and crawled into bed. It seemed as if his body was starting to feel the effects of the part-time job at the construction site he'd taken to finance this trip. I decided not to switch on the reading light and pulled my sheets up to my chest as I looked up at the ceiling.

The light of the moon and stars shining into the room dispelled the darkness. A vague light covered my pillow, as the window curtains nearest my head had not been drawn. The noise of waves came washing in through the window and I attuned my ears to the breathing of the sea.

Thinking that, beneath this same roof, Maria might also be listening to the same sounds gave me a strange sensation. "It's as if this small island turns into its own separate world, drifting away in the universe." She's quite the chatty romanticist.

I knew three people who were in love with her. Some of them even thought somehow that I was her boyfriend and were jealous of me. They were wrong though.

How would my other two seniors be doing back in the frying pan that is Kyōto in the summer? They might be having sleepless nights about their friends and the *moai* puzzle. Sorry about that.

Meandering thoughts came to me one by one, only to be washed away.

It was almost midnight when I fell asleep.

Thus ended the night of the first day.

CHAPTER TWO: LOCKED ROOM PUZZLE

1

'I found it, I found it. Look, it's hiding behind that tree over there.'

I turned in the direction Maria was pointing and there indeed was another *moai* statue. Our exploration of the island was going well. We had got off our bicycles and gone into the thickets. Because there might be yellow-spotted pit vipers around, Maria was wearing capri pants so her legs wouldn't be exposed.

'This one's facing north-north-west precisely.' I'd waited until the trembling of the compass needle had stopped to say that. 'Maria, did you get that? North by northwest. Hitchcock's *North by Northwest.*'

'Yes, I wrote it down.'

On the map with the locations of all the *moai*, Maria drew an arrow indicating the direction. We'd only just begun the job. As we'd agreed last night, Egami, Maria and I were cycling around the island and checking the statues near the road and the direction each one of them was facing. This was the fifth one.

'We're almost near the centre of the island, and there's a place with a fantastic view there. Kashikijima's own observation platform. If this island was a tourist spot, you'd definitely have a gift shop and a bus stop there.'

While Maria was saying that, she put the map in her loose leaf notebook and fastened it to the carrier rack of her bicycle. It seemed a lot of work for a simple piece of paper, but she had no choice, as these bicycles didn't have any baskets.

'Sounds good.' I climbed on my bicycle. 'Looking forward to it.'

'And there's another statue there too. That one was made with special care and is also quite a bit larger than the others. As if it's significant. What could it be hiding?'

We wouldn't know until we saw it.

There was dark green on either side of us. The wind which blew into our faces occasionally carried the heavy smell of grass in the summer. But it also contained the smell of the tide. With the humming of the sea as our background music, we cheerfully continued our cycling. After a while the road curved gently to the left. It was going around the foot of the small hill up ahead. Sitting on top of that hill was what Maria called the observation platform. We had gone a bit farther when Maria slowed down.

'We'll stop here.'

I noticed a small path branching off to the right, which seemed to lead to the top of the hill. We left our bicycles at the base and followed the path up to the top.

'Look.'

Halfway up, Maria stopped and pointed to the branches of a nearby tree.

'I think Alice will like this one too.'

It was there, five metres away, at eye-level. The slender body was only about five centimetres long but, with its legs extended, it was twelve or thirteen centimetres long: it was a big—no, gigantic—spider. It wasn't moving at all, just sitting in the middle of the web it had weaved as a display of its craftsmanship.

'If you're so afraid of snakes, you're probably not a fan of spiders either.'

'I'm fine,' I forced myself to say. 'Not a problem at all. I might jump if I saw it crawling on the wall of my bedroom, but I'm fine seeing it here outside. They belong here.'

'Oh good, you're not as big a scaredy-cat as I thought. Well then, take a good look. This is the giant golden orb weaver, Japan's largest spider. Don't worry, they live outdoors.'

A giant golden orb weaver? That didn't sound very cute. True, I wasn't good with any insects or spiders. "Something in the insect seems alien to the habits, morals and psychology of this world as if it had come from some other planet, more monstrous, more infernal than our own," a Belgian poet had once stated fearfully about insects, and I was in complete agreement.

We continued up the hill. It rose gently, following a round shape, like a tumulus. The top was completely free of trees—even though there were no signs of any having been cut down—and it offered a near-360-degree view.

Turning towards the direction we'd come from, we could basically overlook the complete island. A gigantic pair of arms was hugging the bay, which stretched from High Tide Cape on the right (east), to Low Tide Cape on the left (west). Happy Fish Villa and Panorama Villa sitting on top of those capes looked like pieces of a Monopoly game I could simply pick up. Happy Fish Villa, built in a lodge style, was buried in the nature around it, but the white-walled Panorama Villa stood out from the surrounding greenery. I followed the road that had brought us to the foot of the hill with my eyes and, between the trees, I could see fragments of the road leading all the way back to Panorama Villa.

I fell in love with this view, which made me feel like I myself was a piece inside a scale-model of an island. But it would clearly be impossible for us to check the direction each of the *moai* statues was facing from here. Near the edge of the island I could recognise two or three figures which appeared to be statues, but I couldn't make out which way they were facing.

'Let's rest a bit,' said Maria, and she pointed to an arbour built on the sea side of the plateau. A roof of coconut palm leaves gave it a south sea island feeling and beneath that were a lauan table and four chairs made to look like tree stumps. Absolutely perfect.

Looking down at the sea to the south, I spotted the strange rock formations Maria had mentioned, all in a row, being washed by the waves. There was one rock that looked like the diamond mark of a playing card, only with the lower half extended down. It was about ten metres high. Slightly away from that, two other rocks stuck out from the sea, half the size of the first rock, but wider. It was an amazing view, enough to put all those something-something-rocks at second-rate tourist traps to shame.

'The left one, the tall one with the large head is the Candle Rock. Those on the right are the Twin Rocks.'

'These rocks in the middle of nowhere have names?' laughed Egami. 'But I'm rather disappointed by your naming sense.'

'My grandfather named them. He knew they were unoriginal names, but he probably wanted to give them the kind of common names you'd hear anywhere.'

The hill dropped steeply down to the sea. There was a rocky stretch right below. If you were careful, you could make your way down, but climbing back up looked very daunting, so we just looked.

It was a great island, I had to admit. Drifting in the middle of the deep blue sea, richly filled like a miniature garden, not only did it offer the beauty of Mother Nature, but it was also one gigantic puzzle, harbouring a man-made mystery. I could only describe the island as a universe of its own. The opportunity to enjoy all of this was a true pleasure for us mystery fiction fans.

'What's the matter?' Egami asked Maria, while he was using his left hand to shield the fire of his lighter from the sea breeze. His cigarette finally caught fire and smoke blew in the wind.

'Was I looking sad again? I often came here with Hideto.'

Once again I looked down at the sea with its high waves. It wasn't as if she'd told me that this was the place where he'd lost his life, but the rumbling of the waves breaking on the rocky stretch below felt threateningly brutal.

'I'd just started in middle school, I think. He taught me to play guitar here. For some reason I wanted to learn that summer. I asked him to give me some special tuition, so he brought his guitar to the island for me. And I didn't feel like practicing in the house, because Kazuto would come and make fun of me. So we came all the way out here and practiced for hours. Even when blood was coming out of my fingers, I never said I wanted to quit, and Hideto didn't tell me to stop either. We were all alone here, playing simple chords like C or Am towards the sea, singing out loud. Oh, but I'm not sad, you know.'

Egami had been holding his cigarette in his hand while Maria was speaking and hadn't taken a puff. The long stick of ash scattered in the wind.

She'd said she wasn't sad, but ever since coming to this island, Maria hadn't completely been her usual self. I imagined that Hideto Arima might possibly have been Maria's first love. But the wind that was blowing over the hill now did not carry the sound of a guitar or singing voices.

'I didn't know you played the guitar,' said Egami as he lit another cigarette.

'I do. That summer I learned to play *Estudio – Moonlight* and *Jeux interdits* in one week. I don't think it's because I learned it in secret, but I never really play in front of other people. I only play by myself in my own room.'

Maria started to hum a low *Moonlight*. Egami, too, participated with a harmonising whistle and I listened to them in silence. Their harmony lasted for one chorus.

'Mr. Egami, you're good at whistling.'

'Was Hideto good at that too?'

Egami grinned as he asked that, but Maria shook her head.

'Not at all. He was good with the guitar, but he couldn't whistle or sing either.'

I was perhaps empathising more than necessary with Maria, but I started to like this Hideto Arima, even though I'd never met him or even seen his photograph.

As I realised how strange that was, I turned my head to face the view to the north. It was a complete contrast to the wild waves to the south: a peaceful bay. I noticed a little boat floating there.

'There's a little rowing boat over there. Look, it's going from Panorama Villa to Happy Fish Villa.'

Egami and Maria turned to look.

'Oh, you're right,' reacted Maria. 'Who could it be? Looks like a man.'

'Not the doc. And that person's head is all black, so it can't be your uncle Kango either. Perhaps it's Junji who got all upset yesterday, or perhaps Kazuto?'

'We're heading to Happy Fish Villa anyway, so we'll find out when we're there. Oh, I almost forgot. You also need to see the *moai* statue on this hill first.'

The statue was at the very top of the hill, so it stood at the highest point of all of Kashikijima. As we approached, I noticed several points about it that made it different from the five other statues we'd already checked. It was about thirty centimetres taller and also wider. It had been chiselled out more carefully and had been completely coated with varnish, giving it a lustrous sheen. I couldn't help but think it held the key to something important. At some point in the process of solving the code, there would come a moment when this *moai* would dramatically show the way, I was sure of that. Or perhaps this *moai* was the starting point of everything.

'Alice, get your instrument out.'

As instructed by Egami, I took the compass out of my pocket. I stood behind the statue and checked the direction it was facing.

'Almost north-west. About ten degrees closer to the north. Now, Maria, get your map out.'

'Ah, I left it on the carrier of my bicycle. I'll write it down when we get there.'

What was the *moai* looking at from the top of this hill? I followed its line of sight and lined up Panorama Villa.

'Panorama Villa? It's looking over there?'

'No, I think you're wrong. Isn't it facing too much to the north for that? It's only off a bit, but it seems a bit sloppy if this *moai* was really intended to be looking at Panorama Villa.'

Now that Maria mentioned it, she was right. But even if he had been looking at Panorama Villa, I still wouldn't know what that meant.

'I'll write down that it's facing slightly north of north-west. Let's go down.'

We descended the hill. The spider hadn't moved an inch, still hanging there in its web.

2

The artist Hirakawa's lodge, Happy Fish Villa, came into view. It was a cabin constructed with large logs. A rocking chair on the oak terrace was bathing in the summer morning sun, giving off the scent of wood.

A red bicycle stood in front of the house, as if the mailman had arrived. This probably belonged to maestro Hirakawa himself. Its colour was different, but the model was the same as the three at Panorama Villa. We parked our bicycles next to the red one.

The front entrance was open. Maria knocked on the door and called out to Hirakawa inside.

'Hey, Maria.'

It was Kazuto who stepped out. It was he who had come here to Happy Fish Palace by rowing boat.

'Come inside. Coffee has just been made. The maestro's looking forward to your visit.'

He looked at Egami and me and invited us inside as well.

The wooden floor creaked. An old lamp was hanging from the low ceiling. A man dressed in a white hemp shirt was sitting at the table beneath the lamp. This must be Itaru Hirakawa. The white oak chairs, which looked as if they featured inlaid lacquer, fitted the style of the lodge perfectly. But the table was like the one in Panorama Villa, with a cold glass top. The floor around it was covered by a surprisingly large carpet with of arabesque design, possibly Persian. On top of the glass table were the scattered pieces of a jigsaw puzzle. No kidding.

'It's been so long. You're in college now, I assume?'

The artist looked up from his puzzle and smiled at Maria. He was probably in his fifties. His face was wrinkled, but he had a healthy complexion. This was the first time I'd met anyone from the artistic community, but my first impression of the man made me think of an understanding high school teacher (subject: English). Based on nothing at all, of course, except I seem to remember having a teacher like him in high school.

'And here are the talk of the town, your two friends. Welcome. My name is Itaru Hirakawa.'

Each of his words was perfectly formed and his enunciation was also clear. As if he was about to ask us to repeat after him.

We introduced ourselves and were offered chairs. Kazuto appeared from the kitchen with a tray bearing coffee cups. Hirakawa pushed the puzzle pieces on the table to the side to make room for the cups.

'Have a drink. It's just instant coffee, though.'

'Kazuto, you didn't have to say that.'

Hirakawa grinned. Because all of the chairs around the table were taken, he brought over a chair from the desk near the window and sat down on it.

'Maria, I haven't seen you for three years, but you've grown up to be a perfect young lady. I'm thrilled to see you. What's your major at university?'

'I'm in the law faculty. With Alice. Sumako studied there, too.'

'Ah, Sumako also studied law, indeed. I'm just from an art university, so to me the words "law faculty" have a dark, stiff image. I think lately more women have been studying law, but you're probably still in the minority among all those men?'

'We're about ten percent. There are a lot of girls there who are daughters of lawyers. I know two girls, both of them called Noriko. One of them you write with the characters for "law" and "child", the other with "rule" and "child."' Maria wrote the characters down on her palm with her fingers to show Hirakawa which characters she meant. 'I'd understand if their parents wanted their daughters to take over the business after them, but they actually hope their daughters will find some intelligent man at university who can take over their business. Don't you just think that's pathetic?'

'Oh, I thought it was the same for you, Maria?'

Maria gave Kazuto a dirty look, but continued.

'I entered the law faculty because I know nothing about how the world works. I want to grasp the structure of our society through the study of law. You know that, here in Japan, all the laws are found within the Complete Book of The Six Major Legal Codes? While the interpretation might change with the times, everything starts and ends with that one book. I find that fascinating.'

'I've no idea what you're talking about,' Hirakawa laughed. 'But anyway, study as hard as you can. At your age, you still have the time.'

I'll just mention it here, but Maria's grades are, in a word, excellent. It's because her own interests line up perfectly with the law. I, on the other hand, have a very wide range of interests and can readily become immersed in a topic, so sometimes I come up with masterpieces like reports on the influence of sociocultural evolution on social thought for History of Sciences, or on the word-building capacity of the Japanese language for Language Studies, even if I'm rather awful with my major. I might be using my talents in the wrong way.

'Mr. Hirakawa, what are you working on now?'

To answer her question, the artist pointed towards an easel in the back of the room. The leaning painting was facing towards us, and on the canvas I could make out the sea and a cape.

'It's Panorama Villa. Low Tide Cape basking in the morning sun. Some years ago I made one of the night view, so I intend this one to form a pair with it. When it's finished, you'll need to take a picture and make a jigsaw puzzle of it, Kazuto.'

'Do you like jigsaw puzzles too?' I asked him and he waved "no, no" with the hand that was not clutching the cup of coffee.

'Even if I said I liked them, I'm not crazy about them. Well, I was slightly influenced by the previous head of the Arima family, so I spend my days here on the island elegantly playing with jigsaw and sliding puzzles. Anyway, I just like passing the time at my own leisure here.'

The puzzle on the table was also one of about 2,000 pieces and of a famous painting. Unbefitting this artist of Western-style paintings, the puzzle was of Hokusai's *The Great Wave off Kanagawa*.

'You're coming over tonight, aren't you?' Kazuto asked. 'Doctor Sonobe also arrived with Maria yesterday, so that's everyone this summer. Come and have dinner with us. The doctor also brought some Scotch. That'll keep us company until late. You can stay for the night.'

'That sounds good. I haven't been over to your place for five days now. I don't mind the thirty minute bicycle ride, but all of you have been paying me visits the last few days.'

'Have you enough food left?'

'Yes, yesterday morning Reiko brought supplies with the boat. She looked much better than I'd expected.'

'It's been three years.'

Hirakawa hesitated for a moment, then turned to us.

'I hear you're trying to solve the *moai* puzzle?'

'Yes,' answered Egami. 'Maria's asked us to do so.'

'I guess it's still early, but what do you think? What's your starting point?'

'The direction the statues are facing. Maria's cousin Hideto had mentioned that he was closing in on the answer before he died. With that hint, we're now checking the direction each statue is facing.'

'Poor Hideto. He may well have had the correct answer in his head. He was smart. I'm not sure whether he got it from his grandfather, but he'd been good with puzzles and that kind of thing ever since he was a child. I think it was when he was in the fifth or sixth grade of elementary school that he asked me: "Maestro, what is the Golden Mean?" So I explained it to him briefly, but he didn't look satisfied. His next question was: "Who discovered it?" and he followed up with: "Why is it like that?" And I had no answers to offer him.'

He stopped talking and sipped the last drop of coffee remaining in the bottom of his cup.

'I wish you good luck. It's a fact that a priceless treasure is hidden here on the island. Long ago, I got all serious and tried to find it myself, but I didn't manage to get even one step closer to the treasure and gave up. It's impossible for someone as inflexible as me. I'm only good with something like a jigsaw puzzle, which you can eventually solve if you just take your time and keep up with one simple job. I'll take a seat in the audience, and expect to see something come out from the flexible, imaginative minds of you young people.'

Maria looked at the clock and mumbled: 'It's eleven.'

'What happens at eleven?' asked Kazuto.

'I need to go back and help Reiko. I told her I'd help prepare lunch.' She turned to Hirakawa. 'We'll leave now. I hope to see you tonight.'

'I'll drop by. And you puzzlers, do your best. We'll talk another time.'

We said goodbye and left the lodge. Happy Fish Villa stood at the very edge of the cape, so the sea was right behind the house. There was a small sand beach below, with stone steps leading down. A wooden post to fasten a rowing boat was right beside the steps, and the little boat Kazuto had used to cross the bay was moored there, bobbing up and down in the waves.

Thirty minutes later, we'd gone around the island once again and returned to Panorama Villa.

3

As planned, the afternoon consisted of bathing in the sea. We went down to the beach together with Toshiyuki and Satomi Inukai.

Undressed, I could see Toshiyuki had the body of a sportsman, with a broad, muscular chest. Egami had an odd preference for part time jobs consisting of manual labour, so he also had a fine build. I was the scrawniest of the bunch. Satomi appeared to have little interest in swimming, as she avoided the sea, sitting on a towel hidden away in the shadow of a parasol. She'd only come down to the beach to accompany her husband. Meanwhile, swimming was all Maria had in mind, carefully doing warming-up exercises in her blue one-piece swimsuit.

'That's a rather tame swimsuit. I was expecting something like a high-leg swimsuit.'

Maria stopped her exercises for a moment.

'Hah, you really did say it. I was willing to bet on it. If you'd been nicer, I'd have given you my copy of Clayton Rawson's *The Headless Lady*.'

That's one of the infamous out-of-print books from publisher Sōgen Suiri Bunko. Satomi was sitting nearby and the expression on her face when she suddenly heard us talking about some Headless Lady was a sight to behold. If I'd thought Maria was serious about giving me the book, I might have retracted my comment.

We swam a lot. The sea was unbelievably clear and when you dived in you could see the light of the sun piercing through the water surface and then swaying as if it was dancing. It was so beautiful I spent most of the time under water. Egami did the exact opposite and was enjoying drifting along the waves beneath the sun like a sea otter. Toshiyuki and Maria had gone off swimming all the way to who-knows-where. Satomi had only dipped a little bit in the sea, after which she remained beneath her parasol, staring absentmindedly into space.

I said goodbye to the striped pattern the swaying sunlight made on the seabed of white sand, and when I popped out of the sea, I was at a spot where I could look up at Panorama Villa through the trees. Was its master, Ryūichi Arima, taking a nap this afternoon? Kango Makihara had invited Sonobe to come along to catch some fish for dinner at the rocky stretch behind the cape, but would they be able to bring in a good catch? With so many guests to care for, the afternoons, when everyone goes their own way, had to be a time of rest for Reiko. She might be reading a book on the terrace, but I couldn't see her from here. But I did see the figure of someone through one of the hallway windows. I squinted to see who it was.

'What are you looking at, Alice?'

It was Maria who spoke, approaching me from behind, doing a breaststroke. She trod water next to me and looked up at the house as well.

'Nothing. Saw someone standing near one of the windows.'

'Kazuto perhaps? Ah, they're all away. Kazuto might be bored now, because there's nobody to keep him company. If only he'd study. If only.'

I remembered he was a student as well.

'He said he'd a report coming up with a very difficult topic. He's studying politics and he brought a portable word processor and a paperback of Max Weber with him to the island. And as he carried them all the way here anyway, he might as well start on it. Oh well.'

She swam away again, mumbling to herself. I looked over at the beach and saw Toshiyuki Inukai walking towards Satomi sitting beneath the parasol, bringing with him a souvenir from the seabed: a shell.

Egami was still floating around in leisurely fashion.

Right about the time when we'd returned from the beach, taken a shower and were about to return to our rooms, we came upon Kazuto coming down from the attic room. He was holding the rifle in his hand, so I jumped a little.

'I'm going to shoot some rounds now. It's a Remington, a repeating rifle. What about you trying it out as well? It's not often you get to hold one of these, so you can brag about it to your friends.'

'Are you shooting targets?' asked Egami, his hair not yet dry.

Kazuto nodded.

'I'd like to be able to say I'd made a shooting range nearby, but it's nothing much really. I place some juice cans on the ground and shoot standing. Simply a game where I can measure from how far away I can hit the target. I'm an awful shot, but it's fun. Come along.'

'Right you are.'

As I replied, a door farther down the corridor opened and Maria appeared.

'I was just asking these two if they'd like to come along for some target shooting.' Kazuto lifted the rifle in his right hand to show her. 'Maria, you can come along as well.'

'I'll pass. I'm exhausted. But they look like they're interested, so please go. Reading adventure novels might become more exciting if they've actually tried it once. But please stop if you think you're getting too hooked on it.'

So, since it might be educational, we decided to take Kazuto up on his offer. As I passed Maria in the hallway, she whispered: 'Never point your rifle at anyone,' to me. She really did look a bit tired as she disappeared into her room and closed the door.

We passed through the empty hallway and went outside. Two of the bicycles were no longer there: Junji and Sumako Makihara had gone off to the observation platform. Kazuto followed the road, which shone a mesmerising white from the reflection of the strong sunlight, for about fifty metres. He suddenly stopped next to some trees on the left.

'This way.'

We followed him and, crossing through the trees, we came out on a cliff overlooking the northern part of the bay. There was no path on the edge of this side of the cliff, but there was an open space of about a hundred metres wide we could use for shooting.

'I'll prepare the targets, so hold this.'

After giving the rifle to Egami, Kazuto made a short run to a point fifty metres up ahead. The cans of sports drinks and cola lying around there were obviously the targets. Kazuto placed three of them at different distances and ran back.

'I placed them at thirty, fifty and eighty metres. Try shooting the one at thirty metres first.'

Egami handed the rifle back to Kazuto and said: 'A demonstration first, please.'

Kazuto looked as if he was pleased to be asked, and a faint smile appeared in the corner of his mouth.

He fed cartridges into the rifle. His hands were clearly used to the motions.

'It's a stationary target, so the only thing you have to do is to steady the rifle.'

So saying, he spread his feet farther apart than the width of his shoulders and held the rifle at the ready.

'Bend slightly backwards and line the target up using the sight. Don't put your weight on your back foot, but divide it evenly between both legs....'

He stopped there. His tongue protruded slightly from the corner of his mouth and he licked his lower lip. I concentrated on the target.

Bang! Gunpowder flew out and the can thirty metres up ahead flew through the air. One shot, one hit.

'Wow,' I let out, impressed. The smell of gunpowder reached my nose.

'Well, it's easy at this distance,' he said, looking pleased. It was almost childish, shooting at empty cans.

'Fifty metres might be too difficult the first time. I'll go and reset the thirty metres target. But first I'll take care of the remaining ones.'

He raised the rifle again, took some seconds to aim and pulled the trigger. Another shot, and then another. The can at fifty metres and the can at eighty metres flew away one after the other.

Playing at being humble, I thought. This was way more than a children's game. An awful shot, he'd said? He obviously had quite a lot of confidence in his own skills. The proud smile on his face as he looked up from the sight was proof of that. He'd invited us to come along simply because he wanted to show off his own skill.

'I'll go and reset the targets again, so please hold this.'

Kazuto ran away, humming. How many times was he planning to walk up and down there? Or was he not expecting us to hit any targets at all?

Egami had been lost in thought with the rifle in his hands.

'What's wrong?' I asked.

'No, I was just thinking that shooting a few empty cans on the ground wouldn't have me—'

'What?'

'I was watching his face as he was pulling the trigger just now. Every time he made a shot he kept repeating silently "damn."'

What a strange guy. The strange guy had lined up the empty cans again and had come running back in a cheerful mood.

Egami looked over towards the sea. I followed the direction of his eyes, and saw a black line on the horizon. At the same moment that I thought something might be coming close, Egami's hair started dancing in the wind.

After we'd returned to Panorama Villa, Kazuto went upstairs to place the rifle back in the attic room. Egami and I sat down in the chairs by the French windows. There were people out on the terrace. One of them was Maria. Had she come down here after an afternoon nap, or had she not slept at all? The other person was Sumako. The two of them were sitting out on the sundeck, chatting. Carried by the wind, their talk reached our ears.

'Maria, which of them do you like?'

'What?'

'Which of them is your favourite, Mr. Egami or Alice? Or are you still not sure?'

They would only be having this talk because they hadn't noticed we were behind them. Unwittingly, my eyes met those of Egami. Maria was about to answer.

'Sumako, please don't talk about it as if I'm in a store, comparing which of the two men is better.'

'Even I don't choose whom I fall in love with by balancing men on a scale. With simple friends it might be different, but there's no need to be so hesitant about someone you're in love with. Oh, so those two are just male friends?'

'Yes.' Maria leaned slightly forward towards Sumako. 'Sumako, have you never been in love with two men at the same time?'

'No. What? Do I look like such a fickle person?'

Sumako was speaking gently and, while I couldn't see from where I was sitting, I could imagine a smile had appeared on her face.

'I wouldn't say fickle, but someone who falls in love more easily. Like the time you fell in love with Mr. Hirakawa.'

'Watch it.' Sumako raised her hand pretending to be angry. 'Don't talk about that anymore. It's embarrassing, and what if my husband should hear about it?'

'Sorry. You're with Junji now. You and Mr. Hirakawa....'

Maria didn't finish her sentence.

'That's all over,' Sumako said quietly.

The two became silent for a moment, their hair fluttering in the wind.

'It's really nothing now. When we meet now, we just talk normally.'

'You're both adults.'

Sumako shook her head.

'It's all we can do.'

Egami poked me with his elbow. Silently, I nodded and we both sneaked away from there. The two on the sundeck never noticed we'd been there and kept on talking.

We went upstairs, where Junji was leaning against the hallway window, looking outside towards High Tide Cape. It didn't appear as if he'd noticed his wife sitting downstairs on the terrace. Even if he had noticed her, he could never have heard the conversation because of the women's quiet voices.

The door next to the staircase opened and Kango appeared. His eyes met those of Junji, who had turned around, but neither of them reacted to the other. Junji looked out to sea again, and Kango nodded to us and went quickly down the stairs.

4

'Mr. Egami is a natural. Alice wasn't that bad either. But if I praise them too much they might get too hooked on it, so I'll leave it at that,' Kazuto said in a loud voice, grinning.

Our target shooting had become the topic of discussion at the dining table. Our lesson had stopped as soon as Egami and I had both finally managed to hit the thirty metre target. Neither of us had any special interest in guns, so we were content with just the experience of having handled real firearms.

'Kazuto, have you been taking good care of the rifle? What if it should explode in an accident?' Reiko asked, concerned.

'That would be a disaster. A scandal for the Arima family.'

Kango laughed in his hoarse voice. He looked extremely pleased, probably because he and Sonobe had caught a big sea bream. I surmised that he hadn't yet had the unpleasant talk with his daughter about debts. I glanced at Sumako and Junji. Still uncertain about whether they would successfully raise money, neither of them appeared to me to be having a carefree dinner. Junji in particular showed a distressed expression at times. Probably because Sumako was taking her time in talking to her father about their debts. *If you're so desperate, just try and ask yourself...* But then my eyes met those of Junji, and I quickly turned away. Oh no. Oh no. That was way too unnatural.

'You two, let's have a drink tonight,' the doctor invited us from across the table. 'Young and old, let's all get drunk with my Scotch and have a talk. But none of that whisky-and-water stuff.'

'Don't say such rash things, Doctor,' said the artist Hirakawa. 'What if one of us gets acute alcohol poisoning?'

'I'll give you a free examination, haha.'

The doctor laughed with his mouth wide open, probably because of the beers he'd had. He talked tough, but he'd probably be the first to go down. Oh well, even if he did go under, I don't think I'd need to worry about anyone telling me to carry him all the way back to his room, like that time I went out drinking with all of my club seniors. At least that was a relief. Hirakawa might actually have been the heaviest drinker there.

'Maria, you're of drinking age now, aren't you? Won't you join us?'

Maria shook her head in response to Hirakawa's question. 'I don't really drink.'

'Bring out the sake then.' The doctor laughed cheerfully again. Maria pouted.

'I can't take much.'

'Maria, tell us about Kyōto.'

She declined Kazuto's invitation as well. She might still be tired from having swum for so long. Kazuto clicked his tongue lightly and dug into his fried chicken. He obviously wasn't the smooth talker he thought himself to be.

'I heard the typhoon was coming closer. I wonder how that'll turn out?'

Ryūichi had asked the question to no one in particular as he wiped his mouth with a paper napkin. 'Indeed,' said Toshiyuki who got up to switch on the little television set in the corner of the room. It was time for the local news and it was reporting on a traffic accident with two fatalaties on the National Highway near Kagoshima.

'I asked a high school student in Okinawa this morning,' said Kazuto as he was using a toothpick on the pieces of meat stuck between his teeth. 'Said the wind was tremendous. It was moving slowly north-east.'

'You asked by wireless?' asked Maria.

'Yeah. That was at nine this morning, so by now it might be past the shore of southern Okinawa and be heading straight this way. Listen….' He placed his hand against his ear. 'Isn't that the wind blowing now?'

The discussion ceased for a moment, as everyone concentrated on listening. I could hear the trees rustling. It might have been my imagination, but the noise of the waves also sounded louder than yesterday.

'No, you're right. That's the wind starting to build up. It's coming for sure,' said Kango without any sign of anxiety. 'We need to board up the windows.'

'The elderly can stay in their seats. We have enough young men here to do the job,' said Sonobe.

I remembered the black shadow I'd seen on the horizon during our target shooting. That must have been the typhoon. This would be the first time I'd actually seen one, and when I thought how something so sinister and large was heading this way and would soon be right over our heads and swallowing us whole, I felt a chill run down my spine.

'We're still safe tonight. Boarding up the windows can wait until tomorrow. Kazuto, bring the bicycles inside. Mr. Hirakawa's as well.'

'Okay,' replied Kazuto.

'It's the weather report,' said Toshiyuki, turning up the volume. Everyone turned to the television. It showed footage from the weather satellite Himawari, but I couldn't make out the details on the small television. Everyone listened to the announcer.

'At six o'clock tonight the large and violent Typhoon No. 12 reached a point eighty kilometres south-east of Ishigaki Island. The pressure in the centre of the typhoon was 950 millibars and the top instantaneous wind speed reached forty metres—.'

At that rate, the rain and wind would become worse over the course of the night and the island would find itself inside a storm area by eight o'clock in the morning.

'What shall we do? Board up the windows tonight?' I asked, as if I was the representative of all the young men present. Ryūichi immediately replied that there was no need for that.

'We'll probably still have enough time to do it tomorrow morning, and the typhoon might veer off to head for somewhere else in the meantime. There's no need to do all that work right before the rain starts. Both you and Mr. Egami are our guests, so you don't need to worry about that.'

Being their perfect guest, without having to do any work, didn't feel right. But there was nothing I could do but nod and scratch my head.

Raindrops beat on the windows. The long arm of the typhoon had reached Kashikijima just as Ryūichi had finished saying "before the rain starts." However, it was still a soft rain.

'It's starting. How awful that the typhoon comes at night.'

Sumako's face clouded, but next to her Junji was swiggng beer down just as he'd done yesterday, his face all red. As if he didn't care about any typhoon.

'Panorama Villa will be fine,' said Hirakawa gently as if to calm Sumako down.

'I must be rather fortunate to have been invited here tonight. I'll be fine here even if my own abode is taken by the wind. There's an old tradition of enjoying a snowstorm over a drink, so Doctor, let's enjoy the typhoon over a drink tonight.'

Sonobe replied that he was only too ready.

The slow dinner finally ended. Black clouds were gathering.

Every one of us could feel the storm coming through our skins.

Thus the night of the second day...started.

5

A loud bang sounded.

Both Reiko and Maria, who were walking towards the glass top table, ducked.

'Oh, maybe the door to the annex is still open?' said Ryūichi testily, his face flush from too many drinks. 'Hey, Kazuto. It's making a ruckus. Go and close it.'

Kazuto's angry frown was visible to all. Ten cans of Heineken were lined up on the rattan table.

'It's not noisy at all. Can't you just let the door bang all it wants?'

Kazuto, grumbling, stood up and went over to the nearest corridor window, where he made a pretence of looking at the annex building. But that was all he did, and he sat down again immediately.

'It's probably the door of the storage room of the annex that's banging. But there's nothing inside anyway, so who cares whether the rain gets inside or the door gets blown away?'

'Lazy as always.' That was all Ryūichi had to say. The door, however, was not busy constantly, but would only bang once in a while, as if it would forget its job and then suddenly remember to go to work again. The occasional loud bang, just as you'd started to forget about it, was even harder on the ears, but nobody felt like dragging their heavy, alcohol-filled bodies outside in the rain. 'Shall I go?' I asked, but Ryūichi firmly said no.

'You don't need to go. If my son won't go, then that's it. We'll just leave the door banging tonight. It's dangerous to go out in the night. Who knows what the sea is also blowing this way?'

'But if it's me, it doesn't matter if it's dangerous or not, eh?' Kazuto mumbled softly, but by now he'd become rather inarticulate.

It was only eleven, but three people had already drunk themselves to sleep. Sonobe, Junji and Egami were all lying comfortably stretched out in chairs here and there, and would occasionally sit up and take another sip of their drink, or stagger to the toilet. Ryūichi and Kazuto were also moments away from going down. I wasn't able to keep up with the drinking pace of the others, so I was only slightly drunk. Next to me, Toshiyuki Inukai was still busy mixing beer with the Scotch. He must have a high tolerance, because he was still sober. 'Is it really okay? Your wife went back to your room earlier.

Shouldn't you join her?' I asked. He hiccupped once loudly. His eyes looked unfocused now. He was starting to feel the alcohol.

'She, she doesn't sleep well while travelling…She takes sleeping pills to fall asleep. She won't… miss me… hic.'

Hirakawa had started off drinking with gusto, but that was all show and he had been the first to get drunk. Already at ten we'd had to drag him to Sonobe's room. Like us, the doctor had a twin room.

Kango Makihara didn't look like the type who would recklessly drink, and he sipped his whisky-and-water at his own pace. Shortly after ten, he'd announced he was going to bed and had gone upstairs. I'd seen Sumako follow him with a determined look on her face, but she hadn't come back down. Had her plea for money been answered, or refused? Or were they still negotiating? No, maybe she'd missed her chance and gone to her own bedroom. Thus did I meddle in their affairs in my own mind.

'Aliiiiice, still among the living?'

Maria yelled to me from across the hall. I waved back to her silently. Maria and Reiko were having a chat, while sipping from their light whisky-and-water and playing with the jigsaw puzzle.

'Oh, you're still sober. Never knew you could drink that much,' said Maria, teasingly. I smiled wryly, mumbling the words she'd used earlier: 'I can't take much.'

'Maria, let's go up to sleep,' said Reiko, as she suppressed a yawn. 'I'm feeling drunk, too. I might not able to make breakfast tomorrow morning.'

'It's okay, Reiko. Look at everyone now. Their hangovers will keep them away from the dining room until noon.'

Reiko agreed and laughed.

The two of them split up and went around waking up all the unconscious men. When Sonobe woke up, he smiled weakly, said 'I'm so sorry,' and staggered upstairs. One taken care of. The others, however, remained lying around, with no intention of moving.

'Oh, that's why I hate drunks,' complained Maria, even though her own breath also reeked of alcohol. Reiko, too, looked displeased.

'Reiko, just leave us,' Ryūichi mumbled. 'We won't catch a cold in this weather, so it's okay. When they wake up they'll go crawling back to their nests on their own. You're tired, so go to sleep now. You too, Maria.'

Reiko was still hesitant.

'Reiko, I'll stay here as well. Just think of us men as standing by in the hall in case the typhoon does come. You two can go to sleep,' I said.

'Reiko, let's do that,' said Maria, pulling on Reiko's elbow. 'Let's go, let's go to sleep. Ah, if only there was someone here who could drink like a real man. Oh, my beloved Philip Marlowe.'

She's drunk. And aren't there plenty of drunken detectives in hard-boiled detective stories, I wanted to say to Egami. But he was still sound asleep, even though he was almost falling out of his chair.

The door of the annex storage room banged again, twice. It was probably that noise that had woken Kazuto, who was slowly nodding.

'Morning, Reiko and Maria.' His tenor voice rang through the hall. 'I drank too much. Kind of embarrassing you seeing me like that.'

What was he talking about?

'Go to bed now, Kazuto,' said Reiko.

'Ah, I'll sleep in your room then. Take me with you.'

You fool!

'Oh yeah, Kazuto's room is in the annex.' Maria, too, sounded shocked by his suggestion. 'So sleep here, then. Good night. Reiko, can I sleep in your room tonight? I can just sleep on your couch with a cushion. I'm so afraid of the typhoon.'

Oh brother.

'Okay, you come and sleep with me. Just for tonight I'll give you the bed.'

'No, I'm the one intruding. I can't go chasing you out of your own bed as well.'

That's all fine, but Reiko, please take that drunk with you immediately.

Reiko took Maria by the hand and the two of them disappeared down the corridor in the back. I could hear Maria humming *Over the Rainbow* all the way until the bedroom door opened and closed.

The hall turned silent again and I let out a sigh of relief. The howling of the wind outside and the drumming of the raindrops on the windows only heightened the silence. Besides me, there were only five men, drunk and not moving an inch, like a bunch of broken mannequin dolls. Why was I at a place like this?

'There's a storm outside.'

I played with those words on the tip of my tongue.

The night had only just started.

6

'Hey, Alice.' A voice was speaking close to my ear. 'You'll catch cold.'

Someone gently shook my shoulder. I rubbed my heavy eyelids and looked up to see Egami standing in front of me. It seemed I'd dozed off. What was this about catching a cold? Coming from someone who'd been sleeping like a log until just now.

'I said the same when I tried to wake you up. What's the time?'

Egami looked at his watch before answering: 'Just before two.' The third quarter of the Hour of the Ox in the traditional time-system. The time when ghosts are at their most active.

I looked around to see how the others were doing. Kazuto and Junji were still asleep. Ryūichi Arima and Toshiyuki Inukai had left.

'Mr. Egami, didn't you wake up just now?'

'Yes. I don't remember a thing after eleven. And when I woke up, there were just the four of us in the hall. Guess the others made it back to their rooms on their own.'

'So they left us here. On second thoughts, they probably tried to wake us, but to no avail.'

My head felt heavy. I massaged my eyebrows and stood up. A glass of water suddenly appeared in front of my eyes.

'Drink it,' said Egami and I thanked him as I grasped it. Egami, too, drank a glass of water with ice cubes. If we could go to the sauna right now, we could get the alcohol out of our systems.

'The rain's not that bad, but the wind is raging,' said Egami as he walked to the window, glass in hand. The rustling of the trees had become louder, and the wind that came howling from beyond the sea sounded as if it was lamenting or suffering in pain. It even reminded me of a voice from beyond this world. And then the storage room door banged again.

'Haaaooo.' Egami yawned once and closed the curtains. 'Drinks were flowing rather freely. As if we were all drinking for the sake of getting drunk.'

'It was the doc who got us going.' I poured a second glass of water for myself. 'He'd already started drinking in the afternoon. By the time we joined him, he was already pretty drunk, pouring for everyone else, babbling about nothing and gobbling snacks, saying dinner hadn't been enough. One moment he was yelling "Keiō University is king of the athletic field," the next he was reciting the *Rubaiyat*. And somehow he managed to drag us along too.'

*People only set out on this eternal Road
And none return to explain the way.
Do not leave anything at this tavern
Once you leave you will never return.*

Egami leaned against the wall while he, too, recited the *Rubaiyat* in a low voice, as if it were an incantation.

*Oh Saki, those who went down this path,
Are already resting in the triumphant land.
Have some wine and heed my words
What those people said was simply wind.*

The ice cubes in Egami's glass were clinking.
'…Who wrote those lines?'
'Omar Khayyám. An eleventh-century Persian poet. It's well-known that the British writer Saki took his name from that four-line verse.' Egami smiled wryly. 'This poem and Mahler's *Das Lied von der Erde* are enough to drive anyone to drink. Haha.'
It wasn't likely that Egami had memorised the poem from Sonobe's dodgy and barely articulate recitation. It was more likely *Rubaiyat* was one of his favourite books. He emptied his glass and let out a sigh.
'Shall we go to bed, too? Let's wake these two up.'
He gently shook Junji awake and I did the same with Kazuto. They regained their senses, gulped down the glasses of water we poured for them, and then sighed.
'We sure had a lot,' said Kazuto as he blinked his eyes, blinded by the light in the hall. Junji was mumbling something.
'That quack! Drinking like that.'
You're a fine one to talk.
'And the typhoon? Not here yet?' asked Kazuto.
'There's a gale outside now, but it isn't the typhoon. Probably still on its way here,' I said, to which he replied: 'Don't worry. Even if it did hit the island, what could happen? It's not as if we have a mountain on the verge of collapsing behind the house or a river about to overflow. If you're into surfing, this is a once-in-a-lifetime chance. Fantastic waves out there.'
'Do you surf?'

With a sullen expression, he replied in the negative. Oh, that was right, Maria mentioned he couldn't swim and would simply sink. Seems as though I'd hurt his feelings.

'Let's go to bed.'

Junji raised his heavy body. He staggered a little, but did manage to walk on his own. With a 'Good night' he walked to the staircase and with his hand firmly gripping the rail, he slowly went step by step upstairs.

'What do you think of him?' Kazuto asked, after the sound of Junji's slippers had disappeared. 'Junji Makihara. What do you think of him? He always seems so comical to me.'

What a rude expression. I was just thinking about what he meant by that when Kazuto himself, still under the influence, started to explain:

'You know, he's the only one who doesn't fit in our company. He only speaks to his wife and he looks as if he has no idea what he's doing on a small island like this. So, don't come. I guess Sumako dragged him along. His dear little wife. But——.'

Kazuto paused for a second, then decided to say it anyway.

'But that's the whole comedy. Sure, Junji is everything to Sumako now, but she was all lovey-dovey with the man before him as well. And who was that? Our artist fiend, maestro Hirakawa.'

Maria had mentioned this yesterday, but she'd skipped over it quickly.

'I thought they were acting suspiciously that summer four years ago. She stuck to him from morning to night, claiming he would be the one to solve the *moai* puzzle. The following year, she became his model. Must be great to be an artist, it gives you an excuse to be all alone with a girl in a little room. Oh, did you ever hear this one? An artist is busy in his atelier. Not with painting, but with seducing his model. Suddenly, there's a knock on the door. What did the artist say to his model? "Oh no, it's my wife. Quick, take off your clothes." Hahaha. Funny, get it?'

It probably was. But his delivery was so awful I couldn't laugh.

'But there was definitely something going on during that summer four years ago. The old men didn't notice a thing though. Not my uncle, not my father, not even the doctor had a clue. Probably only a mother would notice. Perhaps they hadn't expected something like that to happen between her and Mr. Hirakawa. Maria and I knew right away, though.

'I think that after returning to Tōkyō, the two of them still saw a great deal of each other for several months. But then the affair cooled off and, as a bystander, I was quite relieved. Now she'll probably agree to a marriage meeting set up by my uncle, I thought, but then along came Junji.

'They're not kids anymore, so if they are really in love, my uncle has nothing to say about it, whatever his feelings may be. Junji could simply take Sumako away somewhere. But the fact remains that Junji did marry into my uncle's family, who think very little of him—and the feeling's mutual....'

The pathetic drunkard talked about his shallow ideas concerning the affair. It's easy to say they should have eloped when you're not involved at all. Her father was probably very important to Sumako, and Junji probably wanted to protect his bar even if it meant he had to stay within Kango's reach. Who are you to talk like a bigshot in the first place?

'And so he bickers with his father-in-law on the one hand, while his wife tries to calm him on the other. Now he's here on the island and the man he's sharing a drink with is his wife's former lover.'

Junji had been drinking in silence on his own, and the first person to pour him a drink and try to have a talk with him had been Hirakawa. Kazuto was probably referring to this when he called it all comical.

Someone came down the staircase. There was a noise of slippers hitting the floor.

'Oh, Mr. Makihara, what's the matter?' asked Egami, who was sitting facing the staircase. Kazuto and I both turned round and there stood the topic of our discussion, who'd only just gone upstairs: Junji Makihara.

'No, err, it's a bit odd,' he said hesitantly. 'I tried to enter my room...but it appears to be locked from the inside.'

'Locked? Oh, the latch?' said Kazuto. Our room had a door latch as well. It was a simple model where a bar dropped into a receiving catch, just like the ones you often read about in old mystery novels.

'Yeah, the latch. I guess that Sumako locked the door and fell asleep, even though I was still drinking down here.'

'That's odd,' said Egami. 'Would she really accidentally lock out her own husband? Does she have a habit of locking the door when she goes to sleep?'

'No. That's why I'm a bit annoyed she decided to do it this time.'

'Did you knock on the door and call out to her?'

'Yeah. I couldn't make too much noise in the middle of the night, so I held back a bit. But she should've noticed it and woken up.'

'Does she take sleeping pills before she goes to bed like Mrs. Inukai?'

'She's never taken anything like that.'

'Then it's really odd.'

Egami had a concerned expression on his face. It was indeed strange for her to lock her husband out, go to sleep and not wake up when he called for her. And Sumako hadn't been drunk; she'd hardly touched any alcohol.

'I'm worried. Let's go upstairs.'

Egami stood up and Kazuto and I followed his example. With our heads heavy, we climbed the dimly-lit staircase in single file.

The hallway on the first floor was also in darkness. Yesterday, starlight had shone brightly through the six hallway windows facing east, but tonight the windows were like a line of mirrors reflecting the darkness. Across from the six windows stood six doors. The Makiharas' room was the second one from the staircase.

Junji stood before the door and knocked three times with a tightly clenched fist.

'Sumako. Hey, Sumako.'

He turned to look at us, as if to show that she really wasn't answering. At this point, I felt a slight unease. He grabbed the door knob and pushed hard, but the door wouldn't budge.

Junji knocked louder and called out to his wife five or six times. There was no reaction from inside the room. The noise of the wind outside was all we could hear.

'Definitely strange.' Kazuto pushed up his bangs of hair with his slim fingers. 'Let's open the door. It's just a latch, so it shouldn't be too difficult. Maybe we can just stick a thin strip of wood through the gap between the door and the frame and push the bar up.'

'That's easier said than done,' growled Junji. 'The latch is actually pretty stiff. It's a bit rusty and you need to apply quite a bit of power to lock or unlock it, or else it won't budge. That's why we stopped using it.'

'Well, that makes matters more difficult, but let's try anyway. Where can we find a thin, sturdy strip?'

I had an idea, so I asked them to wait and went back to our room. I found my half-read Patricia McGerr paperback and ran back to the door where Junji and the others were waiting.

'A metal bookmark? That should do the trick.'

Kazuto took the bookmark and inserted it in the space between the door and the frame. It was a very thin metal strip, but even so, it barely fit inside the gap. Once it was in, Kazuto moved it slowly up until it touched the bottom of the latch bar. He tried to raise it by applying an upward movement, but it didn't move as he'd hoped. 'It won't go up,' he said quietly and tried again with more force, whereupon the bookmark broke in two.

'Oh, I'm sorry.'

'Don't worry about that. But what do we do now?'

The door to the left opened. Sonobe's face appeared.

'What are you doing?'

Egami explained the situation and the doctor grimaced.

'Sumako has no chronic diseases, so there should be nothing to worry about, but still….'

He expressed his concerns like the physician he was, imagining the possibility of Sumako having collapsed because of some hitherto unknown disease, not able to stand up or raise her voice.

'Hey, Sumako. Answer me. Sumako!'

Overcome by anxiety, Junji pounded on the door relentlessly, shouting his wife's name loudly. Still no answer from inside, but from the door on the right a surprised Toshiyuki Inukai appeared, as did Hirakawa, who had been sleeping in Sonobe's room on the left. Junji continued shouting.

'This is strange. Shall we go outside and use a ladder to look through the window?' suggested Toshiyuki, but doing that in the rain and wind seemed too dangerous to me. Sonobe probably thought the same.

'No, we should just break the door open. Kazuto, do you have any tools here?'

'We have a hatchet. Err, was it in the storage…no, I left it somewhere near the back door. I'll go and get it.'

He rushed to the staircase in the back and ran loudly downstairs. Those remaining could only wait. The door outside banged again.

Kazuto came back up the stairs with a small hatchet in his hand. Ryūichi, Reiko and Maria followed him, all dressed in their pyjamas. All were sober again.

'I'll just open a hole near the latch. Then we can get our hands inside and open it.'

Kazuto took aim at the door with his hatchet and the blade made a dull sound as it buried itself in the door. Four, then five times. Splinters flew in all directions. Eventually, he opened a hole in the thin door large enough for an arm.

Kazuto inserted his right arm and felt for the latch.

'Urrgh, it's really stiff,' he groaned, to which Reiko, who'd been standing back, replied: 'Of course it's stiff. The latch of that room is broken....'

Obviously, a lock that would need so much effort to open and shut would be utterly useless. The broken latch had been forcibly locked somehow.

'What's the matter?'

Satomi Inukai had finally woken up and come out of her room. She had probably been in a very deep sleep because of her sleeping pills. She frowned as her husband explained what was going on.

Eventually a metal click could be heard and the door was unlocked. Kazuto had been leaning on the door with his upper body, so the door swung open inwards. We all tried to look inside together.

A noise something like 'Whaaa....' escaped from Sonobe's throat.

For a moment, I couldn't comprehend what had happened in the room. My eyes registered the scene perfectly, but my brain was unable to process it.

I realised that two people were lying, one on top of the other, in a pool of blood near the window. Red stains reached all the way to the door. The person on the floor was Kango Makihara. On top of him lay Sumako.

7

Sonobe went straight towards the two, followed by Junji and Egami. The others remained frozen near the door.

The doctor checked the pulses of the two victims and remained speechless for a moment.

'...It's too late for either of them.'

'You mean she's dead!?' Junji yelled. Maria, too, cried out that it couldn't be true.

'What do you mean, dead? Wha—what happened?'

'Just stay calm now,' Sonobe told Junji, wiping the beads of perspiration from his forehead.

'Sumako! What happened? Sumako!'

The Murder Scene

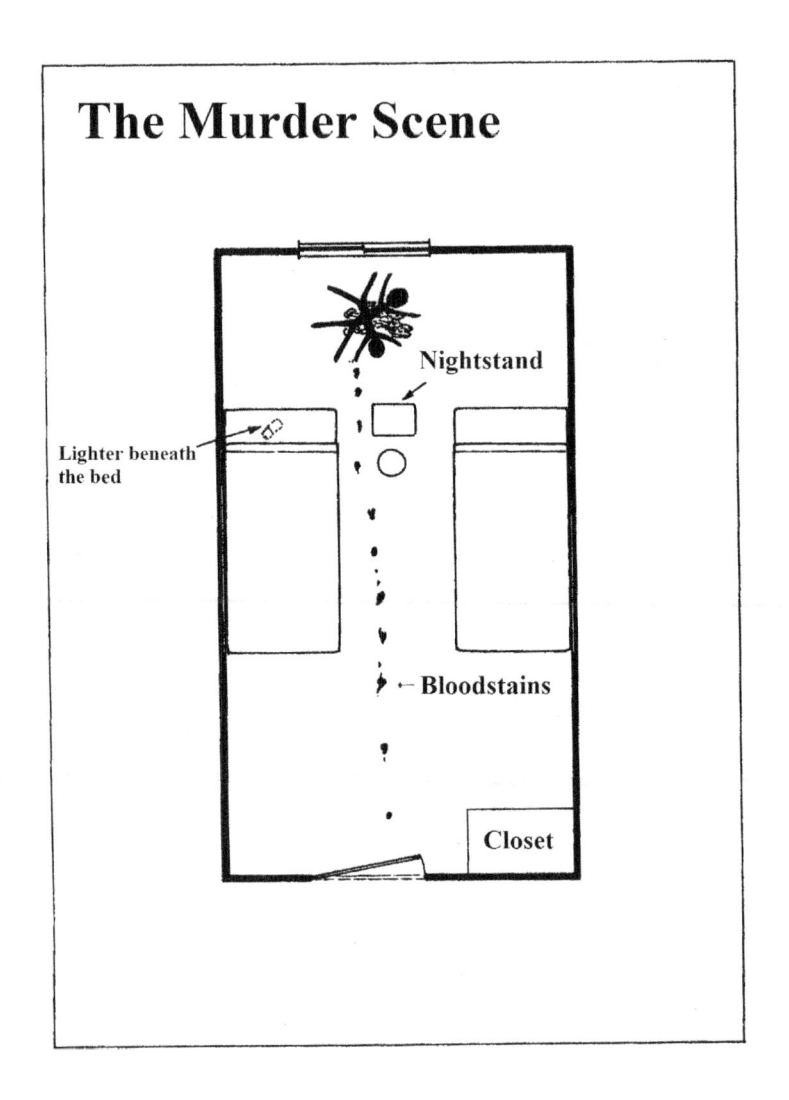

Lighter beneath the bed

Nightstand

Bloodstains

Closet

84

Junji knelt down and feverishly shook the hand of his deceased wife. The scene, set beneath a starless window, reminded me of the finale of a tragic play. But this was not a theatre performance.

'A double suicide of parent and child.'

It was Toshiyuki who mumbled those words. A double suicide of parent and child. Was that what had happened? Was that really it?

'Doctor, what did they die from?' asked Egami, as Sonobe placed his hand on Junji's shoulder. 'I need to check.' Junji staggered to his feet, and Reiko walked over to him and took his hand. She sat him down on the bed and told him gently to get a grip on himself.

The doctor separated the two bodies and examined the origin of the pool of blood. He removed Kango's pants and exposed Sumako's chest. Both of their faces looked relatively calm, and the expression on Sumako's face, in particular, made it appear as if she was resting in peace.

'I can't believe it...this is horrible.' The doctor looked up with a pained expression. 'It's a gunshot. They were both shot to death.'

'Shot to death?' repeated Egami. Everyone remained silent in utter amazement.

'Kango was shot here once,' said the doctor, pointing to the right thigh of the deceased. He pointed at Sumako. 'Sumako has a gunshot wound here on the left side of her chest. It's a large wound. Not a pistol. And not a shotgun... She was shot by a rifle.'

'You can't mean they were shot by my rifle? It can't be....'

'Of course it was your rifle,' growled Ryūichi at the bewildered Kazuto. 'How many of those things do you think we have lying around in the house? Look at what happened because of your rifle.'

'After our target practice this afternoon, you put the rifle back in its usual place, didn't you?'

Kazuto nodded in response to Egami's question.

'Alice, go and check.'

I flew straight out of the room without stopping to answer. When I reached the attic room and looked at the spot next to the door, I saw the rifle wasn't there. An unpleasant sensation filled my mouth.

When I returned to the room and reported the absence of the rifle, a horrified expression appeared on Kazuto's face.

'My rifle...they died because of my rifle....'

'Isn't the rifle here in the room?'

Sonobe's question had us looking all over, but we didn't see it. Egami and I pulled the bed sheets away, peeked inside the closet and dropped to the floor to look beneath the beds, but there was no rifle anywhere.

'But that's strange. Then this can't be a double suicide. If it were, the rifle should be here somewhere,' Maria said, dissatisfied.

She was right. It didn't make any sense for the rifle not to be in the room.

'No, it could still be a double suicide. One of them could have shot the other, then themself and thrown the rifle out of the window. There's nothing but sea outside,' mumbled Ryūichi. Was that possible? My eyes automatically went to the window.

'The window's locked.' Egami pointed to the aluminium sash crescent lock. 'See?'

'What are you implying?' asked Ryūichi irritably. 'The person who shot the other probably threw the rifle away through the window and locked it with their last ounce of strength. Sonobe, is that possible?'

'Wait,' Reiko interrupted. 'Please stop talking about this in front of Mr. Makihara's and Sumako's remains. Let's put them on the beds and cover their faces.'

Sonobe, Ryūichi and Egami looked at each other. They appeared to have been caught off-guard, but eventually Egami opened his mouth.

'You're absolutely right. We can discuss what happened here in detail downstairs. But before we put their remains to rest, there's something I think the doctor should do first, so we can clear up what happened here. A medical examination.'

Reiko agreed. 'Well then,' said the doctor and he kneeled down near the bodies and resumed his examination. He gave a muttered commentary about all he saw, felt and noticed.

'Death occurred between two and four hours ago. It's two thirty now, so the estimated time of death is between ten thirty and twelve thirty. As for the cause of death, Kango died of blood loss. I can't say for certain about Sumako. There's little loss of blood in her case, despite being shot in the chest, so it might've been pericardial tamponade...I can't say without an autopsy. Both have only one rifle wound. Kango was shot through an artery in his thigh, that's why he lost so much blood. Both wounds are penetrating gunshot wounds, so the bullet didn't pierce completely through the bodies. And...yes, Kango was hit hard on the back of his head. Did he hit his head on the floor? No, it was the night stand next to this bed. He hit his head when he fell to the floor after being shot in the thigh. You, please check.'

In response, Egami took a look at the corner of the night stand.

'There's some hair stuck here.'

'Yes? Then that's it. He hit his head here and lost consciousness. His thigh went on bleeding and he died.'

'What's the cause of Sumako's death?' asked Egami.

'Pericardial tamponade? I don't dare say for certain without a detailed examination, but basically, she didn't bleed on the outside, but on the inside. Blood flows inside the pericardium and stops the pumping of the heart. That's why she lost so little blood.'

'She didn't die immediately?'

'It would have taken a little while.'

'And the wound on Mr. Makihara's head was made by the corner of this night stand? He wasn't beaten by a club or anything like that?'

'To be honest, I can't be completely sure. That's what I conclude from my preliminary examination.'

'Doctor, just one more thing.' Egami raised his index finger. 'Do you know which of them was shot first and which of them died first?'

The doctor grimaced.

'There's no way to check for that now.'

'Thank you for all your answers.'

There was a short silence. Finally, Toshiyuki spoke out hesitantly: 'Shouldn't we leave the remains as they are until the police come? Or have I been watching too many crime dramas?'

'But that would be too horrible,' objected Reiko, carefully. 'Even if Kazuto is able to report this to Amami right away on the wireless transceiver, no boats or helicopters can reach us now the typhoon is near. That's why I think we shouldn't leave them like this.'

We agreed with Reiko and carried the two bodies over to the beds. We put our hands together after we placed white cloths over their faces and then went downstairs to the hall.

8

We placed the table with the glass top and the rattan table together in the centre of the hall and sat around them. Reiko and Maria made some hot, strong coffee and brought it out. A tea party at three in the morning....

'What happened in that room?' Egami's voice was the first to ring through the hall. It was followed by the sound of spoons being stirred wearily in cups, and it took a while before anyone answered his question.

'Mr. Egami, you are the most clear-headed of us all at the moment. Won't you please lead the discussion?' said Sonobe, massaging his own neck. Being suddenly asked to become the master of ceremonies, Egami answered first with simply a vague 'Oh.' But then he continued:

'So what happened in the room upstairs? To quote Mr. Inukai's initial reaction, it looks like some sort of double suicide. Is that possible, Doctor?'

'Hard to say,' the doctor replied, this time massaging his shoulders. 'I can't think of any reason why the two of them would want to commit suicide. No, even if I ignore that and bring it down purely to a matter of whether it's possible from a medical point of view, even then I have my doubts. One shoots the other, and then shoots themself. Then they throw the rifle out of the window, lock it, collapse and finally die. Just like that. It is not impossible. And if that's indeed the case, who did what becomes clear as well. Sumako was lying on top of Kango, so she would've been the one to shoot him first, and then herself in the chest....'

Sonobe stopped himself. He had realised the contradiction in his own story.

'But, Doctor, that would be odd.'

'I know, I know, Mr. Egami. That would be impossible. Sumako couldn't have shot herself. Her wound showed no sign of gunpowder burns. She only had a penetrating gunshot wound. That wound could only have been made from a distance of fifteen centimetres or more. *Sumako didn't commit suicide.*'

'And if the roles were reversed? Mr. Makihara shoots Sumako first, then himself in the thigh and then throws the rifle away?'

'That's very unlikely.'

'Because he was also shot from more than fifteen centimetres?'

'No. Well, yes, his wound is like that too, but remember, he was shot in the thigh, not the chest. You'd have to take an unnatural pose, but it might be possible to shoot yourself in the thigh from more than fifteen centimetres away. And the wound entrance was—I mean the bullet also entered his body from high to low, so that would also fit. And the cause of death was blood loss from the wound in his thigh, so opening the window and throwing the rifle away would've been easier for him than for Sumako, a woman shot in her chest. However—.'

'Yes. However, if that was the case, *why was Sumako lying on top of Mr. Makihara*? It should have been the other way around.'

'Precisely....'

The two of them fell silent and Toshiyuki raised his hand.

'This is just a thought, okay? I doubt it actually happened, but… First Sumako shoots her father in the thigh. And then something happens and Mr. Makihara gets hold of the rifle. He shoots Sumako from a distance and then opens the window—.'

'And throws it away. Can't agree with that.'

Kazuto shook his head, a cigarette in one hand.

'Why are you discussing this like you're writing some play, ignoring this one little point: whether they shot each other with consent, or it was a forced suicide from one side: *there's not a single reason why they should throw the rifle away through the window*.'

He was absolutely right.

'Yes, I understand that,' replied Egami calmly. 'I'm of the opinion the double suicide theory won't hold water. I've also considered the possibility that, having shot each other, they fought over the rifle until one of them got their hands on it and threw the dangerous weapon out of the window. But that doesn't make sense either. *It wouldn't be necessary to use their last bit of strength to lock the window afterwards*. The double suicide theory only leads us into a dead end.'

'I think we understand what you're implying.'

Egami nodded to Toshiyuki. 'Yes. This was murder. What happened in that room was homicide. The police investigation will probably bring forth more evidence for that. Forensics can test for gunshot residue, for example.'

Not everyone might have known about gunshot residue, so Egami explained. When a gun is fired, gunpowder is blown out both forwards and backwards from the muzzle. This gunshot residue clings to the hand of the shooter. By looking for such traces, the police can determine who the shooter was. In this case, the right hands of both Makiharas, parent and child, would be the focus of such a test—but there was no way for us to check that today.

Kazuto stood up suddenly. He kicked over his chair and headed for the corridor.

'Kazuto, where are you going?' Reiko asked and, with his back still turned to her, he answered: 'Calling the police.' He was going to go in the rain to his room in the annex to use the wireless transceiver.

There was a heavy silence. After a while, we heard the faraway noise of Kazuto opening the back door and going outside. Bang. The storage room door banged again.

'This is a really serious situation,' Hirakawa said as he slowly brushed his cheek. 'Mr. Egami, your mind is still clear, I hope? Do you fully comprehend the situation? I'm sure you haven't forgotten, but that door was locked from inside. Do you know what that means?'

What a roundabout way of talking. There was no way Egami hadn't noticed that.

'I understand. You mean the room was completely sealed. Yes, I know. But I think it'd be wrong to say that, because of that, no murder could have taken place inside that room.'

'Was the murderer still hiding somewhere inside the room when we broke in....?'

The idea Maria had set out to float, however, sank immediately. Right before the door was opened, Satomi Inukai had woken from her deep sleep and shown herself. Everyone on the island—save for the two victims—had been gathered anxiously in front of the door. So who would have been hiding inside? Suppose, for argument's sake, that an unknown person was on the island and that this X was the murderer. Even then, X couldn't have been hiding in that room. The only places where a person could have hidden were inside the closet and beneath the beds, but we'd checked there when we were searching for the rifle and we didn't find even a single rat.

'Mr. Egami, you're fond of detective novels, aren't you? I once read a story about a similar situation. Something about a woman crying out in a blue room or a red room....'

'That's *The Mystery of the Yellow Room*, Doctor. That was one of the classics you read.'

There was the sound of the back door opening and closing. Because the storage room door had stopped banging, I guessed Kazuto had perhaps shut that door as well.

'That was fast,' Ryūichi noted as Kazuto reappeared. He sipped his coffee, which by then was completely cold.

Kazuto stuck his right hand out. In it, he held a bundle of what appeared to be wires.

'The cables were torn out. The transceiver itself is also a mess.'

Several of us cried out....

9

An unbearable silence.
The howling gale.
'This has turned out for the worst,' the artist murmured.

'It really was murder. The murderer has cut off the only method to call for help....' So saying, Toshiyuki asked Kazuto for a cigarette. I didn't know he smoked. Had he given up smoking previously?

'When's the next boat scheduled to come?'

'It's already a new day, so…in another three days,' replied Reiko to Hirakawa's question.

'Everyone on the island is gathered here.' Egami was intent on proceeding with his job as the master of ceremonies.

'That means the person behind the murders must be one of us eleven present here. Well then, who did it? We need to clarify this first. We can then ask the murderer in person why Kango and Sumako Makihara had to die. The first question we need to examine is…who had an opportunity to commit the murders?'

I was, to use a slightly exaggerated word, impressed by Egami's calmness. He was completely clear in his head. How could someone as sharp, as clever and as tough as he was keep on repeating years at university? It was a question that was always in the back of my mind and now it only became more into focus.

It stands to reason to start with an examination of who had an opportunity to commit the crime. But would it be that simple? I turned my mind back to the extravagant drinking party we'd had some hours before, which didn't make me hopeful.

'The estimated time of death is in the two hours between ten thirty and twelve thirty. Anyone who couldn't have gone upstairs in that period, has an alibi.'

'Mr. Egami, can't we shorten the period in which the crime could've been committed?' asked Ryūichi. 'I mean, ten thirty is still early in the night. Most of us were down here drinking, eating and having a talk. If at that time a rifle had been shot twice upstairs, I'm sure at least some people down here in the hall would've noticed.'

'Dad, you've got it the wrong way round,' Kazuto said. 'We wouldn't have noticed the shots while we were in the middle of all that boozing. On the other hand, by the time some of us had dropped out—I was one of them—by falling asleep, or going to their bedroom, that's when we would've noticed a shot blasting through the house.'

'Is there anybody who remembers hearing a shot, probably two shots, one right after the other?' asked Egami.

'I remember having heard something,' Toshiyuki replied immediately. 'I also drank myself to sleep, but I did hear something loud when I was still dozing. Unconsciously I took a look at my watch, and it was a quarter past twelve. I didn't think anything of it, though, and fell asleep again.'

'I also remember something curious.' This time, it was Reiko. 'After I'd returned to my room with Maria and gone to bed, I heard two loud bangs, one after another. But I don't think it was past midnight yet.'

'Oh, a discrepancy,' said Kazuto.

'Actually, I also have a memory of something that might've been the shots,' said discussion leader Egami with a thoughtful expression. 'That was around midnight.'

Hirakawa gave a wry smile. 'Don't know what to believe.'

'What an incredible house! A rifle is shot twice in the middle of the night beneath this very roof and nobody notices it! I'm pretty sure we didn't hold a drinking party during a live heavy metal concert!'

Kazuto looked nervous. But wasn't this to be expected? That is because—.

'It's because we got used to hearing the door of the storage room outside at the back banging. Among all those bangs we heard, who knows which of them were actually rifle shots?'

Toshiyuki sighed loudly. Some of us nodded. That door had suddenly turned into a big problem.

'That's why I told you to shut the damn thing.' Ryūichi was in a bad mood and scolded Kazuto. 'Because you were too lazy—'

'Oh, Dad, you knew someone would die if I didn't close that door? Who's the horrible one here? If it was that important, you could have kicked me until I'd closed the door, or you could've gone yourself....'

'Enough of that!'

Hirakawa calmed the two of them down. This was no time to make false accusations or trip each other up.

'How about the people who went up early to sleep? Mrs. Inukai? Mr. Hirakawa?'

Satomi Inukai cocked her head and looked as if she was quite distressed.

'I...I'm sorry, but I took my sleeping pills just after ten and fell asleep just like that, so I don't remember having heard anything at all. It was only when all of you were making that commotion that I woke up and asked you what was going on.'

I'd expected that answer. I looked at Hirakawa, but he also was wearing a pained expression.

'Mr. Hirakawa, do you also take sleeping pills?' asked Egami.

'No, I don't use anything like that. But even so, I didn't hear anything. You see, the storage room door was distracting me so much from my sleep, I decided to use earplugs. I have them for swimming and I found I had them in my pocket, so that was lucky, or so I thought…. Which means I can't offer you any information either.'

It wasn't just the earplugs. It wasn't only the storage room door that had been loud in the night; the gale had also been doing its job outside.

'It appears it's impossible for us to shorten the estimated period during which the crime was committed.' Egami gave up on pursuing that line of thought. 'Let's go back to the earlier question, then. Was there anyone who could *not* have gone upstairs in the two hours the crime was committed?'

Everyone remained silent for a moment. They were thinking back about either themselves, or about the others.

'My wife took her sleeping pills shortly after ten and went to bed. Do you agree that gives her an alibi?'

Toshiyuki tried to defend his wife, but there was no way that was going to pass muster. We only had her word that she'd taken the pills and gone to bed right after that. In fact, Satomi was the first to disappear from sight and, out of all of us, she was the one who had no alibi for the longest period of time. Naturally, protests were raised.

'I also went to bed early, but that doesn't clear me of suspicion, does it?' Hirakawa admitted himself he had no alibi.

But it wasn't only the people who had gone to bed early who had no alibi. It was possible that someone who'd remained in the hall had actually sneaked upstairs via the back stairs, with the excuse of going to the toilet. Having finished the job, they could have returned wearing an innocent expression—just as in the novels. Another possibility was that someone had remained in the main hall until only those who had drunk themselves to sleep were left, after which they had gone off to commit the crime. Having done that, they could have slipped back into the hall and pretended to be drunk as well.

'And everyone had an opportunity to get hold of the rifle, I think?' asked Egami, just to be sure. At five o'clock in the afternoon of the previous day, Kazuto had placed the rifle back against the wall of the attic room. There was nobody who admitted to having gone up there after that, but still....

'There's one more aspect we need to consider regarding the opportunity to commit the murders. Who wasn't intoxicated last night?'

That was a very difficult question to answer. There was only one person who clearly had not been under the influence of alcohol: Satomi Inukai, who had gone to bed early. Reiko and Maria had only drunk a little. As for the others...I wonder. None of us had merely pretended to drink and secretly spilled their drink on the floor. Everything which had been poured had entered the mouth of someone, but only the consumers themselves would know how far gone they were. One could even imagine that this violent crime had only been committed because of the influence of alcohol. But once you started doubting, anything seemed possible.

'This doesn't seem to lead anywhere, either. One last thing, then. Who could've destroyed the wireless transceiver in Kazuto's room? Kazuto, when was the last time you saw it intact?'

'Before dinner. Before seven. I hadn't gone back to the annex until just now.'

We were just repeating ourselves. Everybody had had a chance. If we were to pursue all possibilities diligently, we could also raise the possibility it was Kazuto himself who had destroyed the transceiver when he went to the annex.

'I give up....' Sonobe let out a deep sigh, blowing out all of his fatigue. He didn't have his briar pipe with him, so he, too, asked Kazuto for a cigarette.

'This really is a nightmare. If we get hit by the typhoon, too....' Then Ryūichi remembered something. 'Reiko, go get a radio. There should be something about the typhoon.'

'Yes,' replied Reiko. As she stood up she turned to Maria. 'Maria, will you come with me?'

'Of course.' Maria was about to get up, but Kazuto stopped her.

'Going alone must be scary. I'll go with you.'

'Nothing dangerous can happen to her if everybody on the island is gathered here in this room,' said Ryūichi. 'But I do feel uneasy. Kazuto, you go get it yourself. It's near the cushion in my room.'

Kazuto scowled, but still followed his father's orders. It appeared that Kazuto was yearning for attention from Reiko and Maria, his beautiful family members. While he and Reiko were not related by blood, she was still his older sister, and Maria actually was his cousin by blood. He was frankly creepy. Had he been left with so many psychological scars by women outside his own family?

Reiko poured some cold tea for all of us while we were waiting for Kazuto to return from his errand. Egami was the first to say 'Thank you' and reach out for a cup, probably because his throat was dry from having talked for so long.

The radio arrived. Kazuto placed it in the centre of the table and switched it on. A voice could be heard amongst all the static. Kazuto and I leaned forward to listen to this voice from the outer world. I hoped it wouldn't be bad news.

'So, Alice? What's it saying?'

'Don't worry, Maria,' Kazuto said, not giving me a chance to reply. 'They say the typhoon went straight east after reaching the main island of Okinawa. It'll pass about 100 kilometres south of us.'

'Thank goodness.' Maria's shoulders dropped and her tension eased a bit.

'So this wind and rain will also subside. That's a relief,' said Hirakawa.

I was glad we'd managed to avoid the typhoon, but we were not in a situation where we could feel any relief at all.

'It's four o' clock now,' Ryūichi said in his hoarse voice, after looking at the wall clock. 'Here in the south the sun comes up late. Let's all sleep for a while.'

With exhausted expressions, we all nodded.

Ryūichi suggested to Junji Makihara that he'd be better off sleeping in Kango's room.

And thus the long night of the second day…finally ended.

CHAPTER THREE: BICYCLE PUZZLE

1

The third day on the island. By ten o'clock, everyone was out of bed and the wind and rain had started to abate. By the time we'd finished our breakfast-cum-lunch, it was already past eleven.

'Did yesterday really happen?'

Those words Maria had accidentally blurted out during lunch had left an impression on me. We'd escaped the terror of the typhoon and, while it was still cloudy, the sky was clear at times. But, to my mind, the residue of yesterday's intoxication still remained. I could very well understand the feeling of wishing it all to have been just a bad dream. But the brutal fact that Kango and Sumako Makihara weren't present at the dining table with us reinforced the painful reality.

After the meal, Egami asked Maria and me to come upstairs with him to examine the crime scene once again. When I tried to reflect on how we'd discovered the bodies, I realised the whole scene had vanished from my memory for whatever reason. Today we would do an on-the-spot investigation of what in heaven had happened in that room last night.

We stood in front of the door, which had a gaping hole in it. Egami grabbed the door knob and easily pushed it open.

'First is the latch.' Egami stared at it. 'I wonder why this stiff—or, as Reiko claimed—broken latch was activated last night in the first place?'

'Mr. Egami,' said Maria, 'last night you all knocked on the door and called out for Sumako several times. There was no answer, so you thought something was amiss. Well, I hadn't arrived then, but was the door really locked from the inside? It's natural to assume a door is locked if it won't open, but isn't it possible something else was preventing it from opening? Perhaps something was leaning against it?'

'Are you suspecting Kazuto?' I asked her. Kazuto was the one who'd made a hole in the door with the hatchet and slid his arm inside to open it, but none of us had actually seen him open the latch. The door had simply opened after he'd put his hand through the hole and muttered things like 'It's so stiff,' 'Just a little bit more' and 'Got it.'

Maria didn't put it in so many words, but she was hinting it may all have been a performance by Kazuto.

'It's not as if I suspect Kazuto of being the murderer, but it's possible it wasn't the latch which was preventing the door from opening.'

She was having difficulty expressing herself. Perhaps she suspected Kazuto was at least involved in the murders in some way.

'That's a very level-headed judgment,' said Egami solemnly. 'But there's no reason to suspect something like that for now. When the door finally opened, there wasn't anything close by that could have been used to prevent it and I didn't notice anything strange about Kazuto's behaviour while he was inserting the metal bookmark in the gap and trying to push the bar up. The very fact that he broke the bookmark shows there must have been something on the door that prevented it from opening. Yet when we finally got it open there was nothing to be seen.'

'So...the door really was locked from inside?'

'Yes,' replied Egami.

We entered the room silently and placed our hands together out of respect for the bodies lying on the two beds.

'Okay, time for us to pretend to be Sherlock Holmes and crawl around on the floor.'

The bloodstains on the floor had turned black. Kango's cause of death had been loss of blood, so the stains near the window where the two had been lying were particularly large and horrible.

'Some smaller bloodstains are spread around the room. They were probably made by Sumako as she moved about after being shot,' Maria noted.

There were five or six spots on the floor where the blood led from the middle of the room to the door. Kango had been shot in the thigh and, as he had been hit in an artery, it's unlikely he could have walked around in the room. There was also a very real possibility he'd lost consciousness after falling and hitting his head on the corner of the night stand after being shot. Sumako, on the other hand, had been shot in the chest, but, according to the doctor, she'd lost only a little blood and hadn't died instantly, so she could have walked around the room in agony, spilling blood on the floor. But for what reason?

'I wonder where Sumako was when she was shot?' I voiced the question. 'I was in such shock last night I didn't even notice these bloodstains at the time, so I assumed that both of them had been shot by the window and fallen there. But that might be wrong. Maybe she was shot near the door and made her way painfully to the window, where she fell on top of her father, who'd been shot earlier?'

'It does look like that,' said Egami after giving it some thought. 'That means Sumako was standing here when she was shot.'

He went over to the bloodstain closest to the door. It was less than a metre away from the door, and you could grab the door knob if you reached out for it.

'That's odd,' said Maria with her finger to her lips, 'Isn't it strange she was shot so close by the door? Suppose Sumako was standing where Egami is now, then the door was open and the murderer shot into the room from the hallway. Sumako was shot from more than fifteen centimetres away and the rifle itself is almost one metre long, so the murderer couldn't have put his back to the door and shot her from inside the room. But that's also very curious. Even if the wind outside was howling loudly and the storage room door was banging about, why shoot from the hallway with the door open?'

She continued: 'If the door was closed and Sumako was standing where Egami is now, with her back to the door, then the murderer would have been standing in the middle of the room. No, that's even more curious. If the two had been in those positions, there's no way Sumako would've stumbled towards the window after being shot. She would've opened the door and fled into the hallway to cry out for help.'

'You're doing well, Patience.'

'Quit joking, Alice. I'm only stating the obvious. It...bothers me that Sumako was shot there.'

'Well then, that's our first problem. *Where was Sumako standing when she was shot?*' Egami continued: 'And the second problem I was about to mention just now: *Why was the latch, which was as good as broken, forcibly locked anyway?*'

I hit upon a good idea.

'I wonder whether my deduction is correct. This is my answer to the first problem: Sumako was shot near the window, or perhaps in the middle of the room. And the bloodstains leading to the door were made when she went over to the door after being shot and...locked it herself.'

'Ah, the classic pattern in locked room mysteries,' said Maria. 'It wasn't some trick of the murderer, but the victim herself who locked the door and then died inside. It does answer the mystery of why the room was locked from the inside. But I don't like that idea either. Why would Sumako first lock the door and then go back to my uncle at the window to collapse there? Was she aware she was going to die anyway, so she wanted to die holding her father?

'I don't believe it. Wouldn't it be more natural for her to open the door and call for help? My uncle was lying there bleeding heavily. What would be the point of clinging to her father? She would cry out for help. Your theory doesn't answer the second problem of why the door was locked.'

'Perhaps she was trying to defend herself from further attacks by the murderer? After the first shot, she could've pushed the killer outside into the hallway and locked the door....'

'Hard to swallow. I can't believe that Sumako, fatally wounded, could've pushed the murderer outside, nor that the murderer wouldn't have pushed his way back into the room while Sumako was still struggling with the stiff latch.'

I could only nod at Maria's arguments.

'There's no doubt Mr. Makihara was shot over by the window,' said Egami, as he followed the bloodstains. 'The problem is Sumako's movements....'

'Maybe there's some physical proof lying around here that will tell us the story,' suggested Maria.

'Okay, everyone on all fours.'

So declared Egami, and he literally started to crawl on the floor, peeking under one of the beds. I looked beneath the other one. Last night, we'd been looking for a rifle, but today I had my eyes wide open for even the slightest clue. And there was indeed something.

'There's something here. It's in the back, so I can't see it very well.'

Egami stood up, and crouched to look beneath this bed from the head side.

'Ah, you're right. Something round. A lighter?'

'My uncle used a cylindrical lighter. It had a strange shape. He said it was a souvenir from Hong Kong.'

Still crouching, Egami stretched his arm out, but couldn't reach the object. He went back to lying on the floor again and finally got hold of it.

'Yes, that's my uncle's lighter.'

'Perhaps he was about to light a cigarette when he was shot,' I suggested. 'That's why he was holding his lighter. And when he was shot and fell down, he let go of it and it rolled down beneath the bed.'

'Probably. He might also have been playing with his lighter while talking with Sumako, as that was his habit. He then let it fall when he was shot.'

Whatever happened, there was no need to look for any deeper meaning regarding the lighter.

After that, even Maria went crawling on the floor, as we went over the room with a fine-tooth comb. But we didn't find anything that could be the key to the problem of what had happened in that room.

2

We didn't want to stay cooped up in the house. Someone suggested going outside. We went downstairs and decided we could go to the observation platform again to discuss the case there. Hirakawa and Reiko were standing in the entrance.

'Mr. Hirakawa, are you going back to Happy Fish Villa?'

The artist turned to Maria.

'Yes. I'll go back to my abode and take another nap. I'm so tired.'

'Can we join you up to halfway? We're going out now as well.'

'Yes, of course.'

Reiko saw the four of us off as we left Panorama Villa on our bicycles. The sky had mostly cleared.

'You were examining the crime scene upstairs again, I understand? Did you find anything?' Hirakawa asked Egami who was pedalling next to him.

'No. We only found Mr. Makihara's lighter under the bed.'

'Is that significant?'

'Probably not. He was either shot just as he was about to light a cigarette, or else he was playing with the lighter as he was talking to Sumako.'

'I wonder what Kango and Sumako were talking about. Sumako left her husband all alone to go upstairs, so she might have had an important talk with her father.'

'Who knows?'

Sumako was of course asking for financial support from her father. Egami was playing dumb. Maria and I were cycling next to each other behind Egami and Hirakawa and listened to their discussion.

'This is a wonderful place, but tragic events have happened here one after another, I heard.' This time it was Egami who began.

'I heard Hideto, Maria's cousin, died in an accident three years ago.'

'Ah, yes.' The artist's voice dropped. 'That was a tragedy. I always considered this island to be a paradise in the south, but that accident was really terrible. And now you say it was murder? I still can't believe it.'

'I'm of the opinion it was murder. I don't like it, but I don't believe it could be anything else. Where did he die?'

'We pulled him out of a stretch of the bay to the north, nearer to Happy Fish Villa than to the centre of the bay. There's a big rock there called the Eboshi Rock, named after those funny high hats court nobles used to wear in Japan. I could never have imagined that someone as good a swimmer as he was could drown like that....'

'You couldn't imagine...?'

'No, what I mean is,' said Hirakawa, flustered, 'I was shocked, but you know, sometimes you get cramp in your legs and swimming in the night all on your own is really dangerous.'

Their talk continued as we passed through the greenery.

'Why was Hideto swimming at night all alone? Did he do that often?'

'I wonder. I'm not sure about that. You'd better ask Maria.'

'He never did anything like that,' Maria said loudly to the two men in front. 'He once took me out in the rowing boat in the night when the moon looked beautiful, but we didn't swim. I remember I said I wanted to get out of the boat to swim a bit and he stopped me, saying it was dangerous.'

The four of us fell silent. This was a bad topic.

'Mr. Hirakawa, are you tired? Are you going to sleep right away when you get back?' asked Maria suddenly. Hirakawa turned his head and looked back at her.

'No, I'm not that exhausted. Why?'

'If it's okay, I'd like to see Sumako's portrait. The one in your studio.'

'That one? It's okay with me.' Hirakawa sounded a bit bewildered.

'Sorry. If you're tired, we can come another time, but I suddenly felt like seeing it. I love that painting. I understand very well this might sound rude to you, as you specialise in painting landscapes, but I think that portrait of Sumako is the best of all your paintings. I even felt jealous of Sumako because of that.'

'Oh,' said Hirakawa, who was facing front again. 'Thank you. Then next time, I'll make a painting of you, Maria. I'll put my heart into it, so it won't lose to Sumako's painting.'

'Thank you. But you don't have to—'

'I want to. But I have to finish the one I'm working on now first. So it will have to be next year.'

'Okay....'

Would Maria be returning to this island next year? Her lifeless answer suggested she herself was doubtful. Kashikijima had become the home of another sad memory.

'Is it okay if we come as well?'

'Of course. You two must come, too. A middle-aged man like me can't hog all the attention of our idol, can he?'

'Oh, Mr. Hirakawa, you can read "Who the heck is our idol here?" all over Alice's face.'

'I didn't say anything.'

'That's why I said we could read it from your face.'

'Are they fighting back there?'

'The two of them are always like that. They get along too well.'

'Mr. Egami!' Maria cried out.

The thirty minutes before we reached Happy Fish Villa were filled chatting about this and that as we pedalled on.

After a while, we arrived at Happy Fish Villa.

We sat down at the table with the glass top, still covered by the scattered jigsaw pieces of Hokusai's painting. As we drank the iced coffee Hirakawa had poured for us, we talked about all kind of topics besides what had happened on the island. As we did, I couldn't help but notice that this artist was almost totally ignorant of the happenings in society. To give an example: he didn't know who the current president of the United States was.

'I feel slightly embarrassed to have been exposed as someone who knows so little of the world. I could pretend that it's proof that I'm a real artist who's dedicated to the arts, but you'd only burst out laughing if a third rate artist like me made such a claim. Simply put, I have trouble placing the human being that I am within the larger society. I'm simply not interested in human society. Human beings, all destined to die; this insight brought despair to me already when I was a child. I was born defective, perhaps. But, well, the world is a strange place and there are wonderful things to be found that appeal to my inner being. Not just art, mind you. I feel attracted to wonderful nature, like on this island and to beautiful women, too. Ah, how I wish I could live surrounded by such wonderful things,' he added philosophically.

We would not be here, had it gone as we had wished.
Who would leave, if it would go as we wish?
If we hadn't come, gone and lived in this shack,
Oh, how much better that would have been!

'I think I've heard that poem before. Is it from the *Rubaiyat*? Dr. Sonobe's speciality.'

Egami answered in the affirmative.

'I like detective novels too, you know. There was a time I read a lot of them.' The artist leaned back deeply in his seat. 'I like Van Dine best of all. But not because the plots of his books are good. I liked that self-satisfied detective Philo Vance. It's called pedantry, I think? The man shows off his knowledge of art and literature from both East and West while he's smugly making grand deductions. A man who can spend his time enjoying art the whole day and studying everything that interests him, because he inherited his aunt's immense fortune. Philo Vance is the embodiment of the life I'd like to live.'

'You don't seem too badly off yourself.'

'There you're wrong, Mr. Egami. A hack like me can just barely make a living. I always wish I had someone like Philo Vance's aunt around, each time I'm worrying where the next meal is coming from.'

'But you're spending your summers rather glamorously here. You have your own house on a faraway island and spend your summers there: aren't you one of the Chosen Ones?'

The artist let out a snort, laughing at himself.

'Actually, I did have someone like Philo Vance's aunt. The person who built Happy Fish Villa was my uncle, a friend of Tetsunosuke Arima. My uncle had no children. So the house became mine when he died. He was quite well off, and the greater part of the inheritance was split among the family. Then they came to me, a starving artist at the time and the black sheep of the family, and proposed giving me this unbelievably inconveniently located house. And this eccentric man did the eccentric thing of happily inheriting it.'

'I think this home fits you really well,' Egami said with a kind expression on his face. 'Have you ever wanted to live here permanently, where it's always summer?'

'Yes. It pains me every year when the day I leave the island comes near. When I was a kid, I'd always get stomach ache the night before the new school period started. The morning of the opening ceremony would be too terrifying and I wouldn't get anything down my throat. Even if I did eat something, I'd throw it up. There wasn't any particular teacher I didn't like, nobody who'd bully me, I wasn't that bad at studying and I had some friends like any other person, but despite that, I felt a terror for school from within the depths of my soul. My stomach would cry out in fear of returning to that cage. Of course, it's not that horrible anymore at this age, but I still feel depressed the day before I leave this island. I'm just a pathetic, childish man who only wants to spend his life surrounded by the things he loves.'

'You say you lament that you were born into this world, but it doesn't appear at all like that to me.' Egami shook his head. 'To me, it seems as though you're taking revenge for being born, by living so well.'

'*Living Well is the Best Revenge*. Some art critic used that as a title for a book.'

The artist picked a jigsaw piece up from the table and fiddled with it. Egami and he had been talking as if they'd been completely alone.

'Maria, didn't you say you wanted to take a look at the painting?'

'I do. I think it's in the back?'

She stood up. It was a simple lodge-style house with a kitchen, washroom and a bathroom, so "in the back" actually meant in the rear corner of the room. Maria walked with her usual wiggle to the back wall, followed by Egami and me. Hirakawa sipped his iced coffee, still leaning back in his chair.

'Nice painting, isn't it?' Maria said. We stood behind her and voiced our agreement.

In the painting, Sumako did not have a wavy haircut, but long, straight hair hanging down to her shoulders. She was wearing a white two-piece dress with a hint of pink, and was sitting in a chair in that very room, her legs neatly crossed. Her slender ankles and the toenails on her bare feet were charming. I looked back at her face. Her head was tilted up as if she was peering into the faraway sky above.

Once again I was reminded that she'd been an attractive woman. I stared for a while at this painting of her made three years ago.

'It's so beautiful…' Maria mumbled again as if in a trance.

'Thank you, I'm happy you like it so much.' Hirakawa said, still with his back to us. 'I like it, too. When Sumako and Mr. Arima said they wanted to hang the painting in Panorama Villa, I had to decline politely. I really felt bad about it, because Sumako had been nice enough to model for me, but I just couldn't let go of it. I just had to keep it here.'

Sumako had been in love with the painter at that time. I wondered what his own feelings towards her had been. Was she just another glass of fine wine to this epicurean, who thought living well was the summit of existence? There was no way to know.

The artist still had his back to us and showed no sign of movement.

'You're always welcome to come and see it.'

I heard him sigh.

'I need to rest now. I'm exhausted.'

3

We were at the arbour on the observation platform.

The three of us were enjoying the breeze as we looked down at the Candle Rock and the Twin Rocks. We had returned to this highest point of the island, as if we were victims of a flood who were about to climb to the arbour's roof to cry for help.

'Perhaps my uncle and Sumako really did commit suicide.... I'm starting to think that might really have happened,' said Maria, as she curled her russet hair between her fingers. I asked her why she'd come to that conclusion.

'I remembered how peaceful Sumako looked in death. If she'd been shot by someone who'd forced his way into her room, why did she die with such a peaceful look? Wouldn't it be more natural to have an expression somewhere between fear and shock?'

'But to go back to the double suicide idea just because of such an impression.... There's something in what you say, but one could also argue she managed to draw her last breath looking so peaceful because she felt relieved she could at least die next to her father. She might've looked different if she was dying all alone. You'd need a better argument to overturn the murder theory.'

I suddenly felt bad for having spoken so lightly about the matter. For Maria, the idea of the two of them having committed suicide together must have sounded better, however slightly, than murder. She might have wished subconsciously for it to be suicide, and there was I, asking her for better arguments. I could probably have been a bit more considerate.

'Would Mr. Makihara and Sumako have any reasons for wanting to commit suicide?' I asked, but Maria shook her head.

'I can't think of any...so I guess it must've been murder after all.'

'If it was murder, who had a motive for killing the two of them?' I asked again. 'Is there such a person?'

'That's even more unthinkable. I have no idea why anyone would want to kill my uncle or Sumako.'

Egami, who had been silent up to that point, opened his mouth. 'I probably shouldn't say this, but if Kango Makihara had been the only victim, there's at least one person with a motive.'

Maria reacted immediately. 'You mean Junji?'

'Yes.'

'They were on really bad terms, but would he really go as far as to murder Uncle Kango? Even supposing he would—and I don't believe it—I can't imagine Junji shooting Sumako as well. He might've said those things two days ago, but he really loved Sumako. It's not possible.'

But it was possible. I understood what Maria was trying to say, but as long as Junji had had the opportunity to murder Sumako and it had been physically possible for him to do so, it meant he couldn't be ruled out as the murderer.

'But it's not as though I have an idea of who else might have done it,' lamented Maria. 'I can't imagine uncle Ryūichi killing his brother-in-law and his niece Sumako, and there's no way Reiko would do anything like that. Kazuto already gets enough excitement just by shooting at cans, so I can't see him doing something as vicious as that, and I think the same of the Inukai couple, Mr. Hirakawa and Dr. Sonobe....'

She was very upset.

Nobody was a suspect. But someone had done it. The murderer was among them.

'I wonder what happened to the rifle.'

Maria was surprised by the question I let slip.

'If they didn't commit suicide, then the question of what happened to the murder weapon comes to mind. It wasn't in the room. Did the murderer throw it out of the window, or did he hide it somewhere?' This was not pleasant to say. 'We're still in danger if they still have the rifle with them.'

'Still the same.' Maria glared at me. 'Little Alice, always full of worries. Are you afraid you're next? It might be a double suicide after all, so you don't need to get all panicky.'

'Not the double suicide theory again?'

'Yes. There's no way to find out what happened in that room because there was nobody there to witness it. Who knows what kind of incredible things could have transpired there? I just said "So I guess it was murder," but I take it back. We just don't know.'

'I take it back too.'

'What?'

'I said "You're doing well, Patience" earlier. I take that back.'

'Take it back all you want. I don't like Patience anyway. She's just a cross-dressing Ellery Queen!'

Let's stop, this is getting silly.

We sat down and remained silent on the hill where Maria had learnt to play the guitar.

'Is that Reiko over there?' asked Egami suddenly.

Maria and I turned to look at the bay to the north, just as Egami was doing. The rowing boat was out there. There was a woman in it, heading towards Happy Fish Villa. It was Reiko.

'Reiko's probably taking something over to Mr. Hirakawa. Whenever he comes over, he always returns with a backpack full of fresh vegetables and other foodstuffs, but he didn't just now. He even forgot his backpack.'

Now that she mentioned it, I remembered Hirakawa's home had no refrigerator.

The waves were higher than yesterday. There was something heroic about the sight of the boat making its way forward while being rocked by the waves.

I turned away and my eyes fell on the *moai* statue. As always, it stood at the highest point of the island, looking down at the world.

'Guess now's not the time to think about the *moai* puzzle,' mumbled Egami, almost incoherently. I sighed. Yesterday, I'd almost felt sorry for leaving two of my seniors behind in Kyōto and coming to this leisure island. My feelings had changed dramatically.

'It's the *moais*' fault,' said Maria. 'Nothing bad, nothing horrible had ever happened on this island until they came here. One summer, my grandfather had workers and engineers come here and had those statues built all over the island, as if he had foreseen his own death. He died the following spring. The year after, Sumako and Mr. Hirakawa had their affair, and the year after that, Hideto died in an accident while searching for the treasure. The last two years nothing happened, but this year another horrible incident occurred.... It's as if those statues have cast a curse on the island.'

'The day we arrived here, you called them the mascot figures of the island, but now you feel differently?'

Maria looked at me and returned a weak smile.

'How silly of me. Taking back all the things I said.'

I looked at the *moai* again. Have you really placed a curse over this island? If so, was it Tetsunosuke Arima who had you built so you would curse the place?'

The *moai* knew something.

The thought suddenly took hold of me.

4

We remained on the hill until close to four o'clock.

We avoided the topic of murder and chatted about things that happened at university and so on. Maria had some unique proposals for recruiting new club members next year, and even declared that from next spring on, the Eito University Mystery Club would become a woman's paradise. One of her ideas was that we should let go of our too direct and rough-sounding organisation name, and consider a trendier one. But what kind of people would be attracted by names like Laughing Daedalus or Murder Land? Strange kid.

When we returned to Panorama Villa we found the doctor in the hall. He was sitting facing the jigsaw puzzle in silence, his face wearing an expression of enlightenment. He was holding his briar pipe in his left hand, but he appeared to have forgotten about it, as only his right hand was busy moving around.

Reiko appeared from the back. She'd probably returned long ago from Happy Fish Villa. She looked refreshed, having changed into denim shorts.

'Welcome back.'

'Thanks. The doctor is all immersed in his game, isn't he?' said Maria and Reiko shot a glance at Sonobe.

'He certainly is. He's been at it since lunch. He's probably trying to get everything out of his mind, but even then, it's amazing how focused he is.'

'Mr. Egami, please come and help me.'

In response to the request, our club president went over to the doctor.

'How are the others doing?' I asked.

Reiko shrugged. 'Everybody seems out of it. Both father and Junji are cooped up in their rooms, only coming out to use the bathroom. The Inukais have been trying to distract themselves by reading or listening to the radio. They're in their room now. The doctor has been like that all day. The only one moving around…,'

Reiko started to say something, but then stopped.

'What's the matter? So the only one moving around is Kazuto? What's he been doing?'

'Well...don't think badly of him, but Kazuto has been searching the house. He says he's going to find the murder weapon: his rifle.'

'Searching the house? You don't mean he's gone into my room and has been going through my stuff, do you? Surely he hasn't gone into Mr. Egami and Alice's room either?'

The expression on Maria's face changed, like a transformation scene in a science-fiction film. Reiko looked embarrassed.

'I'm sorry. I tried to stop him, but he wouldn't take no for an answer. If you're going to get angry, please be angry at me too. Kazuto said that if he went in alone, it'd seem suspicious to the others, so he forced me to come along with him. But I didn't let him take one step inside your room. I had him stand at the entrance while I searched myself. I'm sorry, Alice.'

'When did you search the rooms?' I asked, and she hesitated for a moment.

'Right after you left with Mr. Hirakawa.'

'Unbelievable!' Maria raised her voice in protest. 'So he waited until we were gone to search the house? That's low! Does Kazuto think one of us is the murderer? Or did he do it simply because there was nobody to stop him? I'm going to give him a piece of my mind.'

'Please don't, Maria.'

'No, this is something I won't let slide this easily. Is he in his room?'

Maria walked determinedly down the corridor to the annex as we followed her, telling her to hold it. Maria went out of the back door and stormed into Kazuto's room.

'What's this, without knocking?'

Kazuto was lying on his bed, face up. He had his arms crossed behind his head and only his eyes made any movement towards our party in the doorway.

'We heard you went through our rooms searching for the rifle after we left. What an absolutely self-righteous and horrible thing to do!' Maria's tone was intense. 'I understand that you want to find the rifle, but why didn't you get everyone's permission first? What were you thinking, waiting until we were gone!?'

Kazuto jumped up from the bed.

'Don't get all angry with me. I wasn't really expecting to find the rifle in anybody's room, which would've been an obvious admission of guilt, but we had to search the rooms eventually. Reiko watched me, so there was nothing unfair about it. You just don't like that I skipped some of the paperwork.'

'You've quite a nerve, getting on your high horse.' Maria was appalled. 'You didn't answer my question. I asked why you waited until we'd gone to do it. Didn't you feel bad about that?'

'Not in the least. I am starting to have a little bit of regret now. But I think you're overreacting.'

'Why are you trying to make me feel bad? Here I was thinking you might perhaps offer an apology.'

Maria, drained of energy, let her shoulders sag.

'Okay okay, I'll apologise.'

One "Okay" would've been enough.

'If Alice here is upset too, I apologise. Please forgive me.'

I just mumbled something. Maria had already vented her anger at Kazuto, so I'd already lost my own chance to do so.

'Is it really impossible to fix this?' asked Reiko, indicating the broken wireless transceiver on the desk. Ryūichi and Egami had both come here to try to repair it, but the moment they'd seen the horrible state of the machine, both of them had given up immediately. It was impossible to repair.

'Nothing to be done about it.' Kazuto spat it out, but then smiled maliciously.

'I apologised, so that means we're good. Now please leave me alone.'

'Still in shock? Or are you giving yourself a headache over some deduction or other?'

'I have no ideas at all. I'm expecting something from our Alice here. I'd like to see him expose the truth behind all this, showing off the kinds of deduction you see from great detectives in fiction.'

He grinned. He was making fun of me.

'Let's go.'

Maria poked me with her elbow. She left the annex as swiftly as she'd entered, with Reiko and me in tow.

'Maria, we forgot something important.' I said as I chased her.

'What?'

'We forgot about the wireless transceiver. If it truly was a double suicide last night, who destroyed the machine and for what reason?'

'Ah, you're right.' Maria looked surprised. 'You're absolutely right. The fact it was destroyed blows the double suicide theory away. Oh, what's becoming of my brain? Mr. Egami and you too, how come you didn't notice it either?'

'Yeah, my brain's stopped as well. But perhaps not Mr. Egami's. When you were babbling on about the forced suicide idea up on the hill, Mr. Egami was deep in thought about something, and he didn't hear a single word of our conversation.'

'Babbling? I've had quite enough of you.'

Maria wasn't in a good mood today. Note to self: I need to be nice to girls at a time like this. But playing the nice guy started to feel foolish after a while, and my mouth started to open once again.

Back in the hall we saw the two puzzlers putting their heads together over their game.

5

Maria and I passed the time in the attic admiring the shell collection and solving maze puzzles. That was all we could do. I could never have imagined I'd be looking forward so much to the boat coming to fetch us back.

'Look, it's the sunset,' Maria said. She was leaning on the window sill.

I looked outside. It was the exact moment the huge setting sun was touching the horizon. It was a very rare moment of the day, where you could clearly see the sun moving. It shone brightly as if it was burning up its very last bit of life, and slowly "the day" disappeared. The room itself was bathed in orange in the afterglow and the light drew clear shadows on the walls.

Was the artist also looking at this sunset?

'It's so beautiful, and yet....' Maria muttered as she watched the sun be swallowed up by the sea.

It was the most beautiful and at the same time the most heartrendingly sorrowful sunset I had ever witnessed.

After dinner, Egami and the doctor started working on the puzzle again. Maria and I took a peek, and we saw clear signs of progress. The bewitching snake charmer was already there. I could follow the seductive lines of her waist.

'I love this painting. When I look at it, it feels as if I'm being pulled into the depths of a forest at night.'

I agreed. I couldn't get enough of the painting either. I also liked imagining the melody the snake charmer was sending into the forest with her flute.

'It's really rewarding when you finally have some recognisable parts completed,' said Sonobe, still puffing at his pipe. 'Putting the eyes into this snake charmer in particular was a delight.'

People concentrating on jigsaw puzzles are already a textbook example of people with too much time on their hands, so there can't be anything more foolish than other people who are doing nothing but watching them. That's why Maria and I decided to go upstairs and go back to our own rooms. It wasn't even nine o'clock yet, but Maria disappeared into her room saying 'Good night.' Was she already tired, or was she just not planning to see any more of me that night?

The first thing I did after entering my own room was lock the door. I was still a little bit scared.

I thought about what I'd do next, and I decided to take out the Patricia McGerr I'd placed on the bookshelf near the head of the bed. I was already at the climax of the story, but I still couldn't really get into it. I put the book back and lay down on the bed face up, as Kazuto had done earlier, and let my thoughts wander as I watched the ceiling.

Occasionally, the image of Kango and Sumako Makihara lying on top of each other in a pool of blood flashed through my mind.

What had happened to the rifle? Had it been thrown into the sea?

I got up and went over to the window. The sea had swallowed the sun about two hours earlier, and now it was dark outside, like an open mouth into the void, accompanied by the sound of the waves. But in the night sky, the stars were shining brightly. They flickered as if they were busy with some celebration, singing and calling out to us down here. Whatever they were doing, the world beyond the window didn't belong to us human beings. Our world had been cut off and ended right in front of me.

There was a knock on the door.

'Who is it?' I asked and Maria's voice answered.

'It's me. You've locked your door.'

''Cause I'm scared,' I said as I unlocked it. 'What's the matter? You just said good night. Are you taking that back too?'

'Yep. It's too early to sleep and I start imagining things when I'm alone. It's the same for you, isn't it?' Maria spoke in a soft voice, still standing in the doorway. I came out of the room.

'Let's go out for a walk.'

Maria nodded.

We greeted Egami and the doctor, who were still busy with the puzzle, and left the house. Kazuto was lying absentmindedly in the rattan chair by the side of the window.

A gentle breeze caressed my cheek. We walked side by side for a while in silence, listening only to the sound of our own footsteps.

'Let's go down to the beach.'

If we continued along the path we were on, all we would do was to follow the road and then turn back again, so I agreed with Maria's idea.

We turned around and went to the rear of Panorama Villa. I descended first down the steps, hidden by the lady palms, which led to the beach.

The pounding of the waves came closer, mixed with the melancholy sound of the foam dispersing on the beach.

When we reached the beach, it was so dark I couldn't believe it was the same place where we'd bathed yesterday afternoon. It was like the shore of the river Styx. I walked along by the sea, enjoying the crunching noise of the sand under my feet.

I suddenly realised I couldn't hear Maria behind me, so I turned round. She was crouching far away at the water's edge, scooping water up in both hands. Her russet hair was bathed in moonlight and shone dark scarlet. I walked slowly over, not taking my eyes off her. Water was running through her fingers, and back down to the sea.

'The sea at night is scary,' I said to her, but she remained crouched, gazing into the distance. As if she was looking for the horizon, which had disappeared into the darkness.

'Dying at sea would be scary.' The words that had slipped from her mouth had a heavy feel to them. 'Could Hideto have found his way into heaven, having drowned in such a lonely sea? I hope that people who die at sea in the night can also reach heaven....'

I didn't say anything. Maria was talking to herself. She just wanted me to listen to her talking to herself.

I noticed a small piece of wood near my feet being washed by the sea. It was half buried in the sand and seemed to be fighting to avoid being taken by the waves. I crouched down and picked it up. It had a pentagon shape, like a *shōgi* playing piece, and was about as big as my hand. A rectangle had been hollowed out in the centre.

'That's a Funadama charm.' I was just wondering what it was when Maria looked at it and made the observation.

'Funadama?'

'Yes, Hideto explained it to me. He loved walking around here, checking out the things that wash up on the beach. Funadama is a deity who protects boats and ships. Sailors place this charm in the middle of a ship whenever they go out, praying for safety. You see it's been hollowed out here in the middle? You put objects inside it. Figures of a man and a woman, or a one yen coin, the hair of a woman…. There's more, but I forget. You found something rare, Alice. This is only the second time I've seen one. Hideto said they were probably thrown away from a boat in a scrapyard, but to me they look as though they might've come from some sunken ship and washed up here….'

I dipped the piece of wood in the waves to wash the sand off. I wanted to keep it, I told Maria.

'Chūya wrote a poem which talks about it. Something about picking up a button on a moonlit beach and feeling so sympathetic towards it he can't bring himself to throw it away?'

Maria slowly got up and finally looked into my eyes.

'Alice. Take me out on the boat.'

Her request was rather sudden, but I decided I should just do as she wanted. 'Okay. Let's do that.'

The pier was like a long, narrow stage, sticking out into the sea. We left footprints in the sand as we walked over to it.

The rowing boat had been fastened by a rope. First I had Maria sit in the boat, then I undid the rope and got in myself.

'Here we go.'

I pushed us away from the pier and the boat moved. I picked up the oars and rowed slowly. We went into the raven black sea I had thought so scary.

The moon was above us and the moonlight it threw on the sea swayed in the waves. I looked over the edge of the boat at the water surface and saw sea sparkles floating on the waves like silver sand. I felt as if I didn't mind wherever we went and simply continued rowing the boat without any thought.

Suddenly, a poem came into my mind. It's one of my favourites, but it was almost uncanny how I managed to recite the complete poem.

When the moon shines radiantly in the sky,
Let's go out in this boat.
The waves will lap,
As the wind breezes gently.

Out in the darkness of the bay,
The sound of water dripping from the oars—
Between the pauses of your voice—
Will be a sign of our intimacy.

The "You" in question remained silent.

The moon will listen in at us,
Even descend a bit,
And be right above our heads,
When we kiss.

Maria finally showed a smile. 'Trying to seduce me?' her face said. Both of us knew quite well that was not the case, and I too had to grin.

And you will talk again,
Chatting and pouting.
And I will listen to every single word,
As I row on and on.

This was my answer to Maria. This was also a poem by Chūya Nakahara.

'Alice, that was fantastic. You memorised all of it for a moment like this? I'm impressed. Even I was touched by it. Do it as well as you did just now when you recite it to the girl you love.'

I had rowed us to near the middle of the bay. There I rowed in a big circle around the centre.

'Alice, are you tired? Rest a bit.'

'Don't mind if I do.'

I put the oars down and stopped rowing. We enjoyed the sensation of just floating along the waves.

'Over there. That's where Hideto was found.'

Maria pointed towards a point deep inside the bay. I could see the big, black figure of the Eboshi Rock.

'He washed up on that rocky stretch there. When someone drowns, they first sink down and, after enough gas has gathered in their bodies, they float up again. But it wasn't like that with Hideto. Perhaps it was because he'd drowned near the rocks, but the waves had brought him to the rocky stretch over there. That was a relief. He hadn't become too horrible to look at. He looked just as he always did. He had merely become cold.'

Stop it, I wanted to yell to Maria. It felt as if we were on a boat heading to the island of the dead. Let's stop talking about those who've passed away. If not, I feared the smell of death would rise from the darkness of the night. She'd told me she'd gone out on this boat one night with Hideto. Perhaps she'd asked me to go with her on the same boat, so she could steep herself in those memories. I didn't care what she was using me for. But I couldn't bear those words any more, trying to call back the dead from the dark, faraway sea.

Maria fell silent. And she didn't mention Hideto any more after that.

'Alice, I'll row us back.'

'It's all right, I'll do it.'

'No, baton pass. I'll come over to your seat.'

'I'm not tired. It's okay.'

'But I want to row. Switch places with me.'

She was already half way up. I wanted to click my tongue at her. It was awkward switching places on this small boat.

'Don't get up, it's dangerous. Sit down. Does it really matter who rows us back?'

'No, but I want to.'

'Oh, you're so stubborn. Sit down, I tell you.'

She wouldn't give up, so I had to do it and I, too, tried to stand up.

'Aah!'

I didn't get up properly and fell back on my behind. The boat started to rock. Maria, who was already half standing, cried out as she started to sway as well. The rolling of the boat became heavier. She desperately tried to keep her balance, but those movements only made the rocking worse.

'Oh no!'

She finally couldn't keep it up anymore and with a loud splash, she fell into the sea.

'Maria!'

I wanted to reach out to save her, but the force of Maria toppling over gave the boat the final push it needed, and it finally flipped over. As I was still on it, I was, of course, also thrown into the sea.

'A !' Maria's voice. 'A— !' And water splashing around. 'Alice, you—' Maria's head went up and down in the water.

'Alice. You. Okay?'

What do you mean, 'Alice, you okay?' Worrying about other people while you yourself are still drifting in the sea is just ridiculous! That thought flashed through my mind as I looked at Maria. I myself had swum right away back to the capsized boat and was holding on to it.

I reached out my right hand to help her and she headed towards me, spewing water as she moved. She reached the side, grabbed the boat, took a deep breath and shook her head, surprised at what had just happened.

'Oops. I toppled the boat.'

'That's why I told you not to try and stand up,' I said, but I realised that reproaching her again at this stage was rather pointless, so I swallowed the rest of my comments. 'Let's try flipping the boat back over.'

'I guess we can, but what about the oars?'

'They drifted away, but they shouldn't be far. Look around.'

We turned the boat over and we swam the breaststroke around it, but while I did find one oar, I couldn't find the other. It couldn't have floated away all that far, but I didn't see it. I threw the oar we did find into the boat.

'This is bad. We've lost the other oar.'

'It isn't on this side either,' said the watery voice of my partner on the other side of the boat. I swam to her side, and we floated there for a while like a couple of jellyfish.

'What a pair we are,' said Maria in a high-pitched voice. The fall into the water appeared to have woken her up. 'We just rendered the only aquatic means of transport on this island completely useless.'

'Let's give up and swim back to shore. We can't find that oar in this darkness.'

'I hope we find it tomorrow,' Maria said with a worried expression, as if she was an elementary school student who hadn't understood her homework.

'We'll probably find it in the morning. Let's return here tomorrow. We're both exhausted, so let's go back to the house.'

'What clumsy fools we are.'

Don't use the plural form all the time. This was eighty percent your fault.

With pain in our hearts we abandoned the floating boat and swam back to Low Tide Cape. So, oddly, the adventure ended with us swimming in the sea at night, precisely as we had talked about that afternoon.

'Alice.'

'Yeah?'

'Let's.' 'Go.' 'Faster.' 'Like normal.' Each word leaving Maria's mouth was accompanied by some water.

'We're going "Like normal."'

I told you already. I'm a slow swimmer. Maria didn't reply.

The sound of the water lapping round my ears, and the splash each of my strokes made, gave me a lonely feeling.

'Not.' 'Scared?'

'Of what?'

'Something.' 'Might pull.' 'Your legs.' 'Down.'

That's not what I wanted to hear at such a moment. It's certainly nothing to be proud of, but I am very easily scared. I hope she wasn't about to tell me she could hear Hideto's voice rising from the depths of the sea. The cape was still far away.

'Alice.'

Now what?

'I lost.' 'A shoe.' 'One.'

Don't ask me about your lost shoe. I'm not the prince from Cinderella.

'I hope.' 'I'll find it.' 'Tomorrow.'

That was the last thing she said.

When we came to the area where it was only about one metre deep, we were able to stand up and wade to the beach. It was exactly like an illustration of the monsters arriving in Innsmouth in a story by Lovecraft. I turned to look at Maria to see how she was doing, but she was feeling embarrassed because her tank top was sticking to her body.

'Don't worry, it doesn't show through.'

'Alice, you walk ahead.'

I walked in front, just as I was told. I heard Maria's footsteps following me. The water in my shoes made a sopping noise.

'Maybe I should make use of this precious experience and write an occult mystery story for this autumn's club magazine,' I said, still facing forward.

Maria asked: 'The title?'

'Obvious. *It Swims By Night*.'

'That's stupid.'

We slowly climbed the stone steps and finally reached the back of Panorama Villa.

'What's the time?'

'Don't know.' I didn't have my watch with me. 'Probably not even eleven yet.'

'Let's go to sleep. We've had so much exercise, I'll sleep like a log.'

That was true. She probably wouldn't feel like thinking about what had just happened. Like two drowned rats, we looked at each other and burst out laughing.

'What would the others think if they could see us like this?'

'I beg you, tell them the truth. If you tell them I made a move on you on the boat and it flipped over, nobody will ever believe my story.'

Like students late for the dorm curfew, we sneaked silently through the back entrance. We'd decided to take turns in the shower and went stealthily upstairs to get a change of clothes. I was thinking about what to tell Egami if he was in the room, but when I reached it, he wasn't there. Was he still keeping the doctor company? Anyway, I grabbed a quick change of clothes. I went out in the hallway again, to find that Maria had also sneaked out silently and was just closing her door. Making as little noise as possible, we went downstairs and I let Maria go in the bathroom first. Both of us would feel uncomfortable if I remained there in front of the door, so I went outside. I passed the time strolling around with my clothes in one hand and thinking about what I was doing now, for heaven's sake.

'Sorry to keep you waiting.'

Maria came out looking refreshed, wearing a T-shirt and a pair of short pants. She looked charming with her hair just washed. I bumped her fist for the baton pass and took my turn in the shower.

When I'd changed into my clothes and got out, I saw the back entrance door was still open. Maria had been doing the same as I, loafing around as she waited for me.

'Haven't you gone up to your room yet?'

'That seemed a bit heartless.'

I was not displeased by that. We went outside and stood for a while in the soft breeze from the sea. If we'd stayed there at the back entrance talking, we'd probably be a pain in the eyes and ears of Kazuto in the annex, so we moved to the terrace. Two bicycles were standing next to the French windows. One more bicycle was standing alone near to the front entrance.

'We've been together the whole day today,' Maria said, as she leaned back on the saddle of one of the two bicycles. I wondered why she was sitting on the saddle and not on the terrace but I, too, sat down on the other saddle and said: 'Yeah.' We had been with Egami until the afternoon, and after dinner we had been alone in our rooms for half an hour, but it felt as if the two of us had spent the whole day in each other's company. The guys who were in love with Maria would probably cry if they heard about that.

'The wind's so refreshing,' said Maria, squinting her eyes. It was a very pleasant midsummer's night, as if all the rain and wind of last night had been nothing more than a dream. I felt like talking with somebody all night long. Unless Maria herself said she'd go back to her room, I'd never suggest leaving here.

'You know Akikawa from our language class?' I blurted out suddenly.

'Yes. Why?'

'I heard he likes you.'

She was at a loss of words for a second, but then merely said:'Oh,' as if she'd been told some rumour about people she had nothing to do with. I thought that her reaction was a bit strange, but I also thought I myself was strange, suddenly raising the topic here.

'Why tell me now? Has our messenger of love suddenly remembered a task he was asked to do?'

I didn't know what to answer. I only told her he hadn't asked me to say anything to her, and there it stopped.

'Let's talk about something else.'

'You're odd.'

We chatted on silently, the breeze lapping round us. It felt as though we'd been there for ages. I finally got why she'd sat down on the bicycle saddle. On a night like this, we didn't need to raise our voices, but we could simply whisper to the person right next to us.

I asked her what time it was, and she answered a quarter past twelve. In the end, it was I who drew the curtain and said it was about time we went upstairs.

Maria had lost one shoe and I'd picked up a charm for ships. And the night was over too soon.

6

The fourth day.

When Maria laid out breakfast and my eyes met hers, I had to blush. Thinking back to the previous night, it was as if I hadn't been myself. Maria looked down as she placed the plate with a fried egg and a cup of coffee in front of me, but even when our eyes met for a second, she looked as cool as ever.

'The boat's coming the day after tomorrow, is that right?' asked Toshiyuki Inukai, as he neatly smeared raspberry jam on his toast. From his way of asking, I couldn't make up my mind whether he was glad it was so soon or upset it was still so far away. To be honest, I'd already had enough of waiting all this time. There was also another problem I couldn't mention at the breakfast table. How long would the remains of Kango and Sumako Makihara last upstairs in this heat…?

Junji Makihara appeared to have recovered some of his appetite, but was still eating merely because his body needed it. Dipping pieces of bread in your coffee and eating them is not considered a very elegant way of having breakfast in our country, but I was sure it wasn't customary for him to do so either. His face looked pale and he was obviously disheartened.

Ryūichi Arima said he'd drunk too much before sleep yesterday as well, as he poured himself a second glass of cold tomato juice. He hadn't drunk with anyone, but had just entertained himself in his room until late.

'You can't be like this two days in a row. You mustn't be depressed from the morning on. We need eager faces here at the breakfast table.'

It was Sonobe who reproached Ryūichi. He was putting a special blend in his briar pipe. It was a straightforward way of talking, as expected of old friends. Sonobe himself looked absolutely fine.

Next to him, Toshiyuki was wolfing down his toast. His wife Satomi was using a knife and fork to eat her fried egg neatly. The two of them said nothing and concentrated on their meal. Toshiyuki spoke only once, to say 'Great jam,' to which his wife answered: 'Yes.'

Kazuto had finished his breakfast quickly and, as usual, was waving around the cigarette he held between his fingers. Perhaps he was thinking about something, because he was awfully quiet and simply sat staring at one corner of the room. His lips moved slightly. He was saying something to himself, but he made almost no noise.

After serving breakfast, Reiko and Maria sat down at the breakfast table as well and the two of them chatted about practical but random topics like hair care or how to select shoes. They really looked like close sisters. I heard Maria mention my name once, but I couldn't hear how I starred in her talk.

'Where were you late last night?' Egami asked me as I was observing everyone else. When I'd returned last night at quarter past twelve, he had, of course already gone to bed. But I guess I must have woken him up, because he'd said 'Late, eh?' to me. I'd answered with a vague 'Yeah' and crawled into my own bed. He'd fallen asleep again almost immediately, and that was all we'd said last night.

'Yes, actually—'

I was about to tell him about our adventure with the overturned boat, when Maria stopped me from across the table.

'We'll have to tell everyone anyway, so I'll do it. It's probably better that way.'

She proceeded to tell everyone about our misadventure. All of them reacted with voices of concern about us, and luckily nobody made a big deal about the boat that was still adrift. I made a serious promise to go out with Maria that morning to look for the oar and bring the boat back, but several of them laughed, saying I didn't need to get all formal about it. Oh well, I guess it was something to laugh at.

I looked up when Egami tapped lightly on the table. I wondered whether he was going to make fun of me too, but he merely said he'd help look as well.

'It's just what would happen with you, isn't it, Maria?' said Reiko from the other side of the table. 'I'll help look for the oar, too.'

Satomi whispered something in her husband's ear, and Toshiyuki also offered to help. No good. That wouldn't help at all actually. Luckily, Egami came to the rescue.

'I don't think it'll be necessary to go out to sea with a large search crew. It's my juniors' fault, so I'll take care of it. If we still don't succeed, I might ask for your help later, though.'

Aren't you acting a bit too cool, I thought, but with that the discussion ended. I was relieved. Now all we had to do was find the oar. I turned to Egami.

He had one word for us: 'Dummies.'

After breakfast, everybody moved to the hall for lack of any other place to be. As the others watched television, the three of us went upstairs. We looked over the bay from the hallway windows and saw the boat floating in the waves. It had drifted slightly towards High Tide Cape, but I'd been afraid it might have drifted completely out of the bay. I felt relieved to see it was still there.

We changed into our swimwear, went out through the back and went down the stone steps to the beach. After the murders, I would never have imagined I'd change into my swimwear again.

'Shall we swim out to the boat and use that as our base? We can split up there,' said Egami, turning his neck as a warming up exercise.

'I think that would be too tiring,' said Maria, who already looked exhausted. 'Can't we go somewhere high, like the observation platform, and look for the oar from there?'

'Impossible,' I said. 'Do your best and swim for all you're worth.'

The three of us got in the water and swam to the drifting boat. It felt nice having the sea all to ourselves this morning. Maria called me a slowpoke again, so I did my best to keep up with them.

When we reached the boat, we grabbed on to it, decided who would look in which direction and split up. I say "look", but at that moment I became rather pessimistic about it, as it was quite possible that we'd never see the oar unless, by pure chance, one of us passed close to it. We probably searched for an hour, at times returning to the boat to rest. Just when I started to feel I'd had enough, I heard Egami yell from faraway: 'Got it! Got it!' I returned to the boat, and saw him doing the sidestroke with the oar under his arm. Maria was coming from the other direction.

'Sorry for leaving you swimming all night.' Maria bowed her head and spoke to the boat and the oars. The boat was now restored to its true form, so it was only natural to want to get on it and row back. However, being so small, it couldn't hold three passengers.

'I'll swim back, so the two of you can go back first,' I proposed and the two discussed that.

'But we're almost at High Tide Cape now. Ah, that's it! How about borrowing Mr. Hirakawa's bicycle to go back? You must be tired from all that swimming as well.'

'Oh, that's a good idea.'

I was indeed a bit tired, so I wanted to get on shore.

'But if I do that, I'd need to go back again to return his bike.'

'You can return it after lunch. Then I'll go pick you up with the boat.'

Ah, now I understood. If we followed this plan, nobody would need to swim. Suddenly, Egami burst into laughter.

'What's the matter, Egami?' Maria was perplexed by him laughing out loud right next to her.

He had trouble keeping his laughter under control as he said: 'What kind of idea is that? Why would Alice need to go back and forth on a bike between Happy Fish Villa and Panorama Villa?'

Oh. There was no reason for doing so.

'If Alice is tired, he can go up High Tide Cape and rest a bit with Mr. Hirakawa. Maria and I will first go back to Low Tide Cape with the boat and one of us can just go pick him up again.'

That's it! It was that simple. I was so glad I didn't have to go up to Mr. Hirakawa to explain everything and ask him if I could borrow his bicycle. That's why I'm bad at puzzles.

'Egami,' Maria looked up at him, 'do you think I'm stupid?'

'Not at all. Ah, were your feelings hurt because I was laughing? You're wrong.' Egami flashed a smile again. 'It wasn't that. I wasn't laughing at the silly talk you were having. I was listening to you when I suddenly had to laugh at myself for ever thinking you were smart.'

'That's not flattering either, you know.' Maria clicked her tongue.

It was less than a hundred metres to High Tide Cape. I was thirsty, and I looked up at Happy Fish Villa, pondering whether I should ask for a drink.

'I wonder if he'd think it impolite if we go up to him dressed like this?' Maria asked. 'But we'll be back to pick Alice up with the boat again, so we might as well go and ask if he needs anything. And I'm thirsty now.'

'Sounds fine,' I said. 'You could also have him paint you in a swimsuit or nude.'

'There you go again with the unfunny jokes. It'd just make his creative urge disappear.'

Don't be so sour. Also because I can't tell the difference between her pretending to be sour, and her really being sour.

For some reason we decided that Hirakawa probably wouldn't mind if we visited him dressed in our swimwear, so all three of us came in to land at High Tide Cape. Egami took the oars, while I swam next to the boat.

The pier of High Tide Cape was right next to the stone steps. Egami jumped off the boat and tied it to the post. I climbed on to the pier as well and together we went up the steps.

We went round to the front and Maria knocked on the door, calling out to the artist. After three calls, there was still no answer, and Maria cocked her head.

'Could he be out?'

Mr. Hirakawa's red bicycle was still standing by the side of the house. Maybe he had gone out to do some sketching close by.

'But where could he have gone?' muttered Maria to herself as she grabbed the door knob. Ever since the murders two nights ago, we had all started to lock our doors but, unlike us, the artist had not locked his. The knob made a click and the door opened.

'Mr. Hirakawa, are you there?' Maria asked as she stepped carefully inside. She had opened the door to the main and only room in the whole house, but she was still standing partly in the doorway as she called out.

'Visitors. Mr. Hi—!'

From the back of Maria's throat came a stifled cry. Egami and I looked over her shoulder into the room and we, too, cried out.

Hirakawa was seated in a chair in front of the glass-topped table, his forehead resting on the glass. From that unnatural position, I understood immediately that something was wrong. When I looked more closely I saw that, hidden by his head, a red spot had spread across his chest. The incident two nights ago was still fresh in my mind, so it didn't take me even a second to recognise it as blood.

'Mr. Egami....'

Maria looked up at Egami next to her.

The club president carefully pushed her to the side, and walked over to Hirakawa. He picked up Hirakawa's hanging left arm, checked for a pulse and turned back to us. By a shake of his head he told us it was too late for the artist. A little cry escaped from Maria's lips. I was at a loss for words at this unexpected appearance of Death.

'He's bleeding from the chest. Appears to have been shot like Mr. Makihara and Sumako.'

It was the work of the same person. I felt that instinctively. The thought that this had now become a serial murder case was terrifying, but it was probably still better than assuming two people had planned murders completely separately from each other on this small island.

Yesterday the artist had shown us his painting of Sumako, with his back turned towards us. Was that the last time anyone had seen him alive? When was he shot? He'd died at the same spot where we'd said goodbye to him the day before, so there was no way of telling whether the crime had happened right after we'd left, or long after that. It'd be best if Doctor Sonobe could examine the body as quickly as possible.

'I'll go get the doc.'

'Yes, do that, Alice,' said Egami in a low voice, his eyes still fixed on the body. Then I remembered it wasn't as easy as calling the doctor from the room next door.

'Mr. Egami, are you going to stay here?'

'Yes. You and Maria go back and tell the others. And then you come back in the boat with the doctor. And bring a change of clothes for me too.'

'Okay,' I replied. To Maria: 'Let's go.'

'Mr. Egami....'

Without moving from her spot, she pointed her trembling fingers to the floor near the table.

'Wh—what's that? Scattered all over the floor there.'

I too looked at the floor to see what she was pointing at. There was nothing strange on the floor. In fact, it was only natural they were there. Pieces of the jigsaw puzzle. Lots of pieces.

'Mr. Hirakawa was probably attacked while he was facing the table, playing with the puzzle. When he was shot, he fell forward over the table, and the puzzle pieces he hadn't finished yet fell on the floor,' I said.

'No, the pieces are scattered too widely for that,' replied Egami as he studied the table with a puzzled look. 'I'm sure he'd finished about half of it, but even those pieces didn't remain on the table.'

What did that mean? Had both the finished and unfinished pieces fallen off the table and scattered on the floor when Hirakawa hit the table?

'But don't you think that's odd too? Even if everything on the table had fallen off, would all the pieces really scatter around like this? It's almost as if someone scattered them on purpose....'

'Maria, now's not the time for this. I agree it's odd, but we can talk about it later.'

I urged Maria to come with me. She nodded and we went outside.

'I'll hurry back with the doc.'

Egami simply answered: 'I'll be waiting.'

A single step away from the murder scene, and we were in a landscape brimming with life. How cruel, I thought. The sky was absurdly clear, and the sun was radiant.

The artist had suddenly passed away. Someone had smashed his wonderful life to pieces....

7

I rowed as hard as I could and it took me about fifteen minutes to get us back to Low Tide Cape. By the time we'd hurried up the stone steps and gone through the back entrance, I was completely out of breath. I told Maria to get dressed first, and then rushed into the hall.

'What's the matter? You look as though you've seen a ghost.'

Toshiyuki, who had been watching television, looked up at me. Junji, who was also there, gave me a puzzled look as well, as I was still dressed in my swimsuit. Sonobe was busy with his puzzle, but his reaction was quick and he stood up immediately.

'Did somebody drown?'

'No, not that. Nothing like that. Doctor, you need to come to Happy Fish Villa at once. Mr. Hirakawa is dead. Probably murder.'

'What!?'

The doctor was shocked by the news, but I insisted he needed to come immediately. He understood and nodded.

'What do you mean?' Junji glared at me 'I've no idea what you're talking about. I'll go too, though.'

'Me too.' Toshiyuki stood up. 'Oh, and the boat? Did you find the oar?'

'Yes. I'll take the doctor in the boat. So, Mr. Makihara, Mr. Inukai, I'm sorry, but could you go by bicycle?'

'Okay, we'll do that.'

At that moment, Maria came downstairs. Satomi too. She had apparently been told about what had happened by Maria, because she looked pale. She asked her husband if he'd heard the news.

'Just now. We're going there now on the bikes.'

'We need to tell my uncle too,' said Maria. 'Where could he be? In his room in the back? And where are Reiko and Kazuto?'

'Arima is out,' replied Sonobe. 'He said he'd been in the house all day yesterday, so he needed to get some exercise. As for Reiko and Kazuto....'

While they were talking I went upstairs and got dressed. I was almost out of the room again when I turned back to get Egami his change of clothes. I went downstairs and saw that Reiko and Kazuto had also joined the crowd in the hall. Both of them had been called out of their rooms.

'Okay, the doctor and Alice will go on ahead to Happy Fish Villa,' said Toshiyuki when he saw me coming. 'Mr. Makihara, Kazuto and I will follow by bicycle. Satomi, you stay here with Reiko and Maria and look for my brother. Perhaps he's down at the rocky stretch in the back of the house where Kango and the doctor were fishing previously.'

Everyone quickly started doing as Toshiyuki suggested. I was so anxious to leave I almost tore the doctor's arm off, but he suddenly remembered he had to get his medicine bag and went upstairs, which only annoyed me more.

All in all, leaving Egami at Happy Fish Villa, getting hold of the doctor and returning to the crime scene had taken me almost fifty minutes. It seemed as though Egami must have been looking at the sea all that time and, when we arrived at the pier, he was standing at the top of the stone steps.

'I brought the doctor. And your change of clothes.'

Egami gave me a nod of thanks as he took the clothes and led the doctor into the house.

'This is horrible. It's the same as Kango and Sumako.'

The instant the doctor saw the body of the artist, he put his hand to his forehead and cried out. But then, as you'd expect from an experienced doctor, he immediately got hold of himself and raised the upper body of the artist, resting it against the back of the chair so he could start his examination. Just as before, he muttered out loud about everything he noticed as he went about his duties.

'The gunshot in the chest is the only wound. Slightly right of the *solar plexus*. Just as last time, it was not a fatal shot. Don't think the murderer is a good shot. Estimated time of death is in small hours of the night. Somewhere between midnight and two o'clock. No, better allow for an extra hour on both sides. Between eleven and three should cover it. He probably remained alive for a while after being shot, but sadly there was no way he could've got help in this lonely house. Anyway, it's a wound very similar to what we saw two nights ago. I can't say for sure until we get the bullet out and have it examined, but it's very likely it's the same weapon.'

'From what distance was the shot fired?' asked Egami, his change of clothes still in his hands. Sonobe answered that he could only be certain it was more than thirty centimetres. 'My feeling is it was fired from more than a metre away.'

'And there were no other wounds on the body besides the one made by the rifle? No signs of resistance?'

'A rough examination shows nothing. He was sitting at this table when he was shot from the other side. The bullet hit him diagonally, from high to low, so the murderer was standing.'

'Shot from across the table…so he was shot right here?'

'There's no doubt about that. After he was shot, he wouldn't have been able to get up.'

'Anything else you noticed, Doctor?'

'Nothing. This is about all I managed to find.'

'I see.'

While Egami was getting dressed, Sonobe and I sat down and remained silent for a while. The atmosphere was oppressive.

'So there were no signs of a fight?' I asked, and the doctor simply repeated: 'No.'

'Doctor, do you see all the jigsaw puzzle pieces scattered over the floor? The puzzle had been on the table. When we saw it yesterday, it was half finished. So when I saw the pieces scattered like this, I thought that perhaps Mr. Hirakawa and the murderer had had a scuffle and turned the table over.'

The doctor frowned as he looked at the puzzle pieces all over the floor.

'There wasn't a fight, you say?'

'There was definitely no struggle. There are no scratches or bruises on either the victim's face or wrists. And his clothes were all still neat as well. Just think, a simple town doctor having to do the job of a medical examiner....'

As the doctor had said, the hemp shirt of the victim wasn't wrinkled in any way. And if there really had been a big struggle, during which the table had been flipped over, then it would be natural to assume that at least some of the pieces on the floor would have been stepped on during the fight. Yet I didn't see a single piece which was dirty or damaged. I couldn't help but be bothered by this mystery. Whenever I came across a riddle to which I couldn't find the perfect answer, I'd keep thinking all about it until my hair hurt.

'Oh!' Something else came to mind. 'Perhaps it was the murderer who broke the puzzle and scattered it into pieces? Doctor, you said Mr. Hirakawa had not been hit in a vital spot and so he didn't die right away. So he could've had enough time to leave a dying message.'

'A dying message? Oh, you mean he could've written the name of the murderer before he died? Well, it's certainly possible. But what does that have to do with the puzzle?'

'Mr. Hirakawa mustered his last remaining strength and wrote the name of the murderer on the puzzle with his own blood. There are no writing utensils on this table, so that was the only way he could've written down something.'

'And then?'

'He left a dying message on the puzzle indicating the murderer. But he wrote it down before the murderer had left the room, so unfortunately they noticed and threw the puzzle off the table to break it into pieces. Let's reconstruct the puzzle. The murderer's name might be written on it.'

Sonobe thought about that for a moment. Then Egami, who was dressed by then, joined in the conversation.

'Doesn't sound really convincing. If the murderer had noticed Mr. Hirakawa's dying message, would they really have felt it was enough just to break up the puzzle? If someone reconstructed it, the name would still be there, after all. If it were me, I'd cover those blood letters up with more blood, or take the puzzle with me to throw away into the sea.'

'That sounds reasonable, but the murderer might have been too agitated and not been able to think clearly.'

'I wonder. I think they would want to destroy the message no matter what, if it indicated their name. But, oh well, we might as well try picking up the pieces off the floor and checking them quickly. Pick up the pieces with blood on them and try putting them together. There's no need to reconstruct the whole puzzle from scratch.'

'Okay, let's do that.'

We crouched down and started to collect the pieces, when we heard bicycles stopping in the front of the house. Toshiyuki and the others had arrived.

They gasped when they entered the house and saw the body sitting in the chair, but they also looked in surprise at the sight of us crouching on the floor.

Egami briefly explained the situation to the newly arrived Toshiyuki, Junji and Kazuto, and the three listened to him in astonishment.

'So in the small hours of last night? I wonder if we could've heard the shot?' Kazuto growled. But considering the distance between here and Panorama Villa, even if the noise had carried over there, it would have been very faint.

'The rifle again? So it was the same person?' Toshiyuki posed the question to nobody in particular. A worried frown appeared on his face and he shook his head.

'But what are you doing crawling on the floor? Looking for evidence?'

I was about to answer Junji's question, when Sonobe cried out in surprise.

'Young Alice, I'm afraid your theory won't hold.'

'Why?'

'Look at this.'

The doctor showed me one puzzle piece with blood on it.

'These pieces have a vinyl coating. There's blood on this piece, but see, the blood is repelled by the vinyl. You can't write anything on these pieces unless you have a permanent marker.'

'What about the back?'

'The same as the front. So Mr. Hirakawa didn't leave a dying message on the puzzle. He couldn't have.'

What were the implications of that for the case? I started to reflect again, but it was the doctor this time who proposed a theory.

'Perhaps your theory was half correct. What if it happened like this: Mr. Hirakawa wanted to convey the name of the murderer to us in some way before he died, so he tried to write the name with his own blood on the finished part of the puzzle. He hadn't noticed that he couldn't write on it, because the pieces were coated in vinyl, but desperate to leave the murderer's name, he smeared his finger in his own blood and tried to write the name down. But they hadn't left the room yet. They noticed what Mr. Hirakawa was trying to do, took the puzzle away from him and threw it down on the floor, scattering the pieces all over the floor. How about that?'

That sounded like very plausible reasoning. It was natural to assume the victim wanted to write down the name of the murderer before he died and, as he wasn't able to get out of the chair, the jigsaw puzzle in front of him would've been the first thing to have come to mind to write on. He couldn't reach the walls and he couldn't write on the Persian carpet on the floor. The table was made of glass plate and metal legs, so it was only logical he'd reach out to the cardboard jigsaw puzzle, even if he'd known the puzzle pieces had a vinyl coating. And even if the victim's efforts had been in vain, the murderer must have been surprised when he saw him move and would certainly have reacted by throwing the puzzle on the floor. I had one question, however.

'Having broken up the puzzle, why didn't the murderer—to use a gruesome term—finish Mr. Hirakawa off? Was he simply content that there was nothing in the vicinity any more to write on, with the puzzle scattered on the floor?' I asked.

'Probably.'

Perhaps it did happen like that. The victim probably died right after the puzzle had been swept off the table. Then there would be no need for the murderer to finish him off.

'Doctor,' said Egami carefully as he raised the victim's right hand, 'I'm sorry to keep spoiling your theories, but I think that one is wrong as well. There's no sign of any blood on Mr. Hirakawa's right index finger.'

'What? That's odd. I'm sure he's right-handed.'

'I also checked, just to be sure, but there's nothing on his left index finger either. Nothing on any of his fingers, in fact.'

'So you mean Mr. Hirakawa didn't try to write anything down in blood?'

'Precisely.'

How frustrating. It was a very small problem, but we couldn't find a convincing answer to it. All was very irritating, like when a piece of thread gets stuck between your teeth.

'Let's think about it later. What's important now is to find out what happened to the murder weapon. I find it worrisome that it wasn't left at the crime scene, once again.'

'Mr. Egami is absolutely right,' Toshiyuki emphasised. 'Who cares about some broken puzzle? It probably just fell from the table due to some shock.'

We were already of the opinion that that wasn't the case, but Toshiyuki continued:

'Anyway, it's the rifle we need to worry about. If the murderer is still in possession of it, I'm afraid there's a good possibility they'll strike again. We need to stop them somehow. Shouldn't we think about that, rather than about some triviality?'

'I agree with Mr. Inukai,' added Kazuto. 'At this rate, more of us will be killed. The murderer shot three people with one shot each. There should still be one or two cartridges left.'

'How many have gone?'

Kazuto muttered something vague in answer to Egami's question. He apparently didn't remember in detail.

'…One or two. Perhaps three, but definitely not more than that.'

'That's awfully vague,' Junji said angrily as he glared at Kazuto. 'It's because of that dangerous toy of yours this has happened. That thing should have been kept in a safe place, and not tossed away carelessly somewhere. You hadn't even noticed the rifle was gone until we discovered Sumako and her dad had been murdered, and now you say you can't even remember how many cartridges you're missing? When are you going to take responsibility for this?'

'The—there…' Kazuto seemed to become visibly smaller. 'There's no reason to blame me like that! I wasn't the only person responsible for it, you know. With only upstanding adults who all knew each other in the house, who'd think of keeping that thing in a safe? I know a rifle is a dangerous weapon, but all of us allowed it to be kept like that, so don't talk as though I'm the only person in the wrong here, just because all of this happened and I was the one who happened to bring the rifle here. Remember that when you arrived at the island, you also said it looked like fun and wanted to try it out and do some target practice yourself? You can't have fun then and blame me for everything now. If the murder weapon had been a kitchen knife, would you've blamed Reiko as the one responsible?'

'Are you saying a rifle and a knife are the same?' Junji repeated Kazuto's words with emphasis. 'What country are you from, where they have rifles hanging in the kitchen!?'

Kazuto was upset, but still managed to put up a defence.

'I'm not the only one at fault here. Everyone knew it was kept like that and everyone allowed it to be so. All of us, including you, are to blame.'

'What? What? We allowed it, so we're all responsible? Are you going to blame the National Public Safety Commission if you run over someone with a car?'

'Calm down, you two.' Sonobe stepped in. 'You can blame each other all you want later. Nothing good will come from a fight now.'

Junji didn't look satisfied, but he kept silent and Kazuto looked relieved. I guess that Egami and I, who'd also done some practice shots, were also partially responsible, but even so, it was rather troublesome we didn't even know how many cartridges were missing.

'Finding out who the murderer is, is of the highest priority,' said Toshiyuki and nodded gravely at his own words. His calmness was very reassuring in a situation like this. Perhaps he acted so rationally because it was not only him, but also his wife who was in danger.

'Anyway, now is not the time to let the blood flow to your head.' The doctor asked for a cigarette and Kazuto offered him one and lit it. 'There are only a few people on this island and the murderer must be one of them. If we use our intelligence, we should be able to find out who it is. Right, Mr. Egami?'

The club president mumbled something positive-sounding.

'Let's search for anything the murderer might've left behind,' suggested Toshiyuki. 'Preserving the crime scene until the police come won't do us any good if we're all murdered in the meantime. We need to find material evidence ourselves and confine the murderer as soon as possible.'

'You're right.' Kazuto appeared to have recovered some of his calm. 'We'll be lucky if they left any footprints around the house. Maybe it's impossible to expect to find them now, with the arrival of Mr. Egami and the others before, and now us. But how did the murderer get here anyway? He couldn't have possibly walked here, could he? Did he arrive by bicycle from the front, or by boat at the back?'

'The boat's out of the question.' I stopped him. 'Maria and I were out rowing it before ten o'clock last night. We turned it over at half past ten. The murder happened after eleven, so nobody could've used the boat for the murder.'

'Ah, that's true,' acknowledged Kazuto. 'So the murderer must have come by bicycle. We can just investigate the road up front. If we find tyre tracks and footprints other than those we made just now, then they're those of the murderer.'

'I don't think there'll be such clear prints out there. There was no rain last night,' said Toshiyuki.

'Let's check, just to be sure,' said the doctor as he threw his cigarette out of the window with some regret. 'We're starting from scratch anyway. We can only bet on whatever comes to mind.'

We six men swiftly started to do the work of police detectives.

8

We drew a blank. The murderer had fled from the crime scene without leaving any footprints, not even the smallest trace. Eventually, we agreed that it'd be better to preserve the crime scene for when the police did come, rather than disturb it even more, so we decided to go back to Panorama Villa for the time being. We couldn't bear leaving the artist's remains where they were, so just as with the Makiharas, we put him on his bed.

It was then that I noticed that you had a very good view of the portrait of Sumako from the bed. When Junji followed my eyes and noticed that fact too, he looked shocked. Was the angle just a coincidence? Or did the artist like the painting so much he'd hung it there on purpose? And there was one more thing I noticed. As Junji was looking at Sumako's portrait, I could sense from his eyes, not sadness from seeing a portrait of his late wife, but something closer to malevolent hatred. I became confused. Had this man really been in love with Sumako? I stood still, captured by the strong feeling of hatred I felt in the air.

We left Happy Fish Villa.

Several of us put our hands to our eyes because of the blinding sun.

'Well then, how shall we get back?' asked Toshiyuki, looking at everybody in turn. 'The others back home are probably very curious to know what happened here. Shall we have Mr. Egami and the doctor return by boat first? They can probably explain the situation better than anyone. We'll go back by bicycle. Alice, you don't mind going back on Mr. Hirakawa's bicycle, do you?'

Nobody had any objections. Egami and Sonobe went to the stone steps at the back of the house, while the remaining four of us climbed onto the bicycles. I had a strange sensation as I pedalled on the red one. As Maria had suggested earlier, I was now going back riding Hirakawa's bicycle. But it wouldn't be necessary any more to go back to Happy Fish Villa to return the bicycle to its owner.

We four men said nothing and simply pedalled on. We didn't enjoy talking to each other all that much anyway, and there was a very real possibility one of us was the murderer. It was obvious that any talk would turn into a probing of someone or other.

'Even so....' It was Kazuto who broke the silence. 'I wonder why Mr. Hirakawa was murdered. Of course, it's true for Uncle Kango and Sumako as well: you need a motive for murder. But I can't think of one. That's what makes this so terrifying.'

'A motive, eh?' replied Toshiyuki, who was riding in front next to Kazuto. 'I wonder what it could be. What happened two nights ago still feels like something that could've happened by accident because we all drank too much. An accident conjured up by the storm. But this murder's completely different. The killer has to be one of the people at Panorama Villa so, despite all the risks, they made a round trip to Happy Fish Villa. It takes at least thirty minutes each way so, if we include the time to commit the murder as well, all of it would've taken at least an hour and ten minutes. If it was me, I'd be afraid that somebody would notice I'd been gone for so long. But, despite that, the murderer did it anyway. So it must have been a premeditated attack. This was no crime without a motive.'

'Hmm, I think you're right.' Kazuto nodded. 'The murderer ran a big risk during the night. But I don't think there would be that much danger of somebody noticing your absence if you left Panorama Villa for an hour or so. None of us had slept very well the night before, so many of us had gone to bed early and were sound asleep last night.'

'Maybe, but there were also people like you-know-who who went out at sea in a boat at night and turned it over, so there was still quite some risk involved.'

I felt embarrassed. As if only the two of us had had any fun last night.

'But perhaps,' said Toshiyuki, 'there might there be some special connection between the Makiharas and Mr. Hirakawa? Some fact that connects this series of murders? I don't understand the motives for the individual murders either, but I think we should be looking for something that could connect the two cases.'

'Mr. Hirakawa and Sumako were—' Kazuto started, but then shut up. Perhaps he'd started to say that, three years ago, they'd been lovers. As for why he suddenly stopped, that was of course because he remembered that Sumako's husband Junji was riding behind him.

'Mr. Hirakawa had Sumako model for a painting of his. But that happened three years ago, and I don't imagine it has anything to do with the murders.'

It was a pathetic attempt at correcting himself. But Toshiyuki didn't seem to notice, and said: 'Oh, yeah, there was a painting of Sumako hanging from the wall there. Beautiful painting.'

I stole a glance at Junji, who was next to me, but his face was expressionless. What did those bitter eyes aimed at Sumako's portrait earlier on mean? Perhaps he'd known about the past liaison between his wife and the artist and he was hurt by it? To me, that seemed like the only possible interpretation of those furious emotions which lurked behind his eyes. I could also understand why he'd attacked Kazuto about the rifle. He probably felt even more on edge because he had no one standing by his side anymore. It was a painful sight.

Oh, perhaps that was it?

On the night of the storm, when father and daughter Makihara were murdered, a drunken Kazuto had told us about the past between Sumako and Hirakawa. After he'd finished, Junji, who'd gone up to his room, had suddenly appeared in the hall. He might've heard it all.

Kazuto started to speak again. 'So the murderer pedalled a bicycle in the middle of the night, just as we're doing now? What could've been going through their mind at the time? The ride must've been easy, with the calm sky and the bright moon and stars last night, but thirty minutes to go to murder someone, and another thirty minutes to come back afterwards is pretty long. I really wonder how they felt.'

I, too, tried imagining the scene. The stress and excitement before and after the deed would have their heart beating like crazy and, as they probably wanted to get it all over with and be back in bed as quickly as possible, they probably pedalled at high speed. I could see the image of a lonesome murderer in my mind, perspiring as they hurried through a night in which the wind had calmed down and moonlight was washing down through the sky. The image of the murderer was painted black, however, and I couldn't make out whether it was male or female, let alone who it was.

The road went around the hill with the observation platform, making a curve to the right. Past the hill, the road made another turn and then it was a long straight stretch.

It was there that my eye fell on something. A white object was lying by the side of the road. 'Hold it.' I put on the brakes. 'Hold it! Stop.' As I stopped at where the white object was, I called out to the other three who were moving ahead. They finally stopped about twenty metres farther on and turned around to look.

'What's the matter?' yelled Toshiyuki. I hopped off my bicycle and picked up the white object from the roadside. It was a piece of paper.

'There's something lying here,' I said, as I looked at it. There were cryptic, incomprehensible symbols written on it. Or perhaps it was a pattern. What could it be? I stood next to my bicycle and pondered on its meaning.

'What was it? Did you pick it up?' asked Toshiyuki, still sitting on his bicycle with his head turned my way. They didn't seem to feel like turning back, so I had to go over to them. But there was something I did first. I picked up a stone and marked the tree in front of me with an X at eye-level, so I could find the location again later. I also looked around to memorise the area. Then I stepped on my bicycle and went over to the three who were waiting for me.

'What did you pick up?'

Toshiyuki leaned forward, and Kazuto and Junji tried to steal a glance as well. I handed them the piece of paper.

'Oh, but this is—!' Junji said, and the other two also made similar reactions.

'You mean you've seen this before? Please tell me, what are these strange markings?' I asked. The three looked at each other, and then Toshiyuki started to explain.

'I too have no idea what they mean. But all three of us have seen this piece of paper before. We noticed it just now, on our way to Happy Fish Villa.'

'You noticed this piece of paper? You mean you saw it, but just passed by without giving it any more thought?'

'Think about it. We had just heard about the murder and were desperately hurrying on the bicycles, because we all wanted to know what had happened as fast as possible. Would you suddenly stop simply because you noticed a piece of paper lying around? Impossible.'

'Ah, you're right.' That made sense. 'But you did actually notice this piece of paper lying around?'

'Yes. When we passed by it, I said: "There was something lying there." Kazuto and Mr. Makihara said something like "Looks like a scrap of paper." All three of us saw something lying there.'

'Wait. Mr. Inukai, you just said you passed by it, but there's a bicycle tyre mark on the paper. So to be more exact, you rode over it?'

On the back of the piece of paper was undeniable proof that a bicycle had run over it diagonally.

'No. It was lying here next to the road and we passed by it.... But oh, you're right, there's a tyre mark on it. That's odd. None of us ran over it just now, either.'

This bothered me, but I changed the subject.

'I understand you passed by it on the way as you were in a hurry, but why ignore it now on the way back too? Ah, sorry if that sounded rude. What I meant was: did you have any reason to do so?'

'No.' Toshiyuki looked at Kazuto. 'We simply forgot it was lying there. I guess if we had noticed it again we'd have stopped, but the road's been a straight stretch for a while now and I was facing Kazuto as we were talking, so I didn't notice.'

Kazuto nodded too. Junji, who had been silent, simply answered: 'I'm just not as inquisitive as you.'

That was understandable. Only someone with a curious mind would stop their bicycle because they saw a piece of paper lying by the roadside. But even someone as curious as I wouldn't normally stop their bicycle to pick up something from the ground. It was because at that very moment, I was imagining the scene of the murderer hurrying back on this very same road last night. I'd assumed that the murderer must've left something on the road and immediately put on the brakes. And there was a reason why I'd thought it belonged to the murderer.

'I think this was dropped by the murderer last night. Because yesterday afternoon, the only people who used the bikes were Mr. Egami, Maria and myself. We were on the observation platform until four and we passed by here on the way back. This wasn't lying here at that time.'

The three were silent, contemplating what this meant. Finally, Kazuto said: 'Aha, if that's correct, than this really might have been left by the murderer. But are you sure it wasn't lying here yesterday afternoon? You might not have noticed while you were chatting.'

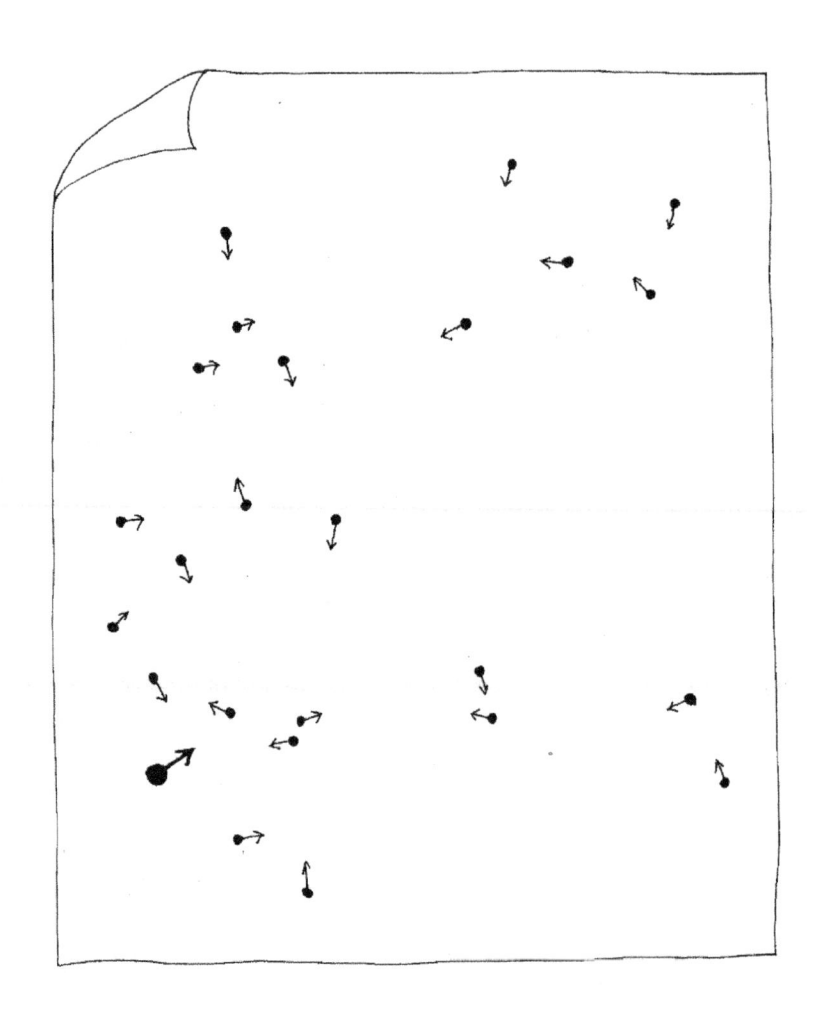

'No,' I said confidently. 'It wasn't there. If you don't believe me, just ask Mr. Egami or Maria.'

Kazuto made a face saying 'Fine, I believe you.'

'If Alice is right and this piece of paper wasn't lying here yesterday afternoon, then I guess it's really something the murderer dropped last night,' said Toshiyuki with a grave expression. 'That makes it a very important piece of evidence.'

'Let me see it.' Junji's interest, too, was piqued. He took the piece of paper from Toshiyuki and stared at it, but all he could do was frown and grumble at it.

'No idea what this is. Looks like some sort of code. Perhaps the murderer and Mr. Hirakawa had been communicating in secret?'

'It's no use discussing it here.' Toshiyuki put an end to the talk. 'Let's take it back to Panorama Villa. Somebody there might recognise it. Alice, you take it with you.'

I took the piece of paper, folded it in four following the existing fold lines and put it in the breast pocket of my polo-shirt.

'It's already twelve-thirty,' said Kazuto as he climbed back on his bicycle.

9

Ten people were gathered in the hall. It was the same scene as that stormy night when we discovered the murders of father and daughter Makihara, but without Hirakawa. There was a heavy atmosphere permeating the air, reminiscent of a wake for the dead. A cool breeze blew through the open French windows, and I stared absentmindedly at the graceful dance of the curtains in the wind.

'It must have been a shock to you when you discovered the body,' said Ryūichi in a gentle voice. 'Especially to Maria. Poor girl.'

At her uncle's words Maria, who was still not feeling well and appeared pale, looked up and answered weakly that she was alright.

'So all of us have gathered here in the hall again just as two nights ago—no, yesterday morning to be precise,' said Sonobe to Egami as he carefully wiped his briar pipe. 'What about it? Will you act as our master of ceremonies this time as well? You were one of the people who first discovered the body, and you can comment on what you yourself noticed or felt.'

Egami accepted the task once again. Everybody seemed to agree he was the one most suitable for the job.

'I've already explained what happened between the time we went out to sea to look for the oar until the time we discovered the body. Doctor Sonobe and Mr. Inukai explained the current situation in detail just now. I assume we all know what happened last night. A second incident occurred, and there was a third murder victim.'

The club president paused for a moment, considering how to begin. During that pause, nobody made any sound, not even a cough.

'Let's go over the basic facts first. The victim, Mr. Hirakawa, was murdered in the period between eleven o'clock at night and three in the morning. The cause of death was blood loss after being shot in the chest with a rifle. The murder weapon was not left at the crime scene, but we assume it's the same rifle that was used in the previous murders. Mr. Hirakawa died sitting in a chair at the table. It appears the murderer suddenly shot him across the table from at least one metre away. There were no signs of either a struggle or the body being moved after death.

'We all want to know why it happened, why Mr. Hirakawa was murdered, but there's one thing we need to find out first: who killed him? We'll examine the problem thoroughly now. I realise it's unusual for a youngster like me to be the one asking the questions, so please forgive me if I sound rude. I'll ask each of you in turn to make a statement about your activities last night. Please tell me everything exactly as it happened. I'd even prefer you to remain silent, rather than give me an incorrect statement or even tell me a lie. If you've any problems with how I ask my questions or how I lead the discussion, please state your objections at that time.'

Everybody seemed intrigued by Egami's eloquence. Even I thought he sounded like a real detective, with his "Examine the problem thoroughly" approach. He was announcing that, if he was going to do it, he'd do it thoroughly.

'I'll proceed in the order of how we're seated. Mr. Arima, could you tell us about your activities last night? From after eight, after we finished dinner, if you please.'

Ryūichi re-seated himself deeply in the rattan chair, put his hands together on top of his stomach and slowly started his testimony.

'Yesterday was absolutely the worst. Because of what had happened the day before, I'd hardly slept. I wanted to take an afternoon nap, but I just couldn't fall asleep, so I spent all day in my room. Oh, you said the night, didn't you? Excuse me. I remained in the dining room for a while after dinner. Satomi was helping Reiko with cleaning the table, and I sat there and had them listen to my boring stories. They finished washing the dishes at around nine-thirty. Then I had a cup of tea with Reiko. We weren't talking about anything in particular, just chatting. We were laughing at how Sonobe and Egami were still busy with the puzzle and how they seemed so absorbed in it. At eleven, Reiko yawned and I said we should go to bed. In my room, I had a bit of brandy by myself. I intended it to be a nightcap, but one glass followed another and I finally passed out. I think I fell asleep before midnight. I'd had quite a few drinks by then and I can only remember until just before that time. That's all I can tell you.'

'Thank you. Now to the person next to you. Reiko, please.'

Reiko nodded and breathed in deeply. It was as if she were about to open her mouth to sing.

'I'm afraid I'll be repeating father, but until nine-thirty, I was cleaning up after dinner with Mrs. Inukai while talking with father. Then, from nine-thirty until eleven I talked some more with my father over a cup of tea. After eleven I suddenly felt tired and started to yawn and my father was kind enough to say I should go to bed. I went to my room immediately and was asleep by half past eleven. In the early morning, while it was still dark, I woke up and went to the bathroom once, but I noticed nothing out of the ordinary then. My head was a bit hazy, so I don't remember exactly what time it was. But I remember that when I went to the kitchen for a cup of cold water, Mrs. Inukai was also there.'

'It was five o'clock,' said Satomi. 'Don't you remember? I said: "Sunrise in the south is really late."'

'Oh, that's right,' replied Reiko. 'Yes, five o'clock. After my glass of water I went to my room to sleep again, and woke up before six. That's when I got up and started to prepare breakfast. Dr. Sonobe came down at five minutes to six for a bath, I remember.'

'And that's all?'

'Yes.'

'Thank you.'

Egami turned to the person next to Reiko: Kazuto.

'If you please.'

Kazuto stubbed out his cigarette in the ashtray, re-seated himself and started talking.

'Unlike dad and Reiko, I just couldn't fall asleep. After dinner, I just hung about in that rattan chair. I tried to think about what had happened to my uncle and Sumako, but my mind wasn't working, and I just sat there staring in front of me. At half past nine I went back to my own room. I think I saw Maria and Alice going out through the entrance then. Back in my room, I tried fiddling around with the wireless transceiver to see if I could fix it somehow, and listened to some music on the radio. Ah, I also played a little card game by myself. Pathetic, isn't it? But what could I do, with nobody to keep me company? Then I got bored and decided to get into bed and go to sleep. I slept for a bit, but I woke up in the middle of the night and couldn't sleep any more. So I got up to get some alcohol in the system and that was…what time was it, Mr. Egami?'

Kazuto threw a question back at Egami. He caught it.

'Just before two o'clock. Remember when we had finished our first whisky-and-water and I looked at my watch and said: "It's already a quarter past two."?'

Kazuto slapped his forehead with his palm.

'Yes, of course. I poured a second glass for you and said: "But it's only a quarter past two." I'd finally found somebody to talk to, so I didn't want to let you go. Our little midnight drinking party for two lasted until four. Right, Mr. Egami?'

'Yes. About ten past four,' confirmed Egami.

'That's all,' said Kazuto, his hands spread in front of him.

'Allow me to add two points,' said Egami. 'During the time Kazuto and I were drinking whisky in the hall, from before a bit before two o'clock until a bit after four o'clock, we didn't hear any gunshots from the direction of Happy Fish Villa, nor did we see anyone suspicious entering or leaving Panorama Villa. Also, we could see the bicycles from the hall and both of us remember that all three bicycles of Panorama Villa were there. We saw two bicycles from the French windows next to this rattan table and one through the window next to the front door entrance. Correct, Kazuto?'

Now Egami threw the question to Kazuto, who answered with a 'Yeah.'

'That's a very important statement.' Sonobe stopped wiping his pipe. 'So you were in the hall from two until four and you didn't see the murderer, but you did see all three bicycles? I'd previously estimated Mr. Hirakawa was murdered between eleven and three, with some leeway, but now it seems that the murderer must have committed the crime before one thirty and had returned to Panorama Villa before two.'

I nodded as I listened, but I suddenly remembered something that made me cry out and I raised my hand.

'We can limit the time of the murder down even further. Maria and I were sitting on those bicycles and talking until quarter past twelve, so the murderer couldn't have used a bicycle until then. Suppose they took a bicycle at quarter past twelve and hurried over to Happy Fish Villa. They would've arrived at around a quarter to one. So that's the earliest time the crime could've been committed. On the other hand, from Mr. Egami and Kazuto's testimony, we know the crime must've been committed before half past one. So that means the crime was committed between quarter to one and twenty past.'

'That's right,' agreed Maria, but Toshiyuki stopped us with a regretful expression.

'Alice, there's one gap in your theory. Aren't you ignoring the possibility the crime was committed much earlier? I mean, the murderer could've killed Mr. Hirakawa sometime past eleven and been back at Panorama Villa already by quarter to twelve. Maybe one of the bicycles you and Maria were sitting on had just returned from Happy Fish Villa.'

'No, that's impossible. Actually, Maria and I had been there since half past eleven. We were sitting on those bicycles and, believe me, all three of them were there. Two near the French windows, one near the entrance.'

'Then it's settled,' said Sonobe firmly. 'Alice here is right. We can assume that the crime was committed between quarter to one and twenty past. That's a lot more precise than the opinion of some quack doctor.'

'Okay. And it's your turn anyway, Alice, so talk about your movements last night from the beginning,' said Egami as he lit a cigarette. Apart from the short period between nine and half past, when I was alone in my room, I'd been together with Maria all the time, so halfway through my story she joined me and we talked about our movements last night in sequence, from how we'd gone for a walk, gone out on the boat and finally overturned it. By the time we'd finished, Egami had turned two Cabin cigarettes into ash.

'The movements of the two of you last night were certainly the most interesting of any of us,' he observed. 'What's more, you didn't see anyone before or after your great adventure, am I right? Not even when you went back to your rooms at quarter past twelve?'

Maria and I said no, in unison.

'Are we getting close to the core of the case?' asked Toshiyuki, but Egami only said: 'I wonder.'

'Well then, let's proceed to the second half.'

10

The Inukais were next. First was the husband, Toshiyuki.

'There's nothing to talk about. My wife helped with washing the dishes while I killed time by watching television. Just after nine, Reiko said she'd do the rest and sent my wife away. We watched a bit of television together and went up to our room at half past nine. Reiko was having some tea in the dining room, and asked us if we'd like a cup, but we declined. Dr. Sonobe and Mr. Egami were hard at work with the puzzle in the hall. It was still early when we reached our room, but my wife took her sleeping pills and went straight to sleep. It was before ten. I got into bed as well and read a book for about half an hour, but it was boring and I got extremely sleepy, so I switched off the light and went to sleep at half past ten. I didn't wake up until this morning, so I didn't notice anything of interest whatsoever.'

His wife Satomi's testimony matched her husband's.

'It's my turn now,' said Sonobe. 'I haven't much to say, either. At my age, you don't become active at night any more, like young Alice and Miss Maria here. Their tale was quite entertaining. As for me, I'm happy to say I found a friend on the island, a young, good friend called Jirō Egami. He was nice enough to keep an old bush doctor like myself company when nobody else cared to do, and chatted to me while we were working on the puzzle. I was happy he wasn't just listening and nodding, but also talked extensively about his own mischievous thoughts. He kept babbling on about his childish opposition to nuclear power, and yesterday I, too, started to have a change of heart... Oh, I did it again. Don't look at me like that, Detective Egami. Anyway, after dinner the two of us had another chat as we worked on the jigsaw puzzle. We had some drinks at eleven and remained in the hall until shortly before midnight. We were just in the middle of another fascinating discussion when I asked him to release me: "I'm afraid my old body can't take much of this anymore. Let's continue tomorrow," I said. What were we talking about again?'

'The pros and cons of Kant's *Ding an Sich*,' replied Egami seriously. I really wasn't able to keep up with their thinking. What was going on in their heads?

'Oh yes, that was it. Well, we can talk about that together at some other time. To continue my story: I went back to my room right after that and went to sleep. I got up once before one o'clock to go the bathroom, but stayed in bed the rest of the time until the morning, except for that. When I came out of the bathroom, I bumped into Maria.'

Maria nodded.

'Yes. I was also on my way there.'

'"I was just talking with Alice on the terrace," she told me beamingly.'

'Why would I be beaming just from chatting with Alice?'

You don't need to deny it so vehemently. But I'd wanted to ask the same question.

'We looked out at the terrace downstairs then and saw the two bicycles there,' Maria said, and the doctor nodded in agreement.

'But from the first floor we couldn't see the third bicycle at the front entrance. After that I fell sound asleep until I got up before six o'clock and took a morning bath.'

'Alright,' said Egami briskly and he moved on to the next testimony.

Junji was the next in line. Despite all eyes being fixed on him, he still wouldn't start talking and stared vacantly into space while rubbing his rough beard.

'My turn, eh? What did I do last night? My head's not really helping now.'

He smiled a little at himself.

'I went up to the attic, to that room with all the stuff in it. There were some rare books, so I stood there, reading some of them and also took a look at the shell specimens there. Then I went to the room where Sumako and her dad were lying and spent some time sitting there. Then I went to my room and crept into bed around half past ten.'

The room he just mentioned used to be Kango's room.

'I think I woke up once in the night. It was past one o'clock. I went to the bathroom, and then watched the sea for a bit through the hallway windows. I stood there for about five minutes, when Egami came out of his room. What time was that?'

'A little after twenty past one,' replied Egami. Sonobe stopped them there.

'Mr. Egami, you're quite the nighthawk. Or are you suffering from insomnia? You just told us you were drinking with Kazuto from a bit before two, but you were gallivanting about the house before that, it seems.'

Egami broke into a wry smile.

'I'm no nighthawk. Last night was just a bit different. I was on my way to the bathroom, sometime after one o'clock, when I came upon Mr. Makihara and had a little talk with him. I returned straight to my room. Mr. Makihara, please continue. You said you were looking out at sea from the hallway windows, which means you were looking in the direction of High Tide Cape. Was there anything you noticed? Perhaps you heard a strange sound, or saw something curious?'

'Now let me think.' Junji hadn't appeared to be very willing to talk, but then his eyes opened wide.

'I did! I did see something!'

'You remembered?' The detective asked, as if he had already expected Junji's answer. For the first time, Junji looked straight into Egami's eyes.

'I was staring in the direction of Happy Fish Villa, when I caught a glimpse of a weak light. That might've been the light of the murderer's bicycle.'

'That has to be it,' Toshiyuki declared. 'Mr. Makihara, try to remember. What time was it?'

'About twenty-five past one, I think.'

'Twenty-five past one.'

Junji and Egami replied almost simultaneously. Egami had something else to add, though.

'However, Mr. Makihara was the only one to see the light. I didn't. Mr. Makihara cried out, so I asked him what was wrong and also looked in the direction of High Tide Cape, but I didn't see anything.'

'Oh, that's right, you didn't see it,' said Junji softly.

'That light, was it moving towards Happy Fish Villa? Or was it moving away from there, towards this place? If it was a bicycle light, it should've been moving.'

'I said I caught a glimpse, but it was really nothing more than that. Hmm, it was… yes, the light was heading towards Happy Fish Villa.'

'You're certain?'

'I'm eighty percent confident. I only saw it for a second or so, and then it disappeared into to the trees. I wasn't standing watch at the windows you remember, so I went back to my room. You did too.'

It appeared that more questions would prove to be fruitless.

Junji's testimony had indeed touched upon a crucial point. But could we trust it? He was the only person to have seen the light that might've been from the murderer's bicycle, so there was room to doubt as to whether he was telling the truth or not. The claim he'd seen the murderer's bicycle heading towards Happy Fish Villa was also an implicit claim to us that he had an alibi, of course.

There was a silence, in which everyone was waiting for Junji to continue. When he finally noticed that, he briefly said: 'That's all.'

'Thank you. And finally, it's my turn.'

Egami adjusted his position on his seat and looked in front of him.

'My movements last night have already appeared partly in Dr. Sonobe's, Kazuto's and Mr. Makihara's testimonies, but allow me to tell you everything from the beginning myself. After dinner, I passed the time talking and working on the jigsaw puzzle with the doctor. That was until slightly before midnight. Then I went to my room, but Alice—whom I thought would already be sleeping—wasn't there. I wondered where he was, but wasn't particularly worried and went to bed. I thought that he and Maria were having a chat and enjoying the evening breeze outside. I was just about to doze off when Alice came back, and fell asleep right away. It was past one when I got up to go to the bathroom. As I already told you just now, I had a little talk with Mr. Makihara in the hallway then and he saw a light near Happy Fish Villa. If you allow me to add one remark: at that time—around twenty past one—I looked down through the window and saw the two bicycles parked near the French windows.'

'Ah, I saw them too.'

Hearing Junji confirm that fact too, Egami nodded lightly and continued: 'I couldn't see the third bike from the hallway. Doctor Sonobe and Maria also testified they only saw two bicycles. A bit before two, I woke up again. For some reason, my throat was all dry, so I went downstairs to the kitchen to have a glass of water. Kazuto arrived too in search of a drink and we had a whisky-and-water together. Around ten past four, the two of us retreated to our rooms. That is all.'

Egami lit another cigarette. He squinted at the smoke he himself puffed out in silence, as if he was putting his thoughts in shape.

'My conclusion is that none of us has an alibi. As the murder happened in the middle of the night, I guess that's only natural. We managed to narrow down the estimated time of the crime considerably, but we didn't find out who the murderer is....'

He was talking to himself.

'Is there any point of interest you've noticed?' Egami asked everyone again, and Toshiyuki answered with a groan.

'Yes?'

'This is different from what we've been talking about, but there is something I want all of you to take a look at. Alice, could you show everyone that piece of paper you picked up with the secret code or whatever it is?'

It was only then that I remembered the piece of paper I'd picked up on the way back. I took it out of my breast pocket, unfolded it and passed it to Egami.

'What's this?'

He gave it a glance and then looked up at me.

'I picked it up on our way back from Happy Fish Villa,' I explained. 'Mr. Inukai, Mr. Makihara and Kazuto had also seen it lying in the roadside on their way over there, but they passed it by because they were hurrying to the crime scene. Mr. Egami, this piece of paper was lying on the side of a relatively straight part of the road, on the Panorama Villa side relative to the hill with the observation platform. It wasn't lying there when we passed by that spot yesterday afternoon, was it?'

'No, it wasn't there. I'm quite certain.'

'Maria, you also remember it wasn't there, right?' I asked her, just to be sure.

'It wasn't there. On this island, anything lying around stands out, even an empty can or a scrap of paper.'

I turned to Egami. 'So that means that it wasn't there yesterday afternoon, and we picked it up this morning. From what we've heard now, it's clear nobody went all the way out to that place on a bicycle during that period. You know what that means, right? This belongs to the person who went out there in the night, but didn't testify about that just now: the murderer.'

'I understand.' Egami looked at everybody. 'Did anyone drop this piece of paper? Is there anyone who might've dropped it who is prepared to claim it has nothing to do with the murder?'

Nobody offered an answer. That meant that the person who had dropped it was indeed the person behind Hirakawa's murder. I had no idea what this scrap of paper meant to the murderer, but whoever they were, they were probably cursing themself at the moment. The murderer couldn't just brush it away, saying the piece of paper was theirs and that it had nothing to do with the murder. If we'd pursued the question further as to why it was dropped there in the middle of the night, the murderer would have had no way to answer.

'Was it the murderer who dropped this...?' asked Egami, pushing the unfolded piece of paper to the middle of the table.

'What's this tyre mark …? Did Mr. Inukai and the others run over it on their way to Happy Fish Villa?'

'No, that's what so strange,' I answered. 'Nobody ran over it. It was lying in the roadside, and they say they only passed it by. It was the same on the way back from Happy Fish Villa. I'd almost passed it by, but then I stopped to pick it up. This tyre mark was already on it. None of us could've made it.'

'That's curious. It means the mark was there already. And it's fresh: grains of sand fall off when I rub it with my finger. This sand got there last night. But I have no idea what that indicates.'

Egami was obviously intrigued by it. I, too, was bothered by the problem, but there was something that piqued my curiosity even more.

'What do these symbols mean?' I asked, and Egami looked up at me in surprise.

'What? But it's obvious. The direction the *moais* are facing.'

CHAPTER FOUR: MOAI PUZZLE

1

'The direction the *moais* are facing…?'

I cried out, almost screeching, in surprise. Egami had answered so casually, I simply couldn't take it in for a moment.

'Quite. Didn't it dawn on you immediately that the points mark the locations of the *moais* on the island? The one that's a bit bigger than the others is the one on the observation platform. There are twenty-five of those symbols. That's exactly the number of statues. I suppose we should check if all the directions are correct, but it's safe to assume they are. That was what we were planning to create ourselves.'

'I understand,' said Maria, 'but who made it? The three of us came here all ready to solve the puzzle, but we'd only just started when those murders happened and we had to let it rest. Who else could have made it? Nobody else had the time.'

'Maria, did you take a good look at it?' replied Egami. 'I don't mean what's on the map itself: I mean the piece of paper. Does it look new to you? Look at the folded lines. There's no way such clean, deep lines could have been made if it had been folded just two or three days ago. The fraying is old as well. This map was made a long time ago.'

Now that Egami had pointed it out, it seemed obvious. The map had clearly been made years ago. That meant….

'Does that mean…it was made by Hideto!?'

Maria cried out in shock and cupped her mouth with her hand. Kazuto and Sonobe hurried over to take a look.

'My brother made this map!?'

'Now that you mention it, I remember Hideto had a habit of pressing too hard when he was writing, even with a fountain pen. Just as on this map.'

Sonobe picked the map up and passed it to Reiko as if to ask her to take a good look at it as well. Fearfully, she took the map in her hands, but as she was looking at it she started to tremble. She was trying to hold down the emotions that were welling up inside.

'It's not a drawing or writing, but what do you think, Reiko? Could it be Hideto's work?' asked Sonobe impatiently.

Reiko's eyes were still fixed on the map. In a weak voice she finally said:

'I don't know. I—I don't know....'

'But you would be the one best able to tell.'

'Stop it!' Maria implored the doctor. 'There's no way Reiko can say for sure Hideto wrote this, just by looking at the markings. She's thinking about it, so stop pestering her.'

The doctor leant backwards, as if Maria's words had hit him straight in the chest, and shut his mouth. She hadn't spoken loudly, but her words had been full of determination.

'I don't know. I can't tell just from this,' repeated Reiko as she gingerly returned the map to the middle of the table.

Sonobe muttered: 'I see.'

I, who had been watching the three of them, felt relieved and a weight being lifted from my shoulders.

'Three years ago, just before his unfortunate death, Hideto made an attempt to solve the *moai* puzzle.' A large part of Egami's cigarette had turned to ash and he let it fall into the ashtray. 'In the weeks before he died, he told Maria he was close to solving the puzzle and that the key lay in the direction the statues were facing.'

'Yes, he'd been going all over the island. But he wouldn't allow Reiko to go with him because of the snakes,' said Maria.

Egami nodded and continued.

'Okay. So it is very possible that the maker of this map was indeed Hideto. But is there anybody here who actually saw him draw it?'

Nobody answered.

'Nobody? Then we'll leave it as a possibility that it was drawn by Hideto. Anyone object to that?'

Nobody answered.

'Anybody who claims they were the one who made the map?'

Nobody answered.

'Then the person who made the map is one of the following: Hideto Arima, Kango Makihara, Sumako Makihara or Mr. Hirakawa.'

Kazuto let out a sigh of relief.

'That's right. It's by no means certain that my brother made it. It could have been Mr. Hirakawa.'

'But, but...,' Ryūichi choked a bit on his words. 'But if this was made by Hideto, why has it just now appeared before us like this, at this time? It didn't come out of the back of a desk drawer or anything like that. It was lying by the side of the road leading to the crime scene. What does that mean?'

'That's just what I don't understand,' said Egami softly. 'Just now, all of us arrived at the conclusion together that this piece of paper was dropped by the murderer. Then we assumed it was a map of the directions the *moai* statues are facing—we still need to confirm that—and have limited the candidates for map creator to Hideto, Mr. Makihara, Sumako, or Mr. Hirakawa. But when it comes to the question of how and why the murderer was in possession of the map, there's nothing we can say about it for the time being.'

If this had been a scene on the stage and we had been in the middle of a performance, then the lighting of the scene would slowly have changed. The case had taken on a completely different character. We didn't know why father and daughter Makihara were killed, and the reason for Itaru Hirakawa's murder was also still unknown. But the *moai* puzzle was a secret code that would lead to the hiding place of a fabulous diamond treasure. Was the treasure the reason for the series of murders?

Several ideas flashed through my mind like static electricity. The murderer had been in possession of a map made by Hideto, who'd been trying to solve the *moai* puzzle and had almost got his hands on the treasure, until he died just before finding it. The murderer had had the map until only yesterday!

The question was obvious: had Hideto Arima's death really been a simple accident? Or had he perhaps been murdered by the same person behind the recent series of murders that had us quaking in our boots? I didn't dare voice the question, however, and had to keep such thoughts to myself.

'Anyone with ideas to share?'

Nobody replied immediately to Egami's question. After a while, Satomi piped up.

'Everyone looks tired, you included, Egami. It's past three o'clock already, and we haven't had any food. In a situation like this, I can understand you might not feel like eating, but I think it's better to have at least something, to keep our strength up.'

'Ah, sorry, I didn't notice you were—.'

'Oh, no, Reiko, you shouldn't mind that much. With all that's happened, it's only natural. Shall we have a break now and prepare some sandwiches?'

'I'll go make them.'

'Reiko, you take a rest if you're tired.'

Maria stood up.

'I'll make them. Reiko, you sit down.'

Perhaps the three women had wanted to leave the depressing discussion. In the end, all three of them got up and disappeared into the kitchen.

'Shall we go and search for the rifle?'

It was Kazuto who broke the silence of the remaining men.

'The murderer is still in possession of the rifle. That's dangerous. We should make a thorough search for it together.'

Some of us agreed, but I felt reluctant. I felt pessimistic about it. I loathed myself slightly for having given up already, even before we had started the search.

The sandwiches were brought in. As the women had been kind enough to make them, we all felt obliged to eat one or two. I winced at the bitter coffee before realising I'd forgotten to put sugar in it.

2

We'd left no stone unturned, but we hadn't found the rifle within the walls of Panorama Villa. By the time we gave up on our search, the hands on the clock were already past five o'clock.

Egami and I went up to our room, joined by Maria. We had a lot to discuss. He and I sat on one bed, and Maria sat on the other. I could sense a sparkle in their eyes that conveyed their commitment to solving the mystery. It was Egami who spoke first.

'What does the fact the murderer was in possession of the map mean?—that's the question. We can infer that the diamond treasure Tetsunosuke Arima buried is somehow connected to it all. And, if this map was made by Hideto, the problem becomes very serious.'

Maria responded briskly.

'Do you mean the murderer may have stolen the map from Hideto three years ago? And it's very likely they weren't given it, but took it by force. Is that what you're saying?'

'This isn't a game of detectives any more. You do understand I'm quite serious about this?' asked Egami, and Maria nodded.

'Let's be open about what each of us is thinking. We can decide if the ideas are wrong or not after they've been discussed. Hideto had almost laid his hands on the diamonds, when he suddenly lost his life in an "accident." Too suddenly. I think there's enough room for doubt as to whether it really was an accident.'

'I agree.'

'Okay, Alice. If the map you found today was made by Hideto, then I can think of the following scenario. Three years ago, Hideto succeeded in solving the *moai* puzzle. Having worked out the location of the diamonds, he went out one night to dig them up. But someone noticed. This person, X, may have followed Hideto when he went out to dig the treasure up, or maybe X asked Hideto if they could help. Or it could be that Hideto himself asked X for help. Anyway, X was there on the scene when Hideto was digging up the treasure. X wanted to keep the diamonds for themselves, so they killed Hideto.... That's one possibility.'

I had the same exact scenario in mind. Maria appeared to have been anticipating Egami's theory, because she showed no signs of disagreement and listened in silence.

'If that scenario is utter nonsense, then so be it. It's not a very pleasant scenario anyway. But I'd like to be sure. I need to ask you some questions, Maria. Is that all right?'

'Yes.'

'Okay then, let's start with the big one. Were there any doubts at the time as to whether Hideto's death really was an accident? It wasn't a natural death, so naturally the police must have come here to investigate.'

'Yes. But their investigation was just a formality. The cause of death was drowning, and they even performed an autopsy, but they discovered nothing out of the ordinary. No unnatural wounds on his body or anything.'

Egami thought for a while. Those were facts that went against his idea of murder, but they had not definitively resolved his doubts.

'Hideto had been looking for the treasure under the assumption the key lay in the direction the *moais* were facing. So then, after his sudden death, did you find anything to show proof of his work? Like a note with the results of his investigations, or something like that?'

Maria looked nervous as she pushed back the bang of hair that was hanging over her forehead.

'We didn't find anything. We were all so stunned by the sudden accident, nobody thought of it. Reiko had collapsed because of the shock, so a lot happened then.... We assumed his notes had got lost in all that confusion, but, after what we found out today, I simply don't know. Maybe it hadn't been lost. Maybe somebody stole it.'

'The confusion....' There was something that bothered me. 'I guess this is the antithesis of the theory that Hideto was murdered, but suppose Hideto's death was indeed just an unfortunate accident and, in the subsequent confusion, somebody happened to come upon Hideto's notes, or something of the kind, and decided to take the treasure for himself? As for why it has only popped up now, three years later, that's a different question. Our map-stealing X went looking for the treasure together with Kango Makihara and Mr. Hirakawa, but they got into a fight about how they were going to divide up the spoils and it turned into murder. Can we agree that's also a possibility?'

Egami groaned. He was placing the two theories, both lacking in evidence, on the scale.

'Well, that's also a plausible scenario. But for now we haven't the data necessary to decide which of them is right, or even whether something else happened.'

'At the moment, we can't say whether Hideto's death was an accident or murder,' said Maria, 'but surely the murders that have happened now must be connected to the *moai* puzzle? Maybe we should go back to the reason why we're here on this island in the first place and try to solve it.'

She pushed her conclusion firmly and awaited our replies. As I looked into her imploring eyes, I thought that Maria might perhaps feel it had been our destiny all along to solve the puzzle. But she was not begging us to help her. She was only asking for our cooperation. She was like that.

'What kind of Mystery Club would we be if we ran away from a puzzle like this with our tails between our legs? Right, Alice?' Egami showed off his white teeth as he said that.

'Of course. Our Boy Detective Club has no little boys, so any trouble we get involved with, we adults can solve by ourselves. That's our motto.'

'That's a pretty stupid motto,' grinned Maria. 'But if we really do solve it, it'll be in the name of our Mystery Club.'

'Even if we solve the puzzle, will we really find the diamonds?' I posed the question. Egami who always finished anything he started, said: 'We're going to solve that puzzle precisely to find that out. If there was a fight when the diamonds were being dug up, then the hiding place might be empty. Be that as it may, we're going to solve the *moai* puzzle.'

The original of the map I'd picked up had been left in Ryūichi's custody, but each of us had a copy we'd made by hand on thin paper sheets—paper for use in a word processor we got from Kazuto.

'I think it's safe to assume this map does indicate the direction the statues are facing, but, as Egami said, it's probably best if we confirm that for ourselves. We checked out five of the statues plus the big one on the observation platform two days ago, and they correspond exactly to the arrows on this map, but shall we go and check a few more?'

It was best to be sure. And if we were going to check them out, then we had to do so as soon as possible. There was still time before six o'clock, so we decided we'd investigate immediately. We decided to try and check out three or four more before sunset.

As we went downstairs, we saw Ryūichi and Reiko sitting in the chairs near the window. They were not talking, but simply sitting in the breeze staring out vacantly to sea.

'Are you going out?'

Ryūichi's voice rang out. We answered in the positive without going into details.

'Are all three bicycles available?' Maria asked Reiko. 'Yes,' she replied. 'Kazuto is out for a walk to clear his thoughts, so nobody's using them right now.'

'Okay. We're going to clear our thoughts, too, by cycling around the island.'

'Be careful.'

With Reiko's words in our ears we left Panorama Villa.

3

Before we climbed on to the bicycles, we discussed which of us would check out which arrows as we looked down at our maps.

We agreed that splitting up would be the most effective way of using the hour and a half we still had until sunset. I took the ones farthest away, near High Tide Cape. Egami was responsible for the centre of the island, which left Maria with the area near Low Tide Cape. I took the only compass; the other two would do their jobs by comparing the directions the *moais* faced with the arrows on the map.

We kept formation for about five minutes, before Maria cut out saying: 'There's one in the back here I'm going to check.' Like Reiko, Egami and I saw her off with a 'Be careful' and then proceeded to ride on side by side.

After a while, we saw Kazuto strolling in our direction. He lifted his hand in greeting, and we stopped

'Where are you going? Don't tell me you're going to Happy Fish Villa to investigate the crime scene again?'

'No,' replied Egami. 'We're going to check whether the map really does indicate the directions the statues face. Checking out ten of them is probably enough.'

'Oh, that's awfully careful of you. I've looked at the map as well and given it some thought. Suppose this is a map of all the *moais*, then what? How does it show the hiding place of the diamonds? Things like that. But I couldn't work anything out. Who knows what it means if one statue is looking this way and another that way? Puzzles and I just don't go well together. I'll leave this one to you.' He continued on his way to Panorama Villa and we went in the opposite direction.

We continued with the sea to our right, and after a while the road curved slightly inland to the left then continued straight for a while in the direction of the hill. We were getting close to where I'd found the map. I'd memorised the location of the tree I'd marked and stopped my bicycle when I saw the X on the trunk.

'Mr. Egami, this is the place. I picked up the piece of paper—the map—here.' Egami looked at the spot but remained on his bicycle.

'So you found it around the roots of that tree? Then it couldn't have been blown far by the wind, which has been blowing north-east since yesterday, so that's why it's been blown to this side of the road. But I don't see anything suspicious here.'

'Shall we go, then?'

'Sure. But keep your eyes on the side of the road as we go. Even though I doubt the murderer was so careless as to have dropped anything else around here.'

We continued our cycling, eyes scanning both sides of the road. But there was nothing of interest by the time the road started to curve around the foot of the hill.

'I'll leave you here,' said Egami and he got off his bicycle. 'There are a couple of *moais* a bit farther north here, off the road. You still have some way to go, so don't overdo it and make sure you're back in time.'

'Okay. I can't check all the statues anyway.'

We separated there.

Three years ago, Hideto had probably used this same road while investigating the statues. The images of him then and myself now overlapped in my mind, but there was no ghost who appeared to lead the way.

He, who as an elementary school student had asked the artist about the Golden Mean. He, who had taught Maria to play the guitar when she was still a girl, and had been a bad singer. He, who had invited his beautiful fiancée to this island and had devoted himself to a treasure hunt for her. He, who had probably discovered the hiding place of the treasure. He, who had lost his life at sea during the night. He, who might have been murdered.

He was seven years older than Maria.
He could focus his mind on one single thing.
He was smart.

Hideto Arima, isn't there anything you want to tell us? But even if you have, you can't, can you? That's all right. We'll find out what it is you want to tell us. So please be patient. We're taking the same road you took three years ago. I know we'll reach you in just a little while….

I started to talk to him in my mind, a person I could now never meet. Yet I'd like to have met him, just once.

I hurried on my bicycle as if I was in pursuit of the setting sun and, by the time I got back to Panorama Villa, it was half past seven. Egami and Maria were sitting in the rattan chairs and discussing the results of their search.

'How did it go?'

'It's clear.' I sat down next to Maria. 'I only managed to check out three of them, but they all corresponded with the arrows on the map. What about yours?'

'Corresponded perfectly, too. Maria and I also checked out three each. If we add up the five we checked out two days ago, that's fourteen out of the twenty-five which check out. I think we can trust these arrows to be correct. Thanks to this map, we don't need to go over the whole island checking all the statues. It's saved us a lot of time and effort.'

'So now all we have to do is figure out what it all means. We know they point to the hiding place of the treasure, but in what way….? Physical labour might be over, but now we need to switch over to mental labour,' said Maria with some satisfaction. 'But we need to have dinner first. You can't solve a puzzle on an empty stomach. I'm going to help Reiko, so you two can sit and think for a while.'

She headed for the kitchen. We rolled our sleeves up and were ready to solve the puzzle, when we realised we hadn't any writing utensils.

'I'll get us something to write with,' I said and I got up from my chair. Egami was already holding the map in his hands and wrestling with the puzzle.

I returned to our room upstairs and switched on the light. The curtains hadn't been drawn yet and I could see the night stretching out beyond the window. I sat down on my bed, took my bag and put it on my knees and searched it. It was rather disorganised, so I couldn't find what I was looking for. I considered throwing the contents on my bed.

When I finally found a mechanical pencil hiding at the bottom of my bag, I felt something strange and heavy around my right shin and ankle. First I thought my bed sheets had covered my leg, but it wasn't that. I put my bag down by my side and took a look at my right leg. And on my jeans, around my calf....

For a moment, I thought it was an illusion, but when I realised what it was, my whole body was hit by shock and fear. A yellow-spotted pit viper had wrapped itself around my right leg.

My first thought was why a pit viper would be been hiding in my room. The snake had wrapped itself almost twice around my leg and had raised its head to complete its second turn. Its red, split tongue was flickering out of its mouth. It didn't just look terrifying, it was also in possession of deadly venom. Shouldn't forget about the deadly venom!

I tried lifting my leg to brush it away, but the snake wouldn't let go. To make sure it wouldn't be brushed away, it wrapped itself around my leg even tighter. I lifted my left leg and tried to kick the snake off my right leg, but it had already crawled up to my knee and I couldn't reach it with my leg. My mouth was completely dry.

I had no choice but to stretch out my trembling right arm and grab the snake tightly around its head. The unpleasant, sticky, cold sensation made me feel sick. My fear and feeling of disgust had reached their limits. I was furious. I felt ashamed my heart had almost stopped beating because of this creature.

Taking no notice of it trying to wrap itself around my forearm, I stood up and walked to the window, which I opened wide with my free left hand. I swung my right arm down with everything I had, as if I was throwing something in the direction of the sea. The snake let go of my arm, leaving only a nasty feeling behind. I didn't manage to throw it into the sea, as I heard the noise of it falling on the ground beneath the window.

I collapsed on my bed. There was still an unpleasant feeling in my right arm and sweat suddenly started to pour from my forehead. I just sat there in dumb surprise, wondering what the hell had just happened. The whole ordeal had taken a minute at most.

The snake had crawled out from under my bed. I suddenly jumped up, as the thought there might be more there crossed my mind. On the other side of the room stood another bed, so I ran to the door, lay down on the floor and, with fear in my heart, peeked beneath both beds. Nothing there.

I put my head to the floor and let out a deep sigh.

I wiped the sweat off my brow, closed the window and went down to the hall. Egami looked puzzled that it had taken me so long. But he noticed I didn't look too well, or was acting strangely, so he put the map down on the table.

'Hey, Alice, what's wrong?'

With an effort, I managed to speak in a low voice.

'There was a yellow-spotted pit viper in our room.'

'A pit viper? As in the snake?'

'Yeah. It was under my bed and it crawled up my leg. I grabbed it by its neck, whirled it around five or six times and hurled it out of the window. Oh man, that was a rather big surprise. What's the matter with this place?'

Egami was not sure what part of my story to believe. He probably wasn't convinced that a pit viper had been hiding beneath my bed.

'Mr. Egami, it really happened. But it's not there anymore, so we can go back up to our room safely now.'

'Sit down.' He pointed to a chair with his chin. I sat down and he lit a cigarette. 'That's a curious story. I don't think a snake would climb the walls and crawl through our window, which you told me was closed, I think? So how and when did it get inside?'

I became sullen. 'How should I know? It was really there, you know. Do you want me to exterminate the termites under the floorboards as well, while I'm at it?'

'What's wrong, Alice?' Maria came out of the kitchen wearing an apron. 'I thought you were trying to solve the riddle and now I see Alice complaining about something. What's the matter?'

'A snake…Just having the word in my mouth makes me feel sick. A long, thin reptile was in our room, Maria. Has that ever happened before? A snake hiding underneath your bed?'

'Never,' replied Maria in surprise. 'You're not pulling my leg, I hope? I just can't believe it. Sure, there are snakes around the house, but they've never gone upstairs. Was your window open?'

'No. It was a yellow-spotted pit viper. I tremble at the thought of being bitten.... Doc Sonobe might be here, but if a serum were necessary, there'd be no way to get our hands on it and I'd be dead by now....'

I had almost died. But, as Egami and Maria had said, it was very curious that a snake had found its way to a room on the first floor. A room whose door and window had been closed. So did that mean the snake could only have been brought there by some person? If so, that person had perhaps tried to kill me or Egami, with the snake as their living weapon.

'But who do you suppose would try to assassinate you using a pit viper? You're overthinking things, Alice. Paranoia, perhaps?'

When I voiced my ideas out loud, Maria laughed and denied it completely. I wasn't really happy with the sinister idea either and I couldn't think of a reason why anyone would want to wipe me out. I had posed the theory without much thought, but there was no evidence to disprove it.

'It might be paranoia, but it might also be a failed attempt at murder. Both are possible, so it can't hurt to be careful from now on. The person behind it couldn't also be the one responsible for all the other murders, could they? Or could they?'

It was time for dinner, and everyone appeared from outside or the floor above and gathered in the hall. They were all about to go into the dining room when Egami gently stopped them. He wanted to tell them the details of the adventure I'd had with the pit viper. Egami told them everything from the beginning, but didn't touch upon the question of whether this was simply a rare incident, or an attempt at murder and finally concluded with a warning to be careful, both inside and outside the house. Everyone looked shocked while they were listening to him, but the individual reactions afterwards were varied.

'How could that snake have got in? That's scary,' Satomi said to her husband, frowning. 'From now on you go inside our room first to see if it's safe.'

'If it was a normal snake, okay, but we're talking about a yellow-spotted pit viper here. Don't just leave it all up to me. Think a little about my life too.'

The Inukai couple were still joking. But Toshiyuki was not happy with it, all the same.

'And how do you suppose a snake found its way inside? Was it some kind of sick prank? If not, then it was attempted murder. This time it was just a snake thrown into their room while they were gone, but we'd all better be careful with locking up if you don't want a venomous snake being brought into your room at night while you're asleep.'

Ryūichi, too, looked dark. 'Never before has a snake crawled inside the house. I ask everyone to be careful.'

'A snake crawling beneath the bed is indeed a bit difficult to believe,' said Sonobe calmly. 'But we don't need to claim that everything was an attempt at murder either. It could've been a prank gone wrong, don't you agree my dear Mr. Egami?'

Egami scratched his head. 'Doctor, I am not that mean. I know very well Alice hates snakes, so while I might sneak an African elephant into our room as a prank, I wouldn't do it with a snake.'

'I think both a prank and an attempt at murder are rather unbelievable.' Kazuto had been silent, but was now glaring at me with a suspicious expression. 'Was there really a snake?'

'You think I'm doing some kind of monkey performance because I'm oh-so-lonely and need all of your attention?'

'Okay, that's enough,' said Toshiyuki.

Why should I be accused of lying by Kazuto? What benefit was there for me to make up a story and cause a fuss about it? I really disliked the illogical accusation he had made so thoughtlessly.

Reiko appeared in the hall to say dinner was ready.

4

Back in our room. The hands of the clock had gone past eleven o'clock.

The ashtray was overflowing with the fifteen Cabin cigarette stubs that had fallen victim to Egami's chain smoking. The ashtray, the exam sheet (the map), a couple of notes, three empty juice cans and the rustling of the cookie bag plus some cookie crumbs on the night stand were proof we were in the middle of a difficult struggle.

We had made some progress. It hadn't taken us long to draw lines extending all the arrows and discover that each *moai* statue was looking towards another one. We drew one continuous line between all the statues. The line started at a solitary *moai* in the north of the island, and ended at the slightly different *moai* statue on the observation platform. The line zig-zagged and crossed over itself in a seemingly random manner, enclosing triangular and quadrilateral shapes with no discernible theme.

Two hours had passed since this first discovery, but we had remained at a standstill. We tried everything we could think of in an attempt to find some kind of a pattern: looking for hidden ratios, measuring the length of each line, and even looking for hidden words, all to no effect. After a couple of hours of experimentation we had to admit failure.

'Guess we're just not good at solving puzzles,' said Maria. She looked tired as she put her hands on her waist and swung her upper body left and right. She hadn't really been occupied with the puzzle before. Perhaps she was starting to think it was out of our league.

In an effort to encourage myself, I said: 'It's a puzzle leading to five hundred million yen that many have tried to solve and failed. We can't just expect to do it in a couple of hours.'

'I guess you're right...I wonder how Mochi and Nobunaga are doing back in Kyōto now? They don't even know the directions the statues are facing, so perhaps they're still struggling with the points.'

'Ah, that's too bad. We at least have advanced to the dimension of lines, but they are still wrestling with the puzzle because they don't have enough data. Racking your brains over a puzzle where you haven't got enough data... Doesn't that just seem to symbolise the drama of human life?'

'All they do is read crappy whodunit mystery stories anyway.'

'By the way, neither of them will be in Kyōto at the moment. Mochi's probably gone back to his parents' home in Wakayama and is fighting with the instructor of his driving school, while Nobunaga's back in Nagoya for his sister's wedding.'

'Ah, so they've escaped Kyōto's torrid nights.'

We'd moved away from the puzzle to simple chatter. Maria suggested we all go to bed.

'Okay,' I agreed. 'Let's continue in the morning.' Maria threw the cookie crumbs into the waste basket, threw the empty cans away and took the bag of cookies with her.

'If I find a pit viper or a tarantula under my bed, I'll come running back. So let me in then, okay?'

It was midnight when Egami and I crawled into our beds and turned the light off.

This was the fourth night on the island. My ears had become accustomed to the lullaby of the waves. Why had bloody murders been committed in a place like this? The tide sounded as if it was laughing at the foolishness of us humans.

I woke up once in the night and saw that Egami was still up. He was sitting on his bed, still dressed in his shirt, studying the map while smoking a cigarette. I saw the grim expression on his face thanks to the light of the stars beyond the window. The rising smoke dancing in the darkness was beautiful. I hesitated as to whether I should call out to him, but decided against it and went back to sleep.

The next time I woke up, it was morning. It was past seven. Egami was already awake, lying on his bed and staring at the ceiling. On the night stand stood the ashtray full of butts and a crushed case of Cabin cigarettes. I said 'Good morning' to him, to which he only replied 'Yeah.'

'Did you start on the puzzle this early? Don't tell me you got up in the night to solve it?'

'Hmm? Oh, well, yeah. Did you see me?'

'No,' I said. 'But this case of Cabins is empty, so I guessed you'd been up.'

'Haha, sharp one, eh, my dear Watson. Without some other clue, we won't be able to solve the puzzle.'

'If you're like this already, I can't begin to imagine how Mochi is doing. Fiddling around with a map that only has dots, and with a copy of *The Origin of Species*.'

'*The Origin of Species*. Evolution theory. A puzzle which evolves. "The person who will solve the evolving puzzle, will inherit the diamonds." Fish, amphibians, reptiles, birds, mammals. Snakes are reptiles…but that has nothing to do with it. A puzzle that can only be solved in stages. One, two, three. Or A, B, C.' Egami started to mumble to himself. We hadn't considered the hint of the "evolving puzzle" last night.

'Ah, so that's it. An evolving puzzle is one you can only solve in stages. That does sound about right,' I commented.

'But we can't get this puzzle to evolve. Or can we? Maybe we did evolve one stage. We connected the facing directions and got this strange figure.'

Egami sat up straight and faced me.

'Remember what you said yesterday. "We've at least advanced to the dimension of lines." We advanced from points to lines. So what's next? After two dimensions….'

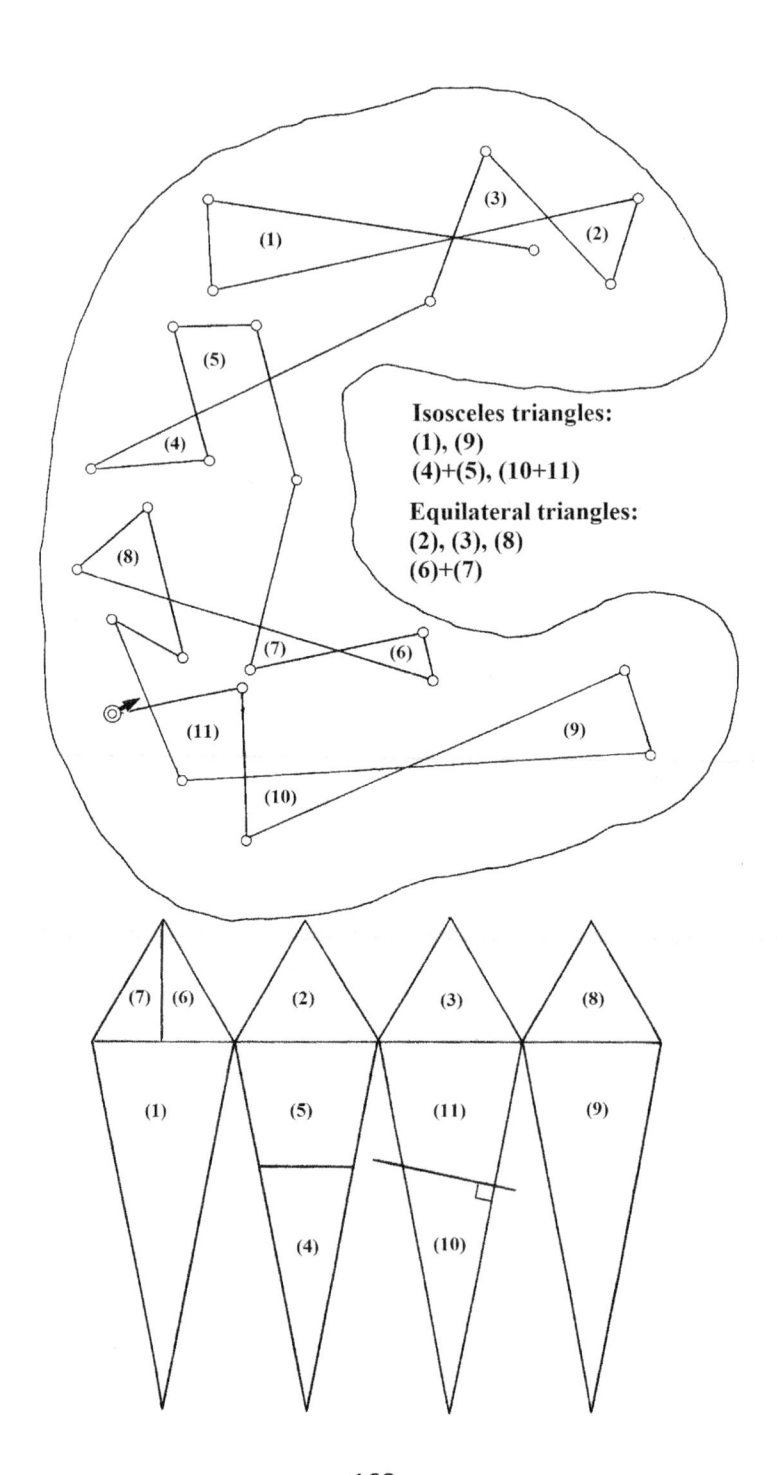

Isosceles triangles:
(1), (9)
(4)+(5), (10+11)

Equilateral triangles:
(2), (3), (8)
(6)+(7)

He reached for the map and I sat down next to him to get a better view.

'One, two, three...eleven. There are eleven closed surfaces here. Nine triangles, and two squares. What are we supposed to do with them? It seems as though there are a couple of them with the same angles...What's it telling us to do?'

Egami let his thoughts run freely again.

'What comes after two dimensions? A solid body. In mathematics, it's zero dimensions, one dimension, two dimensions and three dimensions. That's what you might call "an evolving puzzle." What do think, Alice?'

'I'm with you so far. But what does three-dimensional mean?'

'That we'll have to put this thing together. Have you any scissors? Wait, No need.' Egami searched his toilet bag and produced a safety razor. He removed the blade and, holding it carefully between his fingers, he placed the edge against the map.

'Pass me a ruler.'

I handed him my ruler and he carefully cut along the lines, during which time I could hear our breathing. When he was finished, we had eleven surfaces.

'*The moais were just the base data we needed to extract the surfaces.* Now we can connect them together and make a three-dimensional figure.'

'Mr. Egami, going three-dimensional is a very surprising step, but if this is supposed to be a clue to the hiding place of the treasure, shouldn't it be pointing to somewhere on the map?'

'We'll see when we've built the figure. Perhaps it becomes something very obvious.'

We started by numbering the surfaces from 1 to 11, in order of how you reached them starting from the first *moai* statue. We immediately realised that there were three equilateral triangles 2, 3 and 8, plus a fourth formed by joining 6 and 7 together. We lined them up side by side. The isosceles triangles of 1 and 9 clearly went together as well, but we had to stare for a while at the remaining surfaces 4, 5, 10 and 11 before realising that 4 and 5 formed a third isosceles triangle and 10 and 11 formed a fourth. So we had one set of four equilateral triangles and one set of four isosceles triangles. We were on to something.

We finally put the figure together. It was indeed three-dimensional: an octahedron, elongated as if one apex had been pulled down like a lozenge.

'What is this?'

I scratched my head. The figure looked familiar somehow.

'Hey.' Egami suddenly hit my shoulder with his fist. 'Isn't that Candle Rock?'

It was a very abstract representation, but the proportions were indeed that of Candle Rock. After four stages, we had finally reached our destination, it seemed.

'I'll go get Maria.'

'Wait.' Egami stopped me. 'Maybe you should get dressed first.'

5

We'd barely touched our breakfast before rushing out of Panorama Villa and climbing on the bicycles. Egami and I went so fast, Maria called out from behind us to wait for her. 'Slowpoke Swimmer Alice, wait!'

But my impatience had me pedalling with all my strength. Even I was surprised at how fast we went, but I guess that the excitement of Egami, who was in front of us, had also taken hold of me. We dropped our bicycles at the foot of the hill and ran up the small path to the observation platform.

We were halfway up when Egami suddenly looked as if he'd remembered something and asked Maria: 'Getting down to that rock is easy, but climbing back up might be difficult. Could your grandfather have done that?'

'You mean, could grandfather have climbed back up without anyone's help?'

Egami nodded. 'He thought of this elaborate puzzle all by himself, so I'd expect that when it came to hiding the treasure itself, he also did it alone.'

'Of course. If he'd asked anyone to help, that person might've dug the treasure up themselves and taken it with them.'

'That's why I asked. Now we're here, I'm starting to wonder whether it was even possible for your grandfather to have hidden something on Candle Rock.'

'He hid the treasure and had the *moai* statues created six years ago, soon after my grandmother died, so he was still quite energetic. I think he could easily have climbed up and down the rock. I doubt he could have dived into the sea, though.'

'We don't know how and where he hid the treasure yet, but we can make a good guess as to the limits of where he could have put it. It's not likely he would've dived into the sea and hidden it near the foot of the rock, nor that he would've climbed to the top of the rock and drilled a hole there.'

'No. But up until now, nobody has even considered the possibility it might be hidden on the rock, so maybe it hasn't been searched. Perhaps there's some kind of marker there.'

'That sounds rather over-optimistic,' I observed.

We continued talking as we walked on up and eventually we reached the observation platform. The wind was strong. We looked down at Candle Rock, towering out of the waves. A white sea bird, an albatross perhaps, was resting on the pointed tip.

We'd spent so many hours on this observation platform, yet we'd managed to overlook this large object right in front of our eyes. I mentally took my hat off to Tetsunosuke Arima. The treasure had been hiding in plain sight all the time.

'Let's go.'

Egami went first as we climbed down to the sea. There was no path, but there was no problem finding spots to place our feet. I followed behind him, holding a bag with his and my swimwear and Maria climbed carefully down after me. She probably hadn't wanted to stand waiting for us at the top of the hill. When we reached the rocky stretch of land, she turned towards the sea as we men got into our swimwear.

It was about thirty metres to Candle Rock. As we stepped into the sea, I realised that the rocky stretch actually extended all the way to Candle Rock itself and the water only reached to my waist. That meant even an old man could have made his way there without having to swim.

Once we'd reached the monolith we checked around it to see if there were any markers as Maria had suggested, but there weren't. Next, we went around two or three times looking for traces of burial sites or surface disturbances, but again we drew a blank.

'So? Did you find anything?'

Maria called out to us impatiently. Beads of water flew around as I shook my head. We spread out over a wider area, stretching our backs and arms to the limit, and even tried hitting the rock, but we couldn't find anything odd. It was a very ordinary tall rock.

I started to have doubts whether we'd actually solved the puzzle. Egami stood still and thought as he sucked on his middle finger, which he'd cut on the rock.

'Alice,' he said with his finger in his mouth, 'do you think there's anything special about that *moai* up there on the observation platform? It's bigger than the others and carved out more neatly, it's standing on the highest point of the island and it's the final point on the line when you connect all the statue lines of sight. It stands out so much, there must be something decisively different to the thing itself, I think.'

'I agree. For example, it's looking north-west. Perhaps that means the treasure is hidden on the north-west side of Candle Rock?'

'North-west, eh? But we've gone around this rock at least ten times, and there's nothing on it in any direction. Or does it mean we need to go north-west from Candle Rock?'

'But that's the sea. If you go further you reach the island. Perhaps that wall of rock over there?'

We yelled out our theory to Maria, who was still standing on the rocky stretch. With a compass in her hand, she searched the rock wall north-west of Candle Rock, but that, too, drew a blank.

'But I'm sure the process that led to Candle Rock is correct. The process of evolving from points to lines to surfaces and then getting it to stand up from the paper, that can't be an accident,' I said.

Egami and I sat down in a shaded part of the rock out of reach of the waves, and Maria sat down on a rock as well.

'Maybe we haven't solved the complete puzzle yet. Maybe there's a further stage.'

As I said that, Egami's expression changed slightly. He seemed to have thought of something.

'There's more? *You mean this puzzle will evolve even further*? How is it going to evolve beyond a solid body? Zero, one, two, three, four. Four dimensions. Four dimensions in mathematics. Points, lines, surfaces, solid bodies and now the fourth dimension. *Time*. Hmm, can't proceed from there. Add time to the process so far... If that last *moai* is indicating time, then north-west...no, it wasn't pointing precisely north-west... What time does the angle...Oh, no, this is much simpler of course.'

'*You mean the moai is looking towards Low Tide Cape?*'

Egami stared back at me.

'Precisely. Low Tide. That's the time dimension.'

I wanted to test the theory immediately.

I called out to Maria, who was looking bored. She looked up at my call.

'No idea whether it's high or low water now, but how much of Candle Rock shows above water level when the water is at its lowest?'

If you learned to play guitar on the hill, you should know this. And, as expected, Maria did.

'I think the water should drop another metre. Why?'

I explained our theory of making the puzzle evolve from a solid body to the fourth dimension. She looked very interested and observed: 'Luckily, the water's ebbing now.'

I'd noticed that.

'What about waiting for an hour or so? Then you can see the Candle Rock at low tide.'

We decided to return to the rocky stretch where Maria was standing and wait for an hour. How I wished we could fast-forward like with a video.

When the water had ebbed, you could walk to the Candle Rock with the water level only reaching your knees. This time, Maria rolled up the legs of her pants and came along.

'We just focus on the parts that are visible now the water's gone down, right?'

Maria immediately started touching the rock.

'So, below this line.'

'What about this?' I said, and I put my hand on a part that stuck out of the water now it had become low tide. It didn't feel strange and there was nothing that moved. But this part of the rock that jutted out had several markings that had been made by being hit by something hard. But I couldn't yell 'Eureka' just because of that. I peered more closely at the rock and carefully observed the surface.

'You have something?'

Maria looked over my shoulder. She noticed the markings immediately.

'They look old. What are they? They don't look natural. As if someone had gone at it with a hammer or something.'

I was about to agree with her, when the rock suddenly made a clanking sound and the short tip of the projection moved a little. Both of us cried out simultaneously.

Egami came over from the other side of the rock.

'Did you find something?'

'Perhaps…'

Still not sure, I tried to push it with my hand again, using more force, but this time nothing happened. Just now, the tip had made some noise and moved. It had moved about two centimetres.

'Perhaps you shouldn't push it,' said Maria impatiently. 'Perhaps you should twist it. Try grabbing the part that moved and turning it either way?'

Following her advice, I used my whole hand to grab the tip and twisted it to the right. It made another clanking sound and the tip moved another ten degrees to the right. The lower part had slid about five centimetres apart sideways. When I looked more carefully, I could see an empty space through the gap between the two parts.

'Twist it some more!'

Maria had seen what I'd seen. I twisted it another ten degrees. By that time the lower part had opened about ten centimetres and you could clearly see a cavity five centimetres wide inside. But no matter how much I tried, the rock wouldn't move any further.

'That's it. It won't budge any more.'

I turned to Maria. She was biting her lower lip but suddenly yelled: 'You solved it.'

Egami crouched down and inserted his fingers in the little hole that had appeared. 'It's wide, but shallow,' he said, but it appeared nothing was there and, giving up, he pulled his fingers out.

'Was it empty?'

Egami nodded in response to Maria's question.

'Then this has nothing to do with the treasure?'

That was impossible. A good look told me that excellent work had been done on the rock. It looked as though two rocks that had originally been separate had been put together with a bolt. Not only was the construction sturdy, any trace of it having been a construction in the first place had also been expertly hidden. Why go through all that trouble if not to hide a treasure? It had to have been here.

'Someone got here before us,' I said, at which Maria looked upset. *You can't blame me for this.*

'We did solve the puzzle…,' said Egami as he pointed next to the cavity. We saw something written in paint that had started to fade away.

It said: 'T.A.' in very small letters.

6

We reset the rock to its original position and waded back to the rocky stretch. With heavy legs we climbed up to the observation platform again. We felt as if we'd been in a marathon and been tackled within inches of the finishing line. To an extent, we'd expected it, but it was still a shock.

We sat down in the arbour with the coconut leaf roof and discussed what had happened up until now and what we were going to do next.

First of all, there was no doubt we had indeed solved the *moai* puzzle. The initials of the person who created the puzzle had been written next to the small cavity we found, and the cavity itself was also large enough to hold the treasure. But, unfortunately, somebody else had got there first and taken the treasure with them. Our first topic was who that person could have been.

'It could've been Hideto,' I started. 'We know he managed to solve the *moai* puzzle by himself.'

'Hmm, I wonder.' Egami voiced an objection. 'There's no doubt he'd been trying and had mapped the facing directions of the statues, but we can't be sure he actually made it all the way to the hidden cavity in Candle Rock. Though Maria might not be happy with me saying that....'

'I don't mind.' She shook her head. 'In fact, when you told me the treasure might be hidden on Candle Rock this morning, I noticed something strange. Your explanation of the puzzle sounded convincing, but I thought that if you were right, then Hideto must've been wrong when he said he'd solved the puzzle.'

'Why?' I asked.

'Because we all assumed that Hideto had solved the puzzle correctly, gone out in the night to retrieve the treasure by himself and had then fallen in the sea. So it'd make sense if Hideto had died near Candle Rock, but we found him somewhere else: the Eboshi Rock. So, doesn't that mean he hadn't solved the puzzle?'

'Maybe not,' I said slowly. 'Remember what we talked about yesterday. This might be unpleasant for you, but we speculated about whether Hideto might've been murdered by someone as the result of a quarrel about the treasure? Perhaps Hideto was killed here near Candle Rock, but moved by the murderer to the other side of the island, to the bay to the north.'

'Precisely.' Egami, too, acknowledged the possibility. 'Hideto was found near Eboshi Rock, which might be completely in the opposite direction to Candle Rock, but the distance between them isn't all that great. Suppose the murderer was with Hideto when he found the treasure. It might've been planned, it might've been done on the spur of the moment, but, blinded by greed, they pushed Hideto into the sea and let him drown. The murderer might've been stronger than Hideto, or there might've been multiple people involved, or perhaps the murderer might've caught him by surprise, but in any case, they succeeded in committing the crime. We can easily imagine that after the deed, the murderer—or murderers—didn't want to leave the body there. They'd want to move it as far away as possible from where the treasure had been hidden. Eboshi Rock in the bay up north was a perfect spot. While it's the spot furthest away from Candle Rock if you follow the coastline, it actually isn't far at all if you cross the island overland. Maria, is it possible to get through that forest and reach the bay up north?'

'Yes. Of course it's never easy to get through a forest at night, but this one's not all that dense. It's definitely possible, and listening to your theory I think it's very plausible that the murderer took that route. They crossed the forest carrying Hideto's body...and dumped him in the bay.'

Perhaps the scene had crystallised in her mind, because Maria shook her head two or three times as if to get rid of it.

'This is all just a theory,' Egami emphasised. 'We have a strong suspicion that's what happened, but we haven't any solid proof. And we have no idea who might have murdered him.'

'It's definitely suspicious. And his death three years ago is connected to the murders that are happening now on the island. Because the person behind the murders now was in possession of the map Hideto made. I can come up with several ideas as to how the cases are connected.' Maria mumbled to herself as she drew meaningless figures with her finger on the lauan table.

'Yes,' replied Egami. 'Let's try talking about whatever comes to mind as to how the two cases are connected. Hideto was young and energetic, so we can suppose that there were several people involved in his drowning. Perhaps they've fallen out now, three years after the fact. Maybe one of them wanted a bigger share for some reason, or the one who stood guard was blackmailing the one who did the deed. No, perhaps there was no guard, but a witness. It's also possible one of the murderers couldn't cope with their conscience any more and wanted to confess, but someone else decided otherwise.'

'Mr. Egami, that'd mean that Kango Makihara, Sumako Makihara and Mr. Hirakawa were all three involved in Hideto's death,' I said. 'That sounds a bit hard to believe. Whether they were standing guard or a witness, that'd still mean they were guilty of a crime.'

'I know what I'm saying,' replied Egami. 'I've no idea what we'll discover when we finally do manage to sort out all that's happened here on the island, including what happened three years ago. But whoever the murderer is, the truth will be painful to everybody. Pain is all that's awaiting us at the conclusion of this case. Of that I am convinced.'

'Are you saying that because you have an idea who the murderer is?'

Egami's statement sounded like some kind of prophecy, so I had to ask the question.

'I really don't know. What? Don't look so suspiciously at me. How am I supposed to solve everything based only on what we've discovered so far? Everyone's had a chance to commit the murders, including you, Maria and myself. And only I know for sure that I'm not the murderer.'

'That's a blunt way of putting it,' smiled Maria wryly. 'Are you saying that Alice and I are also suspects?'

'Of course I'm not seriously considering the two of you, but I've nothing to convince others that my juniors aren't murderers.'

'Blunt,' said Maria again.

'Let's get back to the topic.' I attempted to set us back on course. 'We tried examining the link between what happened three years ago, and the murders now, but can't we think of any other possible links?'

'Sure,' said Egami nonchalantly. 'In the case of a fall-out between accomplices, then people not close to Hideto are suspicious, I think. It's hard to imagine that members of his own family, like Ryūichi or Kazuto, or his fiancée Reiko would kill him for the treasure and then have a fall-out between themselves. But there's another way to look at it, and that's when the people closest to Hideto become suspicious. Suppose someone discovered Hideto had been killed and was now committing the murders as revenge.'

'That's just as horrible,' said Maria sadly. 'That'd mean that, whatever the case, my uncle, Sumako and Mr. Hirakawa were involved in the death of Hideto. Now I understand why you said that the truth will be painful for everybody. Everyone will get hurt, but we can't avoid that....'

'Any more ideas?'

I pressed again, but Egami answered in the negative.

'I can come up with a lot more, but it'd be nothing more than conjecture. Shall we talk about something else? When we find out who the murderer is, the motive and all of that will become clear. We can ask the murderer then.'

Putting what happened three years ago to the side and focusing on the case that was still in progress was perhaps the quickest way to the solution.

'Okay, let's start.'

7

'With Mr. Hirakawa being killed after Mr. Makihara and Sumako, I have a feeling at least one question has been answered,' Egami began. 'I mean the question of why someone would commit murders on this isolated island, cut off from the outside world. If the murderer had a motive to kill the Makiharas and Mr. Hirakawa, then it was inevitable they would choose this time for their crime, when all three of their targets would be here to spend their summer. And there'd be more than ten people gathered here, who all knew each other well, so the murderer probably wanted to camouflage themself amongst all the other people, together with their motive. Anyway, I can definitely see why the murders were committed here. If it was all premeditated.'

'Even though the murder weapon hadn't been prepared beforehand? They did use the rifle that was here already.'

Egami answered Maria's question: 'You could look at that the other way around. If the murderer already knew there was a rifle on the island, using it might've been part of the plan from the start.'

'But the first murders were committed on a stormy night when the murderer saw we were all drunk, right? That doesn't sound premeditated.'

'They probably took advantage of the opportunity. But, Maria, surely the third murder had to have been planned? The killer took an hour to go by bicycle to and from Panorama Villa to Happy Fish Villa to kill Mr. Hirakawa.'

Ah, that was true. I could understand why Maria might want to deny the cruel thought of a calculated murder, but the third one had now been shown categorically to have been premeditated.

'And the first two murders. Everybody had an opportunity...that's certain, but there's nothing more we can say about it.'

'I want to solve that locked room,' Maria said with a serious expression. 'We're the Mystery Club, perhaps we can solve the case by focusing on the locked room?'

Egami didn't look interested. He seemed bored by the term.

'The locked room, eh? Sure, it baffles me, but if you focus just on that, you're sure to hit a wall. When I start thinking about what might've happened inside that room, I have the feeling there's no way we'll ever be absolutely sure about what occurred.'

'An indecisive detective....' Maria muttered.

'There's one thing that bothers me,' I said. 'Sumako was shot in the chest, but your uncle Kango was only shot once in his thigh. He did fall over because of that, hit his head, lose consciousness and eventually die of blood loss, but wouldn't the murderer have wanted to make sure he was dead? Why did the killer leave the room, having merely wounded him? That seems very casual. Even if they'd seen Mr. Makihara lose consciousness, I doubt they would've felt relieved just at that. He might've regained consciousness shortly afterwards and crawled out into the hallway to cry for help. There has to be some reason for not finishing him off. Maybe the killer heard someone come up the staircase at the crucial moment.'

The two others agreed there might be something to that idea. In any case, that was all I could come up with. If I'd been asked 'So?' I wouldn't have known how to reply.

'We talked quite a lot about the first two murders on the night they happened and the day after, but we haven't gone thoroughly through Mr. Hirakawa's murder yet,' I said, changing the subject. 'Let's sort out the facts of that case now.'

'We got a lot of testimonies on the spot. I have them all sorted out in my notebook.'

From her waist pack Maria took out a cute notebook that could fit snugly into her palm. It was more a notepad than a notebook.

'Oh, let me see that,' said Egami, and Maria put the notebook open on the table. The neat letters were so small they were hardly legible. Egami and I knocked our heads together when we tried to read. All the testimonies had been organised and put in chronological order.

The third murder (Day 4. 23:00 ~ Day 5 03:00)

22:30 Alice, Maria topple boat.

23:30 ~ 00:15 Alice, Maria sit down on two bicycles standing next to each other near French windows for chat. Third bicycle near entrance. All three bicycles of Panorama Villa present.

Before 01:00 Sonobe, Maria go to bathroom, see each other in hallway. Both saw two bicycles next to each other downstairs.

01:20 ~ 01:25 Egami, Junji talk in hallway. Junji sees moving light near Happy Fish Villa (Bicycle light of the murderer? Optical illusion? Lie?) Both see two bicycles next to each other downstairs (unknown whether the one near the entrance had been there or not).

02:00 ~ 04:00 Egami, Kazuto have drink & talk in hall. Three bicycles.

'After that—in other words after the time period of the murder—
Reiko and Satomi met in the kitchen at five. At six, the doctor came down for a morning bath and Reiko started preparing breakfast. Presented in a time schedule like this it's not that confusing, actually,' observed Egami. 'That mysterious light Mr. Makihara saw makes a lot more sense as well, if you keep this schedule in mind. All three bicycles were at the house before a quarter past midnight and after two, but in the period in between, *one bicycle has no alibi*. And the time Mr. Makihara said he saw the light, was right in the middle of that period.'

We couldn't simply take Junji at his word, of course. He had no alibi either. It was clear that the murderer had used a bicycle because of the tyre marks on the *moai* map. The murderer could only have used it after Maria and I had gone to our rooms, so after a quarter past midnight. Suppose the murderer had hopped on a bicycle and left for Happy Fish Villa right after we'd gone up. A round trip would've taken an hour, plus another five minutes for the murder, so the killer could've made it back to Panorama Villa by twenty past one. Egami met Junji in the hallway at twenty past one, so perhaps Junji had only just returned from Happy Fish Villa. Then he'd cried out when Egami wasn't looking at the window. Pretending he'd seen something....

'Hmmm, I guess my own alibi doesn't hold either.'

Unfortunately, Egami was right. He might've been a real nocturnal animal, talking with people in the hallway or drinking alcohol in the hall in the middle of the night, but he had no alibi. Just as in Junji's case, it was possible that when the two met in the hallway, Egami had just returned from Happy Fish Villa.

We couldn't think of anything even as we looked at Maria's notes. I tried to change the subject again.

'Let's look at that map again, with the facing directions of the *moais*, which turned out to be so useful in our treasure hunt. Why was it lying there at that particular spot in the first place? It hadn't been there late that afternoon, but it was there the next morning. Earlier, we concluded the killer must've dropped it in the night, but why were they carrying it?'

Maria picked up the thread. 'What I don't understand is why that map still exists today. It means the murderer had kept it safe for three years. They certainly took good care of their stuff. I think it'd be much more natural to have thrown it away once the treasure was found.'

She was right. I didn't understand either why that thing had suddenly popped up now. Perhaps the murderer had some reason for carrying it, one we hadn't thought of yet.

'Having found the treasure, the killer should've wanted to burn the map and pull all the *moais* off the island, shouldn't they?' said Egami. 'The statues look like they're buried so deeply and firmly in the ground, you can't, in practice, pull them out or change the direction they're looking in. But a map is something you can simply throw away. By the way, remember that on the surface of the rock where the treasure had been hidden, there were a lot of marks as if it had been hit by something hard? They were probably marks made by the killer hitting the rock with a hammer or something. I think they tried to erase any traces of the treasure having been there in the first place. They hit the rock, but it wouldn't break, so they had to give up on that.'

'Perhaps,' I said, 'but why did they take such care of the map then?'

I didn't understand anything about it.

'There was something I don't understand about the place where Mr. Hirakawa was murdered.' This time it was Maria who had something to note. 'Pieces of the jigsaw puzzle had been scattered on the floor, all around his chair and the table, but why? The puzzle had already been half-finished when we saw it the day before, so why did someone break it in pieces?'

We'd already discussed that with Sonobe at the crime scene earlier. We told Maria that. The doctor had postulated the theory that Hirakawa had tried to leave a dying message written in blood on the jigsaw pieces (even though you couldn't write with blood on them because of the vinyl coating). The murderer noticed Hirakawa's attempt and quickly broke the puzzle into pieces. But there were some points that argued against that. Hirakawa's fingers, for example, had no blood on them, and if the murderer had been in such a panic, it's odd they hadn't given the victim a final blow to finish him off. In the end, we hadn't managed to work out why the puzzle had been broken up.

'I think the broken jigsaw puzzle was a dying message from Mr. Hirakawa.'

'But I just told you, you couldn't write in blood on either the front or the back of those pieces, and there were no traces of blood on any of Mr. Hirakawa's fingers,' I said.

'No, that's not what I meant. What I meant was that it was Mr. Hirakawa himself who broke up the jigsaw puzzle, and that the act of breaking it up is a dying message of its own.'

I didn't quite understand what she was trying to say. Maria caught my expression, and started to explain her theory in detail.

'I just called it a dying message, but there are all kinds of messages, aren't there? This won't be like Dr. Fell's Locked Room Lecture, but allow me to deliver Maria's Dying Message Lecture. In short, I think we can categorise dying messages into four types. Okay if I organise the messages not by *signifié* but only by *signifiant*? So by the *means* of communication, not the actual *contents* of the message.

'First is a message made up of letters or symbols. This is the one that appears most often in mystery fiction I think. It's when a person on the verge of death writes down something like "MUM" or "King" and then dies. Number two is the spoken word. When, in their dying breath, they say things like "Home" or "Samurai." Third is when objects are used, as when someone is holding sugar cubes or an hourglass in their hands. And number four is a message conveyed through an action. A good example would be Edward D. Hoch's *The Shattered Raven*, where a man on the verge of death can't speak, because he's been hit in the mouth by a bullet, and shatters a statuette of a raven instead. There's some overlap, but that's my categorisation for now. So what I meant was that perhaps Mr. Hirakawa's dying message was of the fourth category, a message conveyed by an action. Even if it's impossible to write on the front or the back of the pieces, even if Mr. Hirakawa had no blood on his fingers, he still could've left a dying message. If so, we'll need to figure out what that message was.'

'Thank you for the lecture.' I was impressed and surprised by the sudden speech. 'But we don't need a lecture on mystery fiction at a time like this, so you could've gone straight to the conclusion. What was Mr. Hirakawa trying to tell us by breaking apart a puzzle that was already half-finished? I'd like to know.'

Disappointingly, Maria hadn't actually thought about that. She suggested we think about it together. I started to think myself a fool for having listened to her dying message lecture.

'A broken puzzle. A puzzle lying in pieces. A broken Hokusai. Hoku. Sai.'

Egami started to think hard. But I felt we should give up on thinking about the dying message so seriously. There was no way we could solve that puzzle with logic alone.

'I have another question.' I tried to move the discussion somewhere else again. 'There was a storm the night of the first murders, so the killer couldn't get away from Panorama Villa afterwards. So where was the murder weapon, the rifle, hidden? The following day, Kazuto searched the house with Reiko as his witness, but he said he couldn't find the rifle. I don't understand how the murderer could've kept it hidden.'

'That's not a difficult problem.'

Maria appeared to have forgotten about her dying message and had moved to this topic, too.

'We didn't search the house right after we discovered the murders. Nobody had expected more deaths would follow and we even thought the rifle might've been thrown out of the window by the murderer. We should've searched the house then. The killer couldn't have left the house in the storm, so the rifle had to be hidden somewhere inside the house. Kazuto and Reiko only searched the house the following afternoon. The murderer could've done anything with it in the interim. It's quite possible they took the rifle out from some hiding place above the ceiling and then hid it in the forest or shrubberies nearby.'

'Ah.'

I shut up. There had been no mystery at all.

'It does bother me the murderer is still in possession of the rifle.'

To help ease Maria's anxiety, Egami said, in a lighter tone: 'We're not sure that they do still have the rifle. Perhaps this time, it really has been thrown into the sea.'

'No, they're still planning something.' I was of the opinion we shouldn't be overoptimistic. 'I was almost poisoned to death.'

'Poisoned to death? Oh, the pit viper.' Maria started drawing on the table again. 'That was creepy too. But it might not have been an actual attempt at killing you. Perhaps the snake had been milked of its venom and it was only used to threaten you.'

'Threaten me? Why should I be threatened?'

'A warning for Mr. Egami and you. Stop looking for the truth, stop thinking about the *moai* puzzle and stop digging into Hideto's death. They tried to scare the pair of impertinent amateur detectives, thinking you'd behave yourselves after that. We'd all better be careful, eh, Alice?'

'Yeah,' I said. Since last night, even opening the door of the bathroom has been absolutely terrifying. Of all the methods they could've chosen, they choose something as dirty as snakes....

'But why give me—no, Mr. Egami and me—such a warning? Today, we somehow managed to solve the *moai* puzzle, but we're still in the dark on all the other happenings. I don't think we're worth the warning.'

'Oh, don't sound so pathetic, saying you're not worth the warning.'

But it was the truth. Even Egami seemed to have no clue as to the identity of the murderer. It was only moments ago he proudly proclaimed that he couldn't work out who the murderer was, based solely on what we'd discovered up until then.

So why did the murderer hide a snake in our room?

'That locked room still bothers me, though. But Egami won't play along....,' sighed Maria.

'The locked room, eh?' Egami mumbled. 'There are many possibilities. In fact, there are so many I can't figure out which one is correct. I wonder in how many hundreds of ways similar locked rooms have been solved in detective fiction....'

'Mr. Egami, are you criticising detective fiction?' Maria asked in surprise. The club president of the Eito University Mystery Club remained silent for a while.

'Moving away from grim reality and talking about detective fiction, yes, a locked room is a sort of utopia within the genre. Even now, I remember the shivers I got when I first read Poe's *The Murders in the Rue Morgue*. But after that, with the hundreds of locked rooms you come across—some with fantastic solutions, some with bad solutions—the more I read, the more I started to forget about that very first sense of excitement I had. So many writers have opened the locked room again and again, like there's a revolving door. The locked room has become a dress-up doll. If you really love detective fiction, then it's alright to say: "Maybe we've had enough." What got us excited in the first place is the locked room itself, not some simple magic tricks. They should stop treating a loved one like some simple dress-up doll. I want to come across a simple, honest locked room again.'

'Don't you like the tricks and solutions of locked room mysteries?' asked Maria.

'Perhaps I like "locked rooms" better than "locked room tricks." How about a mystery story like this? A mystifying, baffling murder is committed inside a locked room. All the people who'd been close by stand there in blank surprise and fear, when finally a detective appears in front of them, and without a word, he starts boarding the place up. He turns to the group and says just: "Well, and off we go."…'

I understood what Egami was trying to say.

'Let's get back to reality. What are we going to do with our case?'

'So, are we going to board the room up and seal it forever?' asked Maria, dissatisfied.

'There's nothing exciting about our locked room. If we catch the murderer and ask them about it, they might just say: "Well, perhaps it was just a fluke?"'

Our discussion came to a stop.

We needed to find out who the murderer was. The murderer was undoubtedly on the island.

Who was it? We didn't know.

Not yet.

CHAPTER FIVE: SUICIDE PUZZLE

1

We ended our half-finished meeting on the investigation and headed for the scene of the third murder, Happy Fish Villa. We thought we might discover something if we examined the place again.

The first thing we did after we arrived was to pray in front of the artist's remains, which were lying on his bed. After that we became detectives again and started searching the room, being careful not to disturb the condition of the crime scene too much. The scattered pieces of the jigsaw puzzle were still on Maria's mind, it seemed, as she stood in thought looking at them while I paced up and down the room like a caged animal.

Egami tried the upper drawer of the desk in the back of the room.

'Anything there?' I peeked over his shoulder. There was only a small key inside, which turned out to be the key of the drawer he'd just opened. He tried the second and third drawers, but besides work notes, there were only single-player games like slide puzzles—famous ones by Sam Loyd—and a deck of well-thumbed playing cards. There was nothing that caught the eye. But I did think it was strange that the only drawer with a lock had been empty.

'I've seen enough. Let's go back.'

'Did you learn anything?' I asked, and Egami pretended to be annoyed. 'Stop pestering me.'

'Egami, Alice, look,' said Maria. She was pointing towards the window, out to sea. There was a rowing boat coming our way, and on it were Toshiyuki and Reiko. What business could they have at Happy Fish Villa, I wondered.

They didn't look too surprised to see us. Perhaps they'd even expected it. Without even asking what we were doing, Toshiyuki explained:

'Reiko wanted to see where Mr. Hirakawa passed away, so I brought her here.'

Reiko was holding a bunch of bougainvilleas. She explained that Hirakawa had loved the bright flowers, which she put in a vase from the kitchen, then prayed briefly at the artist's bedside. Toshiyuki and the three of us clasped our hands together.

'I wanted to bring my wife here, actually. I wanted her to see with her own eyes what had happened. But she said she wouldn't come to a horrible place like this. Reiko heard that and said she would come along instead. Would you like to see Mr. Hirakawa's face? He has a peaceful look.'

'No, please,' murmured Reiko. Perhaps she felt it was enough she'd offered the flowers.

'It's almost as if there's some link between the murders, with Mr. Hirakawa being killed right after Sumako, don't you think?'

Toshiyuki was looking at Sumako's picture as he spoke the words. Reiko simply said 'Yes' as she rubbed her left upper arm with her right hand.

'Could the fact that Mr. Hirakawa and Sumako used to be close have something to do with it?' asked Egami, point blank.

Turning to Reiko, Toshiyuki replied: 'I don't know how close those two really were. Sumako was hanging around this place all the time when she acted as his model three years ago... perhaps I could've phrased that better. It's the truth though, but perhaps we outsiders saw too much into it. What do you think, Reiko?'

'I don't think that something that happened three years ago could have anything to do with the murders now,' said Reiko, her eyes cast down to the floor. 'I admit they were pretty close, but I've the feeling it was just for a very short period of time and I just don't see how that could've become the motive for the murders now.' She looked up and addressed Toshiyuki: 'Was it Kazuto who suggested there was a connection?'

'Well, yes,' admitted Toshiyuki with some difficulty. 'Last night I had a talk with him. He's convinced there's a link. But he doesn't seem to have any particular reason for believing so. However....'

He looked pointedly at the portrait of Sumako on the wall in the back. 'That portrait does bother me. I thought at first it was just a beautiful painting. But now I look at it I can see Mr. Hirakawa put all of his passion for Sumako into his brush when he created this work. And the fact that it's hanging here and not in Panorama Villa, in a place very visible from the bed, makes me feel Mr. Hirakawa still had a soft spot for Sumako. Perhaps what happened three years ago is still casting its long shadow into the present.'

'Were you and your wife the only ones there when Kazuto told you this?' asked Reiko.

'Yes. Oh, I get it, you were wondering whether Junji was there as well? Don't worry. He was taking a bath at that moment. That's right, he didn't know about this part of Sumako's past, did he?'

'I don't think it's big enough to qualify as "a past," but I don't think he knows. And there's no need to tell him, either.'

'You're absolutely right. My wife and I don't talk about it either if he's close by. I only mentioned it now because I don't need to be so careful here.'

We listened in silence to the discussion of the two. Just now, we'd inferred that there might be a horrible truth behind Hideto's drowning three years ago, and that it was the root of the murders this year. And now a love affair of three years ago had entered the stage. How was that connected to it all?

I remembered Junji Makihara's face, right after we'd put Hirakawa on the bed yesterday. His eyes, as he looked at the portrait of his wife, were filled with a pale flame of hatred. Perhaps he did know about his wife, after all.

'We're going back now,' said Egami. Toshiyuki was partly facing Sumako's portrait, but then he turned back to us.

'We're going back as well. It only takes fifteen minutes by boat, so we'll be back first. We'll see you later.'

The five of us left Happy Fish Villa together. We watched Toshiyuki and Reiko go down the stone steps and then we got on our bicycles.

2

When we arrived at Panorama Villa, we found everyone in the hall. I felt the atmosphere was tense and my body stiffened. Reiko, whom we'd just seen at Happy Fish Villa, was the first to notice our return. When the others saw the expression on her face, they also looked up and turned to us.

'They're back now. Kazuto, if you have something you want to apologise for, now's the time.' Ryūichi scolded Kazuto, who was sitting in a rattan chair not facing our way, wearing a scowl on his face.

After a while, Egami asked: 'What's the matter?'

Ryūichi clearly didn't like what he was about to explain.

'I am terribly sorry. We just discovered that it was this fool who put the snake in your room.' He indicated his son with his chin. 'He says he pulled its fangs so it wasn't dangerous, but it was a stupid thing to do all the same. There's no excuse for it, but at least listen to what he has to tell you.'

Kazuto remained silent. Ryūichi yelled at him angrily. It was the first time I'd heard him raise his voice.

'How did you discover it was a prank of Kazuto's?' asked Egami, apparently more interested in that fact. Not knowing how to vent his anger, Ryūichi explained:

'Toshiyuki and Reiko caught him red-handed. After they returned in the boat, they saw him rustling around in the grass with a second yellow-spotted pit viper. Apparently, he'd knocked this one out with a stick and was busy pulling its fangs. I didn't know whether to be sorry for him or afraid of him when I heard the tale.'

'I was so surprised.' Reiko said as she rubbed her left shoulder. 'When we called out "So it was you, Kazuto," he jumped up in shock. We asked him why he was doing it and he threw the snake away and said: "I have the right to remain silent." He hasn't opened his mouth since.'

'If you don't talk, we'll have to consider you to be the murderer, Kazuto.' Toshiyuki, who was standing next to the table, said that as if to challenge him, but Kazuto only responded with: 'It wasn't me.'

'Then why were you doing that?' Toshiyuki had a very grave look on his face. 'To me, it seems perfectly obvious that you're the murderer and you wanted to scare off Mr. Egami and Alice from trying to solve the case. If there's some other reason, you'd better start talking.'

Egami asked Kazuto: 'Did you put the snake in our room last night?'

Kazuto merely replied 'Yes' and went silent again. If it had all been a simple prank, he would've reacted differently. The use of a term like 'the right to remain silent' meant he himself acknowledged his crime had been discovered. Was he really the murderer?

Perhaps he couldn't cope with all the eyes staring at him, because he suddenly stood up and, before anybody had time to stop him, quickly disappeared down the corridor from the hallway.

'Wait!'

By the time Ryūichi had realised what had happened and cried out, we could hear the loud bang of the back door closing. Someone sighed loudly.

'Alice, I'm really sorry.' Ryūichi bowed his head deeply. 'I really have no idea what's going on in his head. He might have some insignificant reason he finds hard to talk about. He's angry as well now, so if you could give my son a bit of time?'

I simply said 'Yes.' It felt as if I, too, was somehow responsible for Ryūichi's burst of anger and I didn't feel at ease. Egami was as calm as ever and Maria looked as if she was absolutely stunned.

'I think I've an idea of what's going on.'

It was Sonobe who suddenly spoke. This time everyone focused on him. From the context, he probably meant he knew why Kazuto had concealed a snake in our room. I wanted to know why.

'It was a prank that got out of hand. But there was a reason why he went that far. What he couldn't talk about, was his envy of young Alice here. Jealousy.'

'Jealousy…?'

I couldn't believe my ears. I had been expecting the most evil of intentions, but the doctor had used a mundane, almost banal word.

'Yes, that old green eyed monster!'

'But why should Kazuto be jealous of me? I'm the smallest fry around here.'

'It's not pleasant for Kazuto if I say all of this, but I guess it can't be helped. He adores Reiko and Maria. He didn't like how Maria and you were getting along so well. You remember how, after Mr. Hirakawa's death, we all talked about what we'd been doing the night before? He had a pained expression on his face while he was listening to your exploits, that you'd gone out rowing in the night together, had toppled the boat and swum back. And you also said that you'd spent the night talking together outside. He was jealous of that romantic night of yours. Perhaps he'd seen you from his room in the annex. Perhaps he'd also become frustrated at seeing you having fun swimming in the sea earlier. He can't swim at all, you know.'

I remembered two things. The morning after we'd caused the boat to capsize, Kazuto had behaved strangely at the breakfast table. Talking little, mumbling to the wall. That was the first. The second was when we'd gone out for the swim. I remembered that someone had been looking down at us from the first floor. Maria had suggested at the time that it was Kazuto, and perhaps it really had been him. He sure wasn't a straightforward guy.

'But that's odd, Doctor,' said Maria with an embarrassed expression. 'Why should Kazuto be jealous because of me? I overturned the boat with Alice. So what?'

'You think it's strange he was jealous because of you? No, it's very likely he did just that. Especially if it had to do with swimming. He has quite a complex about not being able to swim. The fact he's the only person who can't swim among us is even more depressing for him.'

'Actually, my wife can't really swim either,' noted Toshiyuki as he looked at Satomi.

I remembered two more things. Regarding Satomi not being able to swim, I recalled that she'd been sitting under a parasol the whole time Toshiyuki was swimming. Regarding Kazuto's complex about not being able to swim, I recalled that when I'd asked him whether he could surf, he'd looked very sullen.

'Anyway, I think that Kazuto isn't very happy with Alice here. But, deep down inside, he's ashamed he's being jealous about his own cousin. And when you consider that both Maria and you have such a splendid club senior with you…. That's why he harassed you in such a horrible way.'

'But it's just weird, to go all that way for me.' Maria looked embarrassed. *Don't get so embarrassed over this.*

'But this is nothing more than speculation on your part,' said Toshiyuki carefully but firmly. 'He might well have another reason for harassing them.'

There was the sound of the back door opening. Kazuto had returned.

'Have you cooled down? You're—,' Ryūichi started to say, but he had to swallow the rest of his sentence. Kazuto had returned to the hall holding a gun in his right hand.

'Kazuto!'

'You!'

Reiko and Ryūichi cried out and everyone gasped in shock. I also heard a cry escaping from my own mouth. I considered that this time the muzzle might very well be pointed at my chest, and I could feel the hairs at the back of my neck stand up and my body stiffen.

'I've kept this a secret the whole time. I got it together with the rifle. Compared to the rifle, it might be just a toy, but it's still a real Smith & Wesson. I tried it out two or three times, but I only had three shots left, so I've kept it as decoration. But now I'm showing it to you all. I don't know which of you stole my rifle and used it to kill the others, but I want you to take a very good look at what I'm holding in my hand. If you're planning to kill me because I'm the most popular target around here, I'd advise you to think again. I'm not so easy to get. If you come close, I'll shoot. It'd be legitimate self-defence, so I wouldn't hesitate to shoot to kill. Take a good look and keep it in mind.'

'Kazuto!' The veins on Ryūichi's temple seemed about to pop. 'You damn fool, give that toy to me this instant!'

Kazuto ignored him. The gun was now pointing at the floor, but his finger was on the trigger. Anything could happen, so it was best not to excite him. I didn't think he'd really shoot, but I also didn't know Kazuto well enough to be sure of that.

'I won't shoot now. I don't know who to shoot, even though the killer must be one of the few people here. Oh, how frustrating! But I'll be waiting for the killer.'

He turned around, and left as quickly as he'd arrived.

'The idiot….'

That was all Ryūichi could muster. He stood there with his hand to his forehead as if he had a headache. I felt sorry for him.

'I don't mind,' said Sonobe with a pipe in his mouth. 'That kid's always been fainthearted. "Don't treat me like a fool" was his pet peeve when he was still a child. He only said that whenever he was afraid of a stronger opponent, though. Even now, he's so scared he doesn't know what he's doing.'

'But that's why it's so dangerous,' said Reiko anxiously. 'I'd never have guessed he was hiding another weapon. With someone who's trembling in fear and who flies into a rage so easily in possession of a thing like that, who knows what can go wrong?'

Somebody coughed in displeasure. It was Junji, who was standing with his arms crossed.

'I don't think we should assume it's fear that made him act like that, simply because he yelled at us. If I'd come in here brandishing a pistol, you'd all turn white, wouldn't you?'

Sonobe frowned at that. He'd been surprised by Junji's remark.

'Do you mean to say that Kazuto was simply putting on a performance just now and that he might be the actual murderer behind all the killings?'

'Yes. Of course, I only wish to point out that we shouldn't forget that the possibility exists. Consider: he is the person most used to handling a rifle. Is it that strange I think that's a bit suspicious? But who could've guessed he also owned a pistol illegally? Doctor, up until now, we've assumed the missing rifle was the only firearm on the island, but now the pistol has popped up. Could it have been the weapon used in the murders?'

'No, quite impossible. Pistols and rifles leave completely different gunshot wounds. I can absolutely declare that that little thing couldn't have been the murder weapon.'

'But you know, considering how things are going, he might even have a machine gun stacked away somewhere. Perhaps the real murder weapon is among them.'

'No, he can't be holding any more large firearms,' Ryūichi declared decisively. 'When Kazuto first brought that rifle to the island, he carried it in a big and strangely shaped bag. To be honest, everyone wondered what it was at the time. He wouldn't tell. It was only after we'd arrived here that he opened the bag and out came the rifle. It was just that one rifle. So what I mean to say is that whether it was a rifle or a shotgun, he couldn't have brought a large firearm with him without us noticing something. That was the only time he brought a strange bag here to the island.'

'But perhaps somebody else brought a weapon?' persisted Junji.

'It's impossible to bring a bag like that along secretly. It stands out like a sore thumb. Nobody could've done that, not even Mr. Hirakawa.'

'Agreed,' said Sonobe as he packed tobacco in his pipe. 'A pistol is a different story, but you can't bring a rifle along secretly.'

'I'll go his room later and get the pistol. I'm sure he'll give it up when he's calmed down,' said Reiko, at which Junji snorted.

'What if you have Maria go along with you? She can stand in the shadows, negotiating with him through a megaphone.'

Maria put a hand to her forehead, hoping it would all be over soon.

3

After that ordeal, we had another late lunch. Kazuto remained cooped up in his room in the annex, so Reiko and Maria had to bring his lunch to him there. The fool was causing trouble for everyone.

'How is he?' asked Toshiyuki when the two returned, to which Maria shook her head as if it was hopeless.

'He didn't allow us inside. He told us to leave the food outside. He seemed to be sulking still.'

'He was just too embarrassed to show his face,' said Reiko, trying to defend him. 'I bet he's regretting it all right now. He did something really stupid.'

'Fool.'

There was a strange atmosphere at lunch. People talked calmly, as if none of the horrible events on the island had happened and as if Kazuto hadn't appeared with his gun. Toshiyuki explained in simple terms his newly discovered route for importing beef, while Reiko revealed a unique method her friend recently used to quit smoking. Sonobe talked about some misadventure he'd had while travelling in Germany, while Egami put forth his own observations on the psychology of people from Kyōto. It was the liveliest meal we'd had in the last couple of days. Before I even knew it, I found myself talking about the acoustics of the Ōsaka Symphony Hall.

After lunch, the Inukai couple watched television. To be precise, they switched the television on, but continued talking casually. After a while, I noticed something curious. Satomi had to suppress a yawn several times. I'd noticed during lunch as well.

'Do you mind if I go up for an afternoon nap?' she asked her husband. 'I feel a bit tired, with all that's happened.'

My suspicions were confirmed. She hadn't been getting enough sleep at night. But why? Was she out of sleeping pills? No. Although we hadn't been able to call the boat because the wireless transceiver had been destroyed, the couple's original plan had been to stay on the island until tomorrow anyway. She would've brought the necessary amount of medicine with her. She also should have had enough to spare her husband a few. So why hadn't she been getting enough sleep? There was only one answer. She hadn't been taking her medicine. She hadn't wanted to fall asleep at night. Was there something she needed to do at night? The question grew bigger and bigger in my mind.

'Shall we go out onto the terrace?' Maria asked me. I answered 'Yeah' absentmindedly, as I was still preoccupied by my growing suspicions. I followed Maria anyway. Egami was once again busy with the doctor tackling the jigsaw puzzle.

Junji was on the terrace. He was sitting on the sundeck, looking at the sea with both his legs spread out. His eyes were set on the faraway High Tide Cape. He called out to me.

'Did Mr. Egami really not see a light that night?'

He probably meant the light—presumably the light of a bicycle—he'd witnessed on the night Hirakawa was murdered. I could only answer as before. Egami wasn't doubting his testimony, but wasn't prepared to claim to have seen things he hadn't. Junji obviously felt quite frustrated by Egami's answer.

'Sorry, but he clearly said he hadn't seen it.'

'I see. But I really did see that light. That was the murderer. I shudder when I think about it. You know the feeling, right? It happened to me once before. I was in middle school. I was cramming the night before an exam, and when I looked up the light in a room in the apartment building across from my room went out. It was around one o'clock at night. I guessed the person in that room had stayed up late and was now going to bed. I decided to go to bed as well and closed my books. And there it was, the next day, in the late edition of the newspaper. The occupant of that room—a single man—had committed suicide. What I'd witnessed, was the moment just before he'd hanged himself, when he switched off the light. I shall never forget the horror that welled up from inside me when I realised that.'

Junji stared out to sea with an expression that seemed to be lamenting everything on this earth. He was just an empty shell, his mind gone.

Was he experiencing a sense of uncertainty and fear of life, as a man who'd just been robbed of his wife? Or was it something quite different: the lethargic feeling which only comes to a man who's robbed another person of their life…?

His mouth was slightly open and he was murmuring something. I noticed his eyes were shining with tears.

On this island abundant with sun and wind, the tragedy continued to unfold slowly. Nobody could stop it from moving inexorably towards its conclusion. And I felt we were almost there.

4

A gunshot rang out under the blue sky.

That a gunshot would be fired on this day, at this time, was something which must have been decided long, long ago.

Another gunshot.

Something within me had been hopelessly shattered into pieces.

5

The annex.

We stood there bewildered, looking down at the body of a young man lying across the desk. It was Kazuto Arima who had drawn his last breath sitting in the chair.

His right arm was lying across the desk, while his left arm was dangling loosely by his side. Blood had flowed from the black hole in his temple and over his shoulder to his chest. It was already starting to dry. On the desk was the pistol, which appeared to have fallen from his right hand, and a piece of paper. A familiar-looking rifle was leaning against the side of the desk and the faint smell of gunpowder was still hanging in the room.

'I can't believe it.'

Ryūichi held his head in his hands and sat down on the bed. Reiko staggered and held herself up against the wall, and Maria ran over to her and held Reiko's upper arm. Reiko said she was okay and put her hand on Maria's shoulder.

Kazuto's death was completely different from the earlier ones. This time the weapon was present. One pistol and one rifle. Two weapons for one death. Too many weapons. As to which of them had been used to blow Kazuto's brains out, I couldn't tell just from looking. But the moment I saw the scene, I imagined that Kazuto had shot himself in the head and fallen over the desk, after which the pistol had dropped from his hand onto the desk.

'He shot himself with the pistol,' Sonobe said after a quick look at the wound. As I'd suspected. If you wanted to use a rifle for suicide, you'd need to pull the trigger with your toes, but Kazuto was wearing his shoes and seated neatly in the chair.

Egami bent down to look at the pistol on the desk and said simply: 'It smells.' He took a look at the piece of paper near Kazuto's hand. His eyes scanned the paper quickly and he slowly began to read the contents out loud.

I, Kazuto Arima, will end my own life to atone for the sins that I have committed. Kango Makihara, Sumako Makihara and Itaru Hirakawa, were all killed by me. You can hate and curse me for having committed the most vile of human deeds so many times.

I am a murderer who cannot hope for even a sliver of sympathy or compassion. But I ask you to bear with me and continue reading this terrible tale of mine.

The three people I have mentioned are not the only poor souls who have died by my hand. There is one more person whom I have murdered. The fact that that person was my very own brother causes me so much pain, my fingers start to tremble as I type this letter.

The death of my brother three years ago was not an accident, but murder. As a deplorable murderer, I have lived the last three years up until now. And the act of trying to protect myself has resulted in a nightmare where I killed three more people.

I will only write briefly about how I came to commit such a horrible act.

My brother was superior to me in all respects and this had planted and fed a feeling of inferiority within me. Three years ago, when I saw how happy he was to spend the summer with his fiancée on this island, my hatred started to rise like mercury in the middle of summer. And finally, my hatred reached a critical point. He told me he had solved our grandfather's puzzle and had come to ask me to help him dig the diamonds up. I will move on to the conclusion. His solution was correct and we succeeded in getting our hands on the treasure. And that was the moment. Something in my head snapped and before I had even realised, I had kicked him down and was pushing his struggling head down in the water. My brother and I were matched in strength. But because I had caught him by surprise, he did not manage to fight back against me, I who had turned utterly mad. I can't remember why I became like that. After it was over, I stood there dazed. Had I really hated my brother that much?

I will hurry to the end. My crime had been witnessed by Hirakawa and Sumako, who had been enjoying a secret meeting in the night. They stole the diamonds from me, promised me they would keep their mouths shut and helped me move the body to a completely different spot. But this year, Hirakawa came here to ask me for some more money. I felt both fear and anger when he told me to go and ask my father for money. I decided I couldn't leave any witnesses alive in this world and killed the two of them. Uncle Kango just happened to be with Sumako at the time and unfortunately became another of my victims. I had nothing against him. I have no words of atonement, I can only shudder at my own sins.

The evidence is in the drawer of the desk, so please keep it safe.
I will bring the curtain down myself.
Everybody, farewell.
Dad, please forgive me if you can.

Kazuto Arima.

After Egami had finished reading, an excruciating silence took over. He stood still for a moment holding Kazuto's suicide note in his hands, but then gently passed it over to Ryūichi. Crushed by the shock, the father couldn't even bring himself to read the note himself.

'What...do you think?'

Egami asked nobody in particular. It was Toshiyuki who managed to come up with a reply.

'It's a complete surprise. How terrible...It's a tragedy, but it seems everything has come to an end now.'

Yes, everything seemed to have come to an end. But I was still not satisfied. It wasn't that Kazuto's suicide note contained an unreasonable tale. It wasn't that I didn't believe he'd been capable of such a horrible deed. It just felt as if the words "The End" had suddenly appeared in the middle of a film. If appearing in front of us a while ago, swinging a pistol around and crying out that anybody who dared could come straight at him... if all of that had been just an act, okay. But that doesn't square with him saying it was all over and then shooting himself in the head only two hours later. Wasn't this ending too sudden? There was nobody who'd been especially suspicious of Kazuto as the murderer. There was also nobody else who was suspected of being the murderer. If he'd made it this far as a successful murderer, why give up so easily and commit suicide? Was it his conscience at work? I wasn't sure I was satisfied with that explanation.

'Could Kazuto really have murdered four people? I don't believe it....'

Maria's eyes looked unfocused as she muttered that. I understood what she was trying to say. But that could only be described as a thought based on weak evidence. It had certainly been physically possible for him to have committed the crimes. In my mind, I rejected Maria's words.

'This note is strange.'

Everybody looked at Ryūichi after he spoke those words.

'I don't believe it. Even his name at the end is typed with a word processor. No matter how much his bad writing might've bothered him, don't you think he'd at least write his name by hand at the end of his suicide note?'

'I agree,' replied Egami immediately. 'I also find that suspicious. There's no sign of any handwriting there, so there's no evidence at all that Kazuto wrote—or, rather typed—the note.'

Maria's eyebrows quivered.

'So there's a possibility somebody else besides Kazuto typed that note? If so, then that means Kazuto didn't commit suicide, and that, just like Sumako and the others, he was murdered....'

'Wa—wait.' Toshiyuki's expression darkened. 'Maria, please don't just say whatever pops up into your mind. This might be rude, but

Kazuto had a bit of a vain side to him. I think it's quite possible that he disliked his own bad writing and used a word processor to write his name, even in the moments before his death. There's a suicide note here and the rifle, too. I think you'd need something more convincing if you're going to say he was murdered.'

'I agree,' added Junji, who was leaning against the wall with one hand in his pocket. 'What he did a while ago in the hall was nothing more than a desperate performance. I think it all fits. His suicide note might've been a bit brief, but the contents are convincing.'

'We'd better not be too hasty jumping to conclusions,' said Sonobe sharply. 'If this is murder, then this note might've been written by the murderer and the rifle might've been brought here by the murderer who'd hidden it somewhere. We can't say for sure either way for the time being, so let's consider everything more carefully.'

After peering at Kazuto's right hand, Egami announced: 'I smell gunpowder.' Another point in favour of the Suicide Theory. He took a mechanical pen from the pencil holder with his left hand and used that to bring the pistol up to eye level. With a handkerchief in his right hand, he checked the magazine.

'Still one shot left. Kazuto told us earlier he had three shots left, so if that was true, two shots should've been fired. Now I think about it, I think I did hear two shots.'

The whereabouts of one bullet were obvious. It was inside Kazuto's skull. I looked around to see where the other shot had gone and soon found it.

'I think it's over there.'

On the wall to the right of the desk, about two metres away, hung a painting—no, a completed jigsaw puzzle. I pointed to the black hole in the centre of it. It was a scene of Candle Rock and the Twin Rocks, as seen from the observation platform. From the style, I gathered the puzzle was based on a painting by Hirakawa. Hirakawa had asked Kazuto to make a jigsaw puzzle of his painting of Low Tide Cape in the morning sun when it was finished. The puzzle here was probably one they'd made earlier.

One scenario came into my mind. If Kazuto's death was a suicide, then it might've happened as follows. First he took out the rifle he'd hidden and put it against the side of the desk. After he'd finished typing out his suicide note on the word processor, he picked up the pistol. It was then that his eye caught the Hirakawa painting hanging on the wall to the right. It was a painting by a man he hated so much he'd murdered him, of a place that held unpleasant memories for him.

It could've been either hatred or fear that made him point the pistol at the painting and pull the trigger. After making a hole in the centre of the painting, he put the pistol to his temple and put an end to his own life. I was satisfied by this scenario I'd constructed in my own mind.

'Perhaps he hated this painting?' Sonobe muttered as he looked at it. He'd probably envisaged the same scenario as I had. He nodded slightly in agreement with himself.

'We'd better take a look in the desk drawer,' said Toshiyuki loudly. 'Didn't the note at the end say evidence was kept there? We'd better see what it is.'

'Ah, that's right.'

Sonobe clapped his hands together and opened the top drawer. I saw that inside were a pocket book entitled *Politics as a Vocation* and what appeared to be a diary carrying the title *Happy Fish Villa Diary*. Sonobe reached out, not for the pocket book, but for the diary. Everyone had their eyes set on the diary in his hands, expecting it to contain the truth behind the whole case.

Sonobe opened the leather cover and two pieces of paper, folded in four, fell out from between the pages, drifted through the air and landed on the floor. Several pairs of eyes followed their fall.

'What's this?'

The doctor crouched down, picked up the pieces of paper, and unfolded them. A deep frown appeared in his brow for an instant and I could hear him growl.

'What is it, Doctor? Show all of us,' said Toshiyuki impatiently. Sonobe clasped the diary beneath his armpit and held one piece of paper up in each of his hands, turning them left and right for everyone to see.

'It's the *moai* map!' cried Toshiyuki, moving closer. 'This is a follow-up to the map Alice picked up from the roadside, isn't it? Yes, it is.'

He was right. The two pieces of papers were the continuation of my map with the twenty-five arrows. On one of the pieces of papers, the twenty-five symbols had been connected by lines. On the other was a sketch of eight surfaces that had been pieced together to form the figure of the Candle Rock. To the side of it, the words "Low tide?" had been scribbled. This was without a doubt a recreation of the process we'd gone through when we solved the puzzle.

'Isn't this figure the Candle Rock? That means…the treasure is hidden on Candle Rock?' said Toshiyuki, with even more excitement.

As I listened to him, I recalled that Egami, Maria and I had decided to keep it a secret that we'd already solved the puzzle ourselves, had found the hiding place of the treasure and had discovered the diamonds had already been taken by someone.

'Yes, it has to be,' said Junji, after which Reiko, who was standing by the window, added in a soft voice:

'That's Hideto's writing....'

Ryūichi got up from the bed.

'You're sure he wrote this?'

The room fell into confusion. Convincing evidence that Hideto had been the first person to solve the *moai* puzzle had now surfaced and it was also evidence that supported what had been written in Kazuto's suicide note. But now was not the time to get all excited, I wanted to say. Shouldn't we be looking at the contents of the diary?

'Doctor, what's written in the diary?'

Urged by Egami, Sonobe put the pieces of paper down on the desk and turned the pages of the diary over. Egami, Toshiyuki and I stood behind him and peeked inside the diary. I saw the following written on the pages.

July 30 (Tuesday) – Clear and sunny
No guests today either.
Only words like 'Okay' and 'Yes' made their way out of my mouth once or twice. All day making sketches of the sea outside. No compositions, just the wide azure. Learned that there is such a thing as an invigorating feeling of fatigue.

It was indeed a diary. The title it bore was probably a pun on Kafū Nagai's *Begonia House Diary*. The diary also contained the following passage.

August 5 (Monday) – Clear
Mr. Kango and Ms. Sumako visited my abode. My first guests in three days. Perhaps my mouth had been wanting for company. Discussed all sorts of trivial matters. Might have perplexed my two guests. Mr. Kango had an abundance of tales to share. Miss Sumako is looking more and more charming. Thanks to her, this has been a good day.

The line "Miss Sumako is looking more and more charming" attracted my eye. Sonobe looked the page over quickly over and turned to another. As the title suggested, this diary was only used while the artist was staying here on the island. On the ninth of August, it only said "Tomorrow, return to the normal world" and then the date jumped to July 28, 1986.

'1986. Three years ago....' Toshiyuki mumbled.

Sonobe's hands stopped and he now read each page carefully before he turned them over. For example, July 31.

July 31 (Thursday) – Clear
Typhoon avoided.
Sumako visited my abode. Painted for five hours with some pauses. Both of us were tired. Had some tea, talked about puzzles and Hideto and his fiancée.

The word "Sumako" caught my eye. Not "Miss Sumako" any more, but plain "Sumako." Their relationship, or at least the painter's feelings towards her, had changed. The speed at which Sonobe turned the pages had slowed down.

August 1 (Friday) – Clear and sunny
Painting Sumako.
Hideto and his fiancée visited. Four of us had a talk. Starting to feel even younger.

This time it was "Starting to feel even younger" that asked for attention. Even before he'd had a talk with the young couple who'd made him feel younger, there'd already been something that had made him feel like that. I imagined that he and Sumako had started a romantic affair. This diary of a man who had been a firm believer of "living well," but who had also been a practical person, was short and simple, but it was possible to read between the lines.

August 2 (Saturday) – Cloudy, afterwards clear
Sumako's painting is coming together splendidly. Can start on finishing it, save for the background. Perhaps should reconsider being a landscape painter.
I'm grateful to Sumako.
These days have been so pleasant, as if I were a baby floating in amniotic fluids.

The artist had been in a good mood.

August 3 (Sunday) – As clear and sunny as can be
Spent whole day with Sumako.
Mr. Arima had invited me over to stay for a night, but I made up some nonsense reason and asked Sumako to politely decline for me. I don't know why. Perhaps I don't feel at ease facing Mr. Kango. Both of them are crazy about fishing.
Sumako left Happy Fish Villa past ten thirty. Slightly worried about her journey back.

These short, but telling entries continued. We were caught up completely in following the artist's letters in blue ink, and kept on reading, ignoring the others who were also curious as to what was written in this diary.
And then came the fourth of August.
'The day Hideto died,' said Sonobe and he held the diary up so we could all take a good look at the page.
I could tell the writer was in shock from how much more he had written than usual, the change in style and the chaotic handwriting.

August 4 (Monday) – Clear
To turn your back on society and live following your whims, with no other purpose in life than not having a purpose. If that is a sin by itself, then I was born a sinner. By now, I have learnt not to mind the frightful word "sin" any more and have even grown fond of it.
Tonight I was given the promise that my way of life will be safeguarded. Even though my chest feels as heavy as lead, my arms and legs feel light as feathers. I do not know how I will feel when I wake up tomorrow morning, but there is nothing more I can do now the act has been done.
What are Sumako and Kazuto thinking as this night is passing by? I can feel them holding their breath, trying to endure the night, from across the cliff on the other side of the sea. We need to sleep this night. Even if it doesn't want to, time will pass by and eventually change into a usual day.
I am tired. I think I'll sleep even better than usual. Oh, accomplices, let's watch this night pass by soon. I will go to bed first.
I am really sorry for Hideto. What found its way to this world in exchange for your life, will be used for the purposeless life of this man. I will pay for this sin in the underworld.

I will keep your maps as long as I live with me, as proof of your victory, as proof of our sin. But I will have to lock my desk drawer from now on.

Tomorrow will be a sad day. Will I be able to live through it when I wake up? I hope so.

Now I will sleep.

Those who will be sad tomorrow, I hope at least tonight, you will sleep peacefully.

6

Nobody said anything after we'd finished reading. It was abnormal. Why had he penned such a crazy entry right after witnessing a murder, blackmailing the murderer for hush money, helping the murderer take care of the body and coming back home? And why hadn't he destroyed this writing afterwards, which obviously had been written on the spur of the moment? Did he think that by putting his sins down in this diary, he had sealed it away?

'Do you think this was really written by Mr. Hirakawa?'

Sonobe nodded in response to Egami's question.

'Without a doubt. This is his handwriting. We'll know for sure once the police have analysed it. While it doesn't confirm all of what was written in Kazuto's suicide note, it does appear that their stories roughly match.'

He was about to pass the diary around, when Egami stopped him.

'Excuse me, but I think there's more after that entry?'

Sonobe turned the page.

'Yes indeed. He wrote on without missing a day. But the following day it only says "A sad day" and the day after that only has "Leaving the island tomorrow."'

'Let me read all of that later. But for now, I want to see what was written *this* year, the day before yesterday.'

'Hmm, the day before yesterday? This is it.'

August 4 (Friday) – Clear

With fear I read what I wrote in this diary that night three years ago. It is the first time I've read it. No matter how much I try to forget, it's a past that won't fade away. I took the three maps—proof of our sin—out of their holding place. Setting Mr. Kango's death aside, I can't help but feel—even if it's based on nothing—that Sumako's cruel death was the result of our sin that night. Our sin rose up from the past and attacked her. No, that can't be. The poor thing was simply a victim of Mr. Kango. I shed no tears, but I feel pity for her.

Living well.

Revenge for reality.

Young Egami talked about that and it was uncanny. It felt as though he was not talking about me, but about himself.

The wind is calm tonight. Silence.

A boat is out in the moonlit bay. Perhaps a little boat trip, but I don't see anyone.

Past midnight.

The third anniversary of my crime has passed.

That was the artist's final entry. How long after he'd written that had he been robbed of his life? Right after? Nobody knows in advance when death will take them away. This solemn fact became all the more clear to me while reading this diary of the deceased.

'Three maps. So there were three of them.' Egami mumbled feverishly.

There had been three maps in total. Two of them were here, and the other map I'd picked up from the roadside. It added up.

'Have you finished?' asked Sonobe of Egami. He then passed the *Happy Fish Villa Diary* to the others.

'Of the three maps, Alice picked one up....'

While the diary passed from one hand to another, Egami stood still, not moving a single muscle. But I was the only one who thought he was behaving strangely.

'This is material evidence.' I heard Toshiyuki say from my right. 'This was without a doubt written by Mr. Hirakawa. And it contains a vital piece of information. We now know the murder was committed after midnight.'

'My poor father-in-law,' said Junji from my left. 'Getting involved with all of this was just bad luck.'

'But I still can't believe it.' Satomi's voice came from behind me. 'To think that Kazuto would do something like that.'

'The tyre marks....' Egami was mumbling. 'But what could that...?'

'And I can't even begin to understand what went on in Mr. Hirakawa's mind,' muttered Maria from somewhere. 'What was he thinking?'

Reiko's voice came from the same direction. 'But now Hideto, Hideto might be able to find some peace....'

'There were two bicycles.' Egami was looking up at the ceiling. 'Before one o'clock and around twenty past....'

'How did he get rid of the diamonds?' asked Junji of Toshiyuki. 'Could he have known some route to get money for them?'

'Probably,' replied Toshiyuki. 'They probably beat the price down and now he'd gone through all of his money.'

'And that's why he did it again,' said Satomi in a subdued voice. 'That's why he asked Kazuto for money again.'

'Kazuto.' Ryūichi was sitting on the bed. 'Hideto....'

'There's still a lot we don't know,' said Sonobe to nobody in particular. 'But the details will become clear once the authorities start their investigation.'

'This is horrible.' Junji's voice. 'It'll be all over the news.'

Egami walked over to the desk and started going over Kazuto's typewritten suicide note again.

'It's my father's fault,' said Ryūichi painfully. 'That puzzle is what brought forth this tragedy.'

'No, it was Kazuto's fault.' Maria's voice trembled. 'It's all Kazuto's fault. He's the most horrible person in all of this.'

'Stop it,' said Reiko softly. 'Let's stop talking like this.'

Egami put the suicide note down, walked over to the wall and peered at the bullet hole in the jigsaw puzzle.

'He must have been suffering a lot,' said Sonobe to someone. 'Too much tension and anyone can snap suddenly.'

'Still, his suicide came out of nowhere,' answered somebody.

'I was so surprised when I came here,' said a male voice.

'But we're all safe now.' Somebody's voice.

'So it's over now?' Somebody's voice.

'Yes.' Somebody's voice.

'No.'

Egami's voice hushed all the other voices in the room. Everyone looked at him standing by the wall, wondering what he meant.

'No. It's not over yet.'

Several seconds passed, during which everyone remained silent. Finally, Sonobe stepped up as representative of us all and asked: 'What isn't over yet?'

Egami didn't hesitate with his answer.

'The murder case. This case hasn't been solved yet.'

'Nonsense.' Junji raised his voice angrily. 'The murderer left us a suicide note, the murder weapons and the diary and maps as material evidence. Everything is here. Right in front of your eyes. What have you been listening to? What have you been looking at to arrive at such conclusion?'

'This.'

Egami pointed at the bullet hole in the centre of the puzzle hanging from the wall. Everyone's eyes followed the movement of his finger and were pulled into that black hole.

'We already saw that. Kazuto put a bullet in that painting he hated, right before he committed suicide. Have you any problems with that?'

'There is one problem.'

Egami asked Junji to come over to the wall. Because their eyes met, Sonobe was asked over as well. We couldn't all peek inside the hole at the same time, so the others, including me, started to focus on what was being said.

'This hole here was without a doubt made when a bullet was shot from the pistol. Can you see the bullet buried in the wall deep inside the hole? Then look at that, there, to the upper-right of the hole. There's blood there. It's blood spatter which occurred when Kazuto shot himself through the head. It almost coincides with the bullet hole. Now look at the lower-left of that blood stain. *Is the edge of the bloodstain going inside the round bullet hole? Is there blood inside the bullet hole? If not, then there's something wrong.*'

The two didn't answer for a while, then Sonobe raised his head and told Egami his observations.

'No, it's not like that. It's the other way around. *The edge of the bloodstain is missing a part because of the round bullet hole*. A part of the bloodstain was blown away by the bullet. Only a little, but still....'

'Mr. Makihara, your opinion?'

Junji looked up at the question.

'He's right. The bloodstain is missing a little part on the lower-left.'

'Can I take a look too?'

Having realised the importance of this fact, Toshiyuki hurried to the painting. I followed. What the others had said was true.

'You're right. But it should be the other way around. The bullet shouldn't have blown a part of the bloodstain away: blood should have gone inside the bullet hole instead! So it means that the bloodstain on the painting was made by the first shot, and a second bullet was fired at the painting afterwards. That's bad.'

'It isn't a question of good or bad, Mr. Inukai,' replied Egami. 'It's a decisive contradiction. The sequence of the bullet hole and the bloodstain occurred precisely as you just said. *First a bullet was shot into Kazuto's head. Blood spattered on the painting. Then there was a second shot at the painting after that.* Which means that after Kazuto died, someone else shot at the painting. Who could that person have been? Who would've done that, and for what purpose? Even if we don't know the identity of that person, one thing is clear: they are the one responsible for the murder of Kazuto and all the other murders on the island.'

'Kazuto was murdered? You mean somebody killed him?' asked Satomi in utter confusion. Nobody wanted to believe it, but Egami didn't hold back from calmly pointing out the truth.

'Is there any other way to look at these facts? Suppose that Kazuto did commit suicide. And suppose that at that time, someone else had been with him here in this room. Kazuto leans the rifle against the side of the table, puts his suicide note on the desk—or types it out then—pulls his pistol out and shoots himself. Then our witness picks up the pistol that's fallen from Kazuto's right hand and—without any reason, without any reason at all—they shoot at the painting, place the pistol down and leave the scene. I can't believe such a thing happened.'

'Hold it,' said Junji. 'I agree it's hard to imagine such a person was here. But it still could've been suicide. Kazuto shot himself. And as he was dying, that cursed painting caught his eye. With his last ounce of strength, he might've shot the painting.'

'Haven't you been listening?' said Sonobe 'What did I say? Kazuto died instantly.'

Junji realised his mistake and fell silent. But then Toshiyuki started to press Egami.

'But there are still some strange parts in your theory. Okay, let's suppose that Kazuto's death was murder. The murderer shoots Kazuto. They then quickly set out the rifle, suicide note and diary and then, for no apparent reason, shoot the painting. Do you agree? The murderer would have no reason to shoot the painting.'

Egami remained composed and started to explain:

'I think that scenario is more convincing. The murderer had a reason, a justification for shooting at the painting on the wall. This is only conjecture, but I've thought of a very rational reason. But allow me to rephrase myself: *it was necessary for the murderer to shoot a second time*. The target itself didn't matter. It could've been the painting on the wall, the floor, the ceiling, anywhere.'

'Why?' asked Toshiyuki:

'It was necessary to pick Kazuto's right hand up, make him hold the pistol and fire it once. *If they didn't, no gunshot residue would be left on Kazuto's hand.* The murderer figured that, once the police investigation started, they would check that out.'

'Gunshot residue? What's that?'

'But you should know about that. I explained this in front of all of you.'

Egami went over the explanation he'd given after Kango and Sumako had been murdered.

'I told all of you this earlier, so everybody here should be aware of what gunshot residue is. So to make Kazuto's murder look like suicide, the killer had needed to leave gunshot residue on his hand. That's why there was a second shot. It didn't matter what was shot. Mr. Hirakawa's painting was probably chosen because they hoped we'd come up with some story that, in his last moments, Kazuto shot at the painting he hated so much.'

Ryūichi's hoarse voice overlapped with the last of Egami's words.

'So, who...killed Kazuto?'

7

I shall omit the unnecessary details of what happened next. By which I mean I'll just provide a simple summary of the investigation into each of our alibis which we started after we had all moved back to the hall.

To start with the conclusion: nobody was in possession of an ironclad alibi at the time the shot that took Kazuto Arima's life rang out. That was odd. Unlike the previous murders, this crime had been committed in the afternoon, around twenty past five. It wasn't strange that at that time, some of us were resting in our rooms or out on a stroll. What was odd was the coincidence that *all* of us had happened to have been alone then. I was at the beach. Egami was in our room. Maria was doing her laundry. Ryūichi was—.

Nobody had an alibi.

Nobody even saw anyone leaving the crime scene.

Perhaps that wasn't such a coincidence. That time period, late afternoon, was when we would scatter most. Also, because the window of the annex had not been locked, the murderer could've escaped the crime scene through the window and easily hidden themselves in the back of Panorama Villa or behind the trees nearby. Perhaps the plan had been to come out from their hiding place during the chaos when everybody came running there because of the sound of gunshots.

Whether they were meditating or climbing trees, it was all the same. I repeat: nobody had an alibi.

'This has become rather unpleasant,' said Toshiyuki, distressed after everyone had finished competing over how little of an alibi they had. Actually, it had been unpleasant for several days now. The pose of his index and middle finger indicated subconsciously that he wanted a cigarette, having failed to give up smoking. Perhaps it had only just registered that Kazuto, who'd shared his cigarettes several times before, was no longer there.

'How about these?'

Junji held out his late wife's menthol cigarettes. Toshiyuki declined with 'Oh, no, I'm all right,' so Junji put one in his own mouth and lit it.

Sonobe had a pipe in his hand and was seated deep in a rattan chair when he started to speak:

'We know the rough outline of what happened on this island three years ago. A horrible murder and blackmail. By way of proof, we found the diary and more. The problem is how these events connect to the murders that have happened now. Is it revenge for Hideto's murder? Or is it about the money that flowed between Mr. Hirakawa and Kazuto? Or is there something else beyond that? We don't know.

'And there's another problem. The murderer knew about Mr. Hirakawa's diary and therefore about the truth of what happened three years ago. How did the murderer sniff out the secret these three were desperate to keep hidden? That's what I want to know.'

The doctor stopped rocking his pipe left and right, and looked at Egami who was sitting far away.

'Mr. Egami. Why have you been so silent all this time? Don't leave me to lead the discussion. You're so much better at it.'

Egami showed no reaction at all. Sonobe's expression hardened. Perhaps he wasn't pleased at being ignored. Egami was looking out through the window in silence with a distressed expression, lost in deep thought.

'Mr. Egami...?' Maria weakly called out to him.

Egami gave a slight nod.

Beyond the windows facing east, I could see that night had already arrived on the island. If this hall had also had windows to the west, we perhaps could have caught a glimpse of light showing just above the horizon.

'You're tired.' Sonobe interpreted Egami's mood as such. 'How about taking a rest in your room?'

'I will,' replied Egami, but then he turned to Reiko and Satomi.

'There's something I want to ask you. On the night Mr. Hirakawa was murdered, you met in the kitchen at five o'clock in the morning. Did you perhaps look outside through the windows in the hall then? If you did, I'd like to know if all three bicycles were there or not.'

While they didn't understand the meaning of the question, the two confirmed that all three bicycles had been there. Another of Egami's impenetrable questions was addressed at Reiko and Sonobe. Whether they had looked outside through the hall at six o'clock in the morning, and if so, how many bicycles had there been standing there then? Both of them answered all three bicycles had been there.

'So they were all there.'

'Oh, but how about dinner? I'll start on it now. How about going to sleep after dinner?' Reiko said to Egami, who was getting up.

'Thank you, but I don't feel like eating now. I'll eat later. I'm terribly sorry, but if you could leave a little for me....'

From that point Egami's words became indistinct and I couldn't hear the end of his sentence. To me, it seemed his mind wasn't with us anymore.

'I see. Well then, please come down later for your dinner.'

'Thank you.'

Egami thanked her again and bowed his head slightly. I felt I needed to say something to him, but I didn't manage to get the words out of my mouth. I didn't know what to say. As I was looking at the back of his silent figure about to disappear up the stairs, Egami turned round to me.

'Alice.'

I looked up.

'Come to our room later.'

CHALLENGE TO THE READER

Perhaps you thought you knew who the murderer was soon after the story started? There might also be people who made up their minds a third of the way into the story, or perhaps right at the midpoint. Others might only have succeeded in identifying the murderer a little while ago, or maybe only moments ago.

It is most likely that the latter arrived at the correct answer.

I, the author, inform you that Jirō Egami has only just now realised who the murderer is, based on the same facts made known to you, the reader. But I hereby also challenge you. Can you identify the murderer, not based on instinct, but on logical reasoning? Even if you don't manage to find the answers to all of the mysterious events that have occurred, you should be able to work out who the murderer is.

This is my puzzle.

Please bring order to this cosmos by your own hands.

CHAPTER SIX: JIGSAW PUZZLE

1

'Alice, come to our room later.'

I returned to our room at nine o'clock as Egami had requested. The rest remained downstairs.

He was sitting on his bed, leaning against the wall. As I entered the room he turned to me and said slowly:

'Alice, I've something I want you to listen to. About what happened on this island, of course.... If there's anything you think is wrong with what I tell you, I want you to ask me questions about that then. I think I've at last worked out the identity of the person behind the murders. I've been going over my reasoning in my head and I think I'm satisfied. Now I want you to check it. Will you do that for me?'

'Of course, you don't need to make a formal request.' I wasn't sure what to think, being asked something that serious at such short notice. 'My mind is at your disposal. Don't have much confidence in its usefulness though.'

'Sit down.'

I sat down on the opposite bed, but not before locking the door. Not because I was afraid that the murderer would suddenly barge in, but more as a sort of charm to cut us off from the outer world. That was all there was to it.

'Where shall I start?' Egami's way of talking was strangely calming. I felt the tension ebb away from my shoulders.

'After reading Mr. Hirakawa's diary, something became clear to me. And when I followed a line of reasoning based on what I'd read, I realised that only one person fulfilled all the conditions to be the murderer. The diary entry which got me thinking was the one he wrote on the night he was murdered, the fourth of August. He wrote about "living well" and that was indeed something we'd talked about with him in Happy Fish Villa that afternoon. There was also a part about a boat floating in the bay that night. Because of those facts, we know that the date of the entry was correct and that the writer was indeed Mr. Hirakawa himself. Nothing much had happened to him during the day and, as usual, he wrote the entry at night. He'd started to think about what had happened three years ago, and reread and reflected on what he'd written that fateful day. As he did that, he had the three maps of the *moai* statues in front of him on the table. The hands of the clock were showing past midnight. Are you with me so far?'

He was asking me if it was okay to proceed and I told him there was nothing I could see which required reconsideration.

'*Mr. Hirakawa was murdered in Happy Fish Villa.* That was the conclusion of Dr. Sonobe's medical examination and it was obvious even to amateurs like you and me. *And that night, Mr. Hirakawa's diary and the three maps were also present at Happy Fish Villa.* If you agree with me on those two points, I can proceed with my story. What I mean is, can we agree that the murderer had not come into possession of the diary and the maps before that night?

'Moving forward... At some time during the night, the murderer appeared in front of Mr. Hirakawa with the rifle and shot him. After that, the killer took the diary and the maps and left the villa. They appear to have been kept in the locked desk drawer, but the murderer somehow got their hands on them, probably by threatening Mr. Hirakawa with the rifle. No objections so far?'

I had nothing of importance to note, so I shook my head.

'The killer then got on a bicycle and headed back to Panorama Villa. They probably put the maps inside the diary and tied it and the rifle to the carrier rack with string, because none of the bicycles on the island have baskets. They hurried back here because they couldn't risk having anyone notice they'd been away for any length of time.'

Once again the scene of the murderer riding a bicycle in the moonlight came to mind. I somehow felt touched by it and thought that a real painting like that would be nice to have. If there was one, I could make it into a jigsaw puzzle.

'The killer pedalled furiously along the uneven road, slowed to go around the foot of the hill, and when they reached the spot where the road goes straight for a while, they sped up again, not noticing that halfway along that straight stretch one of the maps had slipped out of the diary and fallen to the ground. Humans don't have eyes in the back of their heads, so it's only natural that the loss wasn't noticed. Once back here, they took the diary and the rifle from the carrier, sneaked back to their room and went to sleep. There's something wrong with this story, isn't there?'

Of course there was something wrong. 'It contradicts the fact there were tyre marks on the map I picked up.'

'Precisely.'

Egami looked up at the ceiling.

'Precisely. If it had happened like that, then there would have been no opportunity for the bicycle to run over the fallen map. So that version of the story must be wrong. When I realised that that map had been in Happy Fish Villa on the night of the murder, I became utterly confused. If the map had been here at Panorama Villa, things would've made at least some sense. The murderer might've had some reason to take it along with them to Happy Fish Villa and had accidentally dropped it on the way. Then, after committing the murder, they headed back here, carelessly running over the map they'd dropped earlier. That I would have understood. But instead, the map had been in Happy Fish Villa that night.'

'That's certainly strange,' I agreed. Egami looked me straight in the eye.

'*It isn't strange at all. It proves that only one person on this island could have killed Mr. Hirakawa and I now know who that person is.*'

'Just because of that...?'

I didn't follow him at all. The artist's diary might have suddenly appeared on stage, but it wasn't as if it contained passages hinting at who the murderer might be. So what, if the diary had told Egami that the piece of paper with the tyre mark had been in Happy Fish Villa on the night of the murder? Could he identify one specific person as the murderer based on that one single fact? I had no clue as to how that could be the case.

'I just don't see it. Please explain to me how.'

'That's why I called you, so listen to what I have to say.'

I leant forward as Egami started his chain of deduction....

'The map was at Happy Fish Villa. How could a bicycle have run over it and left a tyre mark on it? I imagine under the following circumstances: the murderer left Happy Fish Villa with the map. And then dropped it on their way back to Panorama Villa. Then went out again, back to Happy Fish Villa, didn't notice the map on the ground and ran over it....'

'Eh? Wha—what? *The murderer returned to Panorama Villa, but then cycled back to Happy Fish Villa a second time*? Why would they do that? That doesn't make any sense. You just said it yourself: they had to return here as soon as possible. Having pedalled so desperately to get here, what reason could they possibly have to go back again to Happy Fish Villa? Did they forget something else besides the map?'

'Of course there was a reason for going back, but I'll return to that later. For now, just focus on the question of whether those are the only circumstances under which a tyre mark could've been left on the map. Okay?'

'No, it's not okay at all,' I said rather forcefully. 'I can think of other cases. For example, if there were multiple accomplices. Suppose there are two of them. Murderers A and B head out on the bicycles to Happy Fish Villa to kill Mr. Hirakawa. After the murder, and having got their hands on the maps, murderer A ties them to their bicycle's carrier and starts back to Panorama Villa with B. And on their way, one of the maps falls off A's carrier and B, who's riding behind A, doesn't notice it and runs over the map. That's also a possibility.'

'No, it's not okay at all.' Egami copied me. 'Alice, remember what everyone testified about that night. What you, Maria, the doctor, Mr. Makihara, Kazuto and I said. You and Maria saw that all three of Panorama Villa's bicycles were here until a quarter past twelve. Shortly before one o'clock, Doctor Sonobe and Maria saw two bicycles parked on the terrace by the French windows. Junji Makihara and I saw the same when we looked down through the hallway windows at twenty past one. And from two o'clock until four o'clock, Kazuto and I were in the hall and witnessed all three bicycles standing outside.

'Do you see? At twelve fifteen, before one, at one twenty, after two... there are witnesses to the fact that during the period when the crime must have been committed, there were always at least two bicycles here at Panorama Villa. *Between twelve fifteen and two o'clock, the bicycle parked by the entrance has no alibi, but the other two bicycles do.*'

I understood what Egami was telling me. If murderers A and B had taken two bicycles to go to Happy Fish Villa after Maria and I had gone to our rooms at twelve fifteen, then the earliest they could've returned was one fifteen, given that one way takes thirty minutes. But around one o'clock, Dr. Sonobe and Maria had seen two bicycles standing next to each other by the French windows. The two bicycles had also been witnessed by Egami and Junji at twenty past one. If, on the other hand, murderers A and B had started on their trip after that time, then the earliest they could have returned would have been twenty past two, yet Egami and Kazuto had testified that all three bicycles were at Panorama Villa at two o'clock. Hence it was impossible for two bicycles to have gone back and forth between the two villas together.

'Okay, I get it. I agree. The murderer must have used one bicycle to go between Panorama Villa and Happy Fish Villa twice.'

Egami shook his head. 'Wrong.'
Did I say something odd?
'You're wrong, Alice.'

2

'Did I just say something odd?'

'Think about it logically. If you think about it carefully, you'll see it's not possible for one bicycle to go and come back twice. Maria and you saw all three bicycles at quarter past twelve. Kazuto and I saw all three bicycles at two o'clock. There's only one hour and forty-five minutes between those times. If one way takes thirty minutes, how could you go back and forth twice?'

'No, it's you who's wrong. The murderer had some reason for returning to Happy Fish Villa. But couldn't the second trip have been made after two o'clock?'

'After two? Kazuto and I were in the hall until ten past four. At five o'clock, Reiko and Mrs. Inukai saw all three bicycles. Reiko and Dr. Sonobe also testified they saw all three bicycles just before six o'clock. Those testimonies, each made by multiple witnesses, show that none of the bicycles was gone from Panorama Villa for more than an hour.'

He was right. I realised I had indeed made a mistake. But what could this mean? All I could do was continue to listen to what Egami had to tell me.

'I'll go back to before your refutation. How was the tyre mark made on the map? The murderer dropped it on the way back from Happy Fish Villa to Panorama Villa, and then later ran over it on the way from Panorama Villa to Happy Fish Villa. Now my story has arrived at an unexpected place. It's clear that someone from Panorama Villa used a bicycle on their way back after they'd committed the Happy Fish Villa murder, and that they also used a bicycle when they went back to Happy Fish Villa a second time, for whatever reason. But if so, *how did the murderer go from Panorama Villa to Happy Fish Villa the first time? And how did they get back from Happy Fish Villa to Panorama Villa the last time?* And, before you answer: *it wasn't by bicycle.*'

'On foot?'

'No. Mr. Hirakawa was alive until past midnight. Suppose the crime happened at midnight. By the time the murderer had walked back here it'd be half past one. Even if they'd jumped on a bike immediately, they couldn't have made it back again to this house by two o'clock. Perhaps they wanted to avoid being away from Panorama Villa too long, or they were afraid of being bitten by a snake. In either case: *it wasn't on foot.*'

I finally understood what Egami was getting at and I let out a short sigh.

'*They swam, didn't they?*'

That was the only answer left. The only means of transportation on the island are the bicycles and the boat. Maria and I had rendered the boat useless earlier in the night—at around half past ten—by overturning it.

'We're almost at the finishing line, so can you still stop my horse?'

'Sorry, it's been a rather one-sided discussion so far.

'I'll continue.'

He smiled faintly.

'The murderer acted as follows. They swam from Panorama Villa to Happy Fish Villa. After the murder, they climbed on a bicycle to get back to Panorama Villa. And then they hurried back once more to Happy Fish Villa by bicycle and finally swam back to Panorama Villa.'

'I can't see the reason for all those movements. Having committed a murder, did the killer decide to train for a triathlon that night?'

'Stop being facetious. What you need to pay attention to is which bicycle the murderer used. The one they used to return to Panorama Villa after they'd swum to Happy Fish Villa was, of course Mr. Hirakawa's red bicycle. And now you know the reason why they had to go back to Happy Fish Villa again. It was to return his bicycle.'

'Mr. Egami, it all sounds so convoluted.'

I paused for a moment. I remembered how Egami had laughed at Maria and me just before we discovered Hirakawa's body. The problem of how we could go back and forth between Panorama Villa and Happy Fish Villa: *The Kashikijima Island Puzzle.*

'Your story makes no sense. Why go pedalling like crazy to return a dead man's bicycle? They could simply have left the bicycle here at Panorama Villa and gone to bed. People might've been surprised at finding it here in the morning, but even if we'd realised the bicycle had been used in the murder, there'd be no way for us to work out who'd used it.'

'But that wouldn't do. I admit it's a bit convoluted, but be patient and stick with me. What would've happened if Mr. Hirakawa's bicycle had been left at Panorama Villa after the murder? People would have reasoned as follows: "The bicycle from Happy Fish Villa is here. The murderer used that to return here. So the murderer swam to the other side. We can rule out the boat because it had been overturned. So that means that the murderer must be someone who can swim...." This is not good for the killer. Why? They'd planned to put the blame for all the crimes on Kazuto and kill him. *The murderer couldn't let it be known that the culprit was someone who could swim, because that would show Kazuto was in fact innocent.*'

It was convoluted, but that wasn't why I disagreed. There were some other fundamental points to Egami's deduction I had trouble understanding.

'Mr. Egami, I still think there are some odd points to your theory. I accept that the murderer swam to Happy Fish Villa. It's faster than going by bicycle, so it's only natural. *But why didn't they also swim back*? I don't see any reason for going through all the trouble of using Mr. Hirakawa's bicycle to come back here, then turn around and go back to Happy Fish Villa on it, and then swim back here again. *What was the trip back and forth in the middle for?*'

'There was a reason. Try imagining what was going on at the time in practical terms and you should realise what it was. *The killer wanted to bring back the diary, the maps and, most important of all, the rifle without getting them wet.* If, the following day, we'd discovered Mr. Hirakawa had been murdered and realised it was part of a string of murders, it would've been impossible to move around with a rifle anymore. The killer needed to bring the rifle back to Panorama Villa before the night was over.'

'Without getting the things wet....Aha, a diary, maps and a rifle. All things you don't want to get wet. I see....'

'So, Alice, are you satisfied with my explanation so far?'

Egami asked me once again to be sure. I said yes.

'Then the next step is our final destination. One person will emerge as our murderer.' Egami paused for a second. 'I guess you couldn't stop my horse getting to the finishing line.'

What was he trying to tell me, saying things like "Can you stop my horse," and "You couldn't stop me."? But what if? What if the identity of the murderer in Egami's mind was unbearable to us? Perhaps he wanted me to drag it out of him. The deduction he couldn't get out of his mind....

'It was most of all the rifle the murderer wanted to bring back here without getting it wet. You could've put the diary and the maps in a small plastic bag and swum back. You could perhaps even have casually brought them back with you the following day, without anyone noticing.

'But because the murderer wanted to keep the rifle dry, they had to make a very dangerous and troublesome extra return trip on the bicycle. Of course, if the boat hadn't been overturned, they would've used that to get to Happy Fish Villa and back.'

'Mr. Egami...,' I said.

'... And here is my final question. I will answer it myself. How then did the murderer bring the rifle along with them when they swam to Happy Fish Villa to murder Mr. Hirakawa?'

'Mr. Egami.'

I called his name once again, but he didn't allow me to interrupt him and started to speak faster.

'If the murderer had had something to keep the rifle waterproof, they could've returned here using that same thing a second time. So, obviously they didn't have anything to keep it dry. Of course, there had been no time to prepare anything like that. It was only when the murderer came down to the beach on Low Tide Cape that they discovered the boat that should've been there was gone.'

'Mr. Egami, what about Maria?'

'Do you understand what that means? It means the murderer didn't bring the rifle along with them on the night of the murder. *They'd already brought it over to somewhere close to Happy Fish Villa—to High Tide Cape—beforehand, sometime in the afternoon.*'

'Why didn't you ask Maria up here too? She'd probably make better objections than I.'

'The murders of Kango and Sumako Makihara were committed the previous night. There had also been a storm raging that night. Everyone remained inside Panorama Villa even after the rain had stopped. The three of us were the exception, as we visited Happy Fish Villa and talked for a long time on the observation platform. And there—'

'Mr. Egami, Maria—'

I felt something hot creeping up from within the depths of my chest, as well as the feeling of wanting to cry out.

'I saw it from the observation platform. You did too. I'm sure Maria saw it as well. The rowing boat heading from Panorama Villa to Happy Fish Villa. *The person who was on that boat was the only person who could've brought the rifle to High Tide Cape that afternoon.*

'No....'

'The murderer can only be Reiko, who was on that boat.'

Both of us fell silent. Through the window, I could hear the tide wash in the silence. I let my head hang and stared at the toenails of my right foot, my mind blown away in disbelief.

'That's why you didn't ask Maria....'

That was all I could finally manage to say. Now I understood why Egami had looked so sorrowful.

'What are we going to tell Maria?'

First I thought it was somebody else mumbling, but then I realised that those words had escaped from my own mouth. My eyes moved to the toenails of my left foot, but my head stayed motionless, looking down.

After a while I raised my head. I somehow felt afraid of meeting Egami's eyes, so I turned my head to look at the window. As always, there was a deep darkness filled with stars. If I could reach out, the world would end there and it would lead to nothingness....

I peeked at our club president. He was still leaning against the wall, also looking at the window. Neither of us had anything to say.

Then it happened.

There was a knock on the door. Both of us turned at the same time.

'Sorry to disturb you.'

A voice came from beyond the door. My heart leapt.

It was Reiko's voice.

3

Egami got up and opened the door. There she stood.

'You don't mind me disturbing you?' asked Reiko, and Egami beckoned for her to enter.

'Come inside. Please sit down.'

She slid silently into the room and sat down on the chair near the window. She rested both hands on her knees as she looked up at us.

Why had the subject of our talks appeared with such perfect timing? I'm sure Egami had only asked me to come to our room later. Perhaps she had no special reason for her visit. Perhaps she'd only come to see how Egami was, to tell him: "Your dinner is ready, won't you come down and eat?" No, that wasn't right. If that had been the case, she wouldn't have sat down on a chair in the back of the room. What could she be here for? I thought furiously about that.

'I wanted to hear about the case.'

That was all she said, and she looked at Egami and me, then back to Egami, who was leaning casually against the wall.

'We've been talking about nothing but that between the two of us. Right before you knocked on the door, we'd concluded that the murderer of Kango and Sumako Makihara, Mr. Hirakawa and Kazuto was... you.

'I've talked a long time with Alice about how I arrived at that conclusion, but he wasn't able to counter my reasoning. Yet I'm not satisfied I've solved everything, merely because he wasn't able to come up with reasonable counter-arguments. There's still a lot I don't understand, and we haven't any physical evidence either. It means the jigsaw puzzle we made is still full of holes. I'd like to fill in the holes and complete the puzzle now, if you'd be so kind as to help us.'

My eyes remained fixed on Reiko as she listened to Egami. When she was told she was the murderer, her shoulders trembled slightly, but other than that she was just as she always was. She didn't act pathetically like a cornered small animal. As I gazed at her, I felt her beauty and brilliance growing.

'You say I'm the murderer? And you want me to help you solve the case?'

Egami nodded in response to her question.

'Yes. Could you please answer one question clearly before everything else? You're the one who killed the four victims, am I correct?'

Even Reiko couldn't help gasping and looking away. Then she quietly let out the single word: 'Yes.'

'I managed to work out that you were the murderer based on all kinds of trivial details. But, as I just told you, there are still things I don't understand. Some I might learn if I ask you, some even you might not know the answer to. Anyway, shall we start?'

'Yes,' she repeated.

'First I want to establish your motive. May I assume it was revenge for Hideto?'

'Yes.'

'Mr. Hirakawa's diary is rather brief, so it's difficult to infer the complete picture of what happened three years ago, but I think it happened as follows. In an impulsive act, Kazuto killed Hideto, who had solved the *moai* statue puzzle. Mr. Hirakawa and Sumako happened to witness the murder and Mr. Hirakawa demanded the diamonds the brothers had dug up to keep quiet. Kazuto did as he was told and Sumako, who was in love with Mr. Hirakawa, also followed the artist's orders and kept silent. They came to an agreement. The three of them carried the body of Hideto to the bay to the north and left it there. And they tried to forget about the crime they'd committed that night. Somehow you came to learn about it. Kazuto was the one you hated the most because he had committed the actual murder, but you couldn't forgive Mr. Hirakawa and Sumako, who had kept silent about the crime, either. So you decided to do the murders, starting with Sumako and Mr. Hirakawa and ending with Kazuto. You planned to put the blame of the first two murders on Kazuto, and then kill him and make his death appear to be suicide.'

Egami's last sentence hadn't been a question, but Reiko still answered: 'Yes.'

'I don't know how and when you came to know the truth about Hideto's death. Right after it happened, a year after, two years after, or perhaps only when you came to the island this year. I don't know. But, no matter when you found out, it was necessary for the island to become the stage for the murders. Kazuto was living under the same roof as you, but you could only meet with Sumako Makihara and Mr. Hirakawa—especially Mr. Hirakawa—on this island in the summer. You decided to begin your revenge with Sumako. And, fortunately, a storm arrived.'

While Reiko was listening intently to Egami, she slowly rubbed her left shoulder, exposed by the sleeveless shirt.

'Everyone had a lot to drink that night. The door of the storage room in the annex was banging frequently and would hide the noise of the gunshot. Junji Makihara was lying dead drunk in the hall and Sumako went upstairs. You decided to commit the crime there and then, and when nobody was looking you slipped upstairs to get the rifle—'

'I went upstairs after I'd gone back to my room with Maria.'

This was the first time Reiko had interrupted Egami.

'Despite my protests, Maria insisted on sleeping on the sofa. With my heart pounding so hard it could've burst out of my chest, I sneaked out of my bedroom and came back after murdering the Makiharas. Maria opened her eyes briefly, and when our fingers touched, she laughed and said "Your fingers are so cold," and fell asleep again. I don't know why I raised my hand to my face and stared at it, but I smelled gunpowder and in a panic I hurried to the sink to wash my hands.'

Egami nodded several times and continued.

'You took the rifle from the attic room and went to Sumako's room. You knew how to handle it. Kazuto told us everyone on the island had done target practice with it. The lock on the door of Sumako's room was broken, so you slipped quickly inside and took aim. And well, this is just my imagination, but you shot her suddenly, didn't you? I think you shot her, a person you hated so much, without telling her why she had to die.'

Reiko looked puzzled. 'How did you know?'

'Simply by trial and error, trying to get all the pieces of the jigsaw puzzle to fit. I've had to jump to a few conclusions. You fired at Sumako instantly and hit her in the chest. So far, so good. But what you hadn't foreseen was that her father, Kango Makihara, was also in the room. You only noticed him after you'd shot her, so in a panic you shot him as well. But because you were so confused, you didn't manage to take good aim at him and the bullet only hit him in the thigh. And why were you so confused? It was probably because, like you, he'd also appeared very suddenly!'

'How—?'

Reiko was about to ask a question, but swallowed it halfway.

'Just a guess. Mr. Kango suddenly appeared from the head side of the bed, did he not? He'd been crawling on the floor looking for his lighter which had fallen underneath the bed, when he suddenly heard a gunshot and jumped up. And when you saw him, you were surprised as well. You'd been seen, this was bad, shoot. But, because it had all happened so suddenly, you missed and hit him in the thigh. He fell over because of the shot, hit his head on the corner of the night stand and fell unconscious. It was total chaos. With the blood rushing to your head, you told yourself you'd got both of them and ran as quickly as possible away from the crime scene. With all kinds of other thoughts buzzing in your head, you didn't think to make sure both of them were dead. Perhaps you were afraid that three shots, one after another, would definitely be noticed by someone.'

Reiko confirmed Egami's account. Before she'd gone back to her bedroom, she'd hidden the rifle in the ceiling space above the attic room—where the rifle had originally been kept. After that, she'd sneaked into Kazuto's room and destroyed the wireless transceiver. But how had the murder scene been transformed into a locked room?

'What happened in Sumako's room after you'd fled? Nobody knows exactly, but I'll hazard a guess. What I'm about to suggest is nothing more than a theory. I have no evidence. I'd be happy if you'd forget it once you've listened to it. After you'd left the room, the two people left inside were Mr. Kango, who was unconscious and bleeding from the thigh, and Sumako, who had been fatally shot in the chest. And that room became a locked room. *It becomes painfully clear who locked the door.*

'It was Sumako, of course. *And it all comes down to the question: why did she do it?* We have a jigsaw puzzle here. Piece 1: her father was wealthy. Piece 2: her husband was in need of money. Piece 3: her father had been shot in the thigh and was losing blood rapidly. Piece 4: Sumako's own wound was in the chest and was fatal. Piece 5: Sumako had studied nursing and law. By combining these five pieces, I formulated the following theory.

'First of all, Sumako realised that she herself couldn't be saved, but there was a good possibility her father could be, if his bleeding was stopped. In other words, if she opened the door to get help, she wouldn't be saved but her father probably would. Nevertheless, she didn't do it.

'That was because she realised that by not doing so, her death would have more favourable consequences. She was going to die anyway, so she would have her father die with her. *And she would make it appear as if her father had died before her.* That way, she would inherit from her father. Then, if she was perceived to have died after her father, even if it was just one second later, her beloved husband would inherit everything through her. She used her last remaining strength to stagger to the door and force the stiff lock shut. Now you now understand why the door wouldn't open. *She couldn't allow anyone to prevent her father and her from dying.*'

Reiko seemed stunned by what she was hearing for the first time, and she stopped rubbing her left shoulder.

'After Sumako had made it impossible for anyone to enter, she lay down on top of her unconscious father, who was lying on the floor. Perhaps she'd wanted to beg him for forgiveness, even if he couldn't hear her any more. And perhaps she wasn't afraid to die if it was by his side. But I think the most important reason for her lying on top of him was in order for us to us to assume that she'd had been shot after him, and that her father had died first. When asked which of them had been the first to die, Dr. Sonobe had said it was impossible to tell.

'Which means this is a case in which it's difficult to discern the order of death medically. Sumako was aware of that, and that's why she faked the scene. I heard there was a case once where a family had been buried in a landslide and everyone had died. It was obvious the times of death must have been very close, medically speaking, but they needed to determine the order because of the inheritance. How do you think they did it? They decided that the person buried deepest down had died first, and so on.'

As a not very serious law student, this was the first time I'd heard about the case, but perhaps Sumako had known about it. Maybe she'd remembered just before she died and hoped the same reasoning would be applied in her case. Of course, now she was dead, we'd never know.

'Sorry, that was a very uninteresting story I made up. Let's forget it. I'll get some boards and nails and seal the room up. I'll place a sign, saying it's a mystery room and nobody should go inside.'

I sensed a tone of resignation in Egami's words. Perhaps he himself also noticed it, because his manner of talking changed back again.

'And now for the next murder.'

4

'The murder of Mr. Hirakawa. Let's talk about the murder where you had to go through ordeals at least as perilous as the first one. That day, after the storm had passed and the weather had cleared, you took the rifle outside the villa, so you'd be safe even if the house was searched. You had plans to kill Mr. Hirakawa that night and you intended to hide the weapon near the future crime scene beforehand, is that right?' asked Egami.

Reiko ran her hand through her short hair.

'Yes. At that time, most were of the opinion the Makiharas had been murdered, but nobody mentioned the possibility of more murders to follow. Furthermore, they assumed the rifle had been thrown into the sea. So, before anyone made a serious attempt to search for it, I decided to hide it in the forest and then take it over to High Tide Cape in advance. Luckily Mr. Hirakawa had left his backpack behind when he'd left, so I had an excuse to take it over to Happy Fish Villa.'

'And when Kazuto said he wanted to search the house to look for the rifle?'

'I'd already hidden it in the forest. I thought I'd need to get it over to High Tide Cape as soon as possible, before he proposed searching in the vicinity of the house as well, so I went over to Happy Fish Villa as soon as we'd finished searching the house.'

'I see. Then let's go over what happened later that night. You could head out to commit your crime empty-handed because the weapon was already in the vicinity of Happy Fish Villa. You sneaked out of the house, but you got a severe shock at the bottom of the stone steps because the boat wasn't there.'

Drawing the scene in my mind, I imagined how Reiko must have felt. Beads of sweat gathered in the palm of my hand.

'There were two options you could take at that point. Go back up the steps and take a bicycle. Or swim to the other side. Perhaps you'd decided on the former originally, but in the end you decided not to use that method. Was it because you didn't want to risk being seen leaving on a bicycle? Or was it because Maria and Alice were still sitting on the bicycles, with no idea as to when their long chat would finally end?'

Reiko answered, hesitantly.

'Because Maria and Alice were there.'

'And that's why you decided to swim. You could have chosen to commit the crime at a later time, or on another day, but you chose to go ahead.'

'I wanted to get it over with as soon possible. I was also afraid the rifle might be found if I postponed it to another day.'

'Aha, so that's why. You swam across the bay in the night. A T-shirt, short pants and short hair. You probably found the swimming wasn't all that inconvenient. You came to shore on High Tide Cape, picked up the rifle you'd hidden beforehand and entered Happy Fish Villa. The door wasn't locked. What was Mr. Hirakawa doing at the time?'

'…He was busy with a jigsaw puzzle.'

'That puzzle of an *ukiyo-e* by Hokusai? I can't even begin to guess whether you shot him without any warning as well, or whether you had a talk first.'

Reiko started to say something, but she then looked down. The night had filled the window behind her completely and cast a dark shadow over her back.

'When I pointed the rifle at him, he looked at it and said only: "Revenge for Hideto?"'

The artist had grasped the situation immediately. Even while he'd been wallowing in the good life, somewhere in the back of his mind he'd always known that the hammer of justice would come down on him.

'I simply answered "Yes" and stood facing him for a while, with my finger on the trigger. He said "Please give me a minute." and slowly got up. He walked over to the desk, unlocked the drawer and took something out of it. I was afraid he would take out a hidden pistol, but it was something else. He held the diary and the three maps in front of me and said: "This is the confession of my sins and a memento of Hideto. If someone found these, you'd be in trouble, and they're also shameful to me. Please dispose of them as you see fit." I took them and he returned to his chair, closed his eyes and smiled mysteriously. And, as the thoughts of why I couldn't forgive him arose in my mind, I...I shot him.'

Reiko stopped talking, her eyes still down, and Egami looked at her. They remained like that in silence for a while, but then Egami started again.

'After you'd committed the murder, you thought about how you'd return to Panorama Villa with the diary, the three maps and the rifle. You couldn't swim back across the sea. It would risk ruining the evidence and the rifle. Walking back was dangerous because of the snakes. With no other option left, you decided to borrow Mr. Hirakawa's bicycle and you returned to Panorama Villa with all three items fastened to the carrier rack. You didn't need to stop your bicycle in front of Panorama Villa. You could have got down off the bicycle a bit before that, hidden the evidence and rifle somewhere in the forest and sneaked back inside the house on foot. But there remained another problem. The fact that Mr. Hirakawa's bicycle was here at Panorama Villa meant that someone had crossed the sea and, because the boat was out of action, it would be obvious someone had swum to the other side. But if you wanted to put the blame of the murders on Kazuto, you couldn't have people conclude that the murderer had swum across the bay. Even though you were exhausted both physically and mentally, you decided you had to go back to Happy Fish Villa on the bicycle.'

'How do you know about my movements in such detail?' Reiko must have thought it creepy.

'Because of the tyre mark on the map you dropped on the way back to Panorama Villa. My inferences were guided by that map.'

'Yes, I'd dropped one of the maps. I only noticed it when I'd returned to my room and opened the diary, but I never even considered going back to search for it. I didn't know where I'd dropped it, but I thought that even if it was found, it wouldn't be a clue that could connect me with the crime. Oh, I forget to tell you, that night I was wearing gloves so gunpowder wouldn't be left on my hands, so I hadn't left any fingerprints on the maps when I took them. But despite that....'

'If you'd only dropped the map, I wouldn't have been able to deduce you were the murderer. It's only because you ran over it and left a tyre mark that a crack formed in your impregnable defence.'

Egami carefully explained his chain of reasoning to Reiko.

She listened silently, asking no questions.

'You returned to Happy Fish Villa solely to put the bicycle back in its proper place. And then you swam back across the sea once more to get back to Low Tide Cape. Am I correct?'

Reiko answered: 'Yes,' and it was at this point I joined the conversation for the first time.

'Just a second. There's something I want to ask.'

Reiko cocked her head slightly as she turned to look at me.

'Why was the jigsaw puzzle Mr. Hirakawa had been working on scattered all over floor? Did Mr. Hirakawa himself break the puzzle in pieces? Or was there another reason?'

Reiko hesitated to answer. I glanced at Egami.

'I'd like to know as well,' he said. 'I've no idea why the puzzle was in that state.'

'There's no way you could've known,' she said warmly, as if to defend the detective. 'Only someone who was there could know.'

'Please tell us,' the detective asked the murderer.

'Mr. Hirakawa appeared to have been prepared to die when I shot him. But his feelings of resentment, his hatred towards me were something he couldn't get rid of. When I went back to Happy Fish Villa to return the bicycle, I went inside rather gingerly. I wanted to make sure he really had died. Because, once again, I'd left the crime scene without making sure my victim was dead. Mr. Hirakawa really had died and was lying over the table. But he hadn't simply died, he'd left a message revealing I was the murderer.'

Where could he have written anything like that? He couldn't have written any message in blood on the table, the floor, or the puzzles pieces. I was pondering over this when Egami suddenly muttered: 'Oh…I get it. He used the jigsaw puzzle.'

'Yes.'

Reiko nodded. I voiced my questions: weren't the puzzle pieces coated in vinyl? Hadn't Hirakawa's fingers been clean of any blood?

'Not like that, Alice. He didn't write with his blood on the puzzle. He used the puzzle itself to write something,' said Egami.

'…What?'

'*He took pieces out from the left side of the puzzle, which he'd already finished and left his message via the empty spaces, didn't he?*'

Reiko nodded.

'Yes. The empty spaces spelled out "REIKO." I was so surprised I cried out. He was already dying, so he'd had to improvise to compose the message. The letters weren't very neat, but they did spell "REIKO" quite clearly. I was relieved the bad luck of me having to return his bicycle had turned into the good luck of me discovering his dying message. For a while I couldn't make up my mind as to how best to destroy it. A lot of people knew he'd half-finished the puzzle, so the best solution would've been to put the couple of dozen pieces back in their places. But they'd been thrown together with the hundreds of other loose pieces, and there was no time for me to search for the right ones. So, with no other choice left, I threw the whole puzzle on the floor and scattered the pieces around.'

So it was a dying message. And it's no wonder I couldn't solve it. To be exact: *those pieces were the remains of a dying message.*

'You went to commit the crime while Alice and Maria were still chatting outside.' Egami summarised. 'So that means before midnight. Let's say you arrived at High Tide Cape at ten minutes past twelve. The murder and other activities took fifteen minutes, so you got back to Panorama Villa and hid the evidence and the weapon at five minutes to one. You turned around and reached Happy Fish Villa again at twenty-five minutes past one. That corresponds with what Mr. Makihara said, that he saw a bicycle light moving near Happy Fish Villa at that time. And after parking the bicycle, you discovered the dying message and broke the puzzle apart. You swam back to Panorama Villa and returned here at a quarter to two. You had quite a busy night.'

'Appearances to the contrary, I'm a very active woman.'

Thus spoke the murderer, who exchanged a slight smile with the detective.

5

'Only Kazuto's murder left now,' Egami continued. 'The scenario had already been written. He would take the blame for all the crimes by confessing to the murders in a note and then committing suicide. Before you committed your final murder, you typed out the suicide note on a word processor. What you hadn't expected was that Kazuto was in possession of another firearm. However, he appeared to have a soft spot for you, so that didn't prove to be a major obstacle. Perhaps it suited you even better, because if you could work out a way to use his pistol, the "suicide" would be perfect. You saw your opportunity when everyone started to go their own way, so you headed to the annex to put a sudden end to the case, taking along the rifle, the other evidence and the fake suicide note.'

'And,' interjected Reiko, 'I didn't wait for Kazuto to drop his guard, so I pointed the rifle right at him and took the pistol from him. There was no time, so I didn't go into some longwinded explanation of how much I hated him. He was the complete opposite of Mr. Hirakawa and cried out "Why? Why?" He couldn't even get up because he was so frozen with fear. I put the muzzle of the pistol to his temple and pulled the trigger.'

Egami took over from there.

'You then put the pistol in his right hand and, in order to leave gunpowder on his hand, you took a shot at something random. And the target just happened to be the painting puzzle hanging on the wall.'

'I suppose that was another mistake....'

'Indeed it was. You left the evidence, suicide note and the weapons in the annex and fled the scene. And with that, everything had finally ended...at least, that was what you were probably thinking.'

'Everything had already ended three years ago for me.'

This was the first time Reiko had spoken sharply.

'I had been going to spend the rest of my life with Hideto. I'd been all alone in the world, but I'd finally found my own family. That was what I thought, but then he suddenly died. From that day on, living has been like hell to me.'

Unexpectedly, tears started to flow from her eyes.

'Right after his death, I had a mental breakdown. Perhaps I would've been happier if I'd really gone mad then, but I didn't go that far. I felt as if I was being cruelly tortured and that even my pleas of wanting to die right away weren't being answered. I wouldn't have taken the lives of those four if I'd committed suicide then, but I hadn't done that. To let everyone know, to let myself know how deep the pain was of having lost Hideto, I wanted...to go crazy.'

I winced at her unbearable words.

'The pain became worse with every day and I awaited the day I would truly go mad. Kazuto, Sumako and Mr. Hirakawa, who came to visit me in my private room in the institution, must've thought my case was hopeless. Feeling sorry and afraid for me, Sumako started to cry. She started to blame herself out loud, saying that she couldn't have known this would happen. That's when I began to realise what had actually happened. I decided that only revenge could give meaning to my life.'

Egami listened to her with his eyes closed. The darkness behind Reiko looked deeper than before. Even though it was a night of falling stars.

'I'm sure that Sumako drifted away from Mr. Hirakawa because of what happened. I think she left him saying she wouldn't talk, but she couldn't be with him any more. She must have been suffering as well. You might think I could have at least forgiven Sumako. But that was something I couldn't do. She might have had a painful parting with Mr. Hirakawa, but she soon found a loved one after that and regained her smile again. I couldn't forgive her....'

Reiko's tears kept falling.

'Haven't you considered the consequences of what you did even just a little?'

Egami said this mildly, but the meaning of his words was grave.

'You're talking about my father? You want to ask me if I hadn't thought about the pain my father would suffer, having first lost Hideto and now Kazuto? I did think about it. But I couldn't stop myself despite that. As I hadn't died after Hideto did, I decided I'd spend the rest of my life together with my father to ease his pain, however little. That was what I'd planned to do. But not even once had I considered sparing Kazuto. In the winter two years ago, not even a half year after madness had rejected me and I had been let out of hospital, he timidly tried to make advances to me. When he saw how shaken I was by that, he quickly said it was just a joke. By that time, I'd already pulled the trigger on him dozens of times in my mind. What I wrote in the suicide note about his motive for killing Hideto was not a product of my imagination. He had let slip all of that while in my hospital room. Only the part that Mr. Hirakawa had asked for more money this year was fiction.

'And to be able to take care of your father for the rest of your life, you couldn't have anyone find out you were the murderer,' said Egami in a frustrated tone. 'And I would've needed to deny and laugh away this deduction of mine that's flimsier than a sheet of paper.'

Reiko remained silent.

But if that was the case, why did Egami expose all the crimes she had committed in front of her? As long as Egami didn't talk, she would be safe.

'This is not a warning, saying I will expose you. But when I saw you, I couldn't help but tell you there are people who know about your crimes. I needed to know if you could bear that knowledge. You can't run away from yourself. You yourself have been the one witness to all that you've done. Soon the police will arrive on the island and you'll have to survive an intense investigation. You'll need to be able to withstand that as well. So why, then, couldn't you put up any argument against my tale which is even flimsier than the piece of paper you dropped?'

Reiko stood up without wiping away her tears.

'That's my problem. I need to deal with it myself. I'll think about it.'

She bowed her head slightly, passed in front of us again and went to the door. Without turning round, she said: 'I came here because I had a feeling this would happen. I am grateful Maria wasn't here.'

She raised her chin a little and sighed slightly, with her back still turned to us. She appeared to have made up her mind as she opened the door and disappeared into the hallway.

The artist once wrote this in his diary:

"Tomorrow will be a sad day."

On the day before the boat finally returned to the island, I contemplated those words.

6

After a light sleep, a sad day awaited me.

By the time the morning sun had started to shine through the six hallway windows and be reflected on the doors on the other side of the corridor, Egami and I were already awake. Both of us were looking up at the walls and the ceiling, lying on our beds. For more than an hour, each of us had thought the other was still asleep. Even the noise from the waves of the morning sea hadn't calmed my mind.

And then we began to hear people getting up here and there in the house.

'Let's go downstairs,' said Egami.

We washed our faces, got dressed and went down to the hall. Maria was preparing breakfast in the kitchen.

'Oh, good morning.'

Her energetic voice pained my heart.

'It's not like her at all, but I think Reiko has overslept. I felt sorry for her, as she needs to take a rest too sometimes, so today I'll prepare everything.'

She was cutting slices of ham with a smile on her face, happy that Reiko was sleeping in.

'This morning is kind of strange, don't you think? Egami and Alice getting up first.... But as you're up early anyway and there's still time before breakfast, what about a morning stroll?'

'Let's do that.'

The hairs Egami had missed shaving this morning were standing out on his cheek. We went out of Panorama Villa with heavy steps, as if we had just come home from a night out.

We'd arrived at the steps which went down to the landing place. I glanced at Happy Fish Villa, where the artist was resting, and then looked down at the sea in the morning sun. Then I saw it.

A boat was floating near the centre of the bay.

A feeling of *déjà vu*. I had seen this scene before.

Someone had rowed the boat out there in the night. And the rower had abandoned the boat.

'Mr. Egami ….'

He didn't say anything.

EPILOGUE

Reiko's body had washed up near the Eboshi Rock, where Hideto had also been found. We went out looking for her together; we found her together; we brought her back to Panorama Villa together; and we grieved together.

'And I'd thought that, no matter what, it could never have been Reiko....' The features of Satomi's face contorted as she cried. 'I even doubted my own husband, but I always believed in Reiko....'

Satomi appeared to have been unable to keep everything inside any more and she let it all out to me, as I stood nearby. She said she'd been suspicious of her own husband Toshiyuki and very afraid. Her only reasons for that were that her husband had experience with clay target shooting and that he needed money to ensure the future business of his restaurant chain. She'd only pretended to take her sleeping pills and had stayed up that night to see if he wouldn't sneak out of their room. That was what had caused her lack of sleep the following day.

'I was such a fool. I thought that, as I suffer from insomnia, I could stop taking my sleeping pills and easily stay awake all night to watch him, but precisely at that crucial period, right after midnight, I fell asleep for a while. So not only didn't I get enough sleep, I still couldn't be sure my husband wasn't the murderer.'

Her husband was sitting on the other side of the room, asking Egami for explanations. Elsewhere in the room, Junji said to Sonobe: 'It turned out even more tragic than we could've guessed.'

I could hear the grieving cries of Ryūichi and Maria from Reiko's room.

The motor yacht finally appeared.

The captain was humming a tune and the yacht had almost arrived. What if we were all to go out to where we could look down at the landing place and stand in one line? It would look even more impressive if we'd been holding a banner up:

Welcome to the island of the dead.

Sonobe went to a window that was half open and opened it fully. He said some words to the sea beyond:

It was a journey past countless mountains and rivers,
And we travelled to the edge of the world.
But we met nobody who came from the world beyond,
One only travels down this road, and never will a traveller return.

We are puppets and the sky is the puppet master
This is not a metaphor, but reality.
Once your part has been played,
You will be returned to the box.

The wind blew inside.
On the table far away were scattered the pieces of the jigsaw puzzle which had never been completed.

The summer was over and the season was turning to autumn. Like an operator trying to stop the train silently at the platform, I also slid into autumn.

Part of what had happened on that island became public, part of it was suppressed and the remaining part had spread in the form of stories and rumours that didn't sound familiar at all to me. But that mattered not at all.

Maria had gone away.

No matter how long I stayed staring in the lecture hall after Obligation Law had ended, she would not call out to me and no matter how much I looked, I could not find her among the masses of students who were slowly making their way outside.

Without my even having a chance of congratulating her on her twentieth birthday, the eighth of September passed by.

When I went to the Law Faculty office, a clerk told me they'd received a notice of absence.

I left the campus and ate a light lunch at a café I'd never visited before. I felt listless. I could see the Kyōto Imperial Palace from where I was sitting. I told myself that her pain might have healed a little by the time the trees of the palace turned scarlet, and that she would return.

I hoped so.

That's why until then, I would read the *Rubaiyat* I'd borrowed from Egami and wait for her.

THE END

TRANSLATOR'S NOTES

[i] Villa Lilac refers to *Rirasō Jiken* (The Villa Lilac Case), a 1959 mystery novel by Tetsuya Ayukawa.

[ii] Enkū (1632-1695) was a Buddhist monk who travelled across Japan to help the poor. During his travels, he carved some 120,000 wooden statues of the Buddha. These were crude statues made from tree stumps and other scrap pieces of wood with just a few strokes from a hatchet.

[iii] In Buddhism, Jizō is a Bodhisattva who protects (dead) children, (expectant) mothers and travellers. Statues of Jizō can be found all over Japan near intersections of roads.

[iv] The Boy Detective Club (*Shōnen Tantei Dan*) is a highly influential children's mystery novel series by Edogawa Rampo. The series carries the same title as the second book in the series, first published in 1937.

[v] The Ariake Sea is the home to mysterious ghostly lights called *shiranui*, similar to will-'o-the-wisps. References are made to the *shiranui* in the *Nihon Shoki*, the second oldest chronicle on Japanese history completed in 720. Modern research has concluded the *shiranui* are in fact an optical phenomenon.

[vi] NHK is Japan's national public broadcasting organisation and somewhat similar to the BBC of the United Kingdom. NHK is an abbreviation of *Nippon Hōsō Kyoku*. The English name Japan Broadcasting Corporation is also used.

The poems from *Rubaiyat* which appear in this book are from the Japanese translation by Ryōsaku Ogawa, published by Iwanami Bunko, not the Edward Fitzgerald version.

Printed in Great Britain
by Amazon